MONEY MEN

—— *AND* ——

One-Shot Deal

MONEY MEN

— AND —

One-Shot Deal

Two Novels by

GERALD PETIEVICH

Harcourt Brace Jovanovich
New York and London

To Pam

Library of Congress Cataloging in Publication Data
Petievich, Gerald.
    Money men; and, One-shot deal.
    I. Petievich, Gerald. One-shot deal. 1981.
II. Title.
PS3566.E773M6   813'.54   80-8756
ISBN 0-15-169892-9   AACR2

Printed in the United States of America

First edition

B C D E

MONEY MEN

$/1

The tiny motel room had the odor of mildewed carpet. Charles Carr waited, peeking out occasionally through the yellowed Venetian blind at the room Rico was in. An ancient air conditioner rattled outside the window, filtering warm August smog into cool August smog.

Carr's partner, Jack Kelly, slouched on the bed in rumpled suit and tie, watching the Johnny Carson show on a television set that was bolted and chained to the wall. The room needed painting, and the ceiling mirror reflected a stained bedspread with a cigarette burn.

Each time Carr peeked out he could see the neon sign. It proclaimed SUNSET MOTEL—WATERBEDS, TV, FREE ICE, as if the hookers and their johns who slithered in and out of the rooms cared about such extras. Carr preferred to use the Sunset for undercover operations because the rooms were easy to observe from either of the buildings that faced each other across a small parking lot.

Across Sunset Boulevard was a dingy hot-dog stand surrounded by Hollywood's new breed: runaways with no bras, shirtless punks in vests, skinny men dressed as women. Farther down the street a dwarf hawked phony maps to movie stars' homes.

He remembered bringing dates twenty years—even ten years—ago to the classy theaters on Hollywood Boulevard, stopping for a drink near Grauman's Chinese.

3

Now, he saw the town as a population of crooks and victims. The street people had taken over. The old ladies who lived on the side streets had either moved to Newport Beach or put up wrought-iron window bars.

In fact, eight years ago, when he had first met Sally, she had lived in an apartment in Hollywood. A while back, when she had moved to an apartment near his in Santa Monica, she said it was because of the street people. But Carr knew that was only part of it. She had wanted him to get used to her being close. It had worked.

He wanted to call her tonight, but didn't know quite what to say. He didn't look forward to the explanation of why he hadn't phoned in almost a month. There was no particular reason except that he had been busy making arrests because of Rico. Plenty of arrests: pimps and pushers, blacks and whites, anyone who had counterfeit money for sale.

The underworld had bought Rico hook, line, and sinker. It had been Carr's idea to give Rico plenty of leeway, and it had worked. Rico's answering-service phone hadn't stopped ringing for a month. The word of a solid buyer had spread fast. The project chart showed twenty-one separate hand-to-hand buys in a month. Twenty-one trips to the federal lockup for the sellers. Even in court, with Rico on the witness stand, some of them had difficulty believing the surly Rico was a United States Treasury special agent.

"Why cause misery?" Kelly said during a commercial. "Ever think of it like that?" He folded meat-hook hands behind his head. "Everything we do causes shit for somebody. You get a call to a liquor store . . . somebody passed a phony twenty. You give the liquor-store man a receipt for the twenty. He is pissed off. You find the guy who passed the twenty and arrest him. He is pissed off. You find the printer and arrest him. Now you have enemies. In court the federal prosecutor doesn't like the case, so he's pissed off, and the judge hates you on general principles. So I ask you: Why should we break our ass making cases? Why cause misery?"

"Because it's a lot of good clean fun," Carr said, with a wry smile.

"Yeah, and so is cancer," said Kelly.

4

Carr looked at his watch. It was 11:30 P.M. He tested the volume knob on the Kel Kit radio receiver on the table next to him. If the batteries held out, he would be able to hear every word in Rico's room.

Straddling a chair, he leaned closer to the Venetian blind. He removed the gold Treasury badge from his pocket and clipped it to his coat pocket so it would be in plain sight for the arrest.

The radio receiver blared. Rico's voice was young and upper Bronx. "I'll make the phone call now," Rico said. "Better tell Kelly to wake up." He laughed.

"Wise ass," Kelly said to the television.

Rico dialed the phone.

"Hello, Ronnie? This is Angelo," said the young undercover agent. "I got your message. I'll see you in room seven at the Sunset Motel near California Street within a half hour. I'm ready to deal and I'm not going to wait any longer than thirty minutes. . . . Right . . . I will show you my ten-grand buy money before you show me the funny money. . . . You have nothing to worry about if what you deliver is like the sample you gave me."

Good job, Carr thought. Set the time limit and the rules.

The waterbed made a sloshing sound as Kelly lumbered off it. He looked a little like an old bear. The parts of his body were oversized. Enormous hands and feet, big nose and jowls.

"Sounds like your star pupil is catching on," he said, tucking in his shirt.

Carr nodded and stuck his hand in front of the Venetian blind, giving Rico the thumbs-up sign. Rico returned the gesture, then closed the curtain of his room; standard procedure.

The bedsprings creaked. Rico sat down on the bed in his room to wait. Everything having been planned, everyone having been briefed, there was nothing else to say. The arrest signal would be the usual one. Rico would say, "That seems to be all of it," after he had counted the counterfeit money. Then the door would go down.

"Does Rico have an undercover piece?" Kelly said.

"Two inch in an ankle holster," Carr said. The question caused him to reflect for a moment on the fact that he had found it necessary to remind Rico of safety precautions a little too often. He had chalked this up to the "Elliot Ness syndrome," which he had surmounted over twenty years ago. He figured everyone went through it. Running a finger through flame.

"You know why Rico's been doing so well in this project?" Kelly fiddled with the handcuffs on his belt.

"Why?"

"Because he looks more like a crook than the people who sell him the counterfeit money. Olive complexion, black hair, pinky ring; a real Richard Conte."

"He's too young to know who Richard Conte is," said Carr as he stared out the window at the hot-dog-stand freaks.

"Walking entrapment. That's what Rico is. Some shyster will probably bring that up as a defense someday." Kelly lowered his voice. "Ladies and gentlemen of the jury, look at this mean-looking Italian. He scared my poor client into selling him counterfeit money. How's that for a defense?" Kelly rubbed his barrel stomach. "I'm hungry," he said.

"He sounded real nervous over the phone," Rico said. The transmitter gave his voice a hollow, metallic tone.

Carr wished he could say something back, thought for a moment of phoning Rico's room, but decided against it. The seller would be arriving any minute.

Kelly peeked out the opposite end of the Venetian blind. "This room smells like the dog pound. They should rename this place the Dog Shit Motel. The Hollywood Dog Shit Motel."

Carr shook his head.

Over the radio came the sound of Rico lighting a cigarette.

Kelly began pacing around the room to kill time, running his hand through his salt-and-pepper hair at regular intervals.

"There he is!" said Carr. A young man carrying an attaché case approached Rico's room. The man appeared to be about thirty, medium build, and wore a stylish black leather jacket. He glanced behind him nervously.

Standing at the door, Kelly undid the inside latch and tested the handle, making sure it was unlocked. He pulled his revolver from the shoulder holster and held it next to his leg.

The man in the leather jacket took a final look behind him and knocked on the door. He went in.

Carr turned up the radio.

"Well, here I am," said the man. There was a quaver in his

6

voice. "I've got the funny money right here in the case. Let's see the real stuff."

"Take it easy," Rico said. "I've got the ten grand. . . . Look."

Carr heard the crinkling of the paper bag he had given Rico earlier containing Uncle Sam's marked ten thousand dollars. He guessed Rico had poured the money out on the bed for the count.

Carr turned the volume on the radio even higher. There was the unsnapping of the latches on the attaché case . . . a frenzied moment of scrambling. A loud blast made him jump out of his chair. He instinctively pulled his gun. Ears throbbing, he dashed out the door and across the parking lot to Rico's room, Kelly a few feet behind.

Attacking the motel door with powerful kicks, they entered the room guns first.

Rico was lying on the floor next to the bed, hands clutching his face. Kelly ran to the open window.

No one else was in the room.

Tires squealed outside. "He's gone!" screamed Kelly. He ran to the phone.

Revolver still in hand, Carr moved closer to Rico and began to kneel down. He was involuntarily repulsed. Rico's face was blown back and away like a skinned rabbit. A distorted eye socket was gouged open to meet the ear, and bits of brain matter and blood made a circular design on the corner of the cheap bedspread.

Carr, on his knees, stared at the ruined body.

Kelly yelled, gasped, into the phone, "I want an ambulance! Sunset Motel, Sunset at California Street! A federal officer has been shot."

Carr placed his fingers gently on Rico's neck. No pulse. No breathing. He stared at his fingers, now wet with blood.

Rico's pants leg was up and the small revolver, the undercover gun, was showing. It was still in the holster.

Kelly stood next to him and crossed himself. "Holy Mother of God," he cried, turning his head away. "He must have used a sawed-off shotgun."

To Carr, the squalid room became more unbearable with each group that arrived: ambulance attendants shaking their

7

heads, young policemen running about, and, finally, coroner's deputies in olive-drab overalls.

Later, as police detectives and Treasury agents cordoned off the motel room, combing for evidence, Carr and Kelly stood together outside the door. They were unable to look at one another. The motel lot was full of men and women who had come out of their rooms to gape.

Across the boulevard the habitués of the hot-dog stand pointed and gawked like children watching a puppet show.

A coroner's ghoul walked from a black station wagon carrying a blue rubber body bag.

"Don't use that," Carr said.

"Whaddaya mean?" mumbled the ghoul. He looked at Carr's eyes for a moment.

"Oh, yeah, sure."

A few minutes later Carr stepped out of the way as the man pushed the gurney toward the station wagon. The body of Rico de Fiore was wrapped in a sheet and blanket.

The fatigue had set in.

On the way back to Hollywood from downtown, Carr leaned back in the passenger seat and closed his eyes. Kelly weaved in and out of freeway traffic and rambled fitfully about the lack of clues.

Though early in the morning, it was already hot enough to turn on air conditioning or jump in a pool. They had been up all night, going from county morgue to field office to police department; a headachy night of repeating the story, making reports, phone calls, composite sketches. Kelly pulled into a no-parking curb zone in front of Rico's apartment building. A sign posted in the middle of an ivy lawn read APARTMENT FOR RENT. ADULTS ONLY—NO PETS.

Carr opened a window inside the studio apartment, thus furnishing the room with a shaft of dust-reflecting light and a view of a cement retaining wall. "When you rent a place, make sure there are no windows facing the street," Carr had told Rico, as if the young agent hadn't known better.

The furniture was neat and impersonal: a painted chest of drawers, flower-patterned sofa, and small wooden desk. On the wall above the sofa hung a desert-scene print in an aluminum frame, which came with the room.

The apartment reminded Carr of scores of the easily forgettable "temporary duty" places he had rented in his early career. A trailer in Las Vegas, the two-bedroom hovel in San Francisco's mission district, a brownstone walk-up in Baltimore; the duty was temporary because it ended when everyone except the undercover man was suddenly arrested. He remembered the loneliness brought on as much by the environment of self-interest as by solitude. He had learned to take the edge off the loneliness by working harder, meeting more paper pushers, pressing more strongly for the hundred-grand buys.

Kelly rummaged through pots and pans in the kitchen. He pulled a large roaster pan from a bottom drawer of the stove and removed the lid. "Here's the issue equipment," he said. He sat down at a chrome-legged dinette table and removed items from the roaster pan: a government-issued cassette tape recorder with telephone attachment, a shoulder holster, binoculars, expense voucher forms, government transportation requests. He put the items in a cardboard box.

Carr found one of Rico's phony driver's licenses hidden under army-rolled socks in the chest of drawers. He picked it up and handed it to Kelly.

Carr remembered picking Rico up at the airport two months ago and handing him the license. "Don't forget to memorize the date of birth on the license before you fill out the rental application," he had said. It was always the little things.

Kelly was up and crashing about, pulling drawers out of cupboards, turning them upside down, spilling things. "His daily reports have got to be here somewhere."

"They're here somewhere," Carr said.

He had met Rico late every night at the hot-dog stand on Alvarado to check them. Rico's reports were always up to date.

Carr had said, "Keep the pressure on. Make the seller put up or shut up. It's what real crooks do. Make 'em deliver and give the arrest signal. You know the scenario and they don't. Keep it simple."

"You like to play with their minds," Rico said. "All I want to do is make a few buys, testify before the grand jury, and go home to New York. Times Square at midnight is kindergarten compared to temporary duty in Hollywood." They both laughed.

Rico was the best he had seen—cautious, with the ability to take orders, but, more important, the ability to break them if necessary, to be resourceful, to recognize things as they were and forget the always safe and sure *Manual of Operations* answer. Like Carr, Rico could feel the pulse.

Kelly, trancelike, sat down at the kitchen table again. He talked into the cardboard box.

Then he slammed a fist into an open palm. "Sheeyit!"

$ /2

Carr, a trim man with mournful brown eyes, wove his way through flocks of Chinatown tourists. The smell of incense and fried shrimp was familiar. He headed for Ling's Bar, passing novelty shops with bored-looking Oriental sales people standing in doorways. Having just come from the funeral, he needed a drink.

He paused and noticed his reflection in the window glass of a jade-jewelry shop. He was shocked by his seedy, tired appearance. Darkness under the eyes and a sprinkle of broken blood vessels on his cheekbones. Features fighting age. Temples more gray than brown. Maybe a haircut would help, and perhaps a shoeshine.

Or maybe a new wardrobe. . . . His lapels were outdated. He refused to buy new suits to look stylish while crawling under a house to search for counterfeit money or wrestling a hype.

His appearance had been one of Sally's pet topics. She had even given him a hair blower. He had used it once and retired it to a junk drawer.

As he waited for the light at Hill Street, he thought of the bright stained glass, agents and cops standing in line, the sound of Rico's sisters sobbing.

The light turned green and he continued on, crossing the street among a group of middle-aged women. Hell, he was close to their age. Behind him were twenty years of "street time."

11

Staying on the street, with his sleeves rolled up, had been his own choice. Asking questions and getting answers was what he was good at, climbing the ladder to the printing press, beating the bad guys. Leave the pencil-pushing to those who took their transfers to the ivory tower of Washington, D.C.

Now, things had changed. Because of Rico's murder he knew he was headed for the barn. The first rule of bureaucracy is that somebody always has to take the blame. They would say that his security precautions at the motel had not been adequate. They would transfer him to the Washington, D.C., scrap heap. Had he done the right thing by refusing the promotions that had been offered him through the years?

He passed a penny-stained goldfish pond known as the Chinatown Wishing Well and turned down an alley.

"Charlie!"

A man's voice behind him. Higgins, a muscular man with short blond hair, walked toward him down the alley with a paper napkin tucked over his belt buckle. His pants were baggy and he wore a plaid sports coat with a revolver bulge on the right side. Approaching Carr, he pulled the napkin from his belt and wiped his mouth.

"Just chowing down," he said. "Saw you pass by the window. I need to run one by ya."

"Shoot," Carr said.

"I'm looking for a guy who slit an old lady's throat. Snitch says the guy who did it has a nickname—'Trash-Truck Jimmy.' S'posed to have done time years ago for passing queer twenties and tens. Ring a bell?"

"Jimmy Tortamasi," Carr said. "He did time in Terminal Island about five years ago for passing. Escaped once by hiding inside a trash truck. He walks with a limp now. The truck had a hydraulic compacter, and he figured there was enough room for a body between the pusher and the back wall of the truck."

"I take it he figured wrong."

"Right," Carr said. "It crushed him like a grape. After a year in the prison hospital he was good as new . . . except for the leg. Jimmy should be about forty-five now. When he's out of the joint, he usually lives in one of the fleabags around McArthur Park."

Higgins was writing the name down on the napkin. "T-o-r-t-a-m-a-s-i?" he said.

Carr nodded.

"I told my partner, if the dude was into bad paper, you'd know who he was." He put the napkin in his shirt pocket and stepped a little closer to Carr. Suddenly he looked embarrassed. "I'm sorry about Rico. I didn't get a chance to make it to the funeral. . . ."

"I want to know everything you hear about capers with sawed-off shotguns. Call me night or day."

"That's a promise," said the detective.

Carr swung open the door at Ling's, and glass chimes rattled. Sunlight splashed along the bar, revealing rows of brandy snifters with tiny parasols. On the wall hung a swan-scene tapestry and a photograph of the spectacled Ling and his brother wearing bow ties.

A dusty jukebox in the corner (known to the badge-carrying regulars as Ling's Hit Parade) waited to blend outdated tunes into the usual field office and precinct house chatter. Because of the early hour, the four worn Naugahyde booths nestled against the opposite wall were empty.

Delgado sat at the bar alone. He stood up and greeted Carr with a strong handshake. He had been the agent-in-charge in Los Angeles years ago, before his leadership abilities had vaulted him to Washington, D.C.

It was no secret that Delgado and Carr were old friends. Without a friend in Washington, Carr could never have managed to avoid the bureaucrats' obsessive love of transfers and remain in Los Angeles. Of course, wanting to stay in Los Angeles was a desire few other agents could understand. While most other T-men couldn't wait to buy a set of golf clubs and ship out for three years of "eight-a-day-Monday-through-Friday" in Phoenix or Portland, Carr preferred L.A.'s big-city action. Undercover buys, search warrants, and conspiracy cases were his cup of tea. Besides, Los Angeles, from sandy-floored beach bars to the shady edges of the tract-house valleys, felt like home by now.

"Greetings, *amigo*," said the tall, slim Chicano. "It's been a long time." With his full head of gray hair and pin-striped suit, Alex Delgado could pass for a Latin-American diplomat.

"I guess you knew where to find me," Carr said.

"Right." Delgado laughed curtly. "I came here from the airport. . . . Took the noon flight out of Dulles." He looked ill-at-ease. His complexion had a saddle-soap tinge.

Carr sat down. He looked at the other man's suit. "You dress a little better now that you're a big-shot headquarters inspector," he said with a smile.

"I'm such a big shot that I'm bored to death. My job is nothing but political bullshit, staff reports, and phony statistics. . . . Doctor tells me I have an ulcer." Delgado pointed to his glass. "Look at me. I have to drink Scotch and milk. I had an operation, but it didn't help, so I've been thinking about pulling the pin. I've got my twenty-five years in, and I'm tired of fighting the ass kissers and pencil heads. . . ." He tore pieces from the wet napkin under his drink. "How about you?"

Ling set a Scotch-and-water in front of Carr, who sipped, then said, "Haven't really thought about it."

"Are you still seeing Sally?"

Carr nodded.

"Nice gal. A really classy lady. The wife and I always sort of hoped you two would get married. You go back a long ways with Sally, don't you?"

"I guess so."

"Typical Charlie Carr remark," Delgado said. "Noncommital when it comes to anything personal. No, sir, you haven't changed a bit."

"You have. You used to get to the point a little quicker."

Delgado ignored the statement without so much as a wince. A survival technique, Carr figured, that he had picked up at the School of Beating Around the Bush on the banks of the Potomac; smile, agree, ignore, achieve.

The gray-haired man dug a handkerchief out of his pocket and wiped milk from the corners of his mouth. "I look at retirement as just a change of scenery," he said. "Nothing more. It'll do me good. I don't need the pressure any more. I've done my part. It'll be a welcome change for me. Changes are something we all have to face." He gulped the chalky mixture and continued. "It's just a matter of accepting the stages of life. I mean you and I are of another generation. The new guys don't know how

14

it was years ago, before court decisions: Miranda, Escobedo, outlawing the wiretaps. . . . Things are one hundred percent different from when you and I went to Special Agent School. I'm sure you agree."

Carr didn't answer.

"Seriously. I'm asking your opinion," Delgado said. He patted Carr's arm.

Carr looked at Ling and made the "another round" gesture with his index finger. Ling dug into a sink full of ice with a scoop.

"Nothing has changed," Carr said. "It's the same street, the same bad guys. The same rules. Only difference is that they don't stay in prison as long—and they all carry guns. That's because they watch TV and they think they are *supposed* to carry guns. Other than that, nothing has changed. Everything is exactly the same."

Delgado curtly laughed away from the subject and steered the conversation to small talk. The next two hours were spent talking of ancient cases, almost forgotten girlfriends, and snapping fingers trying to remember bartenders' names at some of the old downtown hangouts.

Though it was one drink after another, neither man became drunk. It was as if it was necessary to pour in the drinks to continue. Carr knew it was Delgado's way.

Then finally came the trunk story. It was almost a ritual between them by now and seemed to grow with every retelling. Undercover Agent Carr, acting the part of a buyer and convincing the seller to accompany him to Big Bear to pick up a package of twenties, Delgado hiding in the trunk of the automobile as protection. Delgado's motion sickness on the mountain roads, the retching sounds coming from the trunk, Carr turning up the radio to cover the sounds—then the punch line. Delgado, covered from head to toe with vomit, jumps out of the trunk, gun drawn, and runs into the mountain cabin to arrest the counterfeiter. When it was over, even *he* had laughed at Delgado's strange appearance.

They chuckled. Delgado slapped Carr on the back. "Charlie, you're one of the best undercover men in Treasury. For twenty years you've made cases that others couldn't make. The counterfeiters fear you. You're known as the Snake out there. . . ." He sipped a fresh Scotch-and-milk. "But guys like you and me have to move along in life. . . . Do you know what I'm saying?"

"Not exactly," Carr said. I'm going to make you say it, he thought.

"I'm telling you the powers-that-be are saying that Charlie the Snake should accept his rightful senior agent status like the others of his vintage and come out of the street. I mean why the hell should you still be out there booting doors, covering buys, taking chances every goddamn day? In that, I agree with what they are saying."

Ling served Carr's seventh Scotch-and-water with a "here comes joke" leer, and said something about Carr's needing to find a new girlfriend since Rose the cocktail waitress was on vacation at Lake Arrowhead. Carr forced a smile. Ling returned to a sink at the other end of the bar and continued scrubbing glasses.

"I guess you know that I'm in charge of the shooting investigation," Delgado said. "That's why they sent me out here."

Carr took a long pull from the drink. "What have they decided to do with me?"

Delgado paused before answering. "Charlie, you know I'm just the one who coordinates the interviews and writes the final report. I can make a recommendation, but what happens in the end is up to the people at headquarters."

"Hogwash," Carr said matter-of-factly. "The Ivory Tower has already decided what they're going to do. Your report will be justification for it. I want to know what's going to happen to me."

Delgado looked at his drink sadly. "They're going to transfer you on the next list. Of course you'll be able to get your choice of offices. . . . I can help with that."

Carr spoke to Delgado's reflection in the bar mirror. "Hold up the transfer until I find who killed Rico."

"You know how headquarters is. . . ."

Carr turned to face the other man. "To hell with headquarters. I'm not taking a transfer until this thing is over."

"No, sir, the years haven't changed Charlie Carr." Delgado sipped his drink. He rubbed his stomach.

16

Carr felt uneasy. He wished he'd been less direct.

"Charlie, what are your ideas on how the investigation should go?" Delgado said at last.

"If Rico's murder had made the papers," Carr said, "we might never find the killer. Luckily, there's been no publicity, so the killer must believe he murdered a hood. He must figure that the cops have nothing to go on except the body of a thief in a motel room. I say that's what we want him to think. Let him believe he killed a hood rather than a cop. Our only chance to bag him is if he tries it again."

Delgado nodded and ordered more drinks.

At 1:30 A.M. Ling began wiping up the bar and locking liquor cabinets. He yammered something about closing time.

"I guess you were pretty close to the young fellow," said Delgado in a soft tone.

Carr cleared his throat twice. "You would have liked him. He was one-hundred-percent T-man. He could have become an inspector like you someday. He could smell green ink a mile away." He spoke imploringly, as if the inspector had the power to change what had happened.

"I'm going to lay my cards on the table," Delgado said, with open palms. "I want the killer caught one way or the other. You know what I mean by that. On the other hand, I don't want to see you end up in Leavenworth in his place."

Delgado got off his barstool, rushed his drink to his mouth, and swallowed. He looked at Carr. "I can postpone your transfer for a few weeks. It's against policy, but I've got my years in and there's not a hell of a lot they can do to me at this point. I'll use the argument that you are the only one who saw the killer and can identify him. All I'm asking you to do is keep your head. I want your word you will keep your head."

Carr, sober, looked him in the eye. "You have my word."

"Ling, two more for the road," Delgado said.

"I'll also give you my word on something else," said Carr. "I'm going to find the one who did it and put him in a box."

Delgado acted as if he hadn't heard the remark.

Carr pushed the buzzer under the name Sally Malone and waited. He was prepared for her not to let him in.

Seconds later, the door buzzed open. He walked upstairs to her apartment. The door was ajar and he walked in almost cautiously. The living room was neat-as-a-pin Mediterranean, with lots of carved wood and modern-art prints. The place was as immaculate as her desk in Judge Malcolm's courtroom.

Sally was standing at the stove stirring mushrooms with a wooden spoon, her back to him. She wore a robe that barely touched her knees.

"Look who's here," she said without turning around. Her voice was soft, almost inaudible, as always.

Carr sat down at the kitchen table and drummed his fingers. Sally stopped stirring, poured a Scotch-and-water and plunked it down in front of him.

"You know this is the first time I have seen you in three weeks," she said after returning to the stove. Admiring her gray-streaked hair and tanned athletic features, Carr thought she looked much more like a dance instructor than a stenographer. They had met because she had asked *him* to lunch, during a counterfeiting trial. He remembered waiting for her to call him the next week, as sort of a people experiment. He finally had to call her. Later, she said she would never have called him for the second date. He always wondered. . . .

"You know how busy . . ." he said.

She turned and faced him. "How busy can someone be!" she interrupted in an angry whisper. "Can you really be so busy that we only see each other once a month? . . . Twelve times a year? The same thing is happening to us again, and I, for one, should know better. Sometimes I can't believe I have known you for eight years."

"It's not like I intentionally didn't call you," Carr said. "You know that." He realized it was a dumb thing to say as soon as the words left his mouth.

"I know *exactly* why you didn't call! You and that crude Jack Kelly are like children who forget what time it is when they're playing. You get a charge out of arresting people and all the crap that goes with it. You are a forty-five-year-old Boy Scout! You like the danger or something. I don't understand you. . . . Did you know that we both live in apartments in Santa Monica and see each other once a month? Oh, hell, what's the use!"

18

She turned back toward the stove, picked up the frying pan, and dumped the mushrooms into the sink. She washed the pan furiously. Nothing was said for a few minutes.

"Did you know the young undercover man who was killed? I heard the judge talking about it." Her tone was sour.

"Yes," murmured Carr. He sipped his drink.

Sally finished up at the stove and placed the utensils in the sink. She grabbed the edge of the kitchen counter with her hands and stood with her head down.

Carr looked at his watch. "I thought we could go to a movie tonight," he said politely.

"Jesus," she said, shaking her head. "No communication *whatsoever*. Why can't you talk to me? I heard you were *there* when it happened. Can't you at least share that with me? Sometimes when I am around you I feel absolutely alone, as if I'm talking to . . ."

Carr stood up and walked toward the door.

"Please don't leave right now," Sally said.

Quietly, Carr followed her into the bedroom.

It was the usual sex scene: the almost perfunctory kisses, clothes in neat separate piles, thrusting tongues, moans of love, her fingernails in the usual place on his shoulders, Carr delaying his orgasm until the proper time. . . . Then the whispers.

"I have two tickets to a charity brunch at Marina Del Rey tomorrow morning," she said. "The judge gave them to me. It should be a real nice affair." She got up from the bed and put on a robe. Her eyes sought his reaction.

"I had planned to drive out . . ."

". . . to Chino," she interrupted. "A two-hour drive to Chino prison to see Howard. After all, you certainly wouldn't want to miss your Saturday visit with him. You've gone out there every Saturday for the past year. Every single Saturday . . . Incredible." She shook her head.

"We could go somewhere on Sunday," Carr said.

She stared at the bedroom mirror. "Sure. To wherever I want. You, as usual, never have any ideas. For once I would like to go somewhere that we both want to go. . . . Though I'm sure you'd much prefer to be sitting at a bar in Chinatown drinking with your pals." She said "pals" as if it were a curse.

$/3

Carr's mind wandered as he drove on the Pomona Freeway toward Chino. He pictured Norbert Waeves (known as No Waves), the pipe-smoking Los Angeles special agent-in-charge, puffing smoke and reading aloud the one-inch newspaper article about Howard. "Howard Dumbrowski, a special agent of the U.S. Treasury Department, pleaded guilty to manslaughter today in Superior Court. Accused of murdering his wife after finding her with another man in their Glendale apartment, Dumbrowski declined to make any statement in his own behalf before being sentenced to two years in state prison." Jumping for joy, the SAIC had tossed the newspaper in the air. "Hooray! He pleaded guilty! No trial! No more bad publicity!"

The visiting-hour trips to Chino were rough at the beginning—forced laughs followed by embarrassing silences.

Carr turned off the highway at the green overhead sign CALIFORNIA CORRECTIONAL INSTITUTE, CHINO. ONE MILE.

The visitors' area was in the open. Metal picnic tables surrounded by a high chain-link fence. It reminded Carr of a grammar-school lunch area. At the tables sat blacks and Chicanos talking with sadly dressed wives. Restless children in T-shirts and tennis shoes wrestled on the yellow grass like bear cubs.

Howard, with a gray crew cut and starched denims, still looked like a cop: stocky, blue-bearded, piercing blue eyes.

20

During the past year his eyes had seemed to become more deep-set.

Carr sat down. Howard smiled. He began dealing gin rummy, a ritual that had started as a compromise to avoid the hurt of conversation. Howard had nothing to talk about any more, and Carr knew that shop talk, even about the old days, brought a sadness to Howard's eyes.

"I got a letter from my daughter yesterday. She told me about Rico de Fiore."

Carr hesitated. "I was his cover. The guy who did it got away from me. He jumped out the motel-room back window."

"Rico was a sharp kid. He had the touch," said the prisoner.

Carr nodded. They looked at each other for a moment.

Howard shuffled and dealt the cards. "Pick up your hand," he said.

At the end of the hand Carr took a small notebook out of his sports-coat pocket, turned to a fresh page, and recorded the score of the fiftieth game.

"I'm going to Eugene, Oregon, when I get out," Howard said. "Lumber-mill job. With the conviction, I figure that's the best I can do. I know I would have beat the rap if I'd gone to trial. Catching her in the sack and all, you know . . . temporary insanity . . . But I didn't want to embarrass my daughter with a trial. You can imagine how the press would have played up the whole thing, how it would have looked to her college friends."

Nothing was said for a long while. Eventually Carr took over as dealer, Howard as scorekeeper.

"Partner, there's something I gotta say," Howard said. The blue eyes flashed. "There were rough times in here, particularly the first few months. I had to fight every day. Once, I found out they were going to put ant poison in my chow. I didn't eat until I found out who it was. A big husky guy. I caught him in the yard and kicked his teeth out. Got almost all of 'em." He hesitated. "I guess what I'm getting at is that I don't know if I would have made it without the card games. I know I can make it now."

"Pick up your cards," Carr said.

"There's something else," Howard said. "Since the day I was

arrested, you're the only one who's stuck by me, and you've never asked me one question about it. I really appreciate that. . . . But I want you to know. A year ago I walked into my apartment with a few drinks under my belt and my old lady is fucking the next-door neighbor. I killed her because I had my gun on. I was a federal cop and my gun was right there in a holster on my belt. Now I'm in the joint for it . . . but I'm the same now as I ever was, and like you and everybody else in the whole goddamn world, I'm never going to change. . . . My wife is dead and I'm alive and one year older. It's as simple as that. A set of circumstances."

A bell sounded. A guard opened a gate in the chain-link fence, and visitors began to depart.

Howard stood up and put the deck of cards in his shirt pocket. They shook hands. "Drop me a line when you get your transfer orders," Howard said.

The Treasury field office was located in the stodgy-looking Federal Courthouse on Spring Street, just a few blocks up from L.A.'s skid row. Jack Kelly waited in the technical shop. He gazed out the window.

The view from the field office was clear, up to a point. Things over a half-mile or so away were blurry. Boyle Heights was in haze the color of oatmeal.

Below, on Spring Street, the "Blue Goose," a large police van, headed toward the tenderloin. Years ago, when Kelly had been on the force, the old-timers used to make the recruits drive the Goose, to avoid the body lice.

He looked at his watch and sipped coffee. For some reason he thought of the Timmy Fontaine incident.

He remembered being on the duty desk the night a young ponytailed hitchhiker marched into the field office and told him about how she was picked up by a "Timmy," who drove her to his Malibu bachelor pad, which had giant stereo speakers.

After she posed for photos in the bedroom, Timmy masturbated while standing over her (Kelly remembered her describing this as being "far out") and then showed her a suitcase full of phony ten-dollar bills. Probably to show off.

Later, the brass said that before Kelly went to a federal judge and obtained a search warrant, he should have determined who Timmy was. The second-guessers figured that if Kelly had known that young Timmy was the son of the Honorable Augustus Fontaine (D., Calif.) he might have handled it differently.

That's where they were wrong. Jack Kelly wouldn't have cared if it had been Prince Charles with the suitcase full of green. He would have done exactly the same thing. Filed the search warrant, knocked on Timmy's door, announced his purpose, kicked Timmy's door down, found the suitcase, and arrested Timmy for possession of funny money, just as though he were any other street punk.

Just that alone would have started a major flap, but it burst into epic proportions when Timmy made the mistake of punching Kelly on the side of his head, during the arrest, breaking a manicured thumb. Kelly counterpunched the unfortunate Timmy on the point of the chin, breaking the attached jaw in two places and causing Timmy's mouth to be wired shut during the trial.

The pressure from above hadn't worked on the judge, and Timmy was sentenced to a year in Lompoc, which Kelly attributed to the fact that the judge had been appointed by a Republican administration.

The honorable congressman got back at them by having one of his old law partners sue Kelly and Uncle Sam in a trumped-up civil-rights and personal-injury case. They even alleged that Kelly broke Timmy's thumb in order to make him talk.

The suit failed, but Kelly ended up in cold storage indexing counterfeit notes and answering calls from bank tellers about what to do if "In God We Trust" was missing from the reverse of a twenty-dollar bill.

After a year he was offered a chance to return to field duties, but he told the agent-in-charge thanks anyway, but that he got the same pay for pushing a pencil as for cracking heads, and that he preferred to remain behind the desk.

It was Carr who had kept Kelly's interest piqued. He eventually enticed Kelly away from the desk and back into the street by little things, such as making sure that copies of interesting reports crossed his desk. Kelly knew what he was up to. Carr was his only real friend.

23

When Carr walked in now, he removed a cassette tape and a plastic envelope containing a counterfeit ten-dollar bill from a file folder marked "Evidence."

Kelly pushed aside a radio chassis and other odds and ends on the workbench and plugged in the tape recorder. He had heard the motel recording many times during the past three days, but realized that when other leads don't pan out a man has to start all over again.

The hours he and Carr had spent looking through mug books of known strong-arm men and rip-off artists had been useless.

They had read the reports of interviews with the residents of the street facing the rear of the motel. No one had seen anything out of the ordinary.

At the Police Crime Lab Kelly had been told there was no physical evidence. No footprints, no fingerprints, no hair. The man in the black leather jacket had walked in the door of the motel room, killed Rico, stolen the buy money, and departed like an actor in the final scene of some bizarre stage play.

Sure, Kelly knew he and Carr had seen the killer, but unfortunately a face is of no use without a name, except perhaps to Kojak or Dick Tracy.

The words floated from the tape machine like the sound of fingernails on a chalkboard.

"Well, here I am. I've got the funny money right here in the case. Let's see the real stuff."

Kelly had already decided there was no detectable accent. No use calling in dialect experts.

"Take it easy," he heard Rico say as the tape continued. "I've got the ten grand. . . . Look." Rico's voice was reassuring. He had learned the lesson well: always show confidence before the buy, to take the crook's mind off protecting himself. Makes him slower to react when the door goes down, gives the arrest team an edge.

Kelly heard the crinkling of the paper bag containing the buy money, then a "ping, ping" sound. Attaché case latches. He figured the case was probably opened on the bed, with the cover facing Rico so he couldn't see the sawed-off shotgun.

With the sound of the shotgun, Kelly crushed the empty plastic cup he was holding and slung it into a wastebasket.

"Turn it off for a second," Carr said with a wave of his hand. Kelly slapped at the plastic buttons, and the tape stopped.

"There was no sound of a round being chambered or a safety being clicked off from the shotgun. That means it was ready to fire when he walked in the door. He didn't come to bluff. He intended to kill somebody."

Kelly nodded and turned on the machine again. By turning up the volume, they could hear the killer slam the case shut, run across the room, scramble out the window. Mixed with the sounds of the door being kicked in, they heard the killer's feet making crunching sounds as he ran down the gravel-covered driveway; then the sound of a car door, squealing tires.

"He must have cased the motel and seen the open window of room seven; otherwise he would have parked in the lot. It would have been easier," Kelly said.

"Wait a second," Carr interrupted. "Play it again. I think I've got something."

Kelly frowned as he snapped the cassette back in the machine. Listening to the tape made him sick to his stomach.

As the tape ran, Kelly noticed Carr looking at his watch. Finally, the tape ran out.

"He didn't start the engine," Carr said. "The sound of footsteps ended and the car zoomed off. The car door hadn't even closed."

"You're right," Kelly said. "He had to have had a getaway driver." Kelly wondered why he hadn't thought of that himself.

The wall phone rang, and Carr picked it up.

"Freddie Roth—are you sure? Okay, thanks."

Carr hung up the phone, walked to the workbench, and picked up the counterfeit ten-dollar bill.

"That was Delgado. A teletype just came in. The D.C. lab says these tens are from an old Freddie Roth printing. It's the first time these particular notes have shown up in over five years."

"Now we have a lead," said Kelly.

$/4

Red Diamond sat on a barstool and sipped straight soda because it was easy on his stomach. The cocktail napkin under the soda read "The Paradise Isle—Hollywood's Friendliest Tavern," though to Red neither the five-foot-tall slimy-haired bartender nor the two puffy-eyed bookies at the other end of the bar looked particularly friendly.

The place smelled like beer-soaked wood and wet ashes.

A wilted cartoon drawing of a giant-headed jockey (the bartender) astride a horse covered part of the spotty bar mirror. It was next to a chalkboard with scribbled messages. "The Commander—call Jimmy J." "Gloria—call your P.O." "Flaco—call the answering service in Vegas."

Red removed a half-dollar-size gambling chip from his pocket and tried to make it finger-walk on the back of his hand. The chip had inlaid red, white, and blue spots and bore a Sahara Club Casino camel trademark. He had discovered the chip in a satchel of personal belongings handed to him by a guard a half hour before he was released from Terminal Island. It had been nine days ago.

Obviously, he had overlooked the chip when he reported to the prison five years earlier to begin serving his sentence. Of course, in those days he considered a ten-spot as nothing more than toke money for the bellman, waiters, bartenders, and cocktail waitresses who had their mitts out when they saw him coming. That's the way it had been before everything went sour.

No period in his life had been more rewarding. For a while it seemed like the suckers had literally been *throwing* their money at him. . . . For once he had been accepted and protected by the big boys, and at home the Cherokee-blooded Mona had wrapped her velvety tippy-toe legs around him every night.

The prison stretch had certainly not been the first, but it had hurt more. Red attributed this to the age factor. After all, what in the world wasn't easier at twenty-five than at fifty-plus?

Red's sensitive colon gurgled. He restrained an urge to run for the men's room because he knew it was just nerves. Ronnie was an hour late. How long could it take to ditch a goddamn car?

The feeling in his bowels reminded him of the time he had posed as a bank courier and convinced a bank branch manager to give him three gold bars for delivery to Canada. As he stood in the bank's churchlike vault filling out the phony paperwork, he felt like he was going to mess his pants right then and there.

It had been mind over matter.

And mind over matter was why, at fifty-four years old, after serving five years flat for extortion, he was still able to come out fighting. He had slipped back five steps, but with a little luck, combined with good planning, he would soon be back in the running.

First he had to pay off Tony Dio, the loan shark.

During his first years in Terminal Island he had made himself believe that by the time he got out Dio would have died or something, and he would no longer owe the twenty-five grand. When he had borrowed it, he had had no problem paying the ten percent per week. Cash flow with the phony desert-land caper had been adequate to cover the nut. Then the rug was pulled out, and silk-tie Tony came to see him in the lockup and told him not to "worry" about paying it back until he got out of prison. Red had been out for nine days and he was worried. Maybe Ronnie's ten-grand score would keep Dio off his back for a while.

Right now, paying Dio back depended a lot on how well Ronnie performed. Ronnie had been useful in the federal pen. Anybody who's over fifty in the pen needed a bodyguard, and Ronnie had benefited by learning about something other than lowbrow, chickenshit bank jobs.

Red looked at his watch again, and scratched his balding pate fiercely. Much of the hair on top had fallen out during the last stretch, though the sides were still red and frizzy. He ordered another straight soda.

The bartender washed glasses. "I've seen you before," he said. His facial features were small, rodentlike, except for a set of oversized, improperly spaced teeth. He wore a long-sleeved polka-dot shirt with underarm stains.

"Think so?"

"Yep. You used to be with Tony Dio a few years back. I was tending bar at the Crossroads in Beverly Hills. You and him used to come in all the time. You guys were always buying rounds."

So big fucking deal, thought Red. "Small world," he said, looking at his watch. Ronnie, where are you?, he said to himself.

The little man filled a glass with ice, poured soda, and placed it gently next to Red's half-full drink. His fingernails were dirty. "I remembered because of the soda. You always ordered straight soda. I never forget a drink. . . . Name's Gabe." He hesitated a moment before sticking out his hand. "You probably remember me."

They shook hands. As Red had feared, the handshake suddenly made things chummy. Gabe rested his elbows on the bar and leaned close to Red's face.

He whispered, "I figure you must have just got out. I remember the case in the papers. Five years ago. It took the bank months to figure out what had happened. What was it? Phony bank loans to get stocks?"

Red shook his head. "Phony stocks to get bank loans."

"Yeah." The bartender beamed. "How did it work?"

"Too complicated to explain." Red looked at his watch again.

"I'm glad to see classy dudes like yourself in here. You ain't got no worries in here. I know most everybody that comes in. What goes down in here stays here. No turkeys in this crowd." He wiped his hands on the front of his pants.

28

Gabe shuffled to the end of the bar and served drinks to some bookmakers who had been alternately using the phone in the men's room. He hurried back to his old buddy.

Red cringed.

"Tony Dio's *big* now. *Real* big," Gabe said. "He can get *any-thing* done."

"That's what I hear," Red said.

Ronnie Boyce walked in the door in a blast of acrid L.A. heat, and Red's entire stomach felt better immediately. He motioned to Ronnie with both hands.

"What took so damn long? I thought you got popped or something. *Jesus!*"

Ronnie sat down on a barstool. "Couldn't find a bus back. I parked it down on Central Avenue. When the cops find it, they'll figure some nigger stole it." He motioned to the bartender.

"Very good. Very good," said Red. He removed a ball-point pen from his pocket and wrote on a cocktail napkin "Recovery operation."

"I'm proud of you, little brother. Stage one is complete," he said. "We're ahead of the game by ten grand. I want you to keep two grand for yourself right off the top. Buy yourself some clothes or something." He spoke as earnestly as possible, not sure if even dumb-as-a-rabbit Ronnie would buy what he said.

"I'll need the rest to start setting up the 'front.' Just like we talked about in the joint. These things take money. For a successful project we'll need a dummy office in Century City or on Wilshire Boulevard—and that takes *money.* You know that. Put the bucks in to get the bucks out. The suckers are out there just waiting. Right, partner?" Red put his arm around Ronnie's shoulder, waiting for a reaction. Ronnie nodded.

Red continued, speaking briskly. "With the getaway and everything, I still haven't got the exact details. I want you to relax and tell me just what happened in the room. After a caper it always pays to check for loose ends."

Ronnie's voice was youthful, soft. "I knocked on the door; he let me in. He was alone. Everything went pretty much just like you told me it would. He shows me the buy money, then I set my case on the bed between me and his. I whip out the sawed-

29

off and let loose. You should have seen it. He flew back all the way across the room. And you know something? When he went down, I saw that he had an ankle gun on. If I wouldn't have done him, he might have done me, right?" Ronnie tapped his chest with his thumb.

Red swallowed hard. "You did exactly the right thing. You just made the big time. I'm proud of you, little brother. Your old Red buddy is proud."

Ronnie smiled broadly. "It really worked, just like you said it would."

Red patted his arm. "And the best part is that there isn't going to be any heat from the cops. When the cops find a stiff in a motel room, the first thing they do is run fingerprints. When they do that, they see that the dude has an arrest sheet. The first thing the cops figure is that it was nothing but a thieves' argument and they close the case. That's as far as they go. See, I know how the pigs think. I used to have a lot of 'em drinking in my place in Long Beach in the old days. I used to hear 'em talk when they didn't think nobody was listening. You see, they actually *like* to find a dead thief. They get off on that kind of shit. And that's no lie. That's how they are. To them a dead thief is just less work."

Ronnie nodded his head without speaking, an athlete listening to the coach after competition.

Red continued. "I want you to take the sawed-off and stash it like I explained, and then enjoy yourself for a couple of days. Go see your old girlfriend like you been talking about. Why don't you meet me here day after tomorrow and I'll fill you in on stage two. As soon as we have enough capital, we'll be able to pull one big con and we'll be set for life, partner." The words flowed easily for Red. It was the same thing he had been telling Ronnie in stir for years, though Red knew that the last thing he would ever do would be to get involved in a confidence caper again. He was well known by the Feds and bunco cops from Hollywood to Fort Lauderdale. Christ, how many confidence men had red hair?

Red was too old to get his own hands dirty and end up doing another stretch.

30

$/5

On the way to the hotel Red Diamond drove past the glass-and-steel high-rise buildings in L.A.'s Century City: twenty-story condominium structures and plushly carpeted office suites for rent or lease. This is where I belong, thought Red. My milieu. He knew that with a few bucks he could rent an office in one of the high-rises again. He could start putting people on "hold" by pushing the lighted buttons on the phone. "Hold, please, for Mr. Diamond," the secretary had said. The high-rise world was a mystery to the pussy-headed group counselors at Terminal Island. "Inflated self-image," one had called it. "Don't you think your schemes could relate to your childhood conflicts?" the counselor had asked him.

Red remembered how he had slowly, carefully, over the period of a full year of tedious prison-counseling sessions, faked coming around to the counselor's point of view. It had been sort of a challenge, not to mention that there was nothing else to do. The pussy-headed dollar-an-hour dumb bastard finally bought his rehabilitation act and at the end of the year gave him a progress rating high enough for parole consideration. The counselor had taken the hook and swallowed it because he was like every other sucker in the world—prone to accept his own fantasy and susceptible to flattery. Red's credo proved true again.

Imagine, Red thought, a two-bit Department of Prisons civil

servant with two semesters of psychology writing a report on the behavior of Mr. Rudolph Diamond, former president of Gold Futures Unlimited, Sun King Recreational Properties Corporation, and the International Investment Bank of Nassau, in the Bahamas, whose buxom young secretary used to blow him as he leaned back on the Danish modern sofa in his office at the Century Building.

Red pulled up in front of the multistoried hotel and handed the car keys to a doorman dressed like a caballero.

He took a deep breath and knocked on the suite door. He was conscious of dampness in his armpits.

The door was opened quickly, chain still on, by a husky man in a flowered shirt. Red noticed a gun bulge at the man's waist.

"I have an appointment with Tony Dio," Red said.

The man unlatched the chain and ushered him over plush, thick carpet to a small balcony. On the balcony, without a word, the man began to frisk him. Ignoring this, Red sat down at the balcony table. He faced the ocean.

"Hey, I'm not finished patting you down, pal."

"Where's Tony?"

"You ain't going to see him until I see if you are wired up, pal."

"Tell Tony he can search me himself if he thinks I'm a snitch. Keep your goddamn hands off me." Red stared at the ocean.

Tony Dio, in a tennis outfit and smoked glasses, walked onto the balcony and flicked his cigar ashes over the rail. He looked as if he had been gaining weight for the past five years—King Farouk in tennis shorts. He did not shake hands.

The man in the flowered shirt walked back inside.

Dio turned and looked down at Red.

"Don't let him bother you. He does that to everybody. You know how things are these days." He stuck the cigar in his mouth.

"All I need is another couple of months," Red said. "I have a project planned and I just need a little time. I'm trying to get back on my feet. You know that."

Dio puffed and blew smoke into the breeze. He did not look at Red.

"Red, in the old days, when we were just little guys, there was no quibbling about a few bucks here or there. It's different now. It's all points, you know, *percentages*. Everything is points and deadlines."

The veins on Red's neck stood out. He clenched his fists.

"I just did a nickel in Terminal Island. I'm fifty-four years old. This is it for me. This is my last shot. I've got a big project planned. When it comes through I'll be able to pay you off with interest for the whole five years. You know I'm good for the twenty-five grand."

Dio turned to him and took the cigar from his mouth. "I know you are good for it. That's why I let the debt ride while you were in the joint. . . . Now you are out. I placed my bet on the 'come line.' " He stared.

Red felt sweat begin to run from his armpits to his waist.

"I wasn't born yesterday," he said. "All I'm asking is more time. I guarantee that I'll . . ."

"How much did you bring with you today?" Dio interrupted.

"Eight grand." Red laid the envelope on the table.

"Take your time with the rest," Dio said. He gazed at the ocean again. "Take another ten days."

Red stood up. "How about thirty days? I mean, there's always last-minute problems. . . ."

"Thanks for stopping by, Red," Dio said.

As Red walked through the living room to the door the man in the flowered shirt stood behind a portable bar, watching. Red wondered if he would be the one to get the contract if he couldn't come up with the money.

In the hallway, waiting for the elevator, Red recognized the falling-away feeling, with its concomitant fire in the intestinal tract. He had made notes about the feeling in his cell and had reread them often. The name falling-away feeling was coined by him because "falling away" was the opposite of things "going one's way," that is, goals being reached, predictions of success coming true . . . big scores.

Red's notes had reflected that the feeling usually, but not always, was present shortly before a disaster, when things started to get out of control. A sucker screams about his money and calls the cops; shortly thereafter handcuffs bite the wrists. Even psychiatrists, actual doctors of the mind, could not predict human behavior one hundred percent of the time.

The falling-away feeling was a signal calling for careful planning to find the way out. And Red knew that there was, in every bad situation, a *way* out. Patience was required. And occasionally (he remembered specifically writing this with an exclamation point in a margin) brute force. In other words, "God helps those who help themselves."

The elevator doors opened soundlessly for Red Diamond. He stepped in and they closed. "The primary objective is to reduce risk," he said out loud.

Ronnie Boyce removed the fancy pink package from the attaché case and placed it in the rental locker. After glancing at the passengers in the bus terminal, he closed the locker quickly, removed the key, and pushed it into the pocket of his leather jacket.

On the way from Red's, he had bought birthday paper and wrapped the sawed-off shotgun. Red had told him it was the best precaution against a general inspection of such lockers. He said they usually wouldn't go to the trouble of opening a gift-wrapped package. Happy birthday, mother fuckers, he thought.

Before meeting Red, he would never have gone to such trouble. Now such precautions were a source of pride. "No bull can prove a murder case without the murder weapon," Red often said.

It was dusk when Ronnie drove toward the Sea Horse Motel. He left the Santa Monica Freeway and headed south on Lincoln Boulevard and smelled salt air. The smell reminded him of Carol's beach apartment six years ago. He pictured her walking around the apartment naked, tits jiggling, talking a hundred miles an hour. He thought of the arrow tattoo.

At a traffic light, a woman in tennis shorts crossed the street in snappy fashion. Her legs were long, like Carol's. Although he remembered Carol's body, he wasn't sure he would remember her face. He had not seen her since the trial, six years ago. She had sat in the dock like a penguin and testified against him. For the first months in stir he had dreamed of escaping just to kill her, but those thoughts had faded into others. Walking the yard was a mind bender.

He knew it had been his fault. After all, he chose to live with her and let her in on the bank jobs. What the hell did he expect her to do? Carol would never ride a beef for a man. She was a loner. She was one of the few broads who had her own reputation. Carol was the Queen of Plastic. She could have written books on how to make two grand a day from a hot American Express card.

He swung into the lot in front of a row of aqua-colored motel rooms and parked. He checked the note in his wallet. Sea Horse, room eleven. She had been easy to locate through the grapevine.

He walked to room eleven and knocked loudly. There was no answer. After looking around, he removed the screwdriver from his pocket, jimmied the lock, opened the door, and stepped into the darkened room. Women's clothes lay on the bed; a brassiere hung on a chair. Closing the door, he moved a chair to a corner of the room and sat on it.

He removed the switch-blade knife from his pocket, flicked it open, and cleaned his nails. The motel room was fairly clean, but small, cell-like. A print of an ocean scene hung over the bed. The room reminded him of the Burbank apartment where he had played as a child. Walls thin as paper. His mother had liked the apartment because it was near the studios, where she had worked on and off as a waitress. He remembered the cheap furniture and the hundreds of tiny bottles and jars on her dressing table, the *Screen Romance* magazines in the kitchen drawer, the enormous photo of Alan Ladd on the living-room wall, the smell of cold cream.

He had spent the first night away from the apartment in Los Angeles County Juvenile Hall. The next day, good old Mom had come to pick him up, carting along a whiskey-breath boyfriend. They dropped him off at the apartment after she scolded him for breaking into a car. She hadn't even taken the trouble to find out that he had broken into a house, not a car.

He had received a telegram about her death when he was in Chino serving three years for some gas-station stickups. After learning the news, he had finished his handball game.

He heard a key enter the lock and he stood up quietly with the knife in his hand.

She did not see him as she closed the door and walked to the dressing table. She turned on the table lamp; her back was to him but she saw him in the mirror and gave a sharp cry. Her hands flew to her mouth and she spun around. They faced each other across the messy bed.

"Ronnie! Oh! Please don't kill me. The Feds made me testify. I didn't want to. They tricked me. Oh, God. NO!" Her knees and thighs were held stiffly together.

He noticed the crow's-feet and the extremely short bleached hair. Her voice was the same, deep, almost hoarse. She wore jeans and a silk blouse.

"I guess you know that I woulda never got convicted if you wouldn't have testified." He held the knife loosely in his right hand.

"I just got out a month ago myself. . . . What . . . are you going to do? What are you going to do to me?"

"I was going to choke you to death. Or maybe just cut off your tongue."

Her fists clenched. After a moment of silence she began speaking, her voice shrill, staccato. "I want you to do it," she babbled, "I want you to kill me right now. I want to get it over with. I deserve it for being a snitch. You were my baby and I snitched. I wanted to write you and tell you what happened but I knew you wouldn't understand. . . ."

"Carol, don't try to con me. You're not talking to some bank turkey to set up a phony account. You're talking to Ronnie Boyce. And I'll tell you right off I'm six years smarter than I ever was. I'm *together* this time: one-hundred-fucking-percent *together*."

She fell silent as he spoke, but glanced toward the door.

"Don't look at the door, woman. You ain't going nowhere." Ronnie sat down nonchalantly on the chair. It seemed that they had been staring at each other for hours.

"I heard you ended up in Corona three years ago. I guess you didn't have anybody to snitch off on that case."

With a moan, Carol sat down on the edge of the bed, hands over her eyes and forehead.

"You were all I thought about the whole thirty months," she sobbed, looking up, then covering her eyes again quickly.

Ronnie was quiet for what must have been ten minutes. "Don't get the idea that you've conned me, Carol," he said at last. "Nobody does that to me. If I came here to ice you, that's just what I would have done."

She looked up.

"I just want to make it up to you," she said softly. Her chest was heaving, thrusting, under the silk blouse. Her eyes were piercing.

Ronnie did not answer immediately. Perhaps without admitting it, he had known all along he wanted her back. In prison, his mind had allowed her many fates. Now that he really was finally out, the choice was either to snuff her because of what she had done or to let her live and have things like they were.

He put the blade of the knife back in the handle and tossed it across the bed into her lap. She looked up, startled.

"I'll make it up to you. Everything will be okay again," she said.

"The only way you could make it up to me would be to go down on it nonstop for six goddamn years." His voice was sad.

She smiled cautiously, stood up, and stripped quickly, efficiently, jabbering away as if nothing had happened, as if the six years had been six days.

No reason to kill her now, he thought, it wouldn't prove anything.

Naked, she walked around the bed and faced him. He stared at the tattooed arrow on the thigh pointing upward toward the hair. Christ, in how many prison dreams had he seen the tattoo? Once, he had drawn the arrow on a photo in *Playboy*.

"I ain't never going to go back," he said.

Quickly, she dropped to her knees in front of him. "Everything's going to be okay again. Come here now, let me see . . ." said Carol, reaching for him. He grasped the sides of her head.

$/6

The federal prison was located on the south end of Terminal Island, the gun tower being positioned next to sea rocks. The prison itself was separated from the steam-belching canneries on the island by various perimeters of chain-link topped with barbed wire. The canneries and dead seaweed along the rocks gave the whole place the smell of rotten eggs.

In the prison's parking lot, Charles Carr locked his gun and handcuffs in the trunk of the government sedan and headed for the two-story administration building. The drab brownstone structure accented a steel door with reinforced hinges. It was the only way in and out.

Inside the building he displayed his badge, signed the visitor's register, and filled out two useless forms.

In an interview room, he reviewed Freddie Roth's lengthy prison file, concentrating on the latest stretch.

Carr remembered his first meeting with Freddie Roth. The door of the print shop had gone down. Freddie was back-pedaling past the press with greenish hands in the air. "Okay. You got me. You got me."

Inside the print shop Carr had holstered his gun and bantered with Freddie for over an hour about where he had hidden the plates. "On my mother's grave," chanted Freddie, "I destroyed 'em. Go ahead and look! Be my guest. You won't find

38

any plates. I burned 'em with a blowtorch and dumped 'em in the ocean. So help me God!"

And there was the blank look on Roth's face when the plates were pulled out of the floor safe—not a smile or a frown, just a business-as-usual, do-my-time, see-you-when-I-get-out-again expression.

The interview room was neat. Two chairs, a table, a tiny aluminum-foil ashtray. The walls were freshly painted light green. The paint odor combined with a hangover caused Carr to feel slightly light-headed. He wished he had eaten breakfast.

He stopped turning the pages of Roth's prison file and looked up. The khaki-uniformed guard stepped in the door carrying a steaming mug of coffee. Carr noticed tattoos on his giant arms, a full head of thick hair combed backward with grease.

"You Carr? Treasury?"

Carr nodded. "I'm waiting for Roth to be brought down from D wing . . . Frederick Roth."

After another loud slurp, which caused Carr to stifle a gag, the guard leaned forward for coffee-breath emphasis. "Before you talk to him, there's something you may want to know. He's been in my office begging for a gate pass for the past month. The pass would allow him to be assigned to the work detail in the minimum-security wing. I was going to approve the pass until I found out about his old lady."

"His old lady?" Carr looked puzzled.

"She wrote him a Dear John last month. We read all the letters coming in. The bleeding hearts haven't taken that away from us yet. Seems she moved in with a colored gentleman since poor old Freddie's been in barbwire city. Freddie tried to smuggle a letter out to her." The guard dug into his shirt pocket. "Here's a copy of it."

Carr read the letter as the guard lapped at the mug.

The last line of the letter read, "I'll be getting out of here sooner than you think, bitch. Then you and your nigger are going to die."

"The reason he's pushing for a gate pass is that the minimum-security wing gives him access to the highway. It's the easiest way to escape. You can rest assured the last thing he will *ever* get is a gate pass." The guard smiled wryly.

With the knock on the door, Carr handed the letter back, and the guard quickly stuffed it in his pants pocket. The guard stood up and motioned Roth to the table, stepped outside, and closed the door. Carr heard the snap of the lock.

A gaunt Freddie Roth sat down and gushed insincere greetings about how pleased he was to see the "old fox." Roth's bald head and his face appeared yellow, cadaverous, just as Carr remembered them. His glasses were much thicker.

"This place is a little different from my pad in Malibu years ago, eh? Remember?" Roth motioned to the green walls as if introducing a choir. "It is really good to see yez. Really, I'm very serious about it. It really is good to see yez." He spoke as if he were selling a vacuum cleaner.

"Got a date yet, Freddie?"

"I was supposed to have a date by now, but they turned over my house during a lockdown and found some seed, so they held up my date. The grass wasn't even mine. . . . What do you want to talk to me about?" He pushed his glasses back on his nose.

"Some of your old twenties have been showing up recently," Carr said.

Roth leaned forward, interested, elbows on knees. The glasses slipped again.

"Which old twenties?"

"The ones you printed just before this stretch."

Roth rubbed a hand across the desert of his scalp. "Yes, the plate had a bad key in the Treasury seal." He shook his head. "I should have burned the whole friggin' batch instead of putting them out on the street. I'm almost embarrassed to say they were my work."

"Santa Anita and Hollywood Park didn't think they were so bad," Carr said.

Roth beamed. "The casinos in Las Vegas put out a notice on them, too, as a matter of fact. I had a friend there who checked for me. . . . I was peddling them for *thirty* points on the dollar. *Six bucks* apiece. And even with that price, my phone was ringing off the hook."

"Who has the rest of the notes, Freddie?" Carr's tone was fatherly.

Roth held out his hands. "Wait a minute! Did you come here to lay a goddamn case on me while I'm in the joint? What the hell do I know about who has a few twenties that I printed three years ago? How do *I* know what's happening on the street right now? I'm in a *cage*, man. I . . ."

"Thanks, Freddie," Carr interrupted. "You can go now. Sorry to bother you."

Roth's yellow jaw dropped. "What?"

"I said you can go back to D wing. I don't have any more questions," Carr said. Through the years Carr had learned that Roth had to be kept on the track.

Roth slid his chair back to stand up. He stopped.

"What if I *was* to remember something about a stash on the outside. What's in it for me?" He sat down again.

"What do you *want* to be in it for you?" Carr said.

Roth put his hands in his lap. "It's like this. I'm on the list to get a gate pass to minimum security so I can work outside on the grass. I'm sick and I need some sun and fresh air; vitamin C. You know how it is. . . . If you could talk to the captain and move my name up on the gate-pass list, I think I might be able to remember something about the twenties. Get the picture?"

"I get the picture," Carr said. "I'll go see the guard captain and see what I can do."

Carr stood up and knocked on the door. A guard unlocked and opened it. He stepped out into the shiny corridor and walked toward the prison-staff coffee room. As he walked he noticed the yellow that was building up along the baseboards. Unnecessary waxing, like the cheap labor of an army headquarters company.

In the empty coffee room, Carr picked up a well-worn copy of the *Los Angeles Times*. He read halfway through a feature article on how a small town in Ohio had lowered the crime rate by arresting all its heroin addicts. He thought of one apartment house near McArthur Park where at least fifty addicts lived. The addicts in that apartment house alone would fill up most small-town jails. He threw the paper down.

Leaning back on the sofa, he thought of the smelly Quonset hut outside Seoul where he first practiced real-life interrogation. The methods were different then, but the motivations the same. It was simply a matter of finding the right chord and playing it no holds barred. Carr closed his eyes.

A half hour later, he got up from the sofa, returned to the interview room, and sat down. He looked Roth directly in the eye.

"It looks like you are in luck. I had to take a lot of jaw from the captain, but he finally agreed to go along with the gate pass if I tell him you cooperated with me fully. The deal is on." Carr continued to peer into the other's eyes, for a sincere effect.

"How do I know you're tellin' me the truth?" Roth said. Using his index finger he made a figure-eight pattern on the table top.

Carr stared at the floor for a moment, then spoke clearly and loudly. "I just went in and made a fool out of myself making a deal for you, clown. Either give me the story right now or you go back to your cell, and I'll be on my way. I don't like people who waste my time. I'm tired of this stinking room. I have a hangover. Fuck you."

Carr stood up, knocking his chair back violently, and walked toward the door.

"Okay," Roth said. "Sit down and I'll tell you the whole thing. But I better not be ripped off. If anybody finds out I'm helping the Feds, I could end up getting shanked. There's guys in here that actually *like* to do it. . . ."

"So I've heard," Carr interrupted. "Who's holding your stash?"

"I don't want to get anybody else involved. I gave my stash to a friend to hold for me. He's got about fifty grand. It was left over from the printing. You guys missed it when you broke down the door. I had it buried two blocks away." Roth cleaned his glasses on his shirttail.

"What is your friend's name?"

Roth put his glasses back on. "This guy is a real friend, man. I don't want to see him drop behind a deal where he was just doing me a favor. You know what I mean?"

"How bad do you want the gate pass?" Carr asked.

Roth closed his eyes, opened them, then spoke. "Virgil Leach. He deals in paper. You can find him at the Paradise Isle in Hollywood. He's called 'Pleach.' That's a combination of 'pimple' and 'leach.' You'll know why when you see him. Gotta girlfriend named Vikki; she has a big habit. Now you know as much as I do."

"Why is Leach holding your stash?"

"He's just a friend, a paper passer from the old days. After you guys busted me I knew there would be heat on the serial numbers. I asked him to hold the stuff for me until I got out of the joint. I wasn't going to pass any. I just didn't know what to do with them." His expression was somber.

Carr nodded, as if he understood. He stood up to leave.

"When do I get my gate pass?" Roth said.

"Just as soon as it's typed up." Carr knocked on the door. It was opened. He stepped into the hallway and told the guard to take the prisoner back to his cell.

$/7

It was dark.

Carr looked through the binoculars at Virgil Leach's small wood-frame house. It was nestled next to a modern-looking, pink stucco apartment house. A Cadillac was parked in the driveway. Except for the apartment house, the neighborhood was run down; property values on the decline. "Urban decay," as *Time* would say.

Kelly dozed at the wheel.

After stopping by the state parole office to pick up Leach's mug photo and current address, they had driven directly to Leach's house and begun the surveillance. It had been a long day.

Carr put the binoculars back in the glove compartment. Out of boredom he picked up the Xerox copies of the parole reports again. Leach's mug shot was stapled to the first page. Carr thought of the "before" photograph in an acne-medicine ad.

Leach was described in the reports as a forty-year-old with a "sociopathic personality with emotional blunting."

Kelly yawned loudly and began rubbing his eyes. "You still reading that bullshit?" he said.

"I thought it was more interesting than listening to you snore."

"Man, am I hungry." Kelly rubbed his stomach.

44

"So what else is new?" Carr smiled, lifting the binoculars to his eyes again. He adjusted the lens.

"I got my evaluation today. No Waves put it in on my desk so he wouldn't have to face me. It was a 'sandwich job' as usual."

"A what?"

Kelly reached into his inside coat pocket and took out a typed Special Agent Yearly Evaluation Form. "Listen to this," he said. "Special Agent Kelly is an experienced senior agent who can be counted upon to fulfill his responsibilities. He is an excellent marksman and has a high record of arrests and convictions. At times his outspokenness causes problems with his coworkers. Kelly has a thorough knowledge of the operations manual and keeps his reports up to date." Kelly folded the paper and stuffed it back in his coat pocket. "See? A sandwich job. He starts with good points, then the bad, then ends with something good. A shit sandwich. Just enough to keep me from getting promoted, but not enough to get me pissed off . . . What did he put in yours this time?"

"Same as yours, except for the bad part. Mine said something like 'Carr has a tendency to be too independent. He objects to proper supervision and has on occasion refused to identify his informants when told to do so.' "

"Good old No Waves. He wouldn't know an informant if one bit him on the ass. The pipe-smoking, briefcase-carrying, ass-licking, back-stabbing prick. Did I ever tell you about the time he interviewed me on a brutality allegation?"

Carr shook his head no even though he knew the story by heart.

"He sits there behind his desk with two inspectors in the room, tape recorder on. The interview was almost over, and he says, 'Well, you know how it is. We have to follow up on rumors.' I said, 'I hear rumors every day.' He said, 'Like what?' So I said, 'Yesterday somebody told me you were a queer.' The friggin' inspectors almost fell off their chairs!" Kelly laughed furiously, caught his breath, and laughed again.

Leach walked from his front door. He wore European-cut trousers that were too small for his chunky frame, and a waist-length leather jacket that would have looked good on a nineteen-year-old.

"Okay. We've finally got some movement," Carr said.

Kelly rubbed his face roughly with both hands and started the engine.

Leach got into the Cadillac. The headlights came on. He backed out of the driveway and pulled into traffic.

Kelly, without headlights, kept at a safe distance behind the Cadillac as it drove along shabby side streets toward Wilshire Boulevard. Carr wished Leach would get onto a larger street so the tandem turns would not be so obvious.

The Cadillac turned west on Wilshire Boulevard.

Carr thought they had lost him for a moment when he made a left turn on Vermont. They caught up to the Cadillac as it entered the freeway. The trip to Marina Del Rey was easy because there were a million cars on the freeway. Carr knew that all headlights would look the same in Leach's rearview mirror; an easy tail.

As Leach pulled into a valet lot at the Captain's Disco he almost ran into a bevy of sun-tanned young women dressed in jeans and tank tops. He got out of his car and handed the keys to the valet. He walked up the steps and in the front door.

"Everybody here is either a pipe smoker or a stewardess," Kelly said. "If Leach brought a pipe, he should fit right in."

"You take the point," Carr said. "I'll wait here."

Kelly took off his suit coat and gun and threw them on the back seat. He trotted up the steps, paid his cover charge at the door, and went in. Carr could hear the faint echo of rock music.

Waiting, Carr turned on the radio and listened to a late-night talk program. The disc jockey's voice sounded bored, sleepy, as he discussed capital punishment with a shut-in who kept coughing. They used the word *deterrent* over and over again. Carr leaned back in the seat.

It was 1:30 A.M. when Kelly came back out. He waved to Carr and headed for a phone booth in the parking lot next door. The phone call was brief.

After Kelly hung up the phone, it was exactly four minutes until a black-and-white police car drove into the parking lot.

Kelly approached it. The uniformed officers inside nodded their heads as Kelly displayed his Treasury badge. After speaking animatedly for a few moments, he pointed toward Leach's Cadillac. After a short discussion, the police car pulled out of the lot and parked down the street.

Kelly trotted back to the car and slid into the driver's seat. He turned off the radio.

"He's ready," he told Carr. "I counted at least seven drinks. He's in there trying to pick up teenyboppers, but they've all shined him on."

Leach walked out the front door and waited for the valet to bring the Cadillac. He looked unsteady on his feet. He seemed to fall into his car as the valet opened the door.

The red lights of the police car went on as soon as the Cadillac passed.

Kelly started the engine. They drove past the flashing red light of the police car and saw Leach, arms outstretched, trying to touch the tip of his index finger to his pimpled nose.

Kelly stepped on the gas.

The black sheriff's deputy shoved Leach roughly into the dark cell.

Carr lay on the top bunk feigning sleep, his face embedded in a pillow that smelled faintly of Clorox. He had decided not to say anything until morning, figuring that Leach would not be too enthusiastic about gabbing with a cellmate at 3:00 A.M. No use rushing it.

Leach walked the four steps to the commode and urinated loudly. He flopped on the lower bunk and dropped his shoes to the floor one at a time. He began snoring within ten minutes.

Carr told himself there was no reason why he shouldn't be able to sleep. He rethought the tack he would use, then dozed fitfully.

An echoing scream woke him. He sat up in the bunk. There was the sound of a scuffle farther down the tier, then a loud moaning. People fighting over a cigarette or perhaps a plastic comb?

Carr rolled over and stared at the flaking ceiling. He thought of bicycling along the beach to Sally's house; he knocked and she wasn't home.

He closed his eyes.

Carr woke up as the tier lights went on. He slid off the bunk, put his shoes on, and washed his face with cold water at the yellowish sink. The cell reminded him of a service-station bathroom: filthy cement.

"How long you been in?" asked Leach, yawning. He stood up from the bunk, stretching. He had no shirt on. His face was a mask of ripe, red infections, his neck a collar of thick purple scar tissue with protruding unshavable whiskers.

"Ten days," Carr answered. He dried his hands on a gray towel.

"What're you in for?" Leach yawned again without covering his mouth.

"Drunk driving," Carr said. "I'm getting out today." ("Chance meetings require common topics," said the agents' manual.)

"No shit," Leach said. "That's what I'm in for. Had a few drinks at a bar. I'm on my way home and the cops give me the red lights. No shit." He made his fingers into a comb and raked his sticky hair.

"The goddamn pigs must of needed one more for their quota," Carr said. Without looking at the other man, he climbed back onto the top bunk, lit a cigarette, and leaned against the wall.

Leach was at the sink now, drinking handfuls from the faucet. He spit water into the sink. "Sounds like you don't get along with the man." Leach looked at his wet hands for a moment, turned, and began drying them on a corner of Carr's blanket.

"Get your hands off the blanket," Carr said matter-of-factly.

Leach stopped drying his hands with the blanket but continued to hold it. He stared amusedly at Carr. "Sounds like you learned some of the rules during the last ten days."

"I learned the rules in Leavenworth," Carr said. "Now get your goddamn hooks off the blanket." ("Don't be afraid to poke the lion," said the T-school instructor.)

Leach dropped the corner of the blanket. "No shit," he said.

48

"How much time did you do in Leavenworth?" He rubbed his hands back and forth on his pants.

"A deuce."

"What for?"

"Passing funny money," Carr said.

"No shit? How'd they make you on it?"

"Feds lied on me in court. Said they found funny money in my car." He paused. "What makes you so interested?"

Leach opened up his palms and furrowed his brow. "Easy, dude! You're talking to somebody who's done time in *Folsom, Atlanta,* and *San Quentin.* Maybe you heard of me. Papers used to call me 'The Drugstore Forger.' I was in the papers and everything before my last case. Name's Leach. They call me 'Pleach.' " He stuck out his hand for the jive handshake.

"Right on," Carr said. He shook hands.

Carr smelled the odor of oatmeal and grease as it wafted along the cell block, mixing with that of humans in cages of concrete. A cement nursery school?

Leach stepped to the bars and grasped them. "My bail bondsman should be waiting in the arraignment court to bail me out," he said.

"I should make the noon release myself. This is my last day." Carr bit his lip, hoping Leach would take the bait.

"No shit."

That was the last thing Leach said for a few minutes.

Finally he spoke. "What do you have planned?"

"Make a few bucks and head back east," Carr said.

"I'm going to pick up some phony cashier's checks soon as I get out. A friend's got a load. They're always easy to down without ID."

"Not as easy as funny money."

"Maybe not, but he ain't got funny money. He's got checks."

"Who's your friend?" He cupped his hand to his ear. "Speak up. I didn't hear you."

"Just testing," said the scarred man.

Nothing more was said for at least a half hour.

"Are you still into funny money?" Leach said at last.

Carr casually swung his feet over the side of the bunk. "You might say that."

$/8

Carr heard the sheriff's deputies walking along the tier as they called out prisoners' names. "Bloodsaw, Tyrone. Zavala, Jesus. Leach, Virgil."

"Here!" Leach answered. The deputy stepped to the bars, checked Leach's wrist tag. "Courtline bus number one," the deputy said, looking at a clipboard.

"Looks like I'll be bailed out in an hour or so. I got the first bus. . . . By the way, what's your name?"

"Charlie."

Leach eyed the deputy. He whispered, "Charlie, think you'd be interested in some nice green stuff? No shit."

"What flavor?" Carr said.

"Number twenty . . . with ten different serial numbers." He held up all fingers.

"What's the price?"

"Eighteen points on the dollar. A hundred and eighty bucks for a grand."

The hydraulic lock snapped open cells farther down the tier. Prisoners shuffled.

"I might be interested."

"No shit. How much can you handle?"

"How much heat is on the batch?" Carr said. "Are the Feds on to the serial numbers?"

"No way, my man. The product is cool. No shit. If you can

50

prove otherwise, I'll give you your money back . . . and that is no shit." Leach stuffed cigarettes in his pocket. He tucked in his prison shirt.

The hydraulic lock buzzed, and the cell door slid open slowly. "You'll make the noon release, right?" Leach said.

Carr nodded.

Leach whispered from the side of his mouth. "Meet me tonight at the Paradise Isle on Hollywood Boulevard. I'll have a sample for you. No shit." He stepped out of the cell.

Carr waited on a barstool at the Paradise Isle. The place was dark and crowded, the jukebox deafening. Kelly sat at the opposite end of the bar, near the rear door. He wore a purple bowling shirt and needed a shave.

Carr felt uneasy. The place was all nicknames and handshakes. A fat blonde touched tongues with the black man next to her, knocking off his knit cap.

"Haven't seen ya here before," the bartender said. "Name's Gabe."

Carr shook the offered wet hand.

"Waiting for somebody?"

"Pleach. You seen him around?"

"He'll be in. Stops by every night. Nuther drink?" A fish smile.

Carr nodded.

Gabe served Carr another drink. He dried glasses for a few minutes before approaching Kelly, the other stranger in the place. He asked the preliminaries.

"I'm waiting for some good-looking cunt to walk in here. That's what I'm waiting for," Kelly said, in his normal tone of voice. The fat blonde looked up.

Gabe offered his hand to the Irishman. Kelly put his glass in it. "Put some booze in it this time, little man."

Gabe frowned.

Carr sipped his drink, wondering whether he and Kelly had passed the bartender's test.

Gabe picked up the phone at the end of the bar and dialed, whispered a few words, and hung up.

Fifteen minutes later Leach came in the back door and walked directly to the bar. Carr's breathing quickened.

51

"See? I showed up," said Leach. "No shit."

"That's good. I don't like to be hung up."

"Don't worry about Pleach. I always take care of business." He swung himself onto a barstool.

"We gonna be able to do some business tonight?" Carr asked.

"That depends." Leach glanced at the black wearing the knit cap. "After I bailed out today I started thinking. I don't know you. Nothing personal, you understand. I just don't know where you're comin' from. I mean like I just met you in County last night and I really haven't had time to check you out. No shit."

The bartender handed Leach a drink. He took a sip.

"In other words, you were just running your mouth this morning and you don't really have a connection. Is that what you're telling me?" Carr smiled.

"No, I didn't say that." Leach smiled back.

"Because if it is, it's no problem. I just talked to another guy today who's got some paper lined up for me. Fifties, with all different serial numbers. Price isn't as good as yours, but he'll come down. What I'm saying is that I can score tonight somewhere else." Carr took a sip and placed the glass back on the wet napkin.

"Oh," Leach said. He picked at his face for a moment, then stopped abruptly. "What if I said I could get you a load tonight? Do you have the four grand right now?"

"Sure. I got the four G's right here in my pocket. I'm sitting here in this toilet with my back facing the door and I've got four grand in my pocket. I'm tired of living. I *want* to get ripped off."

"I don't mean *that*. I mean can you come up with the money tonight if I can get . . ."

Carr leaned over and spoke directly into the other's face. "What did I tell you this morning?"

"I know what you said this morning."

"Well, now it's tonight and I'm sitting here having a drink. I just did ten days in jail and it doesn't make a shit to me one way or the other whether you can score for me or not. I have other sources. Okay?"

Leach turned his head, and spoke to the bar mirror. "Don't get pissed, man. I'm just always a little paranoid about dealing with new people. . . . I'm ready to deal tonight if you're ready. No shit."

"Now that you're through with the cat-and-mouse game, go get me a sample. I'll take a look at it, and then we'll talk business."

"I'll have to take a little trip to get the stuff. After you see a sample, how long before you can have the buy money?" Leach's hand explored his face again.

"It's five minutes away," Carr said.

"Do you have any objections to showing me the money before I go make a commitment to my man? He's going to ask me if I've seen the buy money. . . . You know how it works."

The black man was intently watching Leach. He kept swishing the ice cubes in his drink, trying to look nonchalant. The blonde had moved next to Kelly.

"You'll just have to tell him that I don't show money until he shows a sample. My mother always told me that walking into traps was bad for my health."

"Okay. Okay. I'll go get a sample. I'll be back here inside of an hour. No shit. Be ready to deal in five minutes after I show the sample."

Leach got up and walked quickly out the door.

The black man looked at his wristwatch.

Kelly brushed past Carr on his way to the men's room. He returned to his barstool shortly.

Carr ordered another drink and walked into the stinking men's room. He locked the door. Reaching under the sink he felt for the tape and pulled it off with the note.

Spade is a lookout, shoulder holster. I take him.
Push for parking lot. Too many people inside.

Carr threw the note in the toilet, pulled the handle, and watched it disappear. He returned to his stool.

The bar phone rang. Gabe answered and stretched the cord to reach the black man. He listened, said, "Right on," and gave the phone back to Gabe.

Leach came back within a few minutes. He walked in the

door and looked around nervously. The black man gave a subtle nod.

Leach walked to Carr and handed him an envelope.

"Let's go out in the parking lot. There's too many people in here," Carr said. He placed the envelope in the pocket of his sports coat and walked toward the door. Leach followed him closely, looking about. The black man put money on the bar.

Carr stepped out the front door onto Hollywood Boulevard. He took the envelope out of his pocket, opened it, and saw four twenty-dollar bills. The serial numbers were the same.

Leach was walking ahead of him now, into the parking lot. Carr saw the black man come out the rear door into the dark parking lot with his hand inside his leather coat. Where was Kelly?

Leach stopped suddenly and faced Carr. "You looked at the samples," he said. "Now lemme have 'em back and you go get your fuckin' buy money."

"Sure," said Carr. He handed the envelope to Leach.

Kelly came out the back door. It was time. Carr reached into his back pocket, removed a handkerchief, and threw it to the ground. With a puzzled look, Leach focused on the handkerchief for a moment and then looked back at Carr.

Kelly jumped the black man from behind. They fell, struggling, to the asphalt, behind a row of parked cars.

Carr pulled his .357 magnum and pointed it at Leach's face. "Federal officer! Freeze!" He pulled his coat back, showing the badge on his belt.

Leach dropped the envelope and raised his hands.

The sound of fist striking flesh and the rattle of handcuffs came from behind the parked cars. Kelly stood up, holding a .45 automatic for Carr to see. "I got him," he said, out of breath.

Kelly got in the back seat with the handcuffed prisoners for the ride to the field office.

In the interview room, Leach picked at his face as Carr filled in the arrest forms.

"Is that a two-way mirror on the wall behind you? No shit?"

Carr continued to write.

"Why don't you warn me of my constitutional rights?"

54

"No need to. You are bought and paid for. You delivered four counterfeit twenties to the man."

"I think I was entrapped into the whole thing. No shit. You asked me to score some paper for you in the county jail. I was just doing you a favor. . . . Why were you in my cell in the first place?" He squeezed something on his neck and looked at his fingers. He wiped the fingers on his pants.

Carr completed the last of the redundant paperwork. He put his pencil down and offered Leach a cigarette.

"Thanks. No shit." Leach pulled the cigarette from the pack and hung it from his mouth. He lit it with a flourish.

Carr spoke softly. "Pleach, you've been around. I think you and I can talk turkey. I'll be up front if you will. What *I* want is the names of everybody you've dealt the twenties to, and the location of the rest of the stash. What do *you* want?"

Leach pulled the cigarette from his mouth and looked Carr in the eye. "It doesn't matter what I want or don't want 'cause I ain't saying a fuckin' thing. And that is no shit." His expression was smug.

"You must be one of those freaks who actually *likes* the joint. Is that it?" Carr said. He leaned back in his chair.

"I like the joint about as much as I like sticking my head into a bucket of pure shit. But I've been around long enough to know that since I'm on parole I'm going to be violated. I'll pick up another eighteen months, of which I'll have to do a third. Your case with the four twenties will be dropped by the U.S. attorney in the interest of justice so as not to clog up the court since I'm already going back to prison. After all, four twenties is only eighty bucks. With good time, I'll serve four months, and probably only three, since December is early-out time. So, for ninety days you want me to be a snitch and take a chance on getting a shiv stuck up my ass? No way. No fuckin' way. When I was a kid I once did ninety days for getting caught with one roach. I can do ninety days standing on my head."

Carr knew he was right. "If you don't want to cooperate, I guess I'll have to go to your pad and search it. If Vikki's there with the stash, she gets arrested. Do you want to get her involved?" Carr spoke clearly.

"What the fuck do I care? She's just a dumb hype bitch. A friend of mine gave her to me. If you go there and find counterfeit money, it's hers, not mine. I didn't know what was in the envelope I gave you. Why don't you just book me? Fuck all this yakety-yak. No shit." He folded his arms across his chest.

Carr gathered up the stack of printed forms. He stood up and opened the door.

Kelly was waiting in the hallway, eating a large greasy doughnut. "Any luck?" He spoke with his mouth full.

"Nope. You?"

"The spade says he knows Pleach from the Paradise Isle. Acts as a lookout for him when he does deals. Pleach gives him a few bucks after the deal goes down. That's all he's gonna say." Kelly gulped some of the doughnut. "He's con wise, told me what I already know. He just did six months for killing his next-door neighbor; he's out on an appeal or something. Can you imagine that? Six months . . . I'd like to kill my next-door neighbor's kid. His motorcycle is too loud. Six months couldn't be all that bad." He rammed the last of the doughnut into his mouth and chewed. "I'm going down to the grand-jury room. Pick me up there when you're ready to go."

Carr walked down the hall into the tech shop and switched off the tape recorder labeled "Interview Room #1." He removed the cassette tape, wrote "Arrest interview: Defendant Virgil Leach" on its label, and placed it in his shirt pocket. He looked at his watch. It was 8:00 A.M.

$/9

It was 9:30 A.M. by the time Carr had finished briefing Delgado and making phone calls to the coroner's office. He left the field office and took the elevator to the ground floor.

When the elevator door opened, he walked down the marbled hallway toward a large set of wooden doors with gold lettering that read FEDERAL GRAND JURY. A small cardboard sign hung on a door handle. DO NOT ENTER. GRAND JURY IN SESSION. On one side of the doorway stood four long-haired men, whispering to one another. They wore open-collared shirts, tight pants, gold necklaces and rings. They looked at him as if a badge was pinned to his coat.

Farther down the hallway Kelly leaned against the marbled wall.

"What's it look like?" Carr said.

"That paper-pushing sumbitch Tommy the Hat has been on the witness stand for the past hour and a half," he whispered. "He won't even give so much as his home address. The court stenographer walked out a couple of minutes ago and told me. His asshole friends are standing over there with ants in their pants waiting to see if he is going to give up on them as being the ones who passed the fifties." Kelly spoke in a defeated tone. "But Tommy's being a real stand-up guy. . . . That's because he knows we don't have a good case on him."

"Why not?" Carr said.

"A bad search warrant."

"Dry hole?"

"No. We found thirty-five grand in fifties under his bed. Problem is the typist made a mistake and typed in the wrong date on the search warrant."

Carr shook his head.

The grand-jury doors opened. Curly-haired and freckled, Tommy the Hat, in a French-cut white suit, was the first one out. He tapped a matching Stetson with a silver band onto his friz.

Carr walked directly up to him and grabbed his hand before he reached his friends. Tommy looked surprised.

"Tommy," Carr said, cranking the young man's hand in wedding-reception style. "The truth never hurt anybody. You've kept your part of the bargain, and Uncle Sam will keep his. Thanks again, buddy."

Tommy the Hat pulled his hand away from Carr as if it were a handcuff. The young hoods glanced at one another and turned their backs. They swaggered down the hallway without looking back. "I ain't no fucking stool pigeon!" screamed Tommy. "I didn't say a word in there." He pointed at Carr. "You . . . you . . . mother fucker!"

Carr winked at the now red-faced man and headed down the hallway toward the exit. Walking next to him, Kelly made guttural sounds to try to keep from laughing. They passed through the revolving doors into the parking lot, and Kelly burst into hysterical, booming laughter. "How do you ever think of that shit?"

Kelly parked in front of the stucco apartment house next door to Leach's place.

Carr picked up the microphone from the glove compartment and gave the location. He replaced the microphone and shut the compartment.

"Why don't you take the rear," he said. He opened the door and got out. Kelly drove around the corner.

Carr waited for Kelly to get into position. He heard a loud whisper coming from a ground-floor window of the apartment house. "Are you a policeman? I saw you talk on the car radio." The voice was old.

58

Carr stopped. "Who wants to know?"

"The people in that house are up to no good," said the woman. "The girl is a doper. She passed out on the front lawn once. She lives with a guy who beats her like a dog. People go and come at all hours. I hope you arrest them."

"What's your name?"

"I don't want to get involved," she whispered.

Shaking his head, Carr walked to the front door of the house and knocked.

A tiny peephole was opened by a young woman. "Pleach isn't here," she said.

Carr held up his badge. "Open the door, Vikki."

The face disappeared from the peephole. Carr stuck two fingers in his mouth and whistled. There was the sound of running, the back door opening, a struggle.

"Let me go!" Vikki screamed. "You're breaking my arm! You pig! Put me down!"

The screaming came toward the front door. The door was unlocked. Kelley opened the door, carrying the struggling Vikki under one arm like a calf. His other hand held a black plastic garbage bag with something in it. He handed Carr the plastic bag. It was closed with a piece of string. "She tossed this in the yard. I grabbed her before she went back in."

Carr pulled off the string and opened the bag. The money was in rubber-banded stacks. He guessed the counterfeit twenties at forty to fifty thousand worth.

Kelly sat the pale Vikki down in a bean-bag chair and began looking around the house. She was in a housecoat. Her shroud of thick dishwater hair was near waist length and caused her facial features to appear tiny. She had bony hands.

Carr sat on the couch facing a wall papered with a blown-up photo of Leach and Vikki standing in front of a Cadillac in silly poses. There was a stereo system on shelves and on another wall. The room had the scent of marijuana and dirty clothes.

Carr rested the plastic bag on his lap and read the "Warning of Rights" card out loud.

Vikki stared at the floor.

"Do you understand your rights?" he asked, putting the card back in his coat pocket.

"I've been arrested twelve times. What do you think?"

"Are you willing to answer a few questions for me, Vikki?"

She wrapped hair around a finger, pulled, and let it pop back. She looked at her lap. "I guess."

Carr patted the plastic bag. "Who has Pleach been peddling this to?"

"I don't know what's in the bag."

"Then why did you throw it out the back door?"

"I don't know why. I just got scared."

"Pleach is in jail," Carr said.

"For what?" She looked up.

"For delivering some of the twenties out of this bag. He was setting up a buy."

Vikki sat up straight and folded her arms across her chest. "Pleach is my old man. I ain't going to say anything to hurt him. He's been good to me."

Carr sat for a while checking the serial numbers on the counterfeit money.

A tear rolled down Vikki's cheek.

"How old are you, Vikki?" Carr asked.

"Twenty-two." Her voice cracked.

"Any children?"

Vikki turned toward him and finger-rolled some hair. "A three-year-old boy. He's with my mother because he's hyperactive. My mom didn't like my ex–old man, so she keeps him. He's really wild. It's my first husband's fault."

"What was your first husband like?"

"He used to go berserk," she said.

"How do you mean?"

"Like one time when I was out with the girls and when I came home he jumped up and threw a fishbowl at me, and it broke and all the fish were jumping around on the floor and he was grabbing my hair and hitting my head on the sink. He was bad news. He cut his hand on the fishbowl and started wiping the blood on the walls and everything."

"What happened then?"

Vikki wiped her nose with her thumb and index finger.

"I called the cops. They came and arrested him, and to get back at me he told them there was grass in the cupboard and

60

the cops arrested me, too. I tried to make a phone call to my mom, and the cop grabbed the phone out of my hand and handcuffed my hands behind me, and I was in my housecoat and it was open in front. It was really bad news. It was really gross." She released a finger roll of hair. It sprung back to her head like a rubber band.

"When did you meet Pleach?"

"About six months ago. He was a friend of my ex–old man. The second one."

"Does Pleach score for you?"

Vikki extended her track-marked right arm. She rubbed one of the scabs as if the arm was not attached to her body.

"Yes. But I'm not saying anything else. Pleach is my old man. He told me he'd kill me if I ever snitched. Once he knocked me out. He slugged me in the jaw with all his might and knocked me out, but he didn't mean to. . . ."

"Pleach didn't stand up for you today, Vikki. Why do you think we came here?"

"I'm not going to say anything against my old man." Vikki stared at her scarred arm.

Kelly walked back into the living room and began flipping up sofa cushions.

Carr sauntered into the kitchen area and opened cupboards.

Kelly's tone was disinterested. "When's the last time you fixed?" he said.

" 'Bout twelve hours ago."

"How do you feel?"

"I don't feel good. I might have to throw up."

"You'll have plenty of time to throw up in jail tonight. It'll give you something to do." Kelly chuckled.

"You're really cold, man," Vikki whimpered.

Having checked the drawers and cupboards, Carr stepped into the bedroom. An unmade water bed in a sea of dirty clothes and shoes. He waded through the clothes and opened the window. It didn't help the smell.

The dresser drawers were overflowing with a mixture of clean and dirty clothing. Under a pile of socks he found a stack of Polaroid photos. One was of a naked Vikki spread-eagled on the slimy bed, her hype's arms outstretched. Another showed her inserting a pink rubber dildo. Her expression was passive. He put the photos back under the socks.

In the next drawer down was a well-worn address book. He pulled it out of the drawer and looked under R. No Ronnie. He read every page. No one with the first name Ronnie. He put the book in his coat pocket and walked back into the kitchen.

Vikki was sobbing uncontrollably, her hands over her face.

Kelly looked toward the kitchen and winked.

Carr went back into the living room and sat down next to Vikki. She looked up.

"Can I get you a drink of water, Vikki?"

Vikki shook her head no. She wiped her nose with her hands.

"I wouldn't expect you to answer any questions about Pleach if he had stood up for you, but he didn't. He handed you up."

"You're just trying to trick me into talking. I don't know anything. I don't like that other guy. He's a real prick." She pointed at Kelly. "Pleach has been good to me. He respects me as a person."

"He doesn't respect you as a person."

"How do *you* know?" Vikki whined.

Carr stood up and walked to the stereo-system wall unit. He took the cassette tape from his shirt pocket and popped it into the tape player. He fiddled with the dials and turned up the volume to loudspeaker quality.

"If Vikki's there with the stash, she gets arrested. Do you want to get her involved?"

"What the fuck do I care? She's just a dumb hype bitch. A friend of mine gave her to me. If you go there and find counterfeit money, it's hers, not mine."

Carr turned off the tape player and removed the cassette. He put it in his coat pocket and sat down next to Vikki again.

Her expression was the same as in the Polaroid photographs.

Kelly rambled through the bedroom, slamming drawers.

Vikki began to cry again. "I want to see my little boy."

"Who did Pleach give some of the counterfeit money to?" Carr said.

"Nobody. He was holding the stash for a printer who went to the pen. He didn't want to pass the money because the Feds had the serial numbers. That's all I know. How much time am

I going to get? The bag is Pleach's. Not mine. Honest to God."
A tear rolled off the end of her nose and landed on the front
of her housecoat.

"Think back, Vikki. Did he give even one or two of the twenties to anyone?" Carr's voice was soothing, soft.

"He gave a couple of them to a red-haired guy. 'Bout fifty
years old, balding. He came over a few days ago. Told Pleach he
needed a couple of the bills for a scam or something. I was in
the kitchen, and I heard them talking."

"What kind of a scam?" Carr leaned closer.

"He didn't say, and Pleach didn't ask."

"What was the man's name?"

"Red. That's what Pleach called him. That's all I know. Honest
to God."

"Does Pleach know anybody named Ronnie?"

"Not that I know of." Vikki grabbed her stomach. "I think I
have to throw up . . . right now." Carr followed her to the bathroom. She gagged and wretched into the sink violently.

"The mating call of the hype," Kelly said.

Carr leaned against the bathroom doorjamb.

"We might have just run out of luck," Carr said.

"What?"

"She says the only bills went to somebody named Red. That's
all she knows. I believe her."

"Unless we can come up with a 'Red,' we're at the end of the
road," Kelly said.

Carr nodded.

$/10

At the East L.A. County women's jail, Carr had written "Possession of Counterfeit Notes—Federal Arraignment" on Vikki's booking sheet while Kelly had squirted her vomit off the back seat of the G-car with a garden hose.

After finishing the usual booking procedures, Carr phoned Delgado and filled him in. It was 9:30 P.M.

On the way to the field office, Kelly stopped at a taco stand on Brooklyn Avenue.

They got out of the car and walked to the painted hut. GOMEZ BROS TACOS CARNITAS. A freckled face came to the window and asked for their order in Spanish. Carr and Kelly looked at one another before ordering. The taco man had red hair and was balding. Carr shook his head. It had been a week since Rico had been killed and there still were no real leads. He knew as well as any cop that the longer the investigation took the less chance there was for success. Kelly ate five tacos with extra sauce, and they headed for the field office.

Delgado was waiting in the records room, sitting at a long table covered with stacks of five-by-eight arrest cards, Styrofoam coffee cups, and dirty ashtrays.

"The guys that pulled this caper had to know about how a counterfeit deal is done," Delgado said. "I think it's best if we go through the arrest cards, starting at the most current, and work backward. I've got people at LAPD records checking for the same thing. The arrest card has the color of hair and the date of birth." Delgado picked up a stack of cards and began thumbing through them.

The cards of red-haired men began to pile up in the middle of the table as the night wore on. By 3:30 A.M. they had compiled one hundred forty-six arrest forms of persons fitting the general description. Kelly, using a clerk's push cart, pulled the one hundred forty-six arrest packages from file drawers, and the three agents dug out photographs of each man, tossing them into a pile.

"Listen to this," Kelly said. He read from an arrest card: "Identifying marks: Tattoos of devil shoveling coal on each buttock." Kelly laughed hysterically. "This freak has tattoos of the devil shoveling coal into his ass!" They roared.

An hour later Carr rubbed his eyes. "Let's catch a couple of hours," he said. Kelly's head was already down on the table.

Arriving home a half hour later, Kelly parked his car in the driveway, because the garage was filled with bicycles of various sizes. He went in the kitchen door, switched on the light, and took lunch meat and a beer from the refrigerator.

Sitting at the kitchen table, he chewed slowly, as if in a trance. He was exhausted.

He looked up as his wife walked into the kitchen buttoning her housecoat, removing her long braids from inside its collar.

"Do you want me to fix you something?"

He shook his head and took a long pull from the beer bottle, wiping his mouth with the back of his hand.

"What's new around here?" he said.

"Stevie got an F in spelling. Jimmy and Junior took their bikes apart and left them all over the garage floor. That's about it."

"Uh-huh."

She would not ask him about work. That issue had been resolved early in their marriage. He didn't like to talk about the job, because there were too many things to explain, too many impossible translations. It had been easier to sever the ties between the two worlds.

Such things had really never been a problem between them. They had never tried to change one another.

Removing a crayon and coloring book from a kitchen chair, she sat down, softly rubbing her eyes.

"Do you want to talk?"

"Yeah, uh, sure," he said with lunch meat in his mouth.

"This is the earliest you've been home since it happened."

"I guess you're right." He stopped eating momentarily and unloosened his tie.

"I went to early Mass this morning and prayed for Rico. I've had nightmares about it. I've been worried about you, too." She stared at her folded hands.

"God bless you, Rose." He patted her hands. "Everything will be back to normal pretty soon."

"How could they do that to someone? Take someone's life ... a young man like he was. He'll never be able to have ... raise children, to have a family."

He looked away from his wife's eyes.

"Are you going to come to bed?" Rose said.

"Can't sleep right now. I think I'll watch TV for a while." He put things back in the refrigerator.

Rose got up and went into the bedroom.

Kelly fell asleep after watching ten minutes of a Richard Widmark movie. He awoke an hour later and telephoned Carr at his apartment. No answer. He phoned Sally's place. Carr answered.

"Just thought of something," Kelly said. "There used to be a red-haired stickup man that hung around that bail-bond place on North Broadway. . . ."

"He's in San Quentin."

"You sure?"

"Yes. Delgado thought of him and had him checked out."

"Oh. Uh. Sorry to wake you up."

"Good night, Jack."

"Good night."

Carr hung up the phone on the nightstand.

"Who was that?" Sally said.

"Kelly."

"Do you feel like playing?"

"I don't know. Do you?"

She rolled over away from him and mumbled something.

"What say?"

"I said *never mind*."

Carr thought about the Sunset Motel again.

It was 8:00 A.M. Driving back toward the women's jail, Carr wondered if it would have been better not to try to sleep at all. The fatigue had set in.

"What happens if Vikki doesn't recognize any of the mug shots?" Kelly said, looking blankly at the road.

"Back to square one," Carr said. He yawned.

While putting their service revolvers in the jail safety locker, a hefty matron in a green uniform told them that Vikki had just bailed out. The lady sheriff's glossy lipstick was painted slightly over the edges of her lips, giving her mouth a gigantic appearance.

"Bail bondsman from the San Fernando Valley," she chirped. "He had an order from a judge."

"Well, I'll be god damned," Kelly said. "You might have figured that some Communist judge would screw things up."

"Communist?" the heavily rouged deputy said, smiling.

"That's right, sweet meat. Why else would a judge release a hype on bail? Hypes are sick. They couldn't find their way back to court even if they wanted to."

"Well, they all do it these days."

"That's because they're all Communists. Lawyer Communists. All judges were lawyers once. Don't forget that."

"I guess I never looked at it quite like that." The deputy adjusted a straining bra strap.

Carr and Kelly walked across the parking lot to the government sedan. "I hope Vikki went back to Leach's place," Carr said. "Otherwise we might never be able to find her." He put the stack of mug shots in his coat pocket. He really hoped Vikki was home.

Kelly parked the sedan in the driveway of the pink apartment house next door to Leach's.

"Watch this," Carr said. He stuck his head out the passenger window and spoke in a loud whisper toward the apartment house.

"Is she home?"

"Came in two hours ago in a taxi. She's alone. Why'd you let her go?" said the woman.

"She bailed out," Carr answered. He opened the door and got out of the sedan. Kelly followed.

"Who the hell is that?" Kelly said.

"I don't know," Carr said.

They walked to the front door. Kelly knocked loudly. There was no answer. The house was still.

Kelly stayed at the front door. Carr walked along the driveway and into the back yard. He knocked on the screen door and waited. No answer. Cupping his hands to his eyes, he leaned forward against the screen. Vikki was at the corner kitchen table. Quietly, he felt the door handle. It was unlocked. He opened the door and stepped into the kitchen. Hothouse air. A burner on the gas stove was on.

Vikki was sitting in the greasy wallpapered breakfast nook, in a dinette chair. A fixing spoon, cotton ball, and an open can of dog food decorated the table. She leaned forward, resting her head on the Formica table as if taking a nap, her right arm, palm up, outstretched.

The syringe was still in her arm.

Carr touched her neck with two fingers. He could tell she was dead.

He sat down resignedly at the table, not concerned about disturbing the evidence. It was accidental, and if it wasn't, he knew there was no way to prove otherwise in an overdose.

Kelly came in the back door.

"We're back to square one," Carr said. He looked at Kelly.

Kelly turned slightly pale. He stepped back.

"O.D.?" Kelly's voice was thick.

Carr nodded.

"I'll get to the radio," Kelly said. He trotted out the back door.

Carr removed the stack of photographs from his pocket and shuffled through them.

$/11

The doors of the postwar apartments faced a cement rectangle the width of a boxing ring. On the window sills were red clay pots containing cacti and other succulents, some of which were alive. The area smelled of fried food.

Red Diamond knocked three times on a screen door that had a sign saying MANAGER.

A middle-aged woman in a helmet of hair rollers opened the door. She wore a housecoat.

He asked her about Mona as if he had a right to.

"Mona Diamond?" she said. "She moved out of apartment number four about two years ago. Who wants to know?"

"Routine credit investigation," said Red. "She's applied for a loan with our company."

The woman nodded tediously, as if she had something better to do.

"Was she living with anyone?"

"Lived alone. Seldom saw her with anyone. Once in a great while some man would spend the night and leave the next morning. Different guys. This only happened every couple of months. She kept to herself. Did you know her husband was in prison? Some kind of a confidence man. Apparently he really dumped on her. She hated him."

Red shook his head calmly.

"That's all I know about her. Nice gal. Kept to herself. No parties." The woman took a bobby pin from the pocket of her housecoat and plunged it into one of the hair rollers. "Is there anything else?"

"Where did she work?"

"She was a waitress—you know, coffee shops, restaurants— nothing too fancy."

"Where is she working now?"

"I saw her a couple months ago at a coffee shop about six blocks from here. It's on Wilcox below Hollywood Boulevard . . . the left side. . . . Who did you say you were with?"

"National Credit Bureau," said Red.

"I always ask. You never know who you're talking to these days. There's millions of rapists and stranglers. I hate like hell to even open the door."

"Yes, ma'am," said Red in patrolman style. "Thanks for your help." He walked away holding his breath.

Though dark, it was still sweltering in Hollywood.

Red parked the Cadillac in front of the bay window of the Movieland Coffee Shop. He got out of the car and walked to a sidewalk pay phone without taking his eyes off Mona. Looking bored, she served steaming coffee to customers at the counter. He dropped a dime in the telephone.

A woman answered. "Sovereign Rent-a-Car, Hollywood office. This is June speaking."

Red cupped his hand around the mouthpiece. "Hello, June. This is Dr. Richard Sanders. I rented a Cadillac from you two weeks ago."

"Dr. Sanders . . . uh . . . we've been expecting you to return the car. Your contract was a two-day rental."

"That's what I called about. I'm in Phoenix for a heart surgeons' convention and I just wanted to let you know I'll have the car back to you in another week or so."

"Oh . . . well, I guess that will be okay. It's just that you didn't have any credit cards. . . ."

"Young lady, I certainly wouldn't *call* if I didn't intend to pay for the rental."

"Certainly, doctor. I apologize if . . ."

"No problem. See you in a week."

70

"Thank you for calling, doctor."

Red hung up the phone. He wrote "Heart Convention Phoenix" on a card in his wallet, because he knew that details were always important. Stories *must* be kept straight.

Mona wiped the counter with a rag. Red asked himself how many women over forty could be attractive, yes, *sexually* attractive, dressed in a puff-sleeved waitress uniform? Perhaps it was the combination of the tiny waist and the full, high breasts. Her blonde hairdo was the same as years ago, when she served drinks at the Sahara in Las Vegas.

Red remembered how the high rollers all had their tongues hanging out when she swished between the crap tables with trays of drinks, and the legs of a fashion model.

Though she could have had anyone she wanted at that time, it was he who had ended up at the Chapel of Dreams saying vows, with a young Tony Dio as best man. It was in the frenetic days of casino credit, room service, and quick, solid scores; his partner, Tony Dio, bringing in the suckers from Atlanta and Chicago to buy stock, land, and gold that didn't exist.

Mona flitted along the counter, filling cups again from a steaming glass pot. She was making her best thin-lipped smile.

Red rolled up the Caddy's windows and concentrated for a moment on relaxing, then tightening, his stomach muscles. It was his own device for trying to calm nervous intestines.

He got out of the car and walked across the street to the coffee shop. With a deep breath for sphincter control, he swung open the glass door and walked in. He took a seat at Mona's section of the counter.

Her back to him, she arranged plastic-wrapped crackers around a bowl of soup. Knowing her temper, he would not be surprised if she saw him and slammed the soup and crackers directly in his face. That's the way she was: quiet, almost docile until anger flamed. Once, in the parking lot of the Stardust Casino she almost scratched a would-be mugger's eyes out. "Cherokee Indian blood," she always said.

"Hi, Mona," he said in the softest tone he could muster.

She turned and frowned at him as if she had known he was there. She placed the soup bowl in front of a black man wearing a gas-station uniform farther down the counter. Then she picked up silverware and a napkin from a box and placed them in front of Red.

"I thought I'd just stop by, now that I'm out," he said.

Mona took a pencil and order book from her skirt pocket. "I heard you were out. May I take your order?" She leaned on one foot.

"After all this time you don't have to be so hostile," he said.

"What do you want?"

"I just thought we could talk."

"About what?" Mona snarled. She glanced around to see if anyone was listening. "One of your *big ideas* that everyone else ends up paying for?" Tomahawk eyes.

"I'll take a cup of coffee," Red said.

She served the coffee and kept busy with other customers as he drank it. His guts felt mushy. He restrained the bathroom urge.

"What time do you get off?" he said as Mona flashed by with a pie à la mode.

"Eleven," she mumbled without looking at him.

He sat for a half hour fiddling with cream, sugar, and spoon. Finally she returned.

As she made out the check for the coffee, Red spoke in his best bedside manner. "I want to talk to you about something important. It'll just take a couple minutes. Can I meet you out in front when you get off work?"

"Wait out in front," she said without looking up, and handed him the check.

Outside in the Caddy Red looked at his watch over and over again. He knew he couldn't expect wonders. After all, it had been five years. But looking at it realistically, the foot was in the door, and the first step was always the hardest. It wasn't as if he hadn't conquered her once, tamed her hot little ass and made her legs stick straight up in the air when they screwed. The facts as they stood were that she *had* agreed to meet him. He stuck his hand down in his pants and adjusted his genitals.

At 11:00 he broke into a sweat. He knew once she was in the car it would be easy to talk her into joining him for a drink, and with good ol' Mona, liquor was always quicker. At 11:15 he wondered if his watch was slow.

72

He walked back inside the coffee shop and spoke with a young waitress. "Mona? She just got off a few minutes ago. Went home." She pointed. "Left out the back door. She always goes out that way."

Red barely made it to the men's room.

It was after 9:00 P.M. when Carr arrived at his apartment. The one-bedroom place was generally in order. It contained a sofa, TV, kitchen table and chairs, and not much else. Affordable apartments near the beach were small.

In the bedroom, he took the gun and handcuffs off his belt and laid them in a dresser drawer. The framed picture on the dresser was of his mother and father in front of the old frame house in Boyle Heights where he had grown up. The picture was the only one he had framed. The others, of him and his army buddies, police buddies, agent buddies, mugging around beer-bottled tables, were stuffed away somewhere along with the yearly pistol-marksmanship plaques.

The furniture and carpet had the musty smell that things near the beach get; and the brick-and-planks bookcase in the living room (James Jones, a few spy novels and law-of-evidence books) was visibly dusty. As Sally said, "The whole place could use a thorough and complete cleaning."

The phone rang. It was Sally.

"How about dinner along the strand somewhere?" she said. He could tell she had been drinking.

"Sure."

"Let's ride," she said.

They leaned their bikes against a front window of the restaurant. The foot-high Cyrillic-style letters on the window read PRINCE NIKOLA OF SERBIA—YUGOSLAV FOOD.

Attached to the front door was an almost life-size photo of a tall muscular man wearing wrestler's trunks and a metal-studded championship belt. He was flexing his arms and, with the exception of heavy Slavic eyebrows, was completely bald.

They went in. The tables were filled with tanned beach types. Blonde, stringy-haired young women and frizzy-haired men, all wearing garish T-shirts and sports pants.

From behind a small wine bar in the corner, Prince Nikola of Serbia, wearing a form-fitting T-shirt and white trousers, waved them to a table. He rushed over with menus and a bottle of wine. His accent was heavy. "Sarma—stuffed cabbage—is only thing left that's any good. I tell you truth, Charlie." He poured wine into two glasses.

"Sounds okay to me, Nick," Carr said.

Sally nodded agreement. She picked up the wineglass and drank fully half of its contents.

"Did you read in the newspaper about the man on trial for raping his wife? The judge was talking about it. A landmark prosecution." She swished her wine and sipped.

Carr nodded.

"I hope he gets convicted," she said.

"Uh-huh."

"What do you think about it?" She looked at the ceiling.

"About what?"

"About whether a man can be charged with raping his wife."

Carr looked out the window. "I guess maybe he could be charged with stealing his own car, too. Or with indecent exposure when he gets out of the shower."

Sally shook her head and pursed her lips. She filled her wineglass.

"I want to talk about us," she said.

"Go ahead." Carr hoped Nick would hurry with the food.

Sally's mouth was set straight. It was the "let off steam" look. "It just seems that things have changed between us. We don't talk any more." She sipped her wine. "Not that you *ever* were the most open person in the world. I'm not trying to start an argument." More wine. "I've talked to a lot of other women in my Wednesday-night sensitivity class who have the same problem. There's this hostility now between men and women. Both are afraid to be taken advantage of. It's not that I want to be married; I was married once. It was too restrictive for me. I just think that our relationship could become closer." Her voice cracked. She took another gulp of wine. "We've known each other for years. We just seem to be drifting. We go to restaurants, you just sort of drop in to my apartment now and then. . . .

You're too self-contained. It's almost as if you don't need other people . . . and you don't relate well to new people."

"That's just the way I am," Carr said.

"I *know* how you are. It took me years to understand you. It's because of your background. The army, the police department, then one field office after another as a Treasury agent. All the crap. Your life experiences have made you unable to show emotion."

Prince Nikola of Serbia brought another bottle of wine, winked at Carr, and poured.

"Maybe I should join your sensitivity class. I'm interested in the part where you stand around in a circle and goose the person next to you, or whatever it is they do."

"You haven't understood a word I have said," Sally said. "We are not *relating* to one another right this very minute."

It was more of the same during the meal, Sally picking at her food and drinking wine until her lips had a purplish tinge. By coffee time, she was in the "rut" phase.

"An absolute rut," she said. "You go to the same Thursday-night fights with the same friends. You even go to the same restaurants. The same bars in Chinatown. I mean, do you know how many times we've been to *this very* restaurant?" She was beginning to slur.

"Nick is a friend of mine," he said.

"That's not the damn point!" She slapped an open palm on the table.

Riding back along the dark Santa Monica strand, Sally weaved slightly from side to side and continued to speak. She used the words *need, relate, affection,* and *dialogue* over and over again.

By the time they got to her apartment, she had begun to cry. No sobs, just the usual controlled-anger tears.

Inside, she took a bottle out of the refrigerator and poured wine. Then she sat in the middle of the living-room floor holding her wineglass with both hands.

Carr sat down next to her. He stared at the floor. "There is something serious I've been wanting to say to you for a long time. I just haven't been able to get up enough guts to say it."

Her look was incredulous. She set her wineglass down and

put her hand on his shoulder. "What is it?" she said softly.

Carr leaned close to her face, his lips next to her ear. "I'm a sex fiend," he whispered. He stuck his tongue in her ear and wrapped his arms around her.

Sally tried not to giggle as she made a half-hearted attempt to struggle.

"Charlie, stop! You're making fun of me!"

He kissed her lips and reached to unzip her pants.

They made wine-prolonged love on the living-room floor. Afterward, Carr carried the nude and sleepy Sally to her bed. He pulled a cover over her, and she said "I love you" without meeting his eyes.

"I love you, too," Carr mumbled.

He dressed and bicycled back to his apartment.

After showering, he wrote a note and dropped it in the drawer next to his holster and badge. It read:

1. Check mug books.
2. Ballistics report.
3. Autopsy report.

He went to bed.

$/12

The secretary ushered Red Diamond into a paneled office. The little lawyer sat at a big elevated desk with nothing on it but polish. He stuck out a two-ringed hand and forced a smile.

"Glad to see you out," he said.

"Hi, Max."

Max Waxman's bald head was fish skin stretched tightly over skull, with ear-level black hair falling limply over his collar. He wore thick glasses and a sparse mustache. His tie was white silk. "What can I do for you?"

"Now that I'm out, just thought I'd stop by to say hello."

"Hello." Max looked at his watch. He folded his hands.

Red sat down lightly in the leather chair. He nervously curled his toes inside his shoes. His stomach was sour.

"I might as well get right to the point. I'm getting ready for a big score—an oil-lease project—and I'm looking for backing. I thought I'd give you first shot at it since you and me go way back. I got the project figured for two or three hundred grand in twenty days. I'm planning to bring the suckers in through real-estate people. The pitch is a grand a piece. I got a guy who can make the phony oil-lease charts. . . ."

"Red, *please.*" The lawyer held up his hand. "I know you just got out, how tough it is and all, but these things involve too many people. The cops are on to you. You've been down too many times."

"So you won't even let me finish telling you . . ."

"I'll finish it for you. You need a front. An office, a secretary, a car, juice money for the real-estate people, the boiler room, bleepety bleepety bleep. And you want money from me. I'm sorry, Red. The answer is no. I'm sorry." He adjusted his tie.

Red sat for a moment without speaking. "Okay, then," he said, "will you loan me twenty-five grand? You know I'm good for it."

"The people that put up front money for you five years ago wouldn't think you're good for it. They went to the cleaners. They ended up sucking wind."

Red's face flushed. "And I went to the stinking, fucking joint."

"I'm sorry." Max pressed the intercom buzzer and told the secretary to make golf reservations for four, including Judge Brooks.

"If you need bucks, bring something to me, but please, nothing less than a pound. Coke should be legalized anyway. Or paper, bonds, stocks—something that's tangible. My investigator handles the arrangements. Same as before. I like to stick with the basics. Nice talking with you, Red. I'm really kind of busy today." He leaned forward and handed Red his engraved business card.

Red put it in his shirt pocket. He grasped the arms of the chair tightly. "I wouldn't ask you if I didn't need the money. I've sent you a lot of business through the years. I never handed you up to the Feds in the last project. I could of handed you up to the Feds but I didn't. They asked about you but I kept my mouth shut and walked the yard. You could have been there with me. You know that."

"I also know that the statute has run. I'm a lawyer, Red. I'm home free. They can't arrest me, because the offense happened over five years ago. That's the law. Please don't try to muscle me. Nobody muscles me. Let's remain friends." Max turned his palms up and gave a weak smile.

Red stood up and put his hands in his pockets. He thought it odd that his stomach had suddenly stopped churning.

"Tony the juice man has a long memory, doesn't he?" the lawyer asked. Red felt his head bob up and down. "I told you years ago that it was a mistake to go to him for front money.

I'm sorry you didn't take my advice. I'm really very sorry."

Red walked toward the door.

"Bring something to me! Anything except grass. I have a truckload man who keeps me busy with grass. Anything else! With luck you'll be out of the bind in no time at all. I *am* sorry, Red." Max looked at his watch.

The door closed.

A jukebox played soul music.

Red Diamond and Ronnie Boyce sat in a corner booth with drinks, served by a floppy-breasted waitress who wore nothing but a G-string.

The only light in the bar was a semicircle of pink, which illuminated a small, round stage. On the stage, a naked blonde woman with stretch marks on her stomach arched backward clumsily to give some men at a nearby table a good look at her crotch. The men made drunken remarks of appreciation.

No one else in the place seemed to be watching her. The tables and booths buzzed with whispered negotiations of all kinds. In the next booth an older man with a ponytail and a fat Mexican woman snorted cocaine from a tiny spoon.

Red handed Ronnie the ten-dollar Sahara Casino chip. "Take a look at it, lil' brother. I just got it today. You can't tell the difference between it and a real one. It's a sample counterfeit from the guy who makes 'em. He's an inventor, a genius really."

Ronnie rubbed the chip, tried to bend it. "Can we get some more?"

"That's the problem. The inventor made up this sample for me, but we need cash before he'll go into full production. We're back in a negative-cash-flow situation at this point."

Ronnie looked puzzled.

Red wrote on the paper place mat. "Cash flow → equipment → trip to Las Vegas → $100,000." He turned the place mat around to Ronnie. "This is the way I have it mapped out. We need another score to make this thing move. The dude will make the phony chips for a flat fee and we lay 'em down in Vegas. I figure we can do four or five grand at a time. We'll take our time so the pit bosses don't catch on, then we drive back to good ol' L.A. with a hundred big ones. Fifty for you, fifty for me . . . And by the way—" Red smiled and took the chip out of Ronnie's hand—"passing phony gambling chips is only a *state* crime. No Feds to worry about. Once we come back across the California border we're fucking-ass home free. You like?"

Ronnie gave a noncommittal nod. "Yeah, I guess. But how about the money on the last score? Couldn't we . . ."

Red snapped his fingers. "Damn! Let me apologize . . . I thought I had told you what we have working on that end. I've been so busy. . . . Briefly, things are great on setting up the front. I have things worked out for you and me to have offices in Century City. It looks like the best thing to go for at this point is limited partnerships for food franchises or maybe gold futures. This is what the suckers will probably go for. But I need more marketing research. We can't just jump in without *knowing* we can get the suckers. Too much risk for too little profit. You know what I mean. . . ."

Ronnie looked uncomprehending. "Yeah, sure," he said.

The near-naked waitress set fresh drinks down on the table and walked away.

"Then we're together, lil' brother?" Red said.

Ronnie, with a mouth full of ice cubes, grunted.

"That's good, that's fine," said Red. "We've got a lot of irons in the fire right now, and I want to be sure we are thinking along the same lines, you know, to avoid any fuck-ups. We have to think in terms of a long-range program. To get off the ground it's a simple matter of getting that positive cash flow. . . . That gives us a backup. There's always extras. You remember the story I told you about how I got caught short? The manager of the office building walks in and asks for the rent right when I had a sucker sitting there. I mean like the dumb fuck had his wife sitting out in the car holding his life savings. I was supposed to be selling him half ownership in a gold mine and suddenly he sees I'm behind on my rent! *No way.* It was a good lesson. The farmer and his old lady drove off with their fifteen grand, but I learned a good lesson: don't get caught short. Simple." Red gave Ronnie a pet-shop-window smile.

"Remember me telling you about the lawyer? Here's his card."

Boyce accepted the business card and looked at it curiously.

```
┌─────────────────────────────────┐
│         MAX WAXMAN              │
│       ATTORNEY AT LAW          │
│                                 │
│         SUITE 4101             │
│    SUNSET CONTINENTAL BLDG.     │
│       PHONE 721-0196           │
└─────────────────────────────────┘
```

"Max Waxman is strictly a money man. You talk price with
him, but the hand-to-hand will be between you and his private
investigator. Max never touches anything himself; finances a
couple of dope deals a week the same way. He drives a Rolls-
Royce."

"What size deal should I talk about?" Ronnie put the card in
his pocket.

"Tell him you have a hundred and twenty-five thousand that
you're willing to sell for twelve points. Make him come up with
twenty-five thousand for the buy. Don't go over that or he'll
smell a rip-off. He's shrewd, real shrewd." Red took out an envelope, opened it, and showed Ronnie the two counterfeit
twenties. He handed the envelope to the younger man. "Take
good care of these. They're the last samples we have. The dude
that gave them to me got busted last night and they got his
stash."

"Two phony twenties for twenty-five grand. Sounds like a fair
profit." Ronnie smiled.

"And I know you've got the balls to bring it off just like the
one at the motel." Red gave his best flattery look. "Oh, that re-
minds me. Max will never permit a deal in a motel room. He'll
push for a public place, probably a parking lot or something."

Ronnie nodded, took a bite of toast, and swallowed. "Who do
I say referred me?"

"Drop Stymie's name. Stymie's been a front man for Max for
years. He used to impersonate a cop, take care of the heavy stuff
when Max was shaking down fag movie stars back in the old
days."

"You mean Stymie the old trusty from E wing?"

"That's the one." Red finished his soda water.

"What if Waxman checks me out with him?"

"No problem. Stymie got piped last week; some Mexicans.

He's in the prison infirmary with his head bashed in. He can't talk."

"So there's no way Waxman can check me out?"

"No friggin' way, baby. Old Max is shrewd, but he'll bite once he sees those samples." Red felt a slight churning in his bowels.

"With this score we should have enough, right?" Ronnie asked.

"Wha . . . Oh, yeah. One hundred percent for sure! This will give us enough to set up the counterfeit-chips caper. When that's done, we'll get our phony office, bank account, everything. I've got a guy who can draw up phony oil-field charts, whatever we need for the operation. It will be *big*. We'll have the suckers ringing our phone off the hook to put in their grand." Red took out a ball-point pen and scratched figures on the place mat. "Everything depends on cash flow. We've got to *start out* big to *make it* big. We can't get in the middle and have a cash-flow problem. That's a problem area."

Red underlined some of the figures and pointed with his pen. "See? It works out to one hundred and fifty grand for each of us, after both capers. Twenty days after we start the project. And that's minimum. Complete minimum." As Red spoke the words seemed familiar. He could switch off his mind and the words would continue. Prison chatter.

The woman on the stage bent over and grabbed her ankles. She wiggled.

"This private-eye fucker—is he gonna be heeled?" Ronnie broke a swizzle stick in half.

"Always. Waxman buys him a gun permit from a judge every year. The Red guy is telling you to be careful, very careful."

Ronnie lit a cigarette and put the match in the ashtray. "I got my permit right here." He stuck out his middle finger.

Red laughed nervously.

$/13

"Who gave you my name?" said Max Waxman, fiddling with his teen-ager's mustache.

"Somebody I met in T. I.," Ronnie Boyce said.

"Who is somebody?"

"Stymie."

"What does Stymie look like?"

"He looks a lot like a cop, but he ain't."

Waxman smiled. "You look a little like a cop yourself."

"Your mother looks like a cop," Boyce said.

"Okay, kid, what have you got? I'm busy today."

Boyce handed the envelope to the lawyer.

Waxman lifted the flap and blew into the envelope. Holding it open with one hand, he reached into his desk drawer and removed tweezers. He took the bills from the envelope with the tweezers and examined them carefully, both sides. He tucked them back into the envelope and handed it to Boyce.

"Quantity?"

"A hundred and twenty-five grand."

Waxman wrote on a yellow pad. "I've seen better, but I can offer you ten points for the package. That's twelve thousand five hundred for you."

"Thirty points is the usual price," Boyce said.

Waxman raised his voice. "Where? Off the back of a turnip truck? I'll go fifteen points but . . ."

"Twenty points is what I want. It's what I have to get to make my end. I'll take twenty percent or I walk."

Waxman took a plastic bottle of hand lotion out of a drawer, squirted a fair amount on a palm. He rubbed his hands together until the cream disappeared.

"You're a tough little bastard, aren't you? What's your name?"

"Ronnie. Ronnie Smith," Boyce said.

"And I'm Max Doe, the brother of John. Twenty points it is. I don't have time to quibble over a few bucks. That's twenty-five grand to you. It will be in hundred-dollar bills. My man will show you the twenty-five G's first, so you have nothing to worry about. Tonight, 11:00 P.M. exactly, be at the L.A. airport. There is a phone booth in parking lot D-3. You better write that down. I suggest you get to the phone booth early to avoid any problems. At 11:00 P.M. the phone will ring and you will receive final instructions for the transaction. Be ready to deliver five minutes after you pick up the phone. If the phone doesn't ring exactly at eleven, the deal is off. It means something is wrong. Any questions?" He looked at the palms of his hands.

"Who will do the deal at the airport?" Boyce said.

Waxman took off his glasses and wiped them with a handkerchief.

"One person it's not going to be is me, young man. I'm an attorney at law. You saw the sign on the door. . . . It's been nice talking with you. Come see me anytime you have something."

They shook hands.

Boyce walked through the outer office. A fat man with a full-head black toupee and cardigan sweater made a show of handing something to the receptionist. He stared at Boyce. The screen test, thought Boyce.

Ronnie parked the car next to the airport gas station. Carol looked pale; her lips were colorless.

"You just wait here until I signal you for the case," Ronnie said.

"Then what?" Carol said. She looked at the attaché case sitting between them.

"Then you bring it to me in the parking lot, hand it to me, and go straight back to the motel."

She looked at her watch. "It's ten now. When are you going to want it?"

"A little after eleven. Right now I want you to go across the street and rent another car." He pointed.

"What for?"

"Because this car is registered to *you*. That's why. After I take this guy off, somebody might grab the license plate. Rent a big car and drive it back here. Do you have a phony license that you haven't used for anything yet?"

"Yes."

"Use it." He looked at his watch. "Make it quick. The guy is going to call me at the phone booth in that parking lot at eleven." He pointed to the parking lot behind the gas station.

Carol was silent for a moment. A jumbo jet roared to a landing on the runway across the street.

"You're going to ice him, aren't you?" she said. Her eyes were wide.

After a moment Ronnie spoke with a sneer. "When I tell you to do something, you'd best fucking do it without a lot of chickenshit questions. After I take this dude's money tonight, Red and I are going to have enough to set up a front. We're going to parley the score today into two or three hundred grand. No more chickenshit two- and three-grand capers that cost two or three years. Do you understand?"

She nodded, her head down. He continued.

"All you have to do is rent me a goddamn car and carry an attaché case a hundred feet. Is that too goddamn fucking much to ask?"

She turned to him. "But if everything comes apart, I'll be an accessory. That's life. I've already got a ten-year parole. I don't want to go back. Ronnie, I couldn't take anoth . . ."

Ronnie grabbed her ear lobe and jerked her toward him. His voice was a violent whisper. "Don't give me that *shit* about not wanting to go back. *Nobody* wants to go back. The difference is when you say you are *never* going back. That's the difference. To do that you gotta score big, woman. Your fifty-dollar checks ain't going to keep you out. They'll put you right back in with the bull daggers. Course, I heard you didn't mind it too much this last time. A tongue wash now and then made the time go faster, right?" He shoved her head away from him violently.

She looked at him with no expression, checked her purse for the phony license, and got out of the car. He watched her walk across the street and enter the rent-a-car office.

Fifteen minutes later she drove into the gas station in a new Ford. She handed him the keys, and they exchanged cars.

Carol watched him drive through a toll gate into the parking lot. It was nearly full. The attaché case was next to her on the seat. He wouldn't say what was in it, but she assumed it was a piece, since they had picked it up from a bus-depot locker. She undid the latches and opened it. Sawed-off shotgun. She closed the lid and snapped the latches. Ronnie was nuts. He always had been. She wondered how he had found out about what had gone on in Corona. Was it because her hair was too short? Maybe he was just guessing.

Ronnie's hands were wet on the steering wheel when he stopped next to the phone booth. He turned off the ignition. He tried to think of last-minute details, because he knew that was what he should be thinking about. What if someone tried to use the pay phone?

He got out of the car and locked all the doors. A breeze of jet fuel. His hands trembled. He stepped into the pay booth and checked his watch. It was ten-fifty-eight. A few seconds later the phone rang. Waxman's secretary's voice. She was reading from something. "The man in the sweater is our representative. He is in a black Oldsmobile. Follow his instructions." The phone clicked.

A car door of a black Olds slammed two parking rows away. In the darkness the fat man came toward him in a wrestler's walk. The pompadour wig could have been a hat.

The fat man stopped and looked around the parking lot. "Are you together?" he asked.

"Who the fuck are you?"

"I work for Max. I'm here to do business." The fat man's eyes were riveted to Boyce's hands.

"You should have said so," Boyce said. "I'm together. Where's your buy money?"

86

The man stepped closer. "Max doesn't buy anything without seeing the full package. That's the way it has to work. It's safer for everybody. You understand." The fat man's voice had a flat, disinterested tone, like a cop giving a ticket. He folded his arms across his chest.

Boyce maintained eye contact. "I don't want to get ripped off any more than you do. When I talked with Max, he said I could show you the paper at the same time you show me the buy money. What's wrong with that? Otherwise we stand here jerking each other off about who's going to show first. Right?"

The fat man glanced around the lot. He focused back on Boyce's hands. "If I was to agree to showing at the same time, then you shouldn't have any objection to letting me search you beforehand."

Boyce spread his arms out wide, palms upturned. "Search away! I don't have a piece. You got nothing to worry about from me. The paper is nearby. All I have to do is give the come-ahead."

The fat man glanced around the lot again. He patted Boyce's torso.

Boyce cased the lot. The fat man was alone. No backup near.

"Okay," the fat man said, "you don't have a gun. Now you just stand there where I can see you and give your mule the come-ahead." He pulled up his sweater. Underneath was a canvas money belt and a .45 in a waist holder. "The twenty-five grand is in here." He unzipped the belt and flicked the edges of four stacks of hundred-dollar bills. "Now you signal your mule. If anything goes wrong, I'll kill you first." His hand was on the .45.

"Take it easy, man." Boyce's voice cracked.

He waved his hands over his head. Carol approached with the attaché case. As she came closer he felt sweat running down the middle of his back.

She handed him the case without a word and disappeared quickly into the darkness. Another jet screamed onto the runway.

"Now open the trunk of your car," the fat man commanded. "Lay the case down in it and show me the funny money. I want to count it. While you're doing that I will let you count the money in the belt. If anybody walks by, it'll look like we're just un-loading the trunk or something."

"Fair enough," Boyce said. He opened the trunk with the key. The fat man stepped closer. Boyce smelled tobacco on his breath. Boyce laid the case gently in the trunk and flicked open one latch. "Let's see the money in the belt," he said.

The fat man pulled up his sweater. Boyce flicked open the other latch on the case. The man was looking down at the money belt, trying to take it off.

Boyce slammed his fist into the fat man's jaw, knocking him backward and down. Opening the attaché case with flying fingers, he grabbed the shotgun and pointed it down at the angry fat face. The barrel was in the other man's hands. He gave an animal groan.

Boyce pulled the trigger. Recoil knocked him backward into the trunk. The fat man scrambled on the ground. Boyce fired again. The fire flash spun the man's body over.

Ears buzzing, Boyce dropped the shotgun into the trunk, jumped up, and slammed the lid. He ran to the car door. The money belt! He was on the ground tearing at the sweater and the money belt. *Everything is red! Can't get it off!* The fat man gurgled. He ripped the belt from the body and ran for the car door. He jumped in, threw the car in reverse, and backed out. He felt the car running over the body, back wheels, then front wheels.

Keeping an eye on the speedometer, he drove to see Red. At a stoplight, he stuffed the bloody money belt under the seat. His hands felt sticky.

$/14

Red Diamond was waiting on the bus bench at Sunset and Gower. He was where he had said he would be.

Ronnie sounded the horn, and Red got in.

"Any problems?" Red said. He closed the car door.

"I wasted the private eye," Ronnie said. He pulled back into the Hollywood traffic.

"Where's the money?"

"Under the seat."

Red reached under the car seat. "Drive into that supermarket lot up the street on the right." He pulled out the money belt with two fingers. "Jeez."

He unzipped the belt and pulled out a stack of hundreds and began counting. "Oh, no! Oh, shit! It's a fucking gypsy bankroll! The hundreds are counterfeit!"

Ronnie slammed on the brakes in front of the supermarket. "Let's see!"

Red held out the bills. "Look! Look! We've been fucked! That rotten fucking Waxman was going to trade twenty-five grand in funny money for a hundred and twenty-five grand! Paper for paper! That dirty kike!" Red slammed his fist against the dashboard.

Ronnie had a headache. His ears rang from the sound of the shotgun.

"Maybe you should have gone with me, Red."

"Uh . . . bad idea. Everybody in town knows Red Diamond—they could have followed up on us. You know. Don't worry about what happened. It's just one of those things. You know."

Ronnie shook his head from side to side.

People walked in and out of the bright supermarket. They were talkative. The heat of the day was over.

"Shit, shit, shit," Red said, holding the bridge of his nose with two fingers.

"What are we gonna do now?" Ronnie said.

"We can recover from this if we just use our heads. This is a setback. Gotta come back. Gotta come back fast. That's the problem," Red said. His voice became rhythmic, constant, uncontrollable. He had started one of his lectures. "We can do it," he said. "Never doubt that for a minute! See the turkeys walking out of the store with their bags of potato chips? Every one of 'em has a game . . . a scam." Red pointed to a bald man in a jogging outfit carrying a carton of soft drinks in each hand. "Ten to one he's some kinda businessman. Probably life insurance. I can usually guess. . . . He's got *his* scam. That's what insurance is. They bet you will die, you bet you will live, and they always win. Insurance companies are more crooked and powerful than the whole goddamn Mafia. . . . Go down the street to the Fairfax Towers Hotel and you can see Brother Roper's church bus load up every morning with suckers. All old people with canes. They crawl into the bus at 8:00 A.M., and Brother Roper drives 'em out to the City of Moses, a plot of land off the freeway between here and Las Vegas. There's nothing there but desert. All they have to do is sign over all their money to him and he guarantees them a home in the City of Moses as soon as it's built. He's had the same scam for ten years and never been busted! The bastard has to be a millionaire by now. . . . It's just luck. . . . You and me pull one chickenshit caper and end up with a gypsy bankroll! But we can't let it get us down. We have to be *positive.*"

Ronnie Boyce's ears buzzed.

Carol, in shorts and a halter top, bought a morning newspaper from the sidewalk rack and walked back into the hotel room reading.

"Ronnie, listen to this!" She folded the paper to the second page and read aloud. " 'The body of an unidentified man was discovered in a parking lot at Los Angeles International Airport last night. Police sources said the man had been murdered by a shotgun, in gangland style, possibly as the result of an underworld dispute. A witness told investigators she saw two men talking at the trunk of a car and one brandished a weapon and fired twice. The police investigation is continuing.' "

"Lemme see." Ronnie, in shorts, got off the bed and grabbed the newspaper from her hands. He read, moving his lips, and threw the paper back to Carol. "They don't have anything," he said.

"Don't *have* anything? If they've got a witness, they've got somebody who can *identify* you. Pick you out of a *line-up*! Oh, God, I knew something like this would happen." She crumpled the paper.

Ronnie sat down on the bed. He leaned back against the headboard. "That's always been your problem, Carol."

"What?"

"Your problem is that you lose your cool. You get excited and you lose your cool."

Carol shook her head. "I just don't want to go back to . . ."

". . . to the joint," he interrupted. "Well, you won't have to as long as you keep your shit from getting disturbed. I used to be the same way. Everything was a big deal. But not any more. The only way to keep out of the joint is to relax, take each day as it comes. If a case comes down, you keep your mouth shut and ride the beef. Nine out of ten times if you keep your mouth shut, you can beat the case in court. That's a statistic, an actual statistic." He adjusted a pillow behind his head.

Carol spoke. "I don't want you to think I'm . . ."

"I don't think anything, Carol. I'm just telling you that I used to be dumb. That's right, dumb. Would you believe, the first time I did a bank job I didn't know that banks had robbery cameras? That's being dumb. But I'm not dumb any more. The guy I snuffed last night ain't going to take the witness stand too soon. And he was the only other person that saw what happened. Do you see what the fuck I mean?"

She sat down on the edge of the bed resignedly. "Yeah, I guess."

"It's all evidence. What the D.A. wants is evidence. Without it they can't do diddly shit. It's simple, really."

"How much money did the guy have last night?" Carol said.

"Twenty-five G's in funny money," said Ronnie. "But it's going to set up a front. My partner is a con man. He's the best. Within a month I'm going to be set for life, with no way of getting nailed. Phony land deal. There's only so many dudes that have enough smarts to pull one off. The paperwork is set up so that there's no way of getting convicted even if you stand trial. They can't prove intent."

"Sounds beautiful." Carol got off the bed and stood staring out the window.

"It *is* beautiful. We just needed some front money. I did a guy the same way for ten grand a week ago. No witnesses there either." He scratched under his arm. "Let's go get some breakfast." He went into the bathroom and closed the door. The shower started.

Carol turned on the radio fairly loud and dialed a long-distance number. She stared at the bathroom door.

"Naomi?"

"Yes."

"It's Carol."

"Carol, honey, I knew you'd call. I knew you'd change your mind."

"I gotta get out of L.A.," Carol whispered. "I'm with a guy that's bad news. I'll be there this weekend. I'm gonna lay down all my paper—I've got a stack of cashier's checks—then I'm coming to you. I can't take it here any more. I'm paranoid. Can't talk now." She cupped her hand around the receiver.

"Little sister, when you get here the first thing I'm going to do is turn you inside out. I've missed you so much." A kissing sound.

Carol put down the receiver.

The shower went off.

Ronnie walked back in the room soaking wet. "What's the weird look on your face for?"

"Nothing." She gulped.

"Get a towel." He stood with his hands on his hips.

Without a sound, she picked up a towel from the dresser and

92

began drying him. His back, chest, buttocks, legs, and groin.

"That's the way the screws choke you out in T. I."

"What?"

"With a towel." He snatched the towel from her hands, spun her around, pulled it tightly around her neck. She gagged. He flipped the towel back to her.

"Like that," Ronnie said.

Carol coughed and rubbed her Adam's apple.

"Get your clothes off, woman."

Carol stripped as fast as she could.

Without air conditioning, the field office would have been intolerable. Gray desert air hung outside. Exhaust City.

Carr got up from the desk and stared out the window at the brownstone Hall of Justice. The ninth floor was a jail and had iron windows. Five years ago a prisoner had escaped from the jail by using a homemade rope. If he remembered correctly, the man was caught the same day at his mother's house in Glendale, where he had grown up. Stupid.

"Are you sure Vikki wasn't murdered?" Delgado said. He leaned against a bulletin board with blown-up photographs of counterfeit twenties.

"We talked to the taxi driver who picked her up at the women's jail," Carr said. "He took her straight to Leach's pad. Nonstop. A nosy neighbor saw her go into the house. Coroner set the time of death to within a half hour of when she got home. Everything points toward a simple overdose." He loosened his tie.

"I thought you and Kelly searched the pad when you arrested her. Where'd she get the dope?"

"We missed it when we searched. Inside the door handle on the service porch. It was probably an emergency stash," Carr said.

The phone rang.

"Carr."

"This is Kelly. I'm down here at the morgue. I just talked with the coroner himself. He says it was heroin, not poison or anything, and it was usual strength. She O.D.'d. See you in an hour. I gotta stop for a bite."

"Thanks." Carr put down the phone. "The coroner says she O.D.'d on smack. She wasn't murdered—unless somebody gave her a hotshot on purpose."

"I wonder if she committed suicide," Delgado said.

Carr wasn't listening. He faced Delgado. "Let's look at the big picture right now. We're looking for two suspects: a young guy and a middle-aged, balding, red-haired man. The only witness who can identify the red-haired man just checked out of the world. Leach, the man with the samples, won't talk. We've got a stack of one hundred and forty-six photos of red-haired men. That's what we've got. Nothing more, nothing less."

"Only one way to go," Delgado said.

"One way. We'll check up on every red-haired man. See what he's up to, who he hangs with. One of them has got to fit into the picture." Carr turned to look out the window.

"It's a long shot," Delgado mumbled.

"I know it."

$/15

Carr walked toward a run-down stucco house. A FOR SALE sign was stuck in the middle of the tiny yellow lawn. It was as hot as August can be, and his suit and tie felt like a damp strait jacket.

Of course, without the tie, people would never open the door. It was more important than a badge and credentials. Kelly had proved it on a Chinatown bet once by pasting a picture of a monkey over his credentials photo and conducting a whole day of interviews. No one had noticed. And as he told it at Ling's, one lady had mistaken him for an FBI agent.

Carr rang the doorbell. Immediately footsteps clacked on what sounded like a hardwood floor.

The door was opened by a tanned, middle-aged woman in a bikini bathing suit and wooden sandals. She held a *TV Guide*. Behind her he noticed Danish modern furniture, but no carpeting.

Carr flashed his badge. "Special Agent Carr, U.S. Treasury Department. May I come in?"

"Cute little badge," the woman said. "Come in."

She waited for him to enter and closed the door.

"What have I done to deserve a visit from a T-man?" She walked daintily to a portable bar, picked up a beer glass, and sipped.

"I'm conducting an investigation on someone who lives here

in the neighborhood. I have a photo I'd like you to look at." He removed the photo from his shirt pocket. She sauntered to him and examined the photo, holding it gingerly by one corner. She blushed and handed it back.

"Which one of the nosy neighbors told you to come here?" She spoke with her teeth together.

"I may or may not have talked to your neighbors. Right now I'm talking to you. Do you know this man?" Carr took out a handkerchief and wiped his brow.

"Of course I know him; he lives next door," she said.

"Who lives with him?"

"He has a wife and three children. Is that what you mean? What kind of investigation is this?" she snarled.

"A background investigation," Carr said. "Do you know any of his friends?"

"Maybe."

Carr took out his pen. "How about some names?" he said.

She slammed her glass down on the bar and began shouting. "What do you mean 'How about some names?' Let me tell you something. This may be a low-rent neighborhood but I've only lived here since my divorce. I used to live in San Marino, but I ended up with nothing except some goddamn furniture!"

"Hold it a minute . . ." He raised his hand like a traffic cop. "All I want to know is . . ."

"No! I know one of the goddamn nosy neighbors told you to come here because he and I . . . are friends. His stupid wife started the rumors about us. Did you see the 'For Sale' sign when you walked in? That's why I'm moving."

"Lady, I'm not interested!" The woman looked foolish standing there screaming in her bikini.

"Does this have something to do with his child support? Did his first wife send you here? Can't you people give somebody a break? You've got him in jail on a failure-to-provide warrant. What else do you want—blood?"

"When was he arrested?"

"Two weeks ago. He's been in jail since then."

"Thanks. I don't have any more questions." Carr almost trotted to the door.

"Why don't you do something about dope pushers instead of

nosing into people's private lives!" she shouted.

Carr walked to the car, drove around the corner, and parked. He wrote "In jail past two weeks" on the reverse of the photograph and threw it in the glove compartment with the others that had turned out to be dead-end leads.

His notations on the photos showed that three of the men were currently serving time in prison, and one was in the hospital the day Rico was murdered. Another carrot-top had been dead for over a year.

It had taken Carr all day to find these things out.

By 10:00 P.M., he had eliminated two more redheads. He drove to Chinatown and found Kelly sitting in a booth at Ling's. The bar was full of detectives, because it was federal payday. The atmosphere was rowdy.

"Get this," Kelly said, digging his hand deeply into the bar peanuts. "I showed one of the photos to this guy today and he tells me he thinks the photo looks like *me*. I look at it and by God he's right! Except for the red hair, the picture did sort of look like me. I hadn't looked at it that close before. I felt like a real donkey. He must have thought I was walking around showing mug shots of myself. Do you believe that?" Throwing his head back, he accepted the entire handful of peanuts into his mouth.

Carr almost guzzled his first drink. He had been thinking about it for hours.

Rose stood at the end of the bar under a pink light, lifting drinks onto her tray. Her long black hair contrasted oddly with the bright-blue sheen of her dragon-embroidered cheongsam. Even in high heels, she was tiny, the spread of her buttocks from a tiny waist being her only striking physical quality. In the pink light of the bar, just as up close, she appeared drawn, tired, and less than happy, as if it had taken longer than usual to become forty years old.

She smiled at Carr, and he gave a quick wave. He thought of how he waved at her as he drove away from her house after they had made love the first time. Standing at the window in her kimono she had waved back. He hadn't really wanted to leave. "Very embarrass when children wake up in morning," she had said, with her head slightly bowed.

He wasn't sure why he continued to see her. The meetings were infrequent and always seemed a little strained. They never had a great deal to say to one another. Her husband was dead, and she had to work, and he was a federal cop and lived at the beach. That was about it.

But he kept going back to her wan smile and the way she modestly covered her smallish breasts when she crawled into bed.

She made her way to the booth and handed Carr a Scotch-and-water. Kelly excused himself and got up.

"Sit down for a minute." Carr pointed to the seat.

She shook her head. "Too busy right now. Ling get mad."

"How was Lake Arrowhead?"

"We have a real nice time," she said. Her voice was just loud enough to be heard. "Boys catch fish in the lake. Too bad you couldn't come up one day. You probably busy. . . ."

"Yes. Uh, I . . ."

She saw Kelly coming back to the table.

"You come over tonight maybe?" She looked around to see if anyone was listening.

"Yeah. Okay," Carr said.

She shuffled back to the bar.

The bar phone rang and Ling picked it up.

"Charlie, for you." He held up the receiver.

Carr walked to the end of the bar and squeezed in between two bearded federal narcotics agents.

"Carr here."

"Higgins, LAPD Homicide. I got something for ya. Better roll down to the airport. Parking lot D-3."

"What is it?"

"Last week, in Chinatown, you asked me to let you know about any capers with sawed-offs. Somebody just got blown away down here. Looks like a rip-off."

On the way to the airport Kelly remarked that they had forgotten to pay for their drinks.

Carr nodded at a uniformed policeman and ducked under the rope barrier.

A police portable light illuminated a good portion of the parking lot as well as the heavy body, face down on a blanket of dried blood. Flashbulbs snapped. People stood around wearing uniforms of one kind or another.

Higgins, in baggy pants and a short-sleeved white shirt, which concealed the shoulders of a well digger, appeared formidable in the bright light. He stood next to the body making notes on a clipboard. His belt was an array of holsters and pouches.

He nodded at the Treasury men, tucked the clipboard under his arm, and knelt by the body. He pointed with a pencil.

"See the exit wounds? Definitely a shotgun. There's no way to know for sure whether it was a sawed-off, but that's my bet. Japanese tourist lady on the other side of the lot says she saw the man shoot a . . ."—he glanced at the clipboard—" 'long fat pistol.' From what she says, he shot once, cranked another round, and finished him off, got in his car, and split. She can't give any description. Says it was too dark . . . Looky here." He pointed to the small of the back. "Fresh knife cut right here. Doesn't make sense unless maybe he was wearing his buy money."

"A money belt?" Carr asked.

Higgins stood up. "That's a roger. The wound could be from getting a money belt cut off."

"Who is he?" Carr furrowed his brow.

"His wallet says his name is Michael Sawtelle and he works as a private dick for an attorney named Max Waxman. I called Intelligence just now. They have Sawtelle listed as 'Fat Mike,' a transaction man. His M.O. is to show up at a dope deal as a front man. He has his buy money tied around his waist. He shows his .45 for security, then deals right on the spot. I guess he wasn't short on balls. The deals are supposedly set up by Waxman. He's listed in the files as a money man."

"Wheels?" Kelly asked.

Higgins pointed with the clipboard. "The black Olds over there. It's clean. Registered to a car-leasing outfit in Studio City that doesn't give out info on who leases their cars. It's a caper car, for sure. Fat Mike had the car keys in his pocket."

Carr shook his head. "Doesn't look like you have too much to go on," he said.

"You're right there. I'll interview Waxman in the morning and he'll tell me he didn't know what Fat Mike was up to. I'll leave the case open for a couple of months to see if anybody will drop a dime. If nothing happens, I'll close it unsolved. Sorry, there's nothing much here to help you guys. Although it definitely could be the same guy who did Rico." He raised his voice as a plane flew over.

"It is the same guy," Carr said. He watched a policeman slide thin boards under the body. "The word is that Waxman finances counterfeit-money deals all the time. We've never been able to prove it."

A young detective in a hound's-tooth coat and styled hair motioned to Higgins from behind the rope barrier. Higgins went over to him. Four policemen grunted, hoisting the body onto a wheeled cart.

"Let's go," Carr said to Kelly. They walked to the rope and ducked under.

Higgins stopped talking to the young detective and turned toward them. "Here's one! The Japanese lady is catching the next flight back to Japan. Says she's seen enough of this country in two hours. Can you beat that?"

"See ya," Carr said.

Being careful not to make unnecessary noise, Carr unlocked the back door of Rose's tract house and sneaked down the dark hallway. He passed the door to her sons' room. It was closed.

He tiptoed into a dark, air-conditioned bedroom and sat down on the edge of her bed. He took off his clothes.

"I was waiting for you," Rose whispered. She crawled across the bed and began massaging his neck with miniature hands. Her nipples brushed softly against his back.

Before they made love, Rose stuffed a pillow between the headboard and the wall, as she always did to avoid waking up the children.

It was light. He groped out for his watch. Six.

Rose's head rested on his shoulder. She was awake.

"I've got to get going," he said, trying to bring himself into full consciousness. He eased her head off his shoulder and got out of bed.

Dressing in front of a wall mirror, he noticed the middle-aged flesh around his waist. The children in the other room could have been his if he had married. . . .

Rose lay on her back, her eyes open, arms flat at her sides. "Ling says you maybe get a transfer," she said as he buttoned his shirt.

He turned to the dresser and picked up his holster. He clipped it on his belt and put the revolver in. "Maybe," he said, throwing on his coat.

He walked to the door.

"You come to Ling's tonight?" she said, still staring at the ceiling. Her voice was barely audible, childlike.

"Probably."

"I see you there," she said.

Carr headed down the hallway and out the back door.

$/16

It was 7:00 A.M.

The underground parking lot was cool and drafty. Carr told Kelly to pull in next to a parked delivery van. He did, and turned off the motor. Carr focused the rearview mirror on a sign, RE-SERVED—MAX WAXMAN, on the wall at the other end of the parking lot.

"Why don't we just talk to him in his office?" Kelly said.

Carr shook his head no. "His office is probably wired for sound. I've never seen an attorney that wasn't big on tape recording."

"I hadn't thought about that," Kelly said.

A half hour went by before they spoke again. The car radio buzzed with a freeway surveillance.

"You know why people become counterfeiters?" Kelly said. He was slumped down in the driver's seat, his eyes closed.

"Why?"

"Because they think it's a crime that really isn't a crime. They figure if they can make a counterfeit twenty that's good enough, they can pass it and it will go all the way to the bank. No one's the wiser. What's a few bucks to Uncle Sam? Nobody gets hurt. That's what they figure."

Carr nodded sleepily.

Kelly continued. "Sort of like doctors who give unnecessary operations."

102

Waxman pulled into his parking space at 9:00 A.M. exactly.

Carr waited until Waxman took his briefcase out of the trunk and began to walk toward the elevator before approaching him.

"Mr. Waxman?"

"Yes." The lawyer looked puzzled.

Carr showed his badge. "I just wanted to ask you a couple of questions. It's about the murder of your investigator."

Waxman's tone was condescending. "I've already talked to the police. I have no knowledge of Michael's personal affairs."

"Would you mind joining me in the car for a moment so we can speak privately," Carr said.

"Can't we go to my office?" A deprecating smile.

"I'd rather not," said Carr. "I'll be happy to explain why if you'll just let me have a few minutes of your time."

Kelly pulled up in the sedan and swung open the rear door.

"I don't really understand all the secrecy, but . . . oh, what the hell." Hugging his briefcase, Waxman crawled across the back seat. Carr slid in next to him.

"This *does* seem a little overdone," Waxman said.

Kelly drove up cement ramps to the busy street. "Stuffy down there," he said. "I'll just drive around a little bit."

"What do you people have to do with this thing? I was interviewed last night by the Robbery-Homicide people, and I'll tell you exactly what I told them. I have no control over what my employees do on their own time." He spoke carefully.

Kelly looked at Carr in the rearview mirror.

Carr spoke. "A week ago a Treasury agent was murdered with a sawed-off shotgun when he was working undercover. Someone named Ronnie and a red-haired man about fifty years old were the ones who did it. I think they were the ones who dumped your stooge last night."

Waxman leaned back in the seat with no expression. He cleared his throat. "So?"

"So I want you to tell me who they are." Carr paused. "I'll give you my word that what you say will go no further."

Waxman gazed out the window as if sightseeing. "Gentlemen, you don't really expect me to sit here in the back seat of this car and give you a statement about something I know nothing about, and thus incriminate myself, do you? In case you didn't know, I *am* an attorney at law." He turned to Carr. "Would you like one of my cards?"

Kelly stopped for a light.

"Your card says you're a money man and that you never dirty your hands," Carr said. "My partner and I respect you for that. It may sound funny, but we actually do. We know that if *you* didn't act as a middleman somebody else would. To you it's strictly a business proposition, a way to pick up a few bucks. The people who own Standard Oil and AT & T would do the same thing if they weren't making so much money in other ways. All we're asking is that you do something that is in your best interest. Last night your right-hand man got his guts blown out in a parking lot. It could just as easily have been you. The rip-off artist could have dumped you right in your office. Blown your brains out the window onto Wilshire Boulevard . . ."

Waxman frowned. "You needn't be so graphic."

"I'm not finished," Carr said.

"Excuse me."

"They probably showed you a sample; you made the arrangements and agreed on the price. They met your man and ripped him off. You have nothing to lose by helping us, by telling us what you know," Carr said.

"On the other hand, counselor, I have nothing to gain," Waxman said, smirking.

Carr waited a few minutes before speaking. "Yes, you do."

"What's that?"

"You will have our word that we will not put you completely out of business."

Waxman took out a monogrammed handkerchief and wiped his head, neck, and mouth.

Kelly accelerated onto the freeway at Ninth Street.

"Who are you people? Where are we going? What do you mean put me out of business? Jesus Christ!" Waxman said. He rolled his window down a few inches.

"I'll tell you what I mean," Carr said, leaning back in the seat. "If you don't tell us, the heat will be on full blast the minute you get out of this car. Tomorrow you and your secretary get subpoenas to the federal grand jury. I guarantee TV cameras will be there when you appear. I'll contact every one of your clients and

104

ask them the same questions I asked you. I'll put the word out on the street that you are a snitch; that you're ready to turn on all the big dealers in town. We'll camp out in front of your office and your home. I'll dedicate my life to fucking you over. No one in his right mind would want you to back a deal. You'll be back to chasing ambulances."

Waxman grabbed the front seat with both hands. He spoke to Kelly.

"Stop the car! I want out. Let me out right this minute! Right now! I said *right now!*" He tapped Kelly's shoulder.

Kelly speeded up. "Keep your hands off me, you dirty, shit-eating bastard. You filthy, rotten, mother-fucking Communist shyster," he snarled.

Waxman's eyes became big.

Carr twisted in the back seat and faced him.

"Your crummy little brain has figured everything out, hasn't it?" Carr said. "You are going to pull every political string in town the moment you can get to a phone. You're going to call the United States attorney and every political hack in town and tell them how the T-men threatened you. You think you can get us reprimanded and taken off the case. Well, if your connections are as good as everybody says, you're probably right. We *would* be taken off the case. Nothing else would happen to us though, because you have no evidence. If we'd talked in your office, you could have recorded everything, but as it stands now, it's your word against ours, and I guarantee that we will have our story together."

The lawyer folded his arms and sat back. "I want to go back to my office. Right now. I demand to go back right now. I *insist* that . . ."

"But here's the punch line," Carr said. "After you get us taken off the case, we're going to wait until everything is just right and then we're going to catch you alone and beat you to death."

Waxman's jaw dropped. "What?"

"Beat you to death," Carr said. "We're going to beat you to death with our bare hands because we will be so pissed off. You have so many enemies in town no one will even suspect us."

Waxman turned his head. "You are threatening me," he said to the window.

"That's right, you subhuman, chickenshit pimp," Kelly said. He took the Alvarado Street off-ramp. A few blocks farther he slowed down and stopped next to Echo Park Lake. He turned off the engine. Smog-colored ducks coasted on greenish water. The lake was outlined by graffiti-covered palm trees and overflowing trash cans.

Kelly parked and leaned an arm on the back of his seat. "I say why put off till tomorrow what you can do today?" He smiled strangely at the lawyer.

The lawyer swallowed and turned his head. He stared out the window. He cleared his throat three times. "You people are up tight for nothing. You're off base. I don't know anything that can help you. You may not believe me, but I actually have no information on the topic you are interested in. I swear to God. You're wasting your time talking to me . . . and your threats don't frighten me. You want this guy pretty bad, don't you?" The lawyer's lower lip trembled. He quickly rubbed it with the back of his hand.

"All I want is what you know," Carr said. "No more, no less."

"Once I had a client who was charged with stealing some of those ducks over there; he was charged with grand-theft duck, believe it or not," said Waxman, with a nervous laugh. "He never did say what he was going to do with them. He wouldn't cop out even to me." He paused. "What makes you think a red-haired guy was involved?"

"You first," Carr said.

Waxman spoke in a monotone. "There is a chap named Red Diamond, just out of T. I., a con man, who is hurting for bucks. The sharks are after him. He came to see me a few days ago and wanted money. I shined him on. He's the only red-haired guy I can think of. Ronnie was a walk-in. He came in yesterday. I'd never seen him before. I never would have guessed Red Diamond. Red lives in Hollywood somewhere. That's all I know."

Carr nodded to Kelly in the rearview mirror.

Kelly started the engine and drove in the direction of Waxman's office. During the trip, Waxman told them three times that threats of any kind had no effect on him. Neither Carr nor Kelly spoke. Kelly pulled up in front of the modern glass structure, and Waxman got out without saying a word.

106

• • •

Kelly drove two blocks to a coffee shop. The waitress smiled when he asked for extra hash browns, and an extra bottle of ketchup.

"Do you think he will cause a stink?"

"I don't think so. But that's the chance you take. It's a possibility."

"Jesus, I hope not," Kelly said. "Why do you think he talked?"

"I think he just figured why not? Nothing to lose for him, and after all, they did snuff out one of his people last night."

"What if what he told us was bullshit, and he makes a complaint to the U.S. attorney; says we coerced him?"

The waitress poured coffee.

"As the U.S. attorney would say, that's an 'unsubstantiated allegation,' " Carr said. "Not enough evidence for prosecution. I think we would beat the rap."

$/17

It was dark. Red Diamond's insides fluttered as if a flock of birds was trying to fly out his ass.

He sat behind the wheel of the Cadillac and waited. The coffee-shop parking lot was half full. He watched the back door. It was shift-change time.

He had no particular strategy. It would be strictly "play it by ear."

Mona, looking tired, in a spotted waitress uniform, came out the back door carrying a purse. She headed for a battered Volkswagen.

Red got out of the Cadillac and rushed across the lot. He opened the car door and slid into the passenger seat.

Mona was starting the car engine. "What do *you* want?" Her jaw was set.

"I just wanted to talk for a few minutes."

"Get out of my car."

"I know what you probably think of me, but that's what I want to talk about. This last stretch has brought me to my senses. No lie. I've finally wised up." He wished she would at least look at him.

"Get out of my car." She folded her hands across her chest.

"Maybe you don't have any feeling for me now, but there was a time you did. You shouldn't forget that. You owe yourself a

108

few minutes just to listen. For the sake of the way we used to be."

"You are a liar. You aren't capable of telling the truth. You're sick. Get out of my car."

"All I want to say is that I have some great things in the fire now, some really *positive* things. For once, I actually have cleaned up my act. I know this idea will sound far-out, but I would like to see us together again. I promise you'll be able to live well, even better than when I had the place in Long Beach. I don't like to see you slinging hash. It hurts me. You deserve better. We could move into a nice place in Burbank or somewhere right now. I've got some cash. I mean you wouldn't even have to sleep with me at this point. That would be up to you. Completely your choice."

Her face turned red. She faced him.

He stared at her panty-hosed legs, the tiny waist that his hands once fit perfectly around, the firm breasts that had been his to tease.

"Why should it make any difference if we sleep together?" she said with a strained smile.

"Well, I . . ."

"I mean, it shouldn't make any goddamn difference *who* I sleep with ever again, should it?"

"That was something . . . a one-in-a-million situation. It would *never* happen again, as God is my witness, and I wouldn't say that if I didn't really mean it. . . ."

"You asshole!" Tears glistened in her eyes. "You've *never* meant anything you said! You are sick! You did the one thing to me I could never forgive, and here you are back again. Maybe you've forgotten. I was your wife and you made me turn tricks to pay off *your* debts. I became a whore to save *your* ass! Not that my life had been a bed of roses . . . but I had never been a goddamn whore. Sucking off ten stinking-fat businessmen a night until I got you off the hook. *And what did you do?* Pulled another of your capers, one of your 'operations,' and you went to prison *anyway*." The tears almost jumped from her eyes.

Red put his hand on her waist. He had to touch it. It felt the same as ever. The tears were, psychologically speaking, a good sign, he thought. The barrier was breaking down.

She sobbed loudly. Suddenly, she stuck a hand into her purse and pulled out something with a red wooden handle. "Get out!" she screamed, and stabbed toward his chest with an icepick. He used his hands to shield himself. The icepick pierced his palm. "You asshole! I hate you!" Mona shrieked.

Red sprang out of the car. The ice pick was stuck through his hand. He stared at the speared hand and gave a deep animal moan. "Bitch, bitch, dirty bitch!"

Mona started the rattly engine of the VW. He jumped out of the way. The car sped out of the parking lot.

It took a few minutes to get up the courage to pull the ice pick out of the wound so he could drive himself to a hospital.

"How did it happen?" said a nurse in her thirties with a hair-do like Mona's. She pushed his hand into a mixture of hot water and disinfectant. It stung so much he almost passed out.

"Chopping ice in a freezer at a party," Red said. "Hated to leave. All my friends were there. Henry Winkler, Larry Hagman, the Gabors."

"Really?" She pulled his hand out of the water.

"Actually, they're my clients. I run an advertising agency. TV commercials, that sort of thing."

"Must be an interesting job." She smiled and filled a hypodermic syringe.

"I guess you could say that," he said.

The clerk was prematurely bald and attempted to hide the fact by wrapping his few remaining hairs in a circle on top of his head. He spoke, balancing a pipe between his teeth.

"Sorry, Charlie, I can't allow you to review any files unless you have a warrant or a subpoena. Federal Parole Office regulations in accordance with the privacy act. You know how it is." Having said this, he returned to his newspaper-covered desk and sat down.

Carr and Kelly walked past the clerk and found a file cabinet marked "D." Kelly pulled open the drawer. The clerk turned a page of the newspaper.

There were three files bearing the name Diamond. Only one was current.

Carr glanced quickly over reports in the file: "sociopathic personality," "reacts in a hostile manner," "blunted emotional effect," "lacks positive value judgment," "poor communicative skills."

He opened a large envelope stapled to the inside of the file. He removed a thick stack of typed pages titled "Counseling Session Transcript. Prisoner Rudolph Diamond (#40398654). True Name: Rudolph Spriggs." The first page was a statement signed by Diamond giving permission to record the session for "study purposes."

Carr read:

Counselor: Had this ever happened before?

Diamond: It happened a lot when I was a kid. I think it had something to do with the sound of a train whistle. This may sound weird, but my mother's house was near the railroad tracks and when a train whistle would blow I could feel it all the way through my body, sort of as if the sound entered through the hole in my pecker. I had this terrible feeling of fear at my mother's house. And the train whistle was part of it somehow. I had trouble urinating when I was afraid. That was my first memory of having problems taking a leak.

Counselor: And you believe this affected your working life?

Diamond: After I quit high school I went to work in a bottle factory in Oakland and when I went into the bathroom to piss . . . uh, urinate, I just couldn't. I couldn't relax enough to urinate when other people were around. So I quit.

Counselor: And this affected your subsequent employment?

Diamond: What would you do if you worked in a factory with one of those giant cement bathrooms? You know, lots of urinals, and every time you went in to take a leak there were other people there and you couldn't go. Like there was *no way*. Well, you'd do what I did. You'd quit. This happened to me over and over again. I couldn't hold a job and I started to get into trouble to get money. The first thing was the phony raffle tickets. I sold them and kept the money. I got caught. You can see that on my rap sheet there. I did twenty days. I was just a kid.

Counselor: Uh-huh. What were these other arrests . . . there? In the fifties.

Diamond: Pyramid schemes. You know, chain letters. At the time everyone was doing it. I didn't even know it was illegal until it was too late.

Carr skipped fifteen or so pages.

Diamond: So after I got out . . . it was my second prison sentence . . . I bought this bar in Long Beach. Nice place, but eventually guys I knew from the joint kept coming around and got me involved in phony race-track tickets. I didn't have anything to do with printing, you understand. It was a wrong-place/right-time sort of thing. They got me on a conspiracy.
Counselor: The rap sheet says accessory to murder.
Diamond: That's the way it wound up. It was an argument over the tickets. They used a gun I had behind the bar for protection. . . . I'm not trying to make excuses. I don't want you to get the wrong idea. . . .

Carr began flipping pages rapidly.
"He sounds like a confidence man," Kelly said.
"The urinary-problem act shows great imagination," Carr said. "I wonder if he got the private cell he wanted?"
Finally he found a prison status sheet signed by a counselor recommending that Diamond be provided with a single cell for medical reasons. "Here it is," he said.
Kelly laughed.
Carr flipped through to the last page of the folder. It read:

Details of Offense—Pre-Release Summary
Parolee Diamond acted as a principal in a major stock swindle involving the fraudulent sale of undeveloped tracts of land near the Colorado River. During the course of this conspiracy he was also involved in a confidence scheme involving the proposed sale of nonexistent smuggled gold to a wealthy Los Angeles jeweler. Diamond and two accomplices drove the jeweler from Las Vegas to a pay phone in San Diego to await a phone call from a supposed Mexican gold smuggler, who was to deliver the contraband. The jeweler refused to part with the money in his briefcase until he saw the gold. When the phone rang, the jeweler stepped out of the vehicle to answer it. At this point Diamond and his accomplices grabbed his briefcase from him and departed in their vehicle at a high rate of speed. The jeweler fired at Diamond's vehicle with a .38 caliber revolver, wounding the

112

driver. The driver was subsequently admitted to a hospital near San Ysidro suffering multiple gunshot wounds. He implicated Diamond and agreed to testify for the government, as did the jeweler. Federal prosecution was authorized since Diamond and his accomplices had crossed state lines during commission of the crime. Parolee Diamond was convicted on all counts and completed the full five years of his sentence, no time off for good behavior.

Carr tore Diamond's photograph from inside the folder.

"This is our man. He's a rip-off artist," Carr said. He took the mug photos of red-haired men out of his coat pocket and flipped through them.

"What are you doing?" Kelly asked.

"Diamond's picture wasn't among the photos we were checking out. We would never have found him." Carr dropped the photos into the wastebasket.

"Here's his current address." Kelly took a pen and small note pad from his inside coat pocket. "It's 4126 Marshall Avenue. If I remember right, this should be just above Hollywood Boulevard; toiletland, U.S.A." He wrote down the address and put the note pad back in his pocket.

$/18

Carr closed the folder and put it back in the file drawer.

"We headed for Hollywood?" Kelly smiled and rubbed his hands.

"Not yet," said Carr, leaning against the cabinet. He stared at Diamond's mug shot. "I think we'd better talk to the U.S. attorney."

"But we don't have enough for a warrant on Diamond."

"We do for Ronnie, because we can identify him. We saw him go into the motel room. We can get a John Doe warrant for assault on a federal officer. It's best to have the warrant in hand when we make the pinch. Then there'll be no question about procedure when he goes to court."

"You mean we set up a surveillance on Diamond and wait until he meets with Ronnie, *then* make the pinch, right?"

"Right." Carr flicked Diamond's mug photo with his finger.

"If we start a surveillance," Kelly said, "we might end up following him around from now till hell freezes over and he might never meet up with Ronnie."

Carr said, "What happens if we pick up Diamond and he won't talk? You know the odds. He refuses to cop out and we have to let him go; he calls Ronnie and tips him off. Ronnie splits and we'll never find him."

Kelly rubbed his eyes. "I guess you're right. I just don't like

114

the idea of getting the mushhead U.S. attorneys in on the case too soon. You know how they are."

Carr nodded.

"Well, I guess it's up the elevator to the Ivory Tower." Kelly sighed.

They walked past the clerk.

"Wait a second, you guys!" said the clerk. "Whataya say for the game tonight? Dodgers or Pirates?"

"Pirates all the way," Carr said.

"I hope you're right. I've got ten bucks on 'em." He folded the sports page in half.

"Good luck," Carr said.

In the elevator, Kelly pushed the button for the thirteenth floor.

"Let me do the talking," Carr said.

The elevator door opened onto a large and handsomely carpeted waiting room. Smiling photos of the president and the attorney general stared at one another from spotless walls. Air conditioning made the room chilly.

A frail secretary showed them into a comfortably furnished office with a Stanford diploma on the wall. John Blair was on the phone, thick lips touching the mouthpiece. Blair was a young man with an abundance of what some would describe as baby fat: rosy cheeks, puffy neck, fraternity-house beer belly. He wore the latest gold-wire-frame spectacles. His hair was a styling-salon natural.

"Gotta go now, hon. See you at five-thirty or so, depending on the freeway, ya know." He put down the receiver and pointed to two chairs.

They sat down.

"Well, well, Charlie and Jack, the old guard of the Treasury Department." His voice was youthful. "What can I do for you this fine day?"

"I want a John Doe warrant for the guy who killed Rico de Fiore."

"Have you found the killer?" he said. He doodled on a yellow pad.

"We're starting a surveillance on a residence in Hollywood

where we think he might show up. I want to have a warrant in hand when we take him just so there'll be no legal technicalities popping up later. I want to make sure there are no loopholes in this case."

"I'm glad you came in, Charlie. I've been wanting to get together with you fellas on the prosecution angle ever since it happened. There *is* a problem, ya know." He stopped doodling.

"No, I *don't* know," Carr said. "We watched this Ronnie or whoever he is walk into the motel room. We heard the shotgun. We went in the room seconds later and found Rico shot dead. If that doesn't mean a certain conviction for Ronnie when we catch him, I don't know anything about the law. Rico sure as hell didn't kill himself."

Blair scratched his natural. It appeared stiff with hair spray. "No, that's not the problem. The problem is self-defense. It's a one-on-one situation, ya know."

"How do you mean?" Kelly said.

"If you arrest this Ronnie and he goes to trial, you know he can take the stand and say he drew his gun and fired in self-defense after the other man started to pull *his* gun. Rico was working undercover. He *was* acting the part of a criminal, you know? Don't forget that. All Ronnie will have to do is take the stand and admit that he is a seller of counterfeit money. He'll say that in the motel room this surly-looking Italian, whom he firmly believed to be a Mafia lieutenant, tried to steal his counterfeit money and he had to defend himself. Ya know? He might even say that Rico identified himself as a T-man and reached for his ankle gun but he didn't believe it and defended *himself* from a possible rip-off. The physical evidence shows that Rico's pants leg was up and thus he *may* have reached for his ankle gun. As you know, the defense is entitled to a copy of all the coroner's reports and everything; that's the law. They'll use whatever defense fits the facts the best. Ya know?"

Carr and Kelly sat without speaking.

Blair picked up an expensive-looking fountain pen and made ink dots on the yellow pad. When he spoke again his voice was softer.

"We have to keep in mind that there isn't even a murder weapon. Although the coroner could testify that Rico was killed

116

with shotgun pellets, we can't actually tie Ronnie to a murder weapon. Ya know? All you saw him carry into the room was an attaché case, and he obviously took the weapon with him when he escaped. The final problem with the case is that it will be your word against his. You will be open to a tough cross-examination as to how you recognized him as the person who walked into the room, excluding all other persons who may look like him; et cetera, et cetera, et cetera. Ya know? This guy may even have a brother to bring into court that looks like him. Do you see what I'm getting at? The case is weak. I don't think we can get a conviction on murder *or* assault on a federal officer, and there is no other physical evidence of other crimes except the sample counterfeit bill he gave Rico. And that is inadmissible as evidence because Rico is . . . uh . . . not here to testify about it. Ya know?" He looked at his watch.

"If we find the shotgun, what kind of a case will we have?" Carr said, looking at Kelly.

"Not too good," Blair said flatly. "There is no way we can tie the shotgun to the crime. It's not like a pistol; ballistics doesn't do us any good with shotguns. Even if you find the shotgun, there's no way to prove it was the shotgun that killed Rico. Shotgun pellets are shotgun pellets. Ya know? It's too bad it wasn't a pistol. The case, as it stands, is almost nonprosecutable. This is a fact you will have to accept. . . . I know how you guys feel, but that's it. Ya know?"

"We'll try to dig up some more evidence through our surveillance." Carr stood up. So did Kelly.

Blair rolled his fountain pen between his hands, making a clicking sound each time it hit his oversize college ring. "Ya know it's not that I wouldn't like to give you a warrant, but there's no use arresting somebody we can't take to trial and convict. Ya know?"

They walked out of the room.

"I'm glad you held back," Carr said to Kelly.

"I'm not," Kelly said. "When I was in the police department years ago, we had a deputy district attorney like him. He refused to give my partner a complaint on a guy that slapped him in the face. The D.A. said it 'wasn't aggravated enough'; therefore it wasn't really a crime under the penal code. You know what my

partner did? He slapped the D.A. in the face and knocked him
clean out of his chair. You should have seen the uproar." Kelly
laughed so loud the secretary put a finger in her ear so she
could hear the phone.

The elevator door opened.

"What happened to your partner?" Carr said.

"Six months without pay and lost a stripe. But he always said
it was worth it to him."

"A couple of years from now Blair will go into private practice
and be thinking up phony defenses for his clients just like the
ones he was telling us about."

"How did he ever get into the U.S. attorney's office?" Kelly
said.

"Ever heard of Blair's Restaurants and Pastry Shops? Daddy
Blair was invited to the inauguration."

"Oh!"

The elevator door opened.

On the way to Hollywood, Kelly insisted they stop on Alvarado at Calhoun's Hot Dog stand. Carr placed the order while
Kelly pulled napkins from a dispenser and stuffed them in his
pockets.

A short, fat black man wearing a sweat-stained chef's hat
wrapped everything to go. He set canned Cokes with the food
in a small cardboard box and shoved it across the counter to
Carr.

"Stakeout. Right?" said Calhoun.

"You guessed it," Carr said. He tried to hand Calhoun money.

The chef's rough-looking hands made a practiced "on the
house" gesture. "That old Howard Dumbrowski . . . I bet he was
a good man for stakeouts," he said.

"He sure was." Carr nodded.

Calhoun leaned on the counter with both arms. "Once, Howard Dumbrowski and me was sitting at that table behind you
chewing the fat. It was late at night. Howard was on his way
home and stopped for a coupla dogs. Hot damn if a lady don't
get off a bus across the street and some six-foot-three mutha
fucka snatches her purse and knocks her down. You could see
she was hurt. Old Howard come off from the table like O. J.
Simpson. He was across the street and had the mutha fucka by

118

the collar before he got fifty feet. You could see the old lady had a busted arm—the bone was sticking out. I called an ambulance quick's I could." He smiled, showing a gold front tooth. "Course by the time it got here, I had to call another one for the purse snatcher. Howard was making these little screams with every punch. Had tears in his eyes. Like he was getting his nut or something. Beat that dirty mutha fucka up and down that sidewalk. All types of inspectors and shit came around the next few days. I told 'em that mutha fucka attacked Howard first and Howard just defended hisself." He lowered his voice. "The way I seen it, the purse snatcher attacked Howard's fists with his head and stomach." The black man slapped a hand down on the counter and gave a high-pitched laugh that could be heard for half a block.

$/19

Using one hand to shield his binoculars from the sunlight, Carr watched Kelly as he crept past the front door of Red Diamond's apartment. It was on the second level of an unkempt avocado-colored apartment complex that was a copy of ten others on the block.

Somehow every apartment house in Los Angeles looked the same: stucco, carports, and Dempsey Dumpsters.

Kelly got back in the driver's seat. "He's living there. His name is on the mailbox. I think he's home. I think I heard a radio on inside." He opened a pop can and used the liquid to wash down a hot dog, which he devoured in four bites. He licked his fingers one by one and leaned back in the seat.

Carr continued to use the binoculars.

"He should have given the guy a dollar and told him to go find a better piece of ass," Kelly announced.

"Who?"

"Howard. That's what he should have done when he walked in on his old lady. He should have just taken a dollar out of his wallet, given it to Joe the Grinder, and walked out, instead of blowing her away like he did."

"You're right," Carr said. "But that's just the way Howard is. He couldn't help himself any more than Freddie Roth could hold back if he's near a printing press and somebody offers him

120

ten points on the dollar. Same with Rico's murderer. He'll keep going until he's stopped. . . ."

"Imagine us sitting here talking about old Howard as if he's a criminal?" Kelly said. "If he could hear us, he'd knock our heads together like two coconuts."

"He probably would," Carr said. He laughed.

Kelly closed his eyes for a few minutes. "Listen," he said without looking at Carr. "I know I'm always the one to say the wrong thing at the right time, but there's something we should work out."

"Shoot," Carr said.

Kelly wiped his hand on his shirttail and tucked the shirt back in. "I see the whole thing like this. From what the mushhead U.S. attorney said yesterday, it looks like once we find Ronnie, he is going to walk. If we arrest him, he goes to trial and beats the rap. He will have killed Rico for free. Blair is a hundred-percent right. The jury is going to be made up of a bunch of housewives who watch TV soap operas. When the judge instructs them on reasonable doubt, they are going to say, 'Gee whiz, there must be reasonable doubt because I can't imagine anyone being mean enough to blow somebody's head off.' I can see it now."

"You may be right," Carr said.

Nothing was said for a while.

"You and I have been through a lot," Kelly said finally. He was looking straight ahead. "You can trust me if you think we should go all the way on this one."

Carr put the binoculars down. "Ideas?" he said.

"If we find him—I mean, if it's just you and I alone, with no one else around—I say it's our ball game right then and there. He resists and we cancel his ticket," Kelly said. "We both shoot."

Carr put the binoculars to his eyes. He waited before speaking. "We have to be patient, Jack," he said. "We have to wait till everything is right." He put the binoculars on the dashboard. "And it's probably best if we don't talk too much about it. Eventually we may end up sitting on the lie box. It's better not to have discussed such things. You know what I mean."

"Yeah, sure," Kelly said.

121

When darkness fell, they parked closer to the apartment house, because of the lighting. Using the binoculars, Carr made out a soft flicker of light coming from the opening in a curtain.

"He's watching TV," he said.

"I wish he'd make a move. My ass is sore." Kelly popped open a soda. "Wouldn't it be great if the asshole would get in his car and go to a movie. We could just sit there and watch the movie, or, better yet, a restaurant. . . ."

"Dream on," Carr said.

Clad only in boxer shorts, Red Diamond had been lounging on the fat, smelly sofa all day. His tiny apartment was filled with light and sound from a rabbit-eared portable television. Resting on a dinette table, it provided flickering illumination for the dark, bare-floored room and two plastic-covered chairs, an open suitcase, and a phone with a cord long enough to reach the bathroom.

Red's bandaged hand throbbed with the waves of canned laughter emanating from the set.

He crawled off the couch and stretched. It was time for stomach therapy. In the undersized kitchen he pulled open the refrigerator and took out a bottle of real, not imitation, ginger ale. He opened the bottle at the sink. Throwing his head back, he opened his mouth wide and poured fully half of the icy ginger ale down his throat. The half bottle of bubbles tingled and stung all the way to his sour, rumbling stomach. He quickly placed the bottle back in the refrigerator and put his hands on his hips to wait for the belch. It came moments later as a strident, head-down bark.

The poison worry gas had been emitted. He was sure that if he had been able to get real ginger ale during the stretch in Terminal Island, his stomach problems could have been kept under control.

He went back to the sofa and fluffed up a pillow. It was getting dark outside, but he did not feel that the day had been wasted. Alone, with nothing but the television, he had been able to relax, to think. Having had time to treat his body with ginger-ale therapy, he had not had a loose bowel movement all day.

The television crackled with applause. A cuff-linked, effeminate game-show host held a housewife's hand and pointed to the stage set behind him. "You keep five hundred dollars or try for the wild-card prize in one of the boxes!" he quacked. "Take your choice of Prize *One,* Prize *Two,* or Prize *Three!*" Chewing her fingernails excitedly, the housewife jumped up and down. Her breasts were bouncy, youthful, her waist firm. Perhaps as firm as Mona's? For the fiftieth time he saw Mona in the front seat of the car, the look in her eye as she stabbed him. The hole in his hand throbbed again.

"What will it be?" said the game-show man. "The *money* or one of the *wild-card boxes? Five hundred* dollars or a chance at gifts worth as much as *ten thousand* dollars."

"I'll keep the five hundred dollars," squealed the housewife. She chomped on her knuckles. The box opened. "A new car!" screamed the announcer.

"Dumb bitch," Red said to the television. He got up and turned it off. He knocked a dirty towel off a dinette chair, sat down, and flipped a spiral notebook that was on the table.

He closed his eyes and rubbed his temples. Then he picked up a ball-point pen and wrote the following:

RECOVERY OPERATION

The need for cash flow is now imperative, but falling back to quick con game would be disastrous because of being known by the cops. Cannot trust Gabe—he is probably a snitch; much too friendly. Only one to trust at this point is Ronnie. He has proved himself under fire. Dio's deadline is up and it means that plans must be changed to meet the current needs. Dio is to me a barrier, a stone wall that is holding up all further success. He has shown himself to be what he always has been, a person lacking full understanding of people and situations. He is nothing more than a cheap gunsel who lucked out for a few scores and saved his money, like the peasant wop mother fucker that he is. To deal with Dio is a task requiring full commitment. Yes, an all-or-nothing is now upon me. I have survived before because of my mental speed and ability to decipher the

123

codes of life. I picture myself at this moment as a guided missile fueled by the mental speed energy I have been able to develop using the nuclear resources of concentration. Dio's weakness is that, even in the Beverly Hills days, he accepted other people as stereotypes. He could never change an opinion of someone once it was made. His supposed mastery of power is a sham. I want to stick a burning cigar right into his eye and push it into his activating, rotten shit brain. He has challenged my energy by his failure to understand my mental speed. I must maintain control of the resources at my own command in order to return to the home plate of life. I have waited five years. I have been patient. I have not been remorseful. I have not been anything other than a gentleman who requests his seat at the table back. I am fifty-four years old and the little things mean more to me now. There is no question that I can handle the problem with Mona. Time is a healer. Dio, if he was a man instead of a phony rotten prick, could give me more time by just snapping his fingers—but he won't. I have never been afraid to face the music of life. It is time for a plateau decision.

It took him almost an hour to write this. After completing it he took another ginger-ale-belch treatment. Almost simultaneous with the emission of the worry gas, as if by the magic healing properties of ginger, he was aware of what he had to do. He picked the phone up off the floor and dialed. A woman answered.

"Hello."

"I wanna speak to Tony Dio. This is Red Diamond."

A click. "Hello, Red, this is Tony. What can I do for you?"

"I know tomorrow is the deadline, but something just came up and I wanted to check and see if I could get a slight extension. This is not a stall. I give you my word on that. It's just that I'm in the middle of a project that I have capital tied up in. Right now it would be so much easier if I could just have a little more time. That way I can pull off my caper without having to short-stop the whole thing right in the middle. I'm only asking for a few more weeks."

"Are you telling me you don't have what you are supposed to have by tomorrow?"

Red hesitated. He felt as though a faucet had been turned on in his intestines. "Oh, it's not that. *Not at all.* I have the full amount that I owe you. It's just that for the moment the money is tied up in something, and if I pull the money out right now to pay you, I'll just suffer a loss of possible profit and . . ."

"I don't like to talk on the phone, Red. You know that. Tomorrow is your deadline. I will be open for business in my hotel suite tomorrow. Be there at 7:00 P.M. with the money. Bring me cash. If you aren't there, you will have visitors. Like I said, business is business. Points are points."

"After all the fuckin' years I've known you . . ."

"The story has been told, Red. School is out."

Red's stomach roared. "Okay, okay, if that's the way it's got to be . . . I'll send a guy over with the money tomorrow."

"I don't like strangers. Make sure you are with him. I don't open my door for any fucking strangers."

"All right then. I'll bring the money over, but he'll be with me. I don't like to walk around alone with that much money."

"I understand," Dio said. "See you tomorrow."

Red put the receiver down. His hand throbbed painfully. His stomach was an active, squirming bagpipe filled with worry gas and various poison body liquids. He returned to the sofa and watched television until two in the morning. When he finally got into bed, he couldn't sleep, because his mental speed would not slow down to that of an ordinary man.

By the time the sun started to come up, every muscle in Carr's body was sore.

Kelly snored himself awake in a back seat littered with empty pop cans and chili-stained napkins. He sat up and rubbed his hands roughly over his face and hair.

"Breakfast time," he said. "I'll walk down to that little restaurant at the corner." He got out of the sedan.

Less than a minute later Red Diamond walked out of his apartment and got into a Chevy parked at the curb. He started the engine, made a U turn, and headed toward Hollywood Boulevard.

Carr made the same U turn and followed a half-block behind. He slowed near the restaurant to let Kelly jump in.

"You might know he'd leave as soon as I tried to grab a bite," Kelly said.

125

Carr drove at a safe distance behind Diamond down a deserted Hollywood Boulevard to La Brea.

Diamond turned south and continued past motels and coffee shops, and pulled into a small shopping center.

Carr stopped farther up the street. Kelly used the binoculars.

Diamond opened the trunk of his vehicle and carried something into the small shopping center.

"A Laundromat," Kelly said. "He's going to do his laundry. Just our luck. I know what you are going to say: 'Have patience.' "

"Time sure flies when you are having fun," Carr said. He rubbed the small of his back.

Red Diamond had a headache from lack of sleep. He shoved the bundle of clothes into the washing machine and dropped the quarters into the slot. The machine hummed.

He closed his eyes and leaned on the machine with both hands for a long while. Then he stood up straight, walked to the pay phone in the corner, dropped in a dime, and dialed.

He hung up the reciever in a moment. His head throbbed. Another dime. He dialed a number. It rang five times.

"Hello," Ronnie Boyce said. He was out of breath.

"This is Red. What are you doing?"

"Fucking and sucking about a hundred miles an hour."

"I gotta talk with you in person. Meet me at the Paradise Isle."

"Right on," Ronnie said. "Just as soon as I get off once more." He laughed.

Red hung up.

"He's been in there almost an hour now," Kelly said. "Maybe there's a back door. He might have gone out the back."

"Here he comes," Carr said.

Kelly started the engine.

Diamond got in his car, backed out of the parking space in front of the Laundromat, and drove south on La Brea. Kelly pulled into the flow of traffic a few cars behind him. Red turned right on Sunset Boulevard. The agents followed, making a right turn on a residential street.

126

"He must be heading back up to Hollywood Boulevard," Carr said. Diamond was a block ahead of them.

Suddenly an old Chrysler flew backward out of a driveway directly in front of them. Kelly slammed the G-car in reverse, backed up, and tried to get around it, but was blocked by a car parked at the curb. The blue-haired matron in the Chrysler had stalled. The street was blocked.

Carr wanted to jump out and chase Diamond's car as he watched it round the corner ahead of them. It was out of sight. Kelly sped in reverse for half a block until he could turn a corner. It was too late. They had lost him.

They drove back to Diamond's apartment to see if he was there. No luck.

"We've lost him," Carr said, gritting his teeth.

"Goddamnit to hell!" Kelly exploded. "We just wasted a whole day in this stinking car because of that old maid! *Sheeyit!*" He slammed a fist into an open hand.

"Let's take a shower break," said Carr. "Why don't you drop me off at my place and pick me up in a couple of hours and we'll set up again on his apartment. He's got to come back sometime."

$/20

Carr sat at a window table and watched Kelly finish eating. Kelly, with his mouth full, waved at Prince Nikola of Serbia.

The ex-wrestler, wearing a white butcher's apron, put a second basket of French rolls in front of Kelly. "You eat too much bread. Pretty soon you are three hundred pounds, like Man Mountain Dean." He filled his cheeks with air and made a face. "He used to get winded just climbing in the ring." He gave a mischievous smile.

Kelly's mouth was full. He said "Fuck you, too" in three grunts.

Nick laughed uproariously and headed toward the kitchen.

Kelly finally swallowed. He broke another roll in half and plastered it with butter.

Carr stared out at a mixture of people walking in various directions carrying towels, surfboards, and umbrellas.

"Could you recognize him?" Kelly said.

Carr didn't answer.

"I mean if he walked past the window right now. Right this minute . . . Personally, I'm not sure. He walked up the steps and into Rico's room. I didn't even get a face-on shot of him. I'm just not sure."

Carr continued to stare out the window. "I think I would. . . . But I'm not sure."

128

Kelly bit into the roll and chewed. "Maybe we're not doing the right thing."

"How do you mean?"

"I mean, maybe instead of doing surveillance on Diamond, we should just go up against him. Kick his door in and have a little heart-to-heart with him about who his young pal is. Knock his dick in the dirt if he doesn't cop out."

"If he won't cop out, we're through. We'll have tipped our hand," Carr said. "I say we watch him for a while longer."

The bar was empty. Gabe, the bartender, made squeaking noises as he dried glasses with a brownish rag. A radio broadcast race results.

Red Diamond joined Ronnie Boyce in the red leather booth. He slid across in order to sit close, pulled an ashtray toward him, and lit a cigarette. He coughed once, richly.

"You're in trouble, baby." Red took a fierce puff from his Pall Mall and turned his head to jettison a stream of smoke.

"What do you mean?" Ronnie said.

"A contract."

"On who?"

"On you."

"Who would let a contract on me?"

"Friends of the young guinea you dumped last week. Somebody fingered you." Red picked a piece of tobacco from his lower lip and flicked it away. "Somebody must have been watching when you met in the motel room. Everybody has a backup man. It's probably for sure he didn't show up alone carrying ten grand. Somebody must have seen your face and put you together someway. . . . The word is that there was a lookout near the motel who saw you walk in the room." His words ran together.

"Who told you all this?" Ronnie leaned closer to the older man.

"I got a call from a friend who's connected real good with the big boys. I've known the guy for years. He called to ask me if I wanted twenty cases of bourbon off a truck job. We're just shooting the shit, see, and he asks me if I know a guy named

Ronnie Boyce. Not knowing what is on his mind, I tell him no. He tells me a contract is out on a Ronnie Boyce for icing a San Fernando Valley boy in a rip-off. Seems the guinea you iced was somebody's mule. He was handling paper between here and Las Vegas for the big boys."

Ronnie rubbed his chin. "What do you think I should do?"

"Only one thing to do. Beat the fuckers to the goddamn punch. If they want to fight, I say there's no better time than the present. We move first. We show 'em our shit." Red made a gun gesture with his thumb and index finger.

"What if everybody's got a baby brother?"

"I've already checked it out. The guy that put out the contract is a loner. No family ties. He's just a juice man; a ten-percent-a-week Shylock. He had the Italian kid buying hot paper for him. That's all. No family connections. Nothing like that. He wants to make himself look good by offing you. If we put him out of the way, that would be the end of it. Nobody would take his place. No baby brothers. No revenge bullshit. The problem would be solved." Red sucked in smoke.

Gabe came over with drinks on a tray and said, "Coupla usuals." He put the drinks on the table and slithered back behind the bar.

"How are we gonna do it?" Ronnie said with a puzzled expression.

"The juice man does his business out of the California Plaza Hotel. He rents a suite two days a week and people come to him to do business. This friend of mine can get me an introduction. You will be my bagman. We go to the hotel like we were going to get a loan, and do the fucker right in his room. The sawed-off piece doesn't have any numbers. Drop it in the room, and we walk out nice as can be." Red made the washing-hands gesture.

"He'll probably have a backup, right?" Ronnie said.

"Probably. If so, you'll have to dump him, too. There's no other way."

"Right," Ronnie said. His expression was placid.

"How's it sound to you?" Red said. "I mean, do you feel confident? Do you feel good about it?" He resisted the urge to pat the young man's arm.

130

"What's the guy's name? The loan shark," Ronnie said.

Red's voice was lowered. "Tony Dio. Ever heard of him?"

Ronnie shook his head. "No."

"Very good ... uh ... I mean, why should you? He's nothin'—a piece of shit." Red gulped down half of his straight soda and spat ice back into the glass.

"Red, how do you know your friend gave you the straight scoop about this thing?"

"Because I've known him for years." Red finished off the rest of the drink and wiped his mouth on the cocktail napkin. "He's solid. I trust him just like I trust you. See what I mean?"

"I see." Ronnie turned his glass on the table.

"We've got to handle this just right. I want you to go back to your motel room and wait there. Tomorrow I'll pick you up about 6:00 P.M. We pick up your piece. We drive over to the hotel and get it over with. If we're lucky, he may even have some dough in the room. If so, it'll be that much better for us. Two birds with one stone." Red smiled as hard as he could.

Carr walked up the stairs and opened the door to his apartment. Magazines on the coffee table included a three-month-old journal of criminology and a couple of Sally's *Cosmopolitans.*

He showered and shaved and put on a loose-fitting shirt and slacks. He walked into the kitchen and opened the refrigerator door. Green bologna. He pushed it into the garbage-disposal.

The doorbell rang. When he opened the door, Sally looked slightly embarrassed.

"I can't believe you are home for once," she said with a half-smile.

He lowered his head to kiss, but she walked by him and went to the sofa.

She wore athletic shorts and top and tennis shoes.

"Why aren't you at work?" he said.

"Because it's Saturday. The day when normal people don't work. They ride their bikes along the beach."

"I worked all night," Carr said. "I guess I forgot what day it was."

"That's nothing new for you. A new day is a new pinch, right?" Sally slumped down on the couch.

Carr closed the door. He walked back to the refrigerator and began rummaging.

"I came over here to talk."

"Okay." He tossed out a moldy orange.

Sally folded her arms across her chest. "I've been doing a lot of thinking lately," she said. "The whole relationship is wrong. It's not based on anything permanent. We're just using one another. It's not a mature relationship. It never has been. I think it's self-destructive. You're a very cold person and I am not. I like stage plays and art galleries and you don't. I'm thwarting my own potential." She spoke as if she had written it out ahead of time.

"I see," Carr said. He closed the refrigerator door.

"You're going out with a waitress in Chinatown," she said. "You've been seen with her. Do you want to talk about it?" Her tone was schoolmarmish.

"There's nothing to talk about."

"Do you sleep with her?"

"Yes."

She chewed her lip a moment, watching him. Then she changed the subject. "You've always had the ability to judge right and wrong by your own strange set of standards. When we first met, I was fascinated by that mysterious trait. Perhaps infatuated is the word I mean." She stood up and walked to the window. She stared at the beach. "Lately I feel out of place with you," she said. "As if I might have been sent from an escort service. The barrier you built around yourself gets stronger and stronger. . . ." She turned and faced him. "It's not as if we are married. I'm not some stupid, naggy housewife. I'm not chattel." Her voice cracked. "Why couldn't you have told me about her?"

Carr walked closer to her. He spoke quietly. "I didn't tell you because I didn't want to hurt your feelings."

"The same thing happened to your friend Howard. He built a barrier around himself and stopped understanding people's weaknesses. His view became distorted." She looked at her palms. "What I'm talking about is honesty between two people." She looked up. "Being able to have a meaningful dialogue."

132

"That's a lot of shit," Carr said without emotion.

Sally's jaw dropped.

"Those ideas come from the classes you're taking," he said. "Your teachers are phonies and faith healers whose heads are packed full of mush. They peddle bullshit to people like you, who buy it so you can have something to talk about during coffee breaks. How's that for honesty?"

"What is wrong with the truth?" Sally said.

"The truth? You tell me. You work in a courtroom all day. That's supposed to be Truth City. The only truth in there is that the judge is appointed for life."

"What happens in there has nothing to do with what happens between people," Sally said.

"That's my point."

"This is a stupid conversation. It's my fault. I'm playing a stupid female role." Her eyes were wet. "I came over to see if you wanted to go bike riding. I thought we could stop by Nick's for a drink on the way back." She began to cry.

Carr had a feeling of *déjà vu*—Sally with him somewhere in sleepy darkness and he was whispering things that he would never have said in the light.

A knock on the door. Carr turned from Sally and, without hurrying, walked to the door and opened it. It was Kelly.

Sally's hands flew to her face, and Kelly retreated down the stairs.

The phone rang. Sally slumped on the edge of the sofa. The sobs came in waves.

Carr picked up the receiver. "Hello."

"Delgado here. I think you're on the right track. Records at Terminal Island show that Red Diamond shared a cell for over three years with a young guy named Ronnie. Ronnie Boyce. He fits the description. We pulled his records package, and he's a bank robber. He likes the heavy stuff—a real psycho. He shanked an inmate during his second year in T. I. but they couldn't prove it. His whereabouts are unknown now. He listed a phony address when he was released."

Carr wrote the name down on a pad. "Sounds like he's our man."

"There's something else," Delgado said. "A teletype just came in. You've been transferred to Washington, D.C. You're supposed to report there as soon as possible. I've stalled it by answering back that you have lease problems with your apartment. You're going to have to move fairly quickly. Sorry I couldn't tell you in person."

"Thanks, Alex." Carr put down the receiver. Sally was gone. He looked out the window. She was peddling away along the bike path.

$/21

The bank, like most of the others in Beverly Hills, was spacious and modern, with lots of glass and tapestries on the walls.

Carol, in a conservative gray wig and matching pink skirt and jacket, sat down at a desk marked NEW ACCOUNTS—IUMI ISHIKAWA. A young Oriental woman in ponytail and sundress smiled. On the desk was a framed photo of a middle-aged Oriental couple.

"I'd like to open an account." Carol enunciated each word carefully. Rich-lady talk.

The clerk handed her a signature card. "Please fill this out."

Carol filled in the name and address and got goose bumps. She always did. It would be just her luck that someday she would forget the name on the phony driver's license. Every account meant memorizing a new name. Since 10:00 A.M., when the banks opened, she had memorized four different names and addresses, one for each bank. She had four thousand dollars in cash in her purse.

She handed the signature card back to the young woman.

"How much would you like to deposit?" She rolled the card into a typewriter.

Carol reached into her purse. "I'd like to deposit this check. It's for three thousand dollars."

Iumi Ishikawa put on her glasses and examined the check. "May I see your driver's license?"

"Certainly. Here you are."

"Thank you." She copied the driver's license number onto the signature card and laid the check in front of Carol. "Would you please second-endorse the check."

Carol held her breath, signed "Gladys T. Zimmerman," and exhaled. The goose bumps started to disappear.

"You're cold," Iumi Ishikawa said. "I think the air conditioning is on too high." She rolled a rubber stamp over the check.

"Uh . . . yes . . . uh . . . too high. I would like one thousand dollars in cash. Make the initial deposit for two thousand instead of three. I'll take the remainder in cash. I'm going to buy a used car today. Cute VW. Got it picked out already." Carol smiled pertly.

"Where did you do your banking previously?"

"In Europe. My husband is with the Foreign Service. He's teaching for a year at USC. No use buying a new car and having to sell it in a year."

The clerk wasn't listening. She was staring at the check.

"I'm sorry, Mrs. Zimmerman, but we don't usually allow cash-back transactions on an initial deposit," she said.

Carol put a hand to her chest and gave a surprised look. "Then just how are we supposed to buy the VW today? My husband will *kill* me if I don't get the money for the VW. We're buying it from a student. We're getting a very good deal. Today is Friday. The car could be *sold* over the weekend. Would you prefer that I speak with the bank manager?"

"Well, if you feel that . . ."

"That's really not necessary. Surely you can see your way to bending the rules just a little for me. I would *so* appreciate it. . . . Is that a picture of your mother and father?"

"Yes, it is."

"My parents live with us. That's why we came back to the U.S., to take care of them. My mother has cancer. She has me so worried." Carol looked at the floor.

"I'm sorry," Iumi Ishikawa said.

Carol raised her head. "I assure you the check is good."

"I'll speak with the manager. I'm sure he will approve the transaction once I explain it to him." Iumi Ishikawa gave an embarrassed smile, or was it a nervous smile? She walked to the

136

manager's desk. He was blond, tan, trim as a jogger. She talked with him briefly and came back to the desk. The manager picked up his phone and dialed.

"Is there a problem?" Carol asked, lowering her voice halfway through the sentence.

The manager stared at her while speaking on the phone. The Japanese girl stood at the desk with the check in her hands. She did not sit down.

Carol's knees were shaking.

"If you'll just wait a few minutes, the check will be approved," Iumi Ishikawa said.

"No way!" Carol lunged, grabbed the check, and ran out the glass door.

Brakes squealed as she dodged across the street. Looking behind her, Carol flung herself into a department store's revolving door. She heard a siren.

Out of breath, she mixed in with women in furs and rings, moving from table to table, picking things up and putting them down, as if browsing.

Standing behind a window display, she held up a blouse and looked across the street at the bank. The bank manager and the Japanese girl were standing outside the bank looking around.

A police car pulled up. A black policeman got out and slipped his baton into a ring on his belt. The bank manager pointed down the street toward another store. He was pointing the wrong way!

The policeman and the bank manager trotted down the sidewalk.

Carol headed toward an escalator and realized she was walking too fast. She slowed down.

In front of her was a tiered display of purses. She picked one up and studied every face near her. No one was looking. She ripped off the gray wig, stuffed it in the purse, and set it back down. She ran her hand through her hair and got on the escalator.

On the way up she had a view of the entire first floor. It had three street entrances. There was canned music and the murmur of soap-opera talk from a row of color televisions. A man and woman on TV kissed. She was safe.

If no one had seen her run into the store, they would look around for an hour or so and then go away. She breathed deeply.

She realized the check was still in her hand. She asked a salesman where the rest room was and headed for a door near a group of sofas.

In the rest room she stuffed the check in her bra. Watching the door, she took off the pink jacket and put it in a trash can. She tucked in her blouse. Her watch said it was noon. This was as good a place to wait as any.

Two giggling salesgirls came in twenty minutes later, and Carol left the rest room.

The escalator took her to each floor. She paused at every department and made up questions for the salespeople. In the fourth-floor rest room she spent a full half hour standing in front of the mirror before anyone else came in. In linens she purchased some beach towels. They filled up a shopping bag nicely.

On the third trip down the escalator, Carol began to wonder whether the salespeople were staring at her. Or was it just her imagination? But then again, why take chances?

She looked at her watch. She had been in the store two full hours.

From the display window she could see that the police car was gone from the bank. Everything seemed back to normal. The street was crowded with shoppers.

Carol tapped a young salesgirl on the shoulder. "Excuse me, is there a back way out . . . into the parking lot?"

"Sorry, these are the only customers' doors," she said, pointing to the street entrance.

"Thank you."

A bus stopped across the street and picked up passengers. That was it! She could see a bus two blocks down. Thank God!

She joined a group of women going out the door, and walked in the opposite direction from the bank, toward a bus bench. She sat down.

Was that a police car down the street near the bus? Jesus, it was. It was just cruising. It passed the bus and then stopped for a light. It was too late to get up and run. He would see her.

138

Once she got on the bus she would be home free.

As the police car approached, she could see that the driver was black. She felt the goose bumps. He was pulling over to the curb in front of the bus bench. She turned her head.

The policeman got out of the car and walked around the car to her. The bus passed by.

"Ma'am?"

"Yes, officer," Carol said.

"We're looking for a lady in a pink skirt. May I ask you where you've just been?"

"Just bought some towels for the beach house." She opened the bag and smiled. "See?"

"Thank you. Would you mind walking down the street with me to the bank? It will just take a minute."

"I am in a hurry. I'd really rather not. My husband is waiting for me. He's a producer at the studios." Carol looked at her watch.

"I'm afraid you'll have to come along with me. It'll just take a minute," said the policeman.

"Well, if you insist. Would you mind carrying this bag for me?"

The policeman looked at her for a moment and gave a grudging smile. "Sure."

Carol handed him the bag and kneed him in the balls at the same time. He fell backward. There was the sound of police equipment hitting the sidewalk.

Running down the street, she pulled out the check and shoved it in her mouth. "God help me! Please don't let me go back!" She turned the corner, feet flying. The sound of running came from behind her. Suddenly a black arm clamped around her neck. Her feet stopped and flew forward. Ronnie and his towel!

Her tailbone slammed against the sidewalk. She scratched violently at the arm around her neck. The policeman's sweaty cheek touched her ear. "Spit it out, Mabel," he grunted. She tried to swallow, and a funny sound came out. The vice around her neck tightened. "Okay, bitch, you asked for it. Nighty night," said the policeman. Blackness.

•   •   •

Carr's eyes itched from using the binoculars. Someone once told him it was caused by the light refraction of the windshield glass. Kelly's hulk filled the back seat.

"Here comes Scarlett O'Puke," Kelly said, taking a toothpick out of his mouth. A henna-haired middle-aged woman entered her apartment.

By now each resident of the avocado apartment house had been christened by Kelly. One old man was "Mr. Spitter"; the scraggly young couple on the first floor were "John and Martha Incest"; a spindly, modish bachelor who lived next door to Diamond was "Ensign Tubesteak."

"Not one of these people goes to work. Have you noticed that?" Kelly said.

"Would you hire any of them if you were an employer?"

"Fuck no," Kelly said.

"See."

Kelly changed the subject. "I think Red is planning a caper," he said.

"What makes you say that?" Carr said.

"He's too cautious. The only place he's been in two days was a Laundromat. He's laying low. He's building up to something. Rounders never stay in their pad unless it's for a reason." Kelly used the toothpick again.

"Don't forget," Carr said, "Waxman told us Diamond was into the sharks. Maybe he hasn't made his payment and he's worried. Besides, we don't know where he went when we lost him yesterday."

"Maybe. But I say he's getting ready for a job; thinking, planning, using his noodle. Crooks always like public places."

"Maybe so." Carr exhaled. He looked in the rearview mirror.

A sedan pulled in behind them and parked. Delgado got out and came over and leaned in the passenger window.

"The duty agent just got a call from Wilshire Division. They grabbed a paper hanger in a bank. A broad. She's singing for a deal. Says her ex-con boyfriend has a sawed-off. Here's my keys. I'll fill in here with Kelly while you go talk with her."

$/22

The squad room was a jumble of desks and phones. Uniformed policemen and detectives in short-sleeved white shirts used the telephones. People, mostly black, were handcuffed to benches along the walls. The voices were profane.

Carr lit a cigarette and listened to a policeman whose skin and hair were the color of his uniform. The cop's shoes and badge were soldier-shined.

"She tried to scarf the check but I choked her and dug it out of her mouth," said the policeman. He handed Carr a clear plastic envelope containing a gnawed check. "The bank manager had just got a call from a friend at another branch who was stung by the same kind of check, same M.O. The broad—her name's Carol Lomax, by the way—just had a little bad luck. Her records package says she's on parole from Corona. Got out three months ago. . . . She's talking about a dude with a sawed-off shotgun. Since it's a federal beef, I thought I'd give you guys a call."

Carr handed back the check. "Did she give you her boyfriend's name?"

"She said his name is . . ." The policeman took a notebook out of his shirt pocket. "Boyce . . . Ronnie Boyce."

Carr's muscles tensed. "Ronnie?"

"Why? You know the asshole?"

"Yes," Carr said.

The policeman pointed to a door with a photograph of a black-robed judge on a background of girlie-magazine crotch shots. Police art. "She's in that interview room if you want to talk with her." He turned back to writing his report.

Carr wanted to run into the room. Instead, he took a couple of deep breaths. He walked slowly to the door and opened it casually.

Carol was at the table, her head resting on her arms. The room had a table, chairs, and fiberboard walls. The ashtray on the table was overflowing, though there was a wastebasket in the corner. Next to the ashtray were a few wadded-up pieces of Kleenex with red stains. She looked up at Carr.

"You a Fed?"

Carr showed his gold badge.

Carol looked at the badge, picked up a Kleenex ball, dabbed it under her upper lip, and looked at it. Her white blouse was filthy.

"What's the matter?" Carr said.

"That cop choked me out and stuck his hand in my mouth. My gums are bleeding. First of all, before I say anything I want to know what you can do for me." She dabbed again.

"I can't make you any promises."

"I know you can't promise me that I'll get off or anything. I'm on parole. They got the check. I know I'm going back." Her lower lip trembled. She stared at the ashtray. "If I could have gotten rid of the check, they wouldn't have anything on me." The Kleenex ball touched each eye, then the nose. She cleared her throat. "What I want is a letter to the parole board saying I cooperated with the Feds. I want the letter to be in my parole file."

Carr sat down and laid his hands flat on the table. "That can be arranged," he said, "depending on what you can turn."

"How about a sawed-off shotgun?" she said. "That's a federal beef, isn't it?"

"Sure is. Where is the shotgun?"

Carol rubbed the back of her neck. "In a locker at the downtown bus depot. That's where he keeps it. This guy I know. Ronnie Boyce. He just got out of Terminal Island."

142

"What does Ronnie use it for?" Carr said. He drummed his fingers on the table.

Carol looked at Carr's shoulder as she spoke. "I have no idea. I don't know anything about what he does with it, and I don't want to know. I just know he has it." She crushed the Kleenex.

"Have you seen it?"

"Uh, no.

"Then how do you know he has it?"

"I mean, I've seen it, but what he does with it is his own business."

Carr picked up the brimming ashtray, walked to the wastebasket, and emptied it.

"How do you know it's in the locker?" he said, before turning around.

"He's told me that's where he keeps it, and besides, I've seen the locker key in the motel room."

Carr sat down again.

"What's the number on the locker key?"

"I don't remember." Carol picked at her face. "I don't want him to know I handed him up. He's goofy."

Carr folded his hands. "If you want to do yourself any good, Carol, you'll have to tell me where he is."

"I hope you aren't going to rush over there, break down the door, and tell him I snitched him off." Carol's front teeth were bloody pink.

Carr closed his eyes and shook his head slowly.

Carol rested her ears on her fists. "The Sea Horse Motel in Santa Monica. It's on Lincoln Boulevard. Room eleven." Her eyes searched Carr. "Now that I've told you, are you still going to write the letter? Or were you just bullshitting?"

"I'll take the letter to your parole agent myself." He took out a notebook. "What's his name?" He wrote it down and put the notebook and pencil away.

"Is there any way you could get me into a federal prison so I could do my time there? They have a lot more vocational rehab stuff."

"I don't think so," he said.

"The only reason I got caught was because of my skirt. I

should of changed it," Carol said. She put her head back down.
He left the police station in a hurry, headed for Santa Monica.

Carr drove past the Sea Horse Motel to get a look. Circling the
block, he put the radio microphone in the glove compartment
and glanced around the interior of the car to make sure there
were no signs that it was a government vehicle. He drove into
the motel parking lot and parked near room eleven. In the manager's office, he rang a bell at the counter. A brown cat with a
missing ear jumped off the cluttered desk. Television sounds
floated from a room shielded by a grimy plastic curtain.

Carr guessed the woman who made a grand entry from behind the curtain to be over three hundred pounds. With her
pink curlers and skin-tight sweater and slacks, she looked like
an overinflated pool toy.

She took a register card from a drawer and handed it to him
along with a pen. "You want the room for a whole night or just
a short while? Reason I ask is because a short while is cheaper."

"I might be here a few days."

Her curlers moved as she furrowed her brow.

"You'll have to pay the rent each day. That'll be twelve dollars
for tonight."

"Here you are. I'd like to have a room near the ice machine.
That's where I parked my car." Carr pointed behind him.

"All the same to me. Here's the key to room twelve. Make
sure to pay each day before noon." She pulled her sweater
down to reach the horizon of her pants. The sweater popped
back up an inch. She disappeared behind the plastic curtain.

Carr walked into room twelve, carrying a Handie-Talkie in a
brown paper sack, and sat down at the tiny dressing table with
a phone on it. He removed the Handie-Talkie and turned the
volume on low.

He held it close to his mouth and pressed the transmit button.

"Nine bravo four seven, this is three tango three one." He
turned up the volume slightly.

"This is nine bravo four seven, go ahead."

"Two two this number"—he pulled the telephone closer—
"787-9517."

"Wilco. Four seven out."

He turned off the Handie-Talkie and waited, looking at the double bed with white chenille bedspread and the circus-clown prints on each wall. A heater protruded from the wall adjoining room eleven. Above it was a vent.

The phone rang.

"Hello, Alex?"

"Where are you?"

"Sea Horse Motel on Lincoln in Santa Monica. Room twelve. Ronnie's staying in eleven. His girlfriend copped. Says he has a sawed-off. I haven't seen him yet."

"Red is still in his apartment. I'll go back to the office. Jack will stay here on Diamond. At this point, the fewer people we have involv . . ." Delgado cleared his throat. "Let me know if you need anything."

Carr hung up the phone and switched off the light. In semi-darkness he moved the chair next to the wall heater. He stood on it and, being as quiet as possible, used a flat key to remove the screws from the vent. He took it off the wall and tossed it on the bed.

Through the wire vent cover on the wall of the next room he saw a mirror. In the mirror was a reflection of the man who killed Rico lying on the bed smoking a cigarette.

$/23

Kelly peered through the binoculars at Red Diamond's front door. He said out loud, "Come on out and go somewhere, you dirty son of a bitch." He could hardly believe it when a moment later Diamond appeared. He started the engine.

Diamond backed his red Chevrolet out of the carport. Kelly ducked down on the seat as the car went past. Once Diamond had turned onto Hollywood Boulevard, Kelly made a tire-squealing U turn and picked up speed. He had to make the same stoplight as Diamond.

Diamond turned north on Gower, passing a group of teenagers in transparent blouses. He sloped down between green landscaping to the Hollywood Freeway.

Kelly smiled. Diamond didn't know he was being followed. Kelly stayed way back, shielded himself behind other cars.

Diamond continued to the Harbor Freeway, then veered where the high green sign said SANTA MONICA FREEWAY. Kelly grabbed the microphone from the glove compartment as Diamond swung his car off at Lincoln Boulevard.

"Three tango three one, this is your old partner. My man's coming atcha. We're a couple minutes away. . . ."

Carr's Handie-Talkie was clipped to his belt. He pressed the transmit button twice to acknowledge Kelly's message. He continued to peer through the vent. The tin edge was marking his forehead. His eyes and nose were completely inside the vent

146

opening. He knew full well this was a violation of law. He could hear the judge now. "The defendant had a reasonable expectation of privacy as he relaxed in his room. If the agent could have observed him without removing the vent cover, he wouldn't have violated his constitutional rights. But since the agent removed the vent he infringed . . ."

"We just pulled into the motel," Kelly said.

A knock on the door. Ronnie sat up, swung his feet to the floor, crossed to the door, and opened it.

Red Diamond looked pale. "How ya feeling, baby?"

"Fine," Ronnie said. He backed up. Red came in. Ronnie shut and locked the door.

Red rubbed his hands nervously and looked around. "Where's your old lady? I been wanting to meet her."

"She went out to down some paper," Ronnie said. "Have a seat."

"Do you have any questions?" Red sat down but got right up again. "We should get going."

"Yeah. How does this guy know my name?" Ronnie pulled on pants and shirt. "You and me were the only ones who—"

Red had turned on the radio. Rock-and-roll drowned out Ronnie's words.

Carr turned his ear toward the vent, but it didn't help.

Ronnie walked into the bathroom. Red paced and bit his nails. Ronnie came out a few minutes later, shaved and combed. He sat down on the bed and put on his shoes while Red kept talking to him. He nodded his head over and over again.

Carr looked at his watch. It was 6:00 P.M.

Ronnie got off the bed, collected his wallet and change from the dresser, and put them in his pocket.

Red flipped off the radio.

"Where are we going?" Ronnie asked.

"He's in room twelve nineteen at the Plaza penthouse. I called the hotel just a few minutes ago. I've been there before. There's a fire exit at either end of the hallway. When it's over, we can go down the steps to the next floor and get the elevator there. We'll have our car in the big parking lot outside. We can hop back on the freeway before the cops have a chance to get there."

Ronnie picked up a bottle of after shave from the dresser, poured, and slapped it to his face with both hands. "How much money do you think he'll have in the room?" He capped the bottle again.

"Probably a real load," Red said. "But no matter what, Dio must be snuffed. Him *and* his fucking gunsel. It's them or us. They may know what you look like, so get your piece out as soon as we go in the door. Get the drop on 'em, and we'll search the place. Once we find his poke, dump both of 'em right then, wipe the shotgun, drop it, and we get the fuck out." Red fumbled in his shirt pocket for a Pall Mall and hung it on a sticky lower lip.

"I still can't figure out how they knew it was me last week," Ronnie said.

"Don't matter. They did." The Pall Mall jiggled as Red talked. He looked at his watch, lit the cigarette, and coughed a few times. "We gotta get going."

Ronnie shrugged into a jacket, and they walked out the door.

Carr said, "Pick me up," into the Handi-Talkie.

Diamond and Boyce drove onto Lincoln Boulevard as Kelly pulled in the back entrance of the motel parking lot. Carr ran outside and jumped in.

"Don't lose 'em now, Jack."

"Any ideas where they're going?" Kelly said. He stepped on the gas.

"My guess is the downtown bus depot to pick up the sawed-off."

"Jesus!" Kelly kept his eyes on the road. "Could you hear them talking in there? What'd they say?"

Carr didn't answer.

The traffic was stop and go all the way downtown. Diamond pulled up in front of the bus depot and parked. Boyce got out and went in the main entrance. He blended in with a crowd of old people, sailors, and Mexican illegals.

Carr followed him through the waiting area, then lost sight of him when a group of children rushed by. He was gone.

Carr grabbed a bus driver by the arm and asked where the rental lockers were. He rushed up to the banks of lockers and almost bumped into Boyce removing a heavy black attaché case from a locker. The young man looked around nervously. Putting the case under his arm, he strode carefully, slowly back toward the main entrance.

Carr rushed out of the depot and got back in the front seat with Kelly.

"He picked up his piece," Carr said.

Kelly's eyes were big. He reached for the microphone.

Carr grabbed his hand. "No," he said.

"But shouldn't we tell . . . ?"

Carr shook his head. He stared at Diamond's vehicle, parked up the block. Boyce sauntered out of the depot, the case still under his arm, and got in Diamond's car.

Kelly spoke harshly. "I say let's take him right *now*. He's in possession."

Carr kept his eyes on the other vehicle. Diamond started up and pulled slowly around the corner. Kelly followed.

"I think we should wait," Carr said. "Nothing to lose by waiting a little while."

"Fuck waiting," Kelly said. "Let's run 'em off the road. Right now. If he so much as looks at his attaché case, I'll waste both of them."

"It's not time yet." Carr had his eyes on Diamond's Chevy. Back onto the freeway. Kelly's Irish face was red now, as red as Carr had ever seen it. Kelly kept glancing at Carr as he changed lanes to keep up with Diamond. The red Chevy cruised smoothly in and out of traffic and got off at National Boulevard.

"What the hell is wrong with you?" Kelly said. "I hope you're ready to take the responsibility if this freak stops right now, sticks up a liquor store, and kills the owner. You're acting strange. What's wrong? Maybe you've lost your nerve, but I haven't. We've fooled with these animals long enough. I want to stop 'em and finish the thing here and now."

Carr continued to look at the road.

Diamond's Chevy took a right turn into a hotel parking lot. Carr picked up the binoculars. Boyce did something with the case on the front seat of the car. He threw some crumpled pink paper out of the passenger window.

"You follow them in," Carr said. "I'll meet you in the lobby." He flung open the car door and, being careful to stay out of sight of Boyce and Diamond, ran across the crowded parking lot and into the plush, modern hotel lobby. He found a telephone, picked up the receiver, and dialed.

Ronnie ripped off the last bit of pink wrapping paper. His hands felt sweaty. He pulled the beaver tail back, noted that a twelve-gauge round was chambered and ready to fire. He flicked off the safety. He laid the weapon back in the case and closed the lid gently, clicking only one latch.

"Got any ear plugs?"

"What?"

"Ear plugs. My ears rang for two days when I did that guy in the hotel room. This sawed-off is a loud mutha-fuckin' piece." He was making a joke.

Red forced a laugh. He slapped the young man's thigh. "Ear plugs, ear plugs." He chuckled nervously. "That'd be a real friggin' tip-off, wouldn't it? To walk in wearing a set of ear plugs." His stomach made a powerful growl. He rubbed his navel.

Ronnie stared blankly at the hotel. "I once robbed a bank on the same day I was released from Chino. I took the bus from the pen and got off in San Gabriel. I picked up a piece a guy was holding for me, and stuck up the first bank I saw, then caught another bus. My parole was revoked two months later for some minor shit, but they never made me on that bank job. Never. It was as if it was free. You know, like you do five and get one free. I had a real good feeling for that job, just like I do today. I just knew things were right."

"It's confidence, baby. It's because you've got a whole bucket of balls. That's why you and your old Red buddy are going to move up the ladder. Because of mental speed and balls. There is nothing, I mean *nothing* we can't do. We've got what it takes. The ingredients are there." Red looked at his watch. "It's ten minutes to seven. Any questions, baby?" He cleared his throat.

Ronnie shook his head no. He followed Red into the hotel lobby.

At a bank of elevators, Red pushed an Up button and put his arm around Ronnie. In a fatherly manner he whispered, "You've got to get the drop on 'em as soon as we're inside. That's the

150

important thing. As soon as we clear the door. I know you can do it, babe."

Ronnie smiled. The elevator door opened. They stepped in. So did a bellhop with a tray, and two men in sports coats. One man looked seedy. Had they met him in Terminal Island?

Inside the elevator Red pushed the button for the twelfth floor. The elevator rose smoothly, stopping twice to let off the others.

At the twelfth floor, they got out of the elevator and walked along the hallway to the door of room twelve nineteen. It was open an inch. Red knocked lightly.

"Red, is that you?" The voice was from another room in the suite. "Come on in! I'm just getting dressed!"

Red pushed the door open slowly. He nodded to Ronnie. Ronnie stepped in first, his feet sinking into the thickest carpet he had ever felt.

"Now!" whispered Red. "Get it out!"

Ronnie unlatched the case. The shotgun was in his hands. He crept through the living room, Red following close behind. They were at the bedroom door when Tony shouted matter-of-factly, "Come on in here, Red."

Ronnie's fists gripped the shotgun firmly. His finger caressed the trigger.

Red leaned against the doorjamb and turned the doorknob. The door flew open violently.

Explosions of steel fire crashed through Ronnie Boyce's teeth and chest. He was on the floor, sinking into the carpet. Bullets were deep in his chest and head.

More explosions. Red gave a woman's scream.

Blood surged into Ronnie Boyce's mouth and lungs. He felt nausea, then dizzyness. His tongue was keeping air from his lungs. He tried to move his head to the side but it didn't work. Ruined. More ripping explosions. There was only blackness.

151

$/24

Carr, with Kelly two feet behind him, burst from the stairwell door holding his revolver in combat stance. Approaching the room door, he saw a bullet hole.

"Let's kick it," Kelly said.

"Take cover! They'll be bailing out!"

They hugged the walls on either side of room twelve nineteen.

Down the hallway a woman's voice shrieked, "Operator! People are shooting guns! Send the police!"

The two men who stumbled out of the room were not Boyce and Diamond. They ran toward the elevators. Carr and Kelly cut them off. "Federal officers, lads," Kelly said. "Down on the floor and spread."

After handcuffing both men and securing them in a room a maid had been working in, Carr went back to the room where the shots had been fired. He pushed open the door carefully with his revolver. Red Diamond lay next to the sofa, face down, feet twitching. Boyce was sprawled on his back in front of the bedroom door, the shotgun next to him. Carr bent down. His hand moved to Boyce's throat to test for a pulse.

He pulled the hand back before touching, stood up, walked to the phone, and dialed. "Let me have Central Homicide."

A half hour later Detective Higgins arrived. He looked at the bodies and went into the room where Kelly and a uniformed policeman held Tony Dio and his stocky bodyguard. Carr followed.

"I'll tell you exactly what happened," Dio said to Higgins as he sat on the bed. "Two bastards come up to my room to snuff out me and my friend here and we defended ourselves. I got a right to have a gun. It's registered. I was in my own hotel room. They came to do me in. To waste me." His hands were shaking.

"What happened?" Higgins said to Dio.

Carr leaned against the wall with Kelly.

"We were sitting in my room having a drink and I get a phone call. I didn't know who it was. Man's voice. He says, 'This is a friend. Red Diamond and another guy are coming up to your room to rip you off. The guy with Red has a sawed-off in an attaché case.' Then he hangs up."

Kelly's jaw dropped. He turned toward Carr.

Higgins made notes on his clipboard. "So what did you do then?" he said.

"Me and my friend here go in the bedroom and wait. My friend's got a piece because I carry large amounts of cash now and then." He looked at the bodyguard. "L.A. is a high-crime area, right? I peek out the bedroom door and I see these two guys come in the front door. One guy is carrying a sawed-off piece. So my friend here opens the bedroom door and lets loose. I mean, what would you do? It was simple self-defense."

"That's what it sounds like," Higgins said. "I'll have to ask you to come down to the station to make a written report, but by the physical evidence, it looks like self-defense. The dead guys did have a shotgun. No charges will be filed."

Higgins stepped out into the hallway. Carr and Kelly followed.

"We had Diamond and Boyce under surveillance," Carr said. "That's how we happen to be here."

"That's all I need for my report," said the detective. He walked across the hall into the room with the bodies.

It was four hours before the case was wrapped up.

Delgado arrived and chewed Rolaids while Carr explained what had happened. Per standard operating procedure, Carr and Kelly wrote statements, which would serve as their report of investigation. The statements were concise and almost identical.

153

"Occurrence during a Routine Surveillance" was the title block.

Delgado headed back for the field office to send a teletype to Washington, D.C.

They checked the serial numbers of the money in Ronnie Boyce's wallet and found that the numbers on his six tens and two fives matched Rico's marked money.

Higgins unloaded the sawed-off shotgun and put it in a plastic evidence bag.

The bodies were removed to the L.A. county morgue.

After all the details were completed, Kelly suggested Ling's. Carr accepted.

The drive to Chinatown was pleasant. Little or no traffic, and the heat wave seemed to have given way to cooling, smogless sea air.

"The wife and I are thinking of having a little get-together at my place for you before you go," Kelly said. "You know, steaks and beer. I figured I'd ask five or six couples. Ling and his wife said they'd like to come. Couple of the narcs."

"That'll be real nice," Carr said. "I'll bring Sally, if she still wants to see me."

Kelly stopped for a red light at Hill and Alpine and looked both ways. He drove through before the light changed. Down the street he pulled into a curb parking space two doors from Ling's.

"Charlie," Kelly said.

"Yes?"

"How did you know that Boyce was . . ." He turned off the engine. "Oh, never mind."

They got out of the car.

One-Shot Deal

$/1

Larry Phillips, a diminutive man who in attire other than Leavenworth Federal Prison denims might look like a bespectacled young college professor, had been waiting in line for two hours signing forms, turning things in. He was holding a small cardboard box that contained the contents of his cell.

A hound-jowled guard with a jagged scar circling one of his eye sockets stood behind a metal counter. He gave a little nod. Phillips stepped forward to a white line on the floor. The guard's lips barely moved as he spoke. "Put the box down on the counter," he said. "Take off your trousers and blouse and drop 'em in the hamper behind you." He slammed a plastic bag down on the counter. "These are the civies you came in with. Put 'em on."

Phillips set the box on the counter and undressed.

The guard poured the contents of the box out on the counter and examined each item. He barely looked at the books: *A Collector's Guide to Chinese Porcelain, Clinical Hypnosis: Fact and Fiction,* and a dog-eared copy of *A Stock Broker's Guide to U.S. Government Securities,* and tossed them back in the box. He examined the bathing-suit photograph of strawberry-blonde Melba Rivers carefully and tossed it in along with a letter with an American embassy postmark.

The letter was from Phillips's red-faced mannequin of a father, the only one he had received from him during the eighteen-month stretch. He knew its wishy-washy phrases by heart. In his cell Phillips had visualized his father standing behind his portable mahogany bar mouthing the words in the letter, gesturing with his ever-present glass stirring rod. A diplomat who would never refer even to an enemy with words stronger than "down-to-earth." The glass rod tapped the edge of the martini glass like a deafening chime. . . .

Phillips tossed the stenciled denims and shirt in the canvas hamper. He pulled a black polyester sports shirt out of the plastic bag (it was probably out of style by now) and put it on. He zipped up his pants.

The guard initialed a form and shoved it across the counter with a pen. "Sign-the-form-first-name-first," he mumbled.

Phillips signed his name and picked up the cardboard box.

"Step to the door," the guard said. "If you don't have a ride, there's a bus to Kansas City at the road stop in two hours. Don't loiter in front."

Phillips stepped to the door. The guard pushed a button, and the door lock made a violent snap. The door creaked open, and Phillips got goose bumps that were electric, uncontrollable. He strode out the door and along a sidewalk to the parking lot.

A car horn sounded, and a station wagon pulled up next to the curb. Melba was driving. She was wearing jeans and a sweatshirt, though somehow he had expected her to be in a bathing suit, like the photograph. With a sort of squeal, she rushed out of the car and into his arms. He dropped the box as she kissed him hungrily, her tongue flicking deeply to find his. Their mouths parted. "Mercy," she said with a Texan twang. "A year and a half's a long time." They hugged.

"Did you bring the package?" he whispered.

She lifted her head off his shoulder. "Mercy," she said again. "Same old Mr. Business First."

They got in the station wagon, and Melba started the engine. "It's in the glove compartment," she said, accelerating onto the main highway.

Phillips opened the compartment and pulled out a package the size of a bar of soap. He tore it open and removed business

158

cards that read INTERNATIONAL PAPER INCORPORATED, a California driver's license with his photograph, a Social Security card, and an assortment of credit cards. Everything had the name Lawrence T. Porter.

"I kept it in a safe-deposit box . . . just like you told me to," Melba said.

He put the identification in his pocket and leaned back in the seat.

"Should I stop in a motel?" she said. "Or, if you want, I can just pull off to the side and give you a . . ."

"Let's get some miles in," he interrupted. "It's a long way to Washington, D.C." He was staring at the road.

Nothing was said for a while.

"I know how you feel," she said sympathetically. "You think about everything so much and then one day they set you free and you don't know whether to shit or go blind. . . . I felt the same way when I got out of Terminal Island."

The motel was part of a chain that guaranteed every room to be the same design from coast to coast. Thin bedspreads, thick mattresses, and water glasses in little paper bags.

Phillips stepped out of the shower and dried off. He opened the bathroom door.

Melba was sitting on the edge of the bed wearing only panties. She had put on fresh lipstick.

He walked over to the bed. "I want to tell you all about the project," he said.

Melba raised her eyebrows. "Now?" she said.

"Now."

"Okay. It's up to you."

He sat next to her on the bed and described, in detail, the plan, from the beginning to the walkaway. This took at least fifteen minutes. "The score will be close to a million dollars," he said as a finish to his lecture. "We walk away with a mill. Does that turn you on?"

"I wanna use the name Melissa," she said. "Melissa Diane . . . I've always liked that name."

Phillips stood up naked in front of her. "Now would you like to relax and be at ease?" he said.

She nodded and shut her eyes. "I've been waitin' to hear those words for eighteen months."

He put his hand firmly on her forehead. "Sleep," he commanded. Her neck and shoulders drooped suddenly. He pushed her back gently on the bed, and her heavy breasts sprawled to either side of her chest. "Take a deep breath and let it out," he said. "It's time to relax and do the things you love to do."

Without opening her eyes, Melba squirmed her panties off and tossed them on the floor. She stuck her legs straight up in the air.

Phillips's hands grasped her ankles. They felt smooth, perhaps slightly oiled. "I want you to concentrate on the pleasure thoughts. I know you haven't forgotten how," he said softly.

She moaned.

"First, you will imagine the thousand velvety hands massaging and enveloping your toes and feet and crawling slowly down the ladder of your legs. . . . You are going deeper and deeper into relaxation with each and every breath you take. . . ."

He felt her legs start to sway, no more than an inch. His power had not diminished. Even prison had not affected his mastery.

Once again, by marshaling full and complete concentration, he would *will* events.

August 18

The stubby man with a black mustache pinned on his employee ID before passing the warehouse guard booth. The laminated card read:

> U.S. TREASURY DEPARTMENT OF ENGRAVING AND PRINTING
> Washington, D.C.
> Warehouse Fork-lift Truck Operator—All Access
> Ralph T. Smith (Midnight–8 A.M. shift)

He carried a metal lunch pail, which contained a pair of wire cutters and three sandwiches.

Melissa Diane (he loved the sound of the name) had been on his mind all day.

160

At his locker, Smith peeked at the picture in his wallet, as he had done before leaving his apartment. In the color photo she was dressed casually, in a beige tank top and jeans. He looked at the outline of her nipples; her healthy, strawberry-blonde hair; complexion clean, scrubbed, vital; brooding mouth; hips more bone than flesh. And she had been naked for him and taken him into her and done things he could never have asked her to do. She had given herself to him as a woman and called him "Honeybunch," with the lilt of her full-fledged stewardess's Southern accent.

The work buzzer sounded. He stuffed the photo in his back pocket and the wire cutters under his shirt into the Firmo belt. He had worn the Firmo belt since meeting Melissa. He needed to lose the spare tire. It was guaranteed to make fat simply fall off "without resorting to diet or exercise." When he told her he was wearing it, she had kissed him and stopped his embarrassment.

He had told her everything, even about the toupee. A love relationship should be built on a "house of love, not a house of cards," as Dear Abby might say.

He walked from the smelly locker room onto the vast concrete-and-steel warehouse floor. The foreman, a gaunt, middle-aged man with a protruding Adam's apple, was standing next to a yellow fork-lift truck, reading his clipboard.

"Ralphie, me boy," he said without looking up, "one hundred seventy-two pallets on the dock. They go to rotary press one, another twelve to the letterpress machine. That should do 'er for the shift." He made a mark on the clipboard. "Hear you're gettin' married," he said, tapping his nose with the pencil.

Smith smiled and hopped up behind the wheel of the yellow fork-lift.

"Glad to hear it. We worry about you guys over forty that don't take the plunge." The foreman laughed violently, forming his mouth into an O. He handed Smith the work sheet and loped across the warehouse to the office.

Why don't you jump in the lake, you big jerk? thought Smith. The foreman was a good example of why he didn't talk to the other workers very much. They were jerks, like the foreman. Big on jokes about other people. Ha ha ha.

When Melissa had introduced him to her brother Larry, he had enjoyed *his* jokes. Larry had class, like Melissa. Good family. And what he was going to do tonight was going to help them both. Larry would soon be his brother-in-law and his new boss in the new company.

All Larry needed was some genuine currency paper. A few sheets from one stack, out of the one hundred seventy-two giant stacks that were on the dock. He remembered Larry's exact words: "The paper they make money out of comes from a couple of private companies that have a monopoly on its production. They sell to the government, and no one else can enter the field. If I had a few sheets of the paper, I could analyze it and put it into production myself. I could make a bid for a portion of the Treasury Department's business." His remark had been strictly off the wall. No pressure.

It wasn't like Larry was some crook. Far from it. He stayed at the Hilton and dressed like a movie star. His business card said, "International Paper Incorporated, London, Los Angeles, Paris, and New York," and he paid for everything with a gold American Express card. He was a businessman with European-frame eyeglasses.

Smith drove the fork-lift across to the dock, as he had done for the past seven years, and scooped up a wooden pallet of paper. He pulled back the lift handle. The paper sheets were three by three and in stacks a foot high banded with baling wire.

Across the parking lot was his pickup truck, parked next to the security fence. The streetlight next to it had been out for a week.

He looked at his watch. He had worked alone in the warehouse for years, and prided himself on the fact that he could judge time by how many pallets he had moved to the press area. He was halfway through. Three-fifty-seven exactly. Three minutes to the guard's shift change. The foreman would be in the press area for the first run.

It was time.

Smith thought of the picture in his wallet as he climbed off the fork-lift. He pulled sheets of paper from the middle of the pallet. He rolled them together and fastened them with rubber bands he took from his pocket. Trotting, he went down the

162

loading-dock steps into the darkness. At the fence, he crawled onto a stack of empty wooden pallets and dropped the paper over into the bed of his pickup truck. The thud was deafening.

He jumped down and ran back into the warehouse. His heart slamming back and forth inside his chest, he looked back to the parking lot. No guards. Everything okay. So far.

Removing the wire cutters from his Firmo girdle, he snapped the baling wire on the pallet and got back on the fork-lift. He lifted the pallet neatly, both forks even as possible, being careful not to spill the loose stack of paper. He drove slowly across the cement warehouse floor and into the press area. The presses were grinding awake. He moved along the giant rotary press to the paper intake, where loose stacks of paper waited to be fed into presses that transformed them into money.

The foreman was talking animatedly to the lead pressman; their backs were to him.

Smith pushed the lift level all the way forward and dumped the entire pallet of paper onto the floor, knocking it and two other stacks of paper into a jumble under and around the enormous press. He let out his breath.

"First time I've seen ya do that, Ralphie boy! What a mess! You must have your mind on something else." The foreman's mouth made another O and laugh sounds came out again. He strolled to the fork-lift and leaned on the roll bar. "The problem is," he said, "this shit hasn't been counted. Now that it's mixed up with what has been counted, it would take me the rest of the night to figure it out."

Smith felt sweat under his synthetic hair. His mouth was dry.

"So here's what we do," the foreman continued. "I carry the shit as being counted and I makes my initials, Ralphie boy. The only way anything could happen is if the paper-mill count doesn't match with tomorrow's press count. But that hasn't happened in the past twenty-six years that I've been here, so why should it now? I'm an optimist, Ralphie boy. Gimme a smile, Ralphie. I'm takin' care of ya." A giggle came out of the O.

Smith smiled and took a deep breath. By initialing the count sheet, the foreman would take the blame for the missing paper. Thank God everything was going as planned.

Smith made sure he was the first to the parking lot after the

8:00 A.M. buzzer. At the pickup, he covered the paper with a paint tarp. His hands were shaking. He started the engine and drove out of the parking lot without even so much as a glance at the guard shack.

Driving against the rush-hour traffic spilling out of the Virginia suburbs, he felt somehow fulfilled. What he had done, although a violation of rules, would bring benefit to those who were important to him: his new family.

Arriving at the Alexandria apartment house, he left the pickup on the street, as Larry had told him to do, and took the elevator.

In his small, neat apartment, he flicked on a radio on the bathroom sink as he hurriedly washed and dashed cologne under his arms. He shaved carefully. Melissa would arrive any minute. She had a layover. He felt a tightening, firming, in his groin.

A knock sounded. He quickly wiped his face with a towel and trotted to the door. He opened it. It was Melissa, in skin-tight jeans and a bursting blouse. She came in the door past him. "Melissa," he said, smelling her perfume. She turned, eyes fearful, and looked back.

Larry stepped in and doubled-locked the door.

"Larry, what's wrong? The paper is in the truck," Smith said.

"I know," Larry said. He pulled an automatic from the pocket of his cashmere sports coat and snatched a decorative pillow off the sofa. Melissa's hands flew to her ears.

The pillow came toward Smith's face. "Pop." The floor crashed into the back of his head. Nausea. The smell of perfume and carbide. Other sounds. He was deep under black water.

$/2

The well-furnished apartment was decorated with an oil of Fujiyama and a Picasso print from the National Gallery of Art retail store.

Charles Carr stood up from the tiny breakfast table. Amiko tried to help him into his coat, but he shrugged into it himself and turned to face her finely chiseled Oriental features, framed by a shag cut. She wore a shortie nightgown that could have been a child's size. Wrinkles were only around her eyes.

"Don't forget your gun," she said, pointing to the mantel. Her voice was gentle, devoid of intensity.

"I wouldn't want to forget that," he said. "I might need it to shoot one of the wise-ass trainees in my counterfeiting investigation class." He clipped the holster to his belt.

"I have two tickets to the Kennedy Center for tonight," Amiko said. "A customer gave them to me." She picked up the breakfast dishes and carried them to the sink. "He was drinking and showing off. 'Ah so,' Charlie Chan jokes, the whole bit. Typical Washington cornball. Before he left he gave tickets to all the cocktail waitresses. I think he felt embarrassed." She turned on the water.

Carr walked to the door. "I'll pick you up at seven," he said.

Amiko came to the door and stood on tiptoe to kiss him good-by, her arms reaching around his waist with abandon. She straightened his tie. "You should buy new clothes," she said.

"You're not working undercover in Los Angeles any more."

Carr nodded without smiling. "See you tonight," he said on his way out the door. He took the elevator to the street.

He would not take a taxi to the Treasury Building, because he needed the exercise. He looked at his watch and realized that walking would make him late again. In fact, he had been a few minutes late to his Special Agent Training Division job every day since arriving in Washington a year ago. He figured that by now the pencil pushers had stopped gossiping about it, just as they had stopped gossiping about his disciplinary transfer from Los Angeles.

He jogged across Scott Circle on a yellow light and headed down the street toward Lafayette Park. He was breathing hard.

Such exercise certainly wouldn't have caused him to breathe hard more than twenty years ago, when he was sworn in as a U.S. Treasury agent, fresh out of the army, lean and mean. His years had been spent on field duty in New York, Chicago, and Los Angeles; hassling counterfeiters, passers, money men, and paper pimps. Once, he had even been asked to update the section in the manual on undercover operations. Not a spectacular career, perhaps, but at the Treasury Building young agents avoided the high-ranking pencil pushers and came to him for advice on making buys, setting up surveillances.

Like a lot of Treasury agents, Carr was a man of medium height and weight, with no distinguishing characteristics. Lots of people had grayish-brown hair that could use a trim and scattered broken blood vessels high on the cheeks. His shirt collar was out of fashion. He could have been a carpenter dressed for Saturday night. The darkness under his cop's eyes gave him a solemn appearance.

Perhaps it would have been easier if he could admit that he was just killing time at the scrap-heap training job until retirement. Twenty-five years at fifty-percent highest pay. He had six months to go, six more months of war stories.

A Volkswagen pulled up at the curb next to him, and a man leaned across the front seat. "Want a ride?" The young agent had freckles and razor-cut hair.

"No thanks, George. I can use the walk," Carr said with a wave.

"Just heard your old partner Delgado's got the chief inspector job in the bag. They'll announce it today." The Volkswagen drove off.

Carr suddenly got his wind back. He knew if his pal Delgado got a promotion, he would be in a position to approve a transfer back to the field for him. He suddenly felt like running to work.

He crossed Pennsylvania Avenue and took the steps of the massive Treasury Building two at a time. He flashed his badge to the guard at the door of the gray edifice and headed down a high-ceilinged hallway. The whole building smelled like musty paper. After all, that's what it should smell like, he thought, hundreds of people writing, typing, initialing, and filing, approving memos about various things that people should be left to figure out for themselves.

Yesterday they had distributed a two-page memo on how not to waste paper. Everyone in the Enforcement Bureau threw the memo away and spent an hour or so discussing what a waste of paper the memo had been.

Carr was speaking from behind a podium. He was facing a group of athletic-looking men dressed in white shirts wilted uniformly because of the Washington humidity. Behind him, above a green chalkboard, hung a two-foot-high replica of a Treasury agent's gold badge. It was flanked by official photographs of the shaved-head chief of enforcement and his sallow deputy. Neither was smiling.

Carr was nearing the end of his pat lecture on investigative tactics. Strictly the party line: "call the U.S. attorney when in doubt," "always attempt to corroborate information from informants," "don't take chances"—advice he knew would soon be forgotten by those who would turn into successful T-men. The others would obey the rules, follow any and all advice, learn to write the driest and most guarded of reports, and, like other bureaucrats, be hard as hell to find on Friday afternoons.

He finished the lecture and glanced at his notes. When he looked up, a young man in the front row raised his hand. Carr nodded.

"What's the *biggest* difference between now and when you were a junior agent?" he asked.

Carr was silent for a moment, while he stepped from behind the podium. "It's the same now as it was twenty years ago," he said. "It's the same bad guys doing the same bad things. They just dress a little different now. In the old days it *was* easier to search a house—but we had no M.O. computers. It *was* easier to get a confession—but we were short on cars and radios." He rubbed his chin. "It's the same. . . . Here are some tips that'll make your work easier. One, never forget that everything a crook does will be in his own interest. There will never be an exception. It's just the way they are. Two, remember that on the street it pays to make more friends than enemies. Three, never lie in court. Even though the lawyers and the defendants lie, don't give in to the temptation. Why? Because in the end the judge probably isn't going to send anyone to jail anyway. In other words, why commit rape on a mermaid?" Everyone laughed. Carr made a little salute, which meant that the class was over. The men filed out of the room.

He followed them out the door and down the hall to a windowless office and sat down at a desk. It was cluttered with training photographs of counterfeit money and blow-ups of serial numbers.

There was a note clipped to his pen set: "See Inspector Delgado—ASAP." He grabbed it and headed out the door.

He walked directly into Delgado's office. Though they were the same age, Delgado looked much older. Maybe it was the white hair. His Castilian features were clean: thin lips, aquiline nose. A tall, spare man. His dark pin-striped suit fit perfectly. A Mexican banker. Only the saddle-soap complexion gave any hint of stress.

Carr stuck out his hand. "Congratulations. I just heard."

Delgado stood up. "Thanks, *amigo*." They shook hands. He walked around his cluttered desk and closed the door. They sat down in the chairs in front of the desk.

Delgado leaned forward, elbows on knees, hands gesturing. "The whole thing happened fast," he said. "That pencil pusher Norbert Waeves, your friendly agent-in-charge in Los Angeles, had the promotion sown up until last night. It was down to the wire. His hook was his wife. She was a secretary on Capitol Hill for years and got some strings pulled for him. The chief felt the pressure. He swung it to me last night, using Affirmative Action as a justification. That way nobody can fault his judgment. He'll just say he was following federal guidelines for equal opportunity and promoting a Mexican. No senator or congressman would touch that with a ten-foot pole." Delgado smiled and rubbed his hands together. "I told you working the streets of Los Angeles is nothing compared to the treachery here." He leaned back in his chair. His expression became reflective.

"The only drawback is that now I have to wear the dunce cap for getting a 'minority first' promotion," Delgado said. "But it was either that or the incompetent No Waves Waeves gets the prize, transfers back to D.C., and screws me into retirement. With my wife dead now, I don't know what I'd do if I had to retire." He ran his hand through his hair and stood up. He picked up a report from his desk. "As my first duty as the new chief inspector, I hereby assign you to be in charge of this case." He presented Carr the paper with a flourish.

Carr read it. The case title block was "Paper Shortage at the Bureau of Engraving and Printing." "Probably the usual mix-up," he said. "Somebody must have added some figures wrong at the paper mill."

Delgado pursed his lips and shook his head. "No," he said. "They've recounted six times . . . even measured the rolls at the mill. I've been sitting on this for three days, to see if they could come up with the mistake. No such luck. And there's a warehouse man who's been missing since the bad count. His name is on the poop sheet. If there *is* a mistake, I want you to resolve it *today*. If some paper really is missing, for the first time ever, dig in, and report only to me. We'll have to keep it from the *Washington Post*."

Carr strolled, almost swaggered, down the hall to his cluttered desk in the back room of the Training Division office. He dug his handcuffs out of the bottom drawer and hung them over his belt. His pants hung right for the first time in a year.

The sound of the presses was deafening. After four hours in the clackety din of the auditorium-sized structure that was the Bureau of Engraving and Printing, Carr wondered out loud how they stood the noise.

"That's why I usually work the night shift," said the foreman. He was leaning on an idle paper cutter. His Adam's apple bobbed arhythmically as he spoke. "The presses only run during the day. We just warm 'em up on the graveyard shift."

The man's eyes were red, and Carr thought he had been too cooperative while showing him the warehouse setup, the count sheets and delivery logs. He kept hurrying too much, handling the sheets, taking too many steps as he bustled from one part of the place to another pointing things out.

"How about a cup?" Carr said.

The foreman led him into the warehouse office and closed the door to the printing-press noise. He poured coffee and dropped two dimes in a glass jar. "Don't say I never bought you nothin'," he said. A staccato laugh.

Carr sat down at a desk and sipped coffee. He read through the count sheets again.

The foreman picked at his fingernails.

After a few minutes Carr pointed to a mark on one of the sheets. "Where were you when you counted this stack?" he said.

The foreman leaned over the desk like an ostrich. "On the loading dock," he said.

Carr handed him the count sheet. "Are you sure those are your initials?"

The other man's Adam's apple made a sort of false start. "They look like my initials," he said.

Carr took a sip of coffee. "Yes or no?"

The foreman backed away from the desk. "Yes."

"How do you know you were on the loading dock?" Carr said.

"Because that's where I make my count every night."

Carr shuffled through the sheets without looking up. "Who saw you make the count?"

"I don't know," the foreman said. He sat down on the edge of the chair in front of the desk. He picked his fingernails again.

"Smith works on the dock. Did he see you make the count?"

The foreman stopped picking his fingernails and looked at his hands. "I don't know," he said.

170

"If he works on the dock, he would have *had* to see you, right?" Carr said.

"I guess."

Carr put down the count sheets. "When I talk to him," he said, "I'm sure he can clear up the problem of the stacks falling over that one of the pressmen told me about." He crunched the empty paper cup in his hand and tossed it past the foreman's face into a wastebasket. The foreman flinched. Carr smiled at him.

"Can I go now?" said the foreman.

"You're covering up," Carr said.

The foreman's Adam's apple lifted, bobbed, and sank.

"I know it and you know it," Carr said. "I don't think you had anything to do with heisting the paper. . . . You're too close to retirement. I'm not sure exactly what you did at this point, but here's my best guess. You made your initials on a count sheet at some point without actually counting and you're afraid to admit it." He loosened his necktie. "And that is a mistake," he said. "It makes you involved in the theft of the paper. The reason for the count sheets is to place blame when paper is missing. You made your initials on the last count. You get the blame."

The foreman pointed a finger. "Don't try to pin this thing on me! I've been here for twenty-six years! You're questioning *me* and Ralph Smith hasn't shown up for work in three days. Go talk to him!"

"Why should I?" Carr said. "I can write my report right now. You are at fault."

The foreman's mouth became a straight line. He took a pencil out of his pocket and tapped on his nose. "What if I did, just for instance, *did* make a mistake on the count sheet? What could happen to me?"

Carr leaned back in his chair. "You've been working for Uncle Sam's Civil Service for as long as I have," he said. "You tell me what happens to people who make mistakes."

The foreman looked at his bony hands for a few moments. "Usually nothing," he said. "Nobody wants to fill out all the disciplinary forms. Nobody wants to make enemies."

Carr stood up. He spoke in a subdued voice. "You tell me what happened and it'll be between you and me. I'll put in my report that the findings against you are inconclusive. That's a promise."

The foreman gulped. "And if I don't?"

Carr reached under his coat and pulled the handcuffs off his belt. He threw them on the desk. "Then just put these on your wrists, and I'll drive you down to the Washington field office and book you for theft of government property. I'll prove the case with the count sheets. The pressman will testify against you. He won't take the rap for anyone else."

The gaunt man rubbed his eyes. He spoke as if reading. "Smith tipped over an uncounted pallet in the press area and the paper went everywhere. I initialed the count sheet because I didn't want to spend hours counting the shit. Smith probably dumped the stack over on purpose, figuring that's what I would do. There. Ya happy now?"

Carr took the handcuffs off the desk and hung them back on his belt. "What kind of a guy is Smith?" he said.

"An oddball, a loner . . . He's been here for years and he never says shit. He even eats lunch alone . . . and he's a bachelor. One of the pressmen told me that he hangs out at a bar called the Greenhouse on M Street. It's a singles joint. He goes there every weekend."

"Let's see his locker," Carr said.

In the locker room the foreman held open a large brown paper sack and jabbered something about Smith never having "fit in" at work. "He never even joined the bowling team," he said.

Carr removed the items from the arnica-smelling locker delicately, one by one, and dropped them in the sack. He noted each item in a pocket-size notebook. The list read:

1. One roll adhesive tape (toupee)
2. Matchbook—Greenhouse Bar and Grill, Washington, D.C.
3. Airlines flight schedule with notations
4. Three copies *Midnight Globe* newspaper (underlined phrases)
5. Paperback book *Tillie's Lesson* (porno) (underlined phrases)

172

6. Two letters from Mrs. Ralph T. Smith, Sr., Waukegan, Illinois (underlined phrases)
7. One pipe and tobacco pouch
8. One pair work shoes
9. One shirt
10. One pair pants and belt
11. Magazine clipping—advertisement for "Firmo super weight loss belt"

When the locker was empty, Carr closed it. He took the bag from the foreman.

"He was supposed to be getting married soon," said the foreman.

Carr took out a pen and wrote his initials and the date on the bag. "Who's the lucky girl?" he said.

"Nobody knows. He had a picture in his wallet of a real doll. Young gal, a strawberry blonde. One of the pressmen asked him about her and he said it was his fiancée," the foreman said.

"Where does Smith live?"

The foreman handed Carr a small white index card. "Here's a copy of his emergency notification card," he said. "It's got his address and phone number on it. I called the number for the past three days. No answer."

Carr folded the paper sack and walked toward the door.

"Thanks a lot," said the foreman. His tone was uncertain.

"Yeah, sure," Carr said.

Smith's apartment house in Alexandria reminded Carr of his own a few miles away. A gray functional building with mailboxes that never locked properly and washing machines on every other floor. The street-entrance glass door was operated by a buzzer system. Carr pushed a button marked "Manager."

"Yes," said a woman.

"U.S. Treasury agent. May I come in?"

"Wait there."·

A petite woman without make-up came to the glass door and made him hold up his badge before she opened it. He stepped in. Her college sweatshirt and rolled-up jeans looked clean, new. She had close-cropped mousy hair with bangs that met the tops of oversized eyeglasses. "Who do you want to ask questions about?" she said. "Seems like a day can't go by without some G-man coming here to ask questions. Everyone in Washington, D.C., has some sort of a security clearance. The whole thing turns me off. People checking on other people." She took a hands-on-hip pose.

"I'm interested in Ralph Smith. Have you seen him in the past three days?"

"Who?"

"Short, chubby guy with black hair," Carr said.

She held a hand to her cheek. "Oh, yes. Eighth floor," she

said finally. "What's it about?" she added . Her tone was sharp.

"He's missing."

"From who?"

"From work. Do you have a master key?" Carr said.

"Of course. I'm the manager." She folded her arms across her chest. "But if you think I'm going to let you in his apartment, you are crazy. That's a violation of his rights. For all I know, you are working for the CIA. You could be Gordon Liddy or something."

Carr used his best stroking voice. "If you and I could just go up and check to see if he is okay, I would really appreciate it. He might be sick and can't answer the phone." He stepped behind her and pushed the elevator button.

The woman balanced her elbow in her palm and rubbed her cheek. She stepped on the elevator with him. On the way up she said something about the scourge of narcotics agents on college campuses.

The elevator door opened. The drab hallway was empty. She pointed to a door. "That's his apartment, but I've decided not to open the door for you under any circumstance." She folded her arms across her chest again. "Someone has got to make a stand against these government intrusions. I'm fully within my rights."

Carr approached the door and knocked loudly. No answer. He knocked again. Suddenly he dropped to the floor and put his nose to the bottom of the door.

"What are you doing?" the woman said. She stepped back.

Carr stood up. "Give me the key," he said. *"Right now."*

The woman kept her arms tightly folded. *"No!* I'm not afraid to say no to government spies!" she shrieked. "This isn't Nazi Germany!"

Carr took a step back from the door, lifted his right foot, and with a powerful thrust kicked the door wide open, splintering the jamb.

The woman jumped in front of the door with arms outstretched. "I won't let you in! You are a fascist pig!" she screamed.

An odor, suspended powerfully in warm air, reached out to

them. Carr pulled a handkerchief from his pocket and held it over his nose.

The woman's nose twitched, and she jumped away from the door, gagging. The smell of death filled the hallway. "What is it? What is it?" she screamed.

Carr pressed the handkerchief tightly over his nose and mouth. He stepped inside. Smith's body was on the living-room floor, his head framed in a crusty red ring. His mouth was open, goldfishlike. Carr could tell from the greenish, bloated features that putrefaction had set in. He knelt next to the body. There were entry wounds in the face and the head.

The woman still stood back from the door.

Carr took the handkerchief from his mouth. "Go call the police," he said.

The gagging woman disappeared.

He stood up. Oddly, the living room reminded him of his own. Brandy snifter full of book matches, drink coasters, cheap ashtrays; cheap, durable furniture of the kind a bachelor would collect, some framed photos of antique cars. The corduroy pillow next to the body had holes and powder burns.

Using the handkerchief, Carr opened the living-room windows. It didn't help with the smell.

The bedroom was lean, a single bed. On the dresser a photograph of a bulky, white-haired matron, signed "Love, Mother." Next to it a frame without a photo.

The bathroom had only men's items.

Carr went back into the living room. He knelt again by the body and reached into the back pocket. He removed a wallet. No photo of the fiancée. A parking ticket, work ID, driver's license, insurance card, twenty-seven dollars. He replaced the wallet in the dead man's pocket.

Two young Alexandria detectives in plaid polyester coats were the first to arrive. Carr told them that Smith had been missing from work at the Treasury Department and it was routine to have someone stop by the residence. He gave them a card and began knocking on apartment doors.

Just as Carr had guessed, the neighbors knew nothing of Ralph T. Smith except that he was single and had a government

176

job of some kind, like everyone else in Washington, D.C.

A few of those on his floor knew his name, and some even recognized his description. "He doesn't even nod when you walk by him in the hall. He turns his head so he won't have to nod," said a pimply WAC two doors down.

As for those on other floors, Ralph T. Smith could have lived in Addis Ababa for all they knew.

Carr ended up at the manager's apartment. She was sitting on the sofa, arms hugging knees. He asked to use the phone. The woman nodded to the kitchen table. Carr sat down, picked up the phone, and dialed.

"Hello, Del," he said.

"What ya got, Charlie?"

Carr cupped a hand over the mouthpiece. "Well, it happened for the first time."

"How much?" Delgado said.

"About twelve sheets."

"How?"

"Looks like they conned a warehouse worker. When he made the grab, they snuffed him, and took the paper."

"Damn! Any leads?"

"No good ones," Carr said.

"I'll wait in my office until you come back."

The phone clicked.

"Who is responsible for paying for the broken apartment door?" said the manager. She was staring at the wall.

Carr walked past her and out the door.

The woman followed him. "Why are you ignoring me?" she said.

The bar was in a storefront on a corner a few blocks from where herds of blabby civil servants waited for buses every night.

Carr got out of the government sedan and walked across the bustling street and in the front door. The place was well lit.

Inside, pasty-faced secretaries and hair-over-the-ears joggers stood back to back, jiggling cocktail ice and flaming Virginia

Slims with throwaway lighters. Hanging brass pots full of plastic greenery and walls decorated wtih replica movie posters provided breath-mint ambiance.

Carr wormed his way through elbows, breasts, and nervous cigarette puffs to the end of the bar.

"Yes, sir. What'll ya have?" said the bartender, a well-built young man with a trimmed beard and clear blue eyes.

Carr flashed his badge in a cupped hand. "Let's talk outside," he said.

"Yes, sir," said the bartender. His tone was courteous. He motioned, and a man carrying a tray of glasses put them down and ducked behind the bar.

Carr led the way through the front door.

Outside, the bartender wiped his hands on the front of his pants.

Carr handed him Smith's employee-card photo. "You know him?" he said.

The bartender stared at the photo and gave a few blinks. "He comes in on weekends," he said. "Once in a while on a week night." He handed the photo back.

"When was the last time?" Carr said. He put the photo in his coat pocket.

"Few weeks ago, I think."

"Who was he with?" Carr said.

The bartender shook his head. "I don't remember."

"Who are his friends?"

The bartender took a comb from his back pocket. Making little tugs, he combed his beard. "None of the regulars," he said. "The guy just sits and drinks. Stares at the broads, never makes a move. Staggers out at 2:00 A.M. Never causes trouble. Sometimes he gets friendly after the tenth drink or so, but by then it's midnight and all the broads are taken." He stroked downward on his mustache. "His name is Ralph."

"Thanks," Carr said. "That's all I . . ."

The bartender snapped his fingers. "Wait a sec! The last time he was in, he *was* with a broad. She drank Southern Comfort. Dynamite-looking broad. A real talker. I think she was a stewardess. She used some of the jargon."

178

Carr took out a notebook and pen. "How would you describe her?" he said.

"Five foot five, one twenty, strawberry blonde, early twenties. She's been around some, you know; seen some action. I could tell. She was probably just fishing the little fat man for drinks."

Carr wrote in the notebook. "Probably," he said.

"What'd the guy do?" asked the bartender. He turned his head and blew on the comb.

"Nothing. It's just a security check," Carr said. He put the notebook away.

The bartender nodded with a wolfish grin. "I've heard that one before." He wiped the comb on his sleeve and put it back in his pocket.

Carr smiled. "I've told that one before," he said. "Thanks for your time."

He looked both ways and trotted across the street to his sedan. Someone whistled.

"There's something else," yelled the bartender, his hands cupped around his mouth. "She had big tits!" He clapped his hands to his chest.

"Thanks again!" Carr yelled back.

The D.C. air was wet and sultry—firefly weather.

Carr knocked on the after-hours door at the rear of the Treasury Building and waited. He looked at his watch—8:00 P.M.

A blue-uniformed guard with a sweat-ringed shirt opened the door. He nodded at Carr's badge.

Carr dialed Amiko's number from a phone in an empty office. He felt light-headed. He had forgotten to eat all day. He let the telephone ring ten times. No answer. He continued down the musty hallway to Delgado's office.

Delgado drank the last drop from a pint milk carton and tossed the carton in the wastebasket. He spoke with white at the corners of his mouth. "Let's hear it! I've been sitting here stewing since you called." He wiped his mouth with the back of his hand.

Carr straddled a chair and recited the basic facts in investigative-report fashion.

Delgado rubbed his stomach. "That was the last carton of milk in that damn milk machine." He belched.

"Ulcer acting up?" Carr said.

Delgado nodded. His expression was bilious. "Okay. I want you to start from the beginning." He began making notes. "Number one, are you *sure* the paper is missing? Completely, one-hundred-percent *positive?*"

"Yes," Carr said. "I checked every count sheet. There are twelve sheets missing. All we have to go on is a description of a female who may be a stewardess. Unfortunately, the description of the gal fits just about every stewardess who ever handed out a barf bag."

Delgado put down his pencil. "I have my own ideas, but I want to hear yours first. How do you see the whole thing?"

"My guess is that Smith was just a mark," Carr said. "He was spotted by somebody who wanted a load of security paper. They got next to him."

"And whoever it was went to a lot of trouble," Delgado said. "It was a professional job." The phone rang. Delgado picked it up. "Yes, sir. Yes, sir," he said. "The special agent is briefing me at this very moment. Yes, we have established that the paper is definitely missing." He gulped. "Yes, sir. I'll call you in the morning with my operations plan. Good night, sir." He put down the receiver. "The chief," he said, rubbing his stomach with both hands. "Okay," he continued, "you've just conned or blackmailed a Treasury employee out of some security paper. To cover your trail, you empty a clip into his head. What's next?"

Carr turned his hand like a crank.

"Print what?"

"Securities," Carr said. "He didn't get enough paper to make currency worth his while. Treasury notes or bills, something easy to fence or cash through a bogus bank account."

"Who does the printing?" Delgado said.

"No amateurs. I'd get a pro, who had done it before. I wouldn't want to take a chance with an amateur. He might waste some of the paper on starter runs or messy plates."

"Give me some names," Delgado said.

Carr took off his jacket and hung it on the back of his chair. He counted fingers. "The Red Whale, Grady Parks, The Great

Caruso, or good old Mr. Greenjeans Freddie Roth. No one else is good enough."

Delgado picked up a phone and ordered the arrest files on each man from the Index Room.

It was almost eleven before Carr and Delgado determined that thrice-convicted Albert C. Whale, aka The Red Whale, was still in maximum security at Huntsville and that Enrico Caruso, aka The Great Caruso, was awaiting sentencing on his sixth counterfeiting conviction in the New York Federal House of Detention.

Delgado flipped rapidly through a thick file. "The file says that Grady Parks has a print shop in L.A."

"Freddie Roth is probably in the L.A. area, too," Carr said, flipping pages in a file. "Says here 'whereabouts unknown, possibly residing in Los Angeles.' "

Delgado tossed a file down on the desk. "I want you to head for Los Angeles and find out what these people are doing. We'll handle this as a headquarters' case. Report to me directly. Keep in mind that good ol' No Waves is still the special agent-in-charge in Los Angeles. Because it's his district, he has the prerogative of picking a partner to work with you out there. No Waves hates me and will do everything to screw up your investigation to make me look bad. He thinks that if I get one more promotion, I'll have the clout to force him to retire; and he is right."

Carr nodded. He stood up and put on his coat.

"We need to make this case," Delgado said. "If we don't, we'll both end up shopping for fishing poles. It's as simple as that."

It was almost midnight when Carr knocked at Amiko's door.

"Who's there?" she said.

"Me."

She opened the door barefoot, wearing a strapless white evening dress. A hairbrush was in her hand.

"Sorry about standing you up. I was real busy," Carr said. He couldn't decide whether to step in.

Amiko pulled the door open farther. He went in. She closed the door without the usual latching of the door chain.

"When you didn't come, I went by myself," she said.

"What was the play?" Carr said. He felt stupid for having come over.

Amiko walked to the refrigerator. *"Long Day's Journey into Night."*

Carr slid his hands into his pockets. "How did you like it?" he said.

"It was sad," Amiko said, opening the refrigerator door. "A whole family was messed up." She took out an open bottle of white wine and poured two glasses. She handed one to Carr. "I don't think I want you to stay here tonight," she said gently, staring into her wineglass. "You stood me up. It hurt my feelings." Without looking at him, she walked to the sofa and sat down.

Carr took a sip of wine. "I'm leaving tomorrow on a case," he said. "I just wanted to stop and say good-by."

"How long will you be gone?" she said, her voice barely audible.

"I don't know exactly," Carr said. He looked at the door and tried to think of something to say on his way out.

Amiko sat quietly for a moment. She walked to the door, fastened the chain latch, and turned off the light. Then she went into the bedroom.

They undressed and got into bed. Amiko kissed his cheek. She fell asleep with her hand touching his.

Being careful not to wake her, Carr reached across to the nightstand and set the alarm.

In the morning darkness Amiko woke him, her tiny hands and mouth working feverishly. Soon he was erect and breathing hard. She was under him and he felt her fingernails on his back. With her eyes closed, she strained to meet his passionate kisses. Finally he was spent, and lying on his back.

As his breathing and perspiration subsided, Amiko rested her head on his shoulder.

Suddenly she spoke in a clear voice, as if she had practiced the statement. "When you come back from your trip, I don't want to see you any more. I'm sorry."

She got out of bed and locked herself in the bathroom.

Carr dressed and left.

• • •

Carr was in his bedroom. He had been trying to pack for over an hour.

His weathered suitcase was sprawled open in the middle of an unmade bed. The bedroom itself had nothing on the walls except wallpaper; Amiko had called it a cell more than once. He rummaged through a dresser drawer for socks that matched. He found one Argyle inside an army garrison cap he had never been able to throw away. The cap still had the silver dollar sewn in behind the parachute emblem (for use as a weapon to "snap a man's eye out," as the barroom brawlers used to say).

Though Carr had never snapped any eyes out, more than twenty years earlier he had killed North Koreans, two he was sure of, and received the Bronze Star. The medal itself, along with a gold ring that had belonged to his mother, and a rubber-banded box containing photos of such things as people waving cocktails at retirement parties and armed agents posing around green-inked printing presses was somewhere in one of the large boxes in the corner of the room. If not unpacking such items was a subconscious wish to get transferred back to a field office, then so be it.

Having recovered ten usable pairs of socks, he closed the drawer.

From the nightstand, he removed a battered electric clock, an ankle holster, and a small flashlight. He tossed them in the suitcase and slammed it shut.

He lugged the suitcase into the living room, hesitating for a moment in front of a small bookcase. It contained a stack of criminology journals, all the novels of James Jones, and a few book-club selections he had paid for rather than return. Probably won't have time to read, he thought. He continued across the room and set the suitcase down next to the chrome-legged kitchen table.

He opened the refrigerator and took out an almost-full carton of milk. He poured it into the sink.

On the way out the door he pushed the "Listen" button on a telephone-answering device. The machine buzzed. Sally's voice said: "I just got your message. How about dinner at my place when you get in to L.A.?" The machine buzzed again. A man's voice said: "SAIC Norbert Waeves here. I want a personal briefing before you begin any investigation in the Los Angeles district. I've assigned an agent to pick you up at the airport." The recorder clicked. "This is Delgado. No Waves is making a push for control of your investigation in Los Angeles. Don't go for it. Refer him to me. Beware of the agent he assigns you as a partner. . . . Be sure to erase this tape." The tape recorder stopped.

Carr caught a cab in front of the apartment house. On the way to Dulles Airport he asked the driver to stop by a laundry near the Treasury Building. The four white shirts he picked up barely fit into his suitcase.

Larry drove the rented Chevrolet carefully, watching the speed limit, keeping an eye on the rearview mirror.

The view was of a brown desert horizon cluttered only by sterile sagebrush and telephone lines. The dark morning chill had just given way to glowy, back-of-the-neck sun warmth.

A sign: WELCOME TO CALIFORNIA. Beyond the sign was a jumble of red flashing lights, flares, and automobile wreckage. Larry slowed down into a line of cars inching up to a California highway patrolman in a beige uniform.

Without taking his eyes off the road, Larry grabbed the .32 automatic from the glove compartment and shoved it under the strawberry-blonde wig on the seat.

Melba Rivers was startled awake. She grabbed the dashboard. "Where are we? That's a cop. Mercy Jesus!"

"I want you to sit back and be calm. Don't say a word." Larry spoke to the windshield.

The uniformed man motioned cars to pass by the wreckage one by one. Larry slowly pulled up next to him. The officer looked in the window.

"Going to L.A.?" he said.

"Yes, sir," Larry said. "Heading for Disneyland."

The officer smiled and stared at Melba's bulging sweater for a moment. "Have a nice time," he said, and waved them on.

Melba exhaled fiercely and leaned back again. "How long before we get there?" she said.

"Couple of hours." Larry stepped on the gas. He adjusted the rearview mirror and rubbed a hand across his stubbled chin. As well as a shave, he needed a shampoo and a comb-out. After three twelve-hour days of driving, he had a greasy look, and it bothered him. It was the look of lifers, stickup men, and car thieves, rather than that of a man who could use his head, his wits; a man who at thirty-three had proved that the pen was mightier than the sword. He put the .32 back into the glove compartment.

Melba arched back on the seat with her legs in a comfortable knees-outward spread. She closed her eyes. "I hate L.A.," she said.

"Why?"

"On the circuit, the month in L.A. is always the worst. No big tippers, like Vegas and Reno. They always argue price . . . as if fifty bucks was going to break their balls. . . . One john used to bring a little bag of toys with him, a real kink. He used to have me shove a little toy car up his ass right before he would come. Even *he* used to argue price. Mercy!"

Larry was in a road trance. Melba's words were just sounds: fad phrases, repetition, the communications of a parakeet.

"You know, when I met you for the first time I really believed you were some kind of a big businessman. Being in the penthouse suite at the Hilton and all. In fact, when I got the call from the bellhop, I was expecting to see some fat old salesman, as usual. Funny how we just sort of ended up together."

"Whatsat?" he said.

"As usual, you're not listening to me. Mercy."

Nothing was said for at least a half hour. The white highway line dipped and twisted through brushy desert foothills and the sleepy straightaways of Cajon Pass, finally blending into a bustling freeway with signs saying Los Angeles.

Melba spoke with her eyes closed, leaning back in the seat. "I want to know something," she said.

"Uh-huh."

"After we took the guided tour at the Bureau of Engraving

and Printing, remember how we watched the employees walking out after work?"

Larry grunted. Signs pointed toward the Hollywood Freeway. "What I want to know is how you picked Ralphie from the others. Why him?"

"It's all a matter of psychology," Larry said. "He fit the right profile."

Melba opened her eyes with a puzzled look, and closed them again. "Mercy," she said.

Larry left Melba sleeping in a Van Nuys Boulevard motel room and drove directly to a bowling alley less than a mile away. Located in a shopping mall, the bowling alley had a marquee over the front entrance. It read:

IN THE WINNERS' LOUNGE
DR. EMIL KREUZER—MASTER HYPNOTIST
THREE SHOWS NIGHTLY

The rest of the shopping mall, like the thousand others in Southern California, comprised a beauty parlor, a liquor store, and a pizza shop.

Larry walked into the bowling alley and found the door to the Winners' Lounge in the corner next to some ball racks. Only half the tables in the dimly lit bar were occupied. People were drinking beer from bottles. On a tiny stage, three men and three women sat in hard-backed chairs with hands in laps, chins relaxed on chests. Middle-depth trances, thought Larry.

Emil Kreuzer, a well-fed, middle-aged man with a vin rosé complexion, stood on the stage next to the row of chairs. He wore a purple tuxedo and a ruffled shirt. With a hand that held a microphone he pushed his oversized eyeglasses back up his nose. He held the microphone close to his lips. "And now, ladies and gentlemen, our talented stage volunteers will, *at* the count of three, play 'Moon River' for you like you have never heard it played before."

Larry had almost forgotten Kreuzer's on-again off-again German accent.

"One! Two! Three!" said the hypnotist. He snapped his fingers, and the group of zombies came to life. The women crooned a shower-voice rendition of "Moon River" to the accompaniment of the men cavorting about playing imaginary musical instruments.

The audience roared.

A fat man wearing a string tie fingered invisible guitar strings at crotch level. "Look at Marvin!" shouted someone in the audience.

When the guffaws began to subside, Kreuzer snapped his fingers three times. "Awake! Awake!" he commanded. The music crew stopped suddenly and stared dumbly at one another. The audience applauded.

Emil Kreuzer, the Master Hypnotist, shook hands with each of them as they ambled off the stage. He took a bow and the curtain dropped.

The audience filed out of the lounge with the usual boozy remarks of amazement at one another's antics. The comments reminded Larry of one-night stands: country-music bars and bowling-alley lounges from Bakersfield to Albuquerque and from Fresno to Burbank's Buckaroo Cocktail Lounge. Setting up the chairs, picking the best exhibitionists as volunteers, and filling in for Emil when he was too drunk to go on stage. Partners in show business.

The hypnotist rushed toward him from a door next to the stage and gave him a bear hug. Larry felt the older man's glasses poke roughly into his cheek. "Welcome back, my friend," Kreuzer said. He grasped Larry's shoulders. "I feel bad because I never visited you," he said. His hand touched his heart. "But I am too sentimental. I didn't want to see you in there. . . . Please understand me." He was looking directly into Larry's eyes.

"I didn't need anybody to hold my hand," Larry said.

"I know that. You're a little tiger. Glad to see you. Glad to see you." Kreuzer took him by the arm, and they walked through a door and up some steps onto the stage. He motioned him to a chair and they sat down. "That was the last show," he said. "All the shit kickers are heading home in their pickup trucks. Everything the same as before." He laughed, and caught his breath.

Larry looked around the stage. "Things don't seem too bad for you."

"Yes, but nothing is what it *seems*," Kreuzer said in mock seriousness. He thumbed his glasses back onto his nose.

They laughed.

"I've been dying of curiosity since you called," Kreuzer said. "I know you couldn't talk on the phone. . . . Are you going to come back on stage with me? Some of the groupies still ask about you. 'Course, I tell 'em you're on a European tour."

Larry shook his head. "Not enough money," he said.

"But I'm sure you haven't forgotten the side benefits . . . the pussy . . ."

"I have the *paper*," Larry interrupted. He stared into the other man's eyes.

Kreuzer's mouth dropped open. "You mean *the* paper," he whispered. "Like we always talked about?"

Larry nodded.

"Jesus. How did you . . . I mean, you've only been out a little over a month."

"I told you I would get it when I got out," Larry said. "Well, I'm out and I got it. You told me you had the banking connection I needed. Do you still have it?"

The stage door opened. A teen-ager with a wild hairdo and a nippled T-shirt came in. Her hips barely had an adolescent flare, and she wore braces. "Let's go home, Emil," she whined.

Kreuzer waved by moving his fingers. "You go out and wait in the car, *Liebchen*. I'll be right out," he said.

The girl frowned and left.

"What do you think?" Kreuzer nodded toward the door.

"Uh . . . real nice," Larry said.

Kreuzer smiled. He squeaked a thumb along fingertips. "I get her going and she juices right through her panties. . . . But excuse me, I didn't mean to interrupt your train of thought. What was the question?"

Using a distraction to give himself time to think, thought Larry. Same sneaky Emil. "The question is," Larry said, "do you have banking connections? I need an insider. If you can provide one, I'm prepared to offer you a piece of the action."

"Always strictly business with Scary Larry. You never did like small talk."

Larry maintained a poker face.

"Yes, old friend, I can provide a banker, but I think we should discuss certain details before we . . ."

"Eighty percent to me, twenty to you," Larry said. "I'll cover all expenses with what I have left over from the last caper. No other partners, and you can be there with me when the thing comes off. The way I've got it figured, we stand to walk away with over a million. Risk on your part is minimal." He stood up and rested a foot on the chair.

Kreuzer pulled off his bow tie and put it in his pocket. He loosened the collar of his ruffled shirt. "I've always been impressed with your mind, your capacity for details. As a hypnotist, you were a natural. My best student. I tell everyone that." He stared at the floor and rubbed his hands together nervously. "We've got to maintain better security this time. People are unpredictable. The sheer volume was what killed us last time." He looked at the ceiling. "But that doesn't mean it wasn't beautiful. Mr. Sucker gets a letter from his broker telling him to send in a grand to a special gold account; the timing with the newspaper stories of gold prices going up. Almost half of them took the bait. Definitely *creative* . . . And, like you used to say, *victimless crime.*" He shook his head. "If only we had recognized the problems before it was too late."

"Spilt milk," Larry said.

"Yes, yes, of course." Kreuzer shook his head ruefully. "But I still can't help but feel bad about the whole thing. Me getting probation and you going to the joint and all."

"That was my own fault," Larry said. "I should have copped a plea like you did instead of going to trial." He changed the subject. "Can you get me a banker?"

"Yes, of course."

The blonde teen-ager peeked in the door again. She was pouting. "Emil, I wanna go *home.*"

"Coming, *Liebchen,*" Kreuzer said. He stood up. "Meet me at the race track day after tomorrow; the clubhouse. We'll have a nice lunch." They shook hands.

Larry went down the steps and out the stage door.

The girl lingered on the stage while Kreuzer hung his tuxedo in a small closet. He changed into trousers without back pockets and a shirt that draped down enough to cover the middle-age

190

paunch. The cologne he dashed on his face and neck came out of a cylindrical bottle with gold letters that said "Machismo."

They walked out the back door into the well-lit parking lot. Kreuzer slid his arm around the girl's waist affectionately.

"When can we get married?" she said.

"You're only sixteen, *Liebchen* . . . *sweet* sixteen. We need a marriage license." He gave her firm rear end more of a feel than a pat.

"Before I ran away from home, I met this girl at school who told me phony IDs costed twenty dollars," she whined. "Can't you get me one?"

Kreuzer didn't answer the question, because Tommy Luchese pulled up next to him in a Lincoln Continental. Victor King was in the back seat.

"The man wants to talk," said Luchese out of the side of his mouth.

Kreuzer thought of running, screaming—anything to get away. "I've been trying to get in touch with you people," he said. He wanted to slug himself for letting his voice crack when he spoke.

"Get in," Luchese said. He had Neanderthal eyebrows, and the parking lot's artificial light gave his olive complexion an almost greenish tint.

Kreuzer took his hand off the girl's waist. "Go wait in the car, *Liebchen*. I'll be there in a minute."

She shook her head. "All you ever do is talk secrets. *Jeez*." She strutted away.

Luchese leaned across the front seat and opened the passenger door. Kreuzer got in.

A sleepy-eyed Victor King, fiftyish, with a cherubic face and a pompadour hair style, who looked more like a well-nourished headwaiter than a loan shark, was taking squirrel-sized bites from a candy bar. "You fucked me," he said before Kreuzer could turn around in the seat.

"I don't know what you . . ."

"Before you step on your meat, let me draw you a little picture." King spoke softly. "Six months ago you spent too much time betting the ponies at Santa Anita and got in over your head. You came to me as a friend. I took care of you. Because you were slow in making payments, I went further than that. I gave you a chance to work off the debt by carrying a bag for me. I did you a favor. I trusted you to make a few simple collections. I sent you to see the fat banker. The banker was making his payments real good up until the time I gave him to you. Then all I hear is 'the fat man is stalling . . . the fat man can't pay.' "

Kreuzer suddenly felt cold, as if he had fallen into ice water.

King continued. "But yesterday Tommy visits the fat man, and the fat man says he's been paying right along."

"I'm not going to lie to you," Kreuzer said. "I got the money from him. I needed it for something, but I'm good for it. I really didn't think you'd mind that much."

King nibbled on the candy. "Now you owe me forty grand. That's a lot of money for a guy who's lucky to make three fifty a week." He shoved the rest of the candy bar in his mouth and wiped his fingers on the wrapper. "Maybe it's true a gambler can never be trusted, huh? Izzat true, Emil? Izzat true, cock sucker?" King slammed a fist into Kreuzer's temple. His head bounced into the passenger window, and he saw black spots. Pain jackhammered to the top of his head. Luchese had a gun out. It was screwed into his ear. The car was filled with the sound of heavy breathing.

Victor King leaned against the front seat and whispered. His voice seemed to come from the gun barrel. "I want fifteen grand from you within ten days."

Luchese reached across and released the door handle. He shoved Kreuzer out of the car. The Lincoln drove off.

192

$/5

Larry Phillips pushed his way through the boisterous race-track crowd with Melba on his arm. She wore a pink form-fitting outfit that caused obvious second glances.

"Be nice to him," Larry said, "but he doesn't need to know anything about the caper except what *I* tell him. Do you understand?"

"Don't worry, I'm not *that* dumb. Mercy," Melba said.

Larry handed bills to a man in a booth. They took the elevator marked CLUBHOUSE ONLY.

He found Emil Kreuzer at a table next to an expanse of window with a view of stable boys leading horses around the infield. He introduced Melba.

Kreuzer stood up courteously and shook hands without taking his eyes off her chest. They sat down.

Kreuzer smiled. "I remember you," he said to Melba. "You were the one who delivered the phony stock certificates for us ... in our last project."

"I was Mrs. Brown from the brokerage house," Melba said proudly.

They all laughed.

Kreuzer leaned forward with a sincere expression. He looked Larry in the eye. "Things couldn't look better at this point," he said. "I've come up with an insider for us. . . . You'll have to handle him carefully. He's a gambling degenerate. A shaky guy

193

... but on the hook for enough money that he can't say no to anyone."

He stopped talking as the waiter approached. They ordered drinks.

Kreuzer continued. "He's a bank vice-president and rolled dice in Las Vegas with money from his vault, then tried to play catch-up with a few loans he got from the Vegas sharks. . . . At this point they own his *ass*. To pay off, he's been approving bad loans for them. There's no problem for the time being, but I'm sure you can guess the end of the story."

Larry nodded. "One day they stop making payments, and the roof falls in on his head."

"Right," Kreuzer said. He gulped from a drink and wiped his mouth with a napkin. "He ends up holding the bag," he whispered.

"Where do we come in?" Larry said.

"Victor King is the loan shark. He has agreed to let us use him. King is a power in Las Vegas these days. A heavy. He trusts me. We were in McNeil Island together fifteen years ago."

"Where do we go from here?" Larry said.

Kreuzer smiled. He wiped his mouth with a napkin again. "Always a step ahead of the game, Scary Larry. You amaze me sometimes." His eyes roamed Melba's torso. "Today at 6:00 P.M. he'll meet you in the bar at the Onion Dipper in Beverly Hills. He's a fat guy about thirty-five. His name is Arbogast, Bill Arbogast. You can be whoever you want." He pushed his glasses back onto his nose. "I had forgotten how attractive you were, Melba."

She smiled and looked at Larry.

Horns signaled the start of the racing ritual.

Larry sipped vodka and waited.

The cocktail lounge bustled: men in business suits swishing ice cubes and making their points, short-skirted waitresses rushing drinks and credit cards to and from a cushy bar. A happy-hour sign leaning against a bar mirror depicted a man with a pencil behind his ear peeking out of a martini glass.

Larry felt at home in the atmosphere. He was a merchant in the marketplace, a man who could deal from strength.

194

A fat man in a suit and tie was standing at the bar looking around. His hair was cut in a shag, which accentuated his bloated features; his drooping torso was that of a small-boned man who was not really meant to be fat, and he wore white loafers that looked like a pair Larry had seen advertised in *Playboy*.

Larry waved to the man. Expressionless, he came to the table and sat down.

Larry stuck out his hand. "Thanks for stopping by, Bill," he said.

"What do you people want from me now?" Arbogast spoke in a matter-of-fact tone.

Larry pulled his hand back and picked up his drink. "Just a small favor," he said.

Arbogast looked at the palms of his hands. "I've been doing *favors* for the past two months now. There's got to be a letup. You people are pressing me too hard for things. I understand my situation very well. I'm telling you that I don't like the pressure. I don't deserve this kind of treatment." He looked up. "I just want *out* of this thing, so I'm doing what I am told. I expect to be treated fairly. I'm not a stupid asshole."

A cocktail waitress with tired eyes and a push-up bra came to the table. Arbogast ordered a double gin and tonic. She wiggled away.

"Exactly who *are* you?" the banker said. "People keep coming to see me and I'm the only one who has a name."

Larry whispered, "I'm Larry, and Victor King sent me to ask you for the favor." He smiled. "I mean, it's not like I found your name in the phone book."

The waitress came with a drink. She set it on the table. Larry paid, and she wiggled away again.

"And what happens if I, for once, just tell you people to go pound sand?" Arbogast said. "That I've done enough and that's that. I want to know what happens."

"There's no need for hostility, Bill." Larry folded his hands.

"Answer the question. I want you to answer the question. I'm not afraid of you." There was a fine mist of perspiration on his forehead.

"Then I would just fly back to Las Vegas," Larry said. "I'm certainly not some goon. I hope I haven't given you that impression. I'm just a businessman." He sipped his drink. "Of course, you would be required to pay your debt, in full, immediately."

The fat man stared at his drink as if it were poison. He picked up the glass and drank. He put the glass down. "And if I *didn't* pay, you people would put a bomb in my car and blow my legs off, right?"

"Bill, I don't even like to think about that kind of thing," Larry said. His face had no expression.

The fat man rubbed his hands across his face and through his hair. He exhaled. "I want you to tell your people I don't like the way I'm being treated and that they don't scare me," he said. "I want you to tell 'em that." He stared at nothing in particular as he said this. He wiped his forehead with a cocktail napkin. "This whole thing is like some movie. . . . Jesus."

Nothing was said for a minute or so. Larry waited for Arbogast to speak first. The susceptibility test.

"Well, lay it on me," said Bill the banker, with his eyes half shut. "Tell me what you people want this time." He sighed.

"We need to borrow a Treasury bill from your bank's vault. A one-hundred-thousand-dollar-denomination Treasury bill. You give it to me on a Friday and I return it to you before Monday morning."

The banker shook his head with pursed lips. He poked the ice in his drink. *"No way.* That's playing with fire. A Treasury bill is a U.S. government obligation, a bearer instrument. If you lost it, anyone could set up an account and cash it. . . . What if there was a surprise audit or something? *No way."*

"That's *very* unlikely, isn't it, Bill? I mean, thinking in terms of being *realistic* about it? A surprise audit on the weekend?" Larry said. He crossed his legs.

"Maybe so," said the fat man, holding his drink with both hands. "But it's one thing to approve a load on bad collateral. I mean, as long as the payments are made, no one's the wiser, but this thing. . . . If you failed to show up on Monday, it's a hundred-grand loss. The bank would be crawling with bank examiners, FBI men. . . ."

Larry mustered his most confident tone. "That's not going to happen, Bill. . . . I also need a list of the serial numbers of a hun-

196

dred Treasury bills of the same denomination. Just a list of serial numbers. I give you my word of honor you will have the Treasury bill in your hands again by Monday morning. Be logical. If I didn't intend to return the Treasury bill to you, I would have asked you for more than *one*, right?"

Arbogast stared at his drink for a while. "I guess so," he said.

"How about one for the road, Bill?" Larry said.

The fat man nodded his head dreamily, as if he had just awakened.

The heat and odor of smog were oppressive. A rusty sign suspended between two steel posts said EL MONTE GARDENS, as if a trailer park next to a noisy freeway needed a name.

Larry Phillips parked across the street in front of a junkyard and told Melba to stay put. He got out of the car and walked across the street. Between two rows of sagging trailers a group of filthy children wrestled in the dirt with a cocker spaniel. They were trying to put the dog into a cardboard box.

A trailer with a piece of roofing paper covering a hole above the door sat in space twelve.

Larry knocked on the door, and an emaciated Freddie Roth answered it immediately, as if he had watched him approach. The bald, middle-aged man wore khaki work pants and a sleeveless T-shirt. His thick glasses magnified rheumy, melancholy eyes, and he had the complexion of a tubercular.

"Scary Larry!" Roth said. They shook hands. "Nice ta see ya. Nice ta see ya. Come on in."

Larry stepped in, and Roth motioned him to a sofa as if there were more than one. A wrinkled fat woman in a flowered housecoat sat in front of a blaring television. She gave a nod.

Roth offered drinks and Larry accepted. The bespectacled man fussed at a cluttered sink.

"Use the glasses in the top cupboard," said the toothless woman. She spoke without taking her eyes off the television.

Roth walked in front of the reclining woman and handed Larry iced tea in a peanut-butter glass. "This'll cool ya off," he said.

Larry sipped.

"No stinkin' trailer for Freddie in the old days," said Roth. "Had a place in Malibu right by the fuckin' movie stars. Ronald Colman, Dennis O'Keefe. They lived right up the street. A beach house. I used to deal right out of the place. Had a spot for my lookout right in front. Beautiful setup. I bought the place for cash after my second printing job. In those days I printed tens and twenties and sold everything on my own. No partners. No middlemen, and therefore no *rotten, fuckin' stool pigeons* . . . Things were simpler then. Now the Feds are on ya like stink on shit even before the paper is cut." He drank his iced tea so fast it ran from the sides of his mouth. He wiped his mouth with the back of his hand.

"I'm here because I have a project," Larry said.

"I always liked you in the joint," Roth interrupted. "You are a gentleman. It was a pleasure to have somebody to talk to except some corn-holing goddamn nigger. You are an intellectual. I mean that sincerely." He waved his peanut-butter glass for emphasis. "But before you give me a spiel about your project, I want to tell you the answer is *no*. I've been out four months. You would not believe how many people have been over here with propositions." He pointed with his thumb. "Ask my old lady there. She'll tell ya. Every sumbitch that has a cock dream about funny money comes to see old Freddie. They want Freddie to *print*. Freddie will make the negatives. Freddie will make the plates. Freddie will run off a million and be paid twenty percent of the run. That's fine. But what they don't say is that when the bust goes down, Freddie gets *convicted* of making the negatives, *convicted* of making the plates, and *convicted* of printing the million. Freddie does all the *work*, then goes to jail and does all the mother-fucking *time*. Everybody else skates by making a deal with the Feds to hand up Freddie the printer. This is my life story. . . ." He sipped more tea. "So I'll tell ya the same thing I've told everybody else. I'd rather sit here in this stinking trailer until I catch cancer and die rather than chance going back to the joint again. I'm too old for that shit. There's too many mean niggers. It's not like it used to be."

The woman reached forward and turned up the volume on the television set. She leaned back again. Men with guns blasted away at a stagecoach.

198

"Why don't you turn the fuckin' thing up all the way!" Roth screamed. The woman muttered something to the TV.

Roth stood up and shook his head angrily. He opened the front door and stepped out. Larry followed.

The mud-caked children rushed past pulling a cardboard box containing the barking spaniel. The dog was trying to keep its balance.

"This project would be the most profitable and interesting you have ever worked on," Larry said. "You're the only guy who can do it."

"Young man, there's nothing I haven't printed. Cashier's checks, money, bonds, stocks, birth certificates, passports . . ."

"I have actual government security paper," Larry whispered.

Roth tossed the ice cubes out of his tea into the dirt. "If you do, young man, you're the first thief in history to get his hands on any. Sorry, I don't buy that. Nothing personal."

Larry folded his arms. "Would it be safe to say that you might be interested if I had that kind of paper?"

"There would be no way to get caught if you had the real paper," Roth said. "I could print it so even bank people could never tell. It would be like printing up the real thing."

Larry put his arm around Roth's shoulders. They walked toward the car. "I want to show you something," he said.

At the car, Larry looked both ways and unlocked the trunk. He slid the rubber bands off the rolled sheets of paper and handed them to Roth. The printer took off his glasses, breathed steam onto the lenses, and cleaned them on the front of his T-shirt. He held the paper up to the light and pulled it to within inches of his thick glasses. He put the sheets back in the trunk.

"Good goddamn," he whispered. "The real thing, red and blue fibers and all. How did you ever get your hands on . . . ?"

Larry closed the trunk lid. "I thought you'd be impressed," he said. "You're the only printer who could do it justice."

Roth turned and stared across the street at the trailer park for a long time. "There's not enough paper to make much funny money," he said finally.

"My project calls for bills—one hundred U.S. Treasury bills in one-hundred-grand denominations. I also need two passports," Larry said.

"The passports are no problem, but where are you going to get a hundred-thousand-dollar Treasury bill for me to copy?" Roth looked puzzled.

"That's already laid on through a banking connection," Larry said. "I'll have a sample T bill for use this weekend."

"Who else is in on this thing?"

"No one," Larry said.

Roth pointed to Melba. "What about the broad in the car?"

"She's in on the project and helped me get the paper," Larry said. "She can't snitch without incriminating herself. She's part of it. There's nothing to worry about with her. I've known her since before I did my stretch. She fell behind an aiding-and-abetting in my last case and did six months in T. I. without opening her mouth. She's not a snitch."

The printer nodded. "You make things sound pretty solid."

"I need you on this, Freddie," Larry said.

Roth was silent. He kicked some pebbles into the street. His hands plunged in and out of his pockets. "I want five grand up front for supplies and equipment and fifteen when the load is printed," he said. "The only reason I'll go through with it is because you were nice to me in the joint."

Larry opened the trunk again, removed a wad of hundred-dollar bills from a small black briefcase, and counted them. He handed the money to Roth. "Five grand," he said.

The printer licked a thumb and counted the money rapidly. He stuffed it in a pants pocket. "Meet me in front of the Oasis Motel in Palm Springs at 10:00 P.M. Friday night," he said. "Bring groceries for two days, the sample Treasury bill, and color photographs, two by two, for the passports. I'll take care of everything else. Make damn sure you aren't followed. You can bet your ass the Feds are looking for that paper right at this very moment. They've probably put out reward promises to every snitch in the country. I know how they work. They don't fuck around."

The two men shook hands. Freddie Roth headed across the street to the trailer court. He walked briskly.

Larry got in the car and started the engine.

"What did he say?" Melba was fanning herself with an astrology magazine.

200

"He'll do it. The ace was the real paper. He just couldn't refuse to work on Uncle Sam's real paper. For him, it's a wish fulfillment, an ego-gratification thing." Larry made a U-turn and headed for the freeway.

Melba had a puzzled look. "Mercy," she said.

Larry dropped Melba off in front of a record shop and drove across the street into a service station. He got out of the car, dropped a dime in a pay phone, and dialed.

"United Merchants Bank."

"Bill Arbogast, please."

"Hold the line, sir."

"Mr. Arbogast speaking."

"This is Larry. Do you have the material we discussed?"

"Uh, yes. Everything is in order."

"Are you free to leave the bank for a few minutes?"

"Yes."

"Walk to the record shop down the street from your bank. Go in the shop with the material. Buy a record album. As you walk out of the shop, stuff the material into the bag with the record. After you walk out, a woman with strawberry-blonde hair will bump into you. You will both drop your packages. She will pick up yours, and you pick up hers. Return to the bank. Do you understand?"

"Yes. Please have it back by Monday."

"I will call you at 10:00 A.M. Monday and return the material. You have nothing to worry about. I want you to keep your cool and be relaxed."

"Okay."

Larry hung up the telephone and looked at his watch. He got back in the car.

Arbogast walked out of the bank a minute later, his sluggish gait almost hesitant, his basset-hound shoulders drooping, and his double chin looking as if it had been stuffed into his collar to make it fit. He crossed the street and shuffled into the record shop. At least ten minutes went by.

Larry took deep breaths to remain calm—hyperventilation. What if the bank's phone was bugged? he thought.

Ten minutes later the banker snail-paced out of the record

shop, carrying a flat package under his arm. He looked around sheepishly. Melba was close behind. She almost knocked him over. The packages dropped, and the odd pair almost bumped heads picking them up. They said something to each other, and the fat man jiggled back toward the bank.

Melba waited for a light and crossed the street. She got in the car, and Larry started the engine. She looked around nervously.

"Open it," he said.

She opened the bag and took out a Treasury bill, its embossed scrollwork accentuating the words *One Hundred Thousand Dollars*, and a typed list of serial numbers. She handed the items to him.

"Beautiful," Larry said.

"All right!" Melba squealed. "A Hank Snow album! I was so nervous I didn't even look at the one *I* bought."

Larry took a turn toward the Santa Monica Freeway.

"How far to Palm Springs?" Melba said.

"About three hours, going the speed limit." Larry pulled into the fast lane.

Melba fiddled with the radio dials until she found a country-and-western station. "Listen! A Hank Snow tune. What a coincidence!" She leaned back in the seat. "That dude was really nervous. When I bumped into him he stiffened up like somebody stuck him with a cattle prod."

"Quite normal," Larry said.

$/6

Carr trudged out of the crowded baggage-claim area, carrying his suitcase and a well-worn leather garment bag. He peered around for someone who looked like a special agent. Certainly after twenty years he should be able to pick a Treasury man even out of an airport horde.

A horn blast came from an antennaed sedan parked at the curb. A balding, gray-haired man, who sat slumped behind the wheel, motioned to him without sitting up. Carr walked over to the vehicle and peered into the passenger side.

"You Charlie Carr?" The man had very little chin and a ball nose that made his tiny eyes seem to peer over it. With the exception of redness on the nose and the rims of his eyes, his complexion had no color. Carr had never seen him before.

"Yes," Carr said. "Are you from the L.A. field office?"

"No. I'm a fruit trying to pick up you guys," said the special agent.

Carr opened the rear door and loaded his bags into the back seat. He got in.

The man stuck out his hand.

"Cecil True—call me Buck. I'm going to be your partner." His eyes seemed to seek a reaction to his name. They shook hands.

"Funny we've never met," Carr said in a sincere tone. "I mean, after all these years . . ."

True started the engine. His eyes were on the rearview mirror. "The reason you say that is because you think I'm your age. I'm not. Just so you'll know right off the bat, I'm thirty-one years old and I'm five foot five inches tall. That's because at age twenty-nine my hair turned gray and fell out and I lied about my height to get the job."

Carr suddenly remembered. Buck True. The stories about him had been going around for over a year.

True guided the G-car through stop-and-go airport traffic, across the Sepulveda bridge, and onto Century Boulevard.

"How about a drink somewhere?" Carr said.

Carr and True ended up sitting at the bar at Ling's, in Chinatown. It was still the Feds' watering hole, and within walking distance of the Federal Building. The only light in the cramped place emanated from a few bulbs in the bar cabinet and a jukebox near the door that Carr would have sworn had the same record selection as a year ago. The bar mirror, which reflected the shadowy red faces of the detectives in the place, was decorated with a bright-green fluorescent dragon whose tail had flaked off. The facing wall had a couple of dusty tapestries—swans swimming on a blue thread lake. Ling, the bartender, a seedy-looking Oriental in a mandarin jacket decorated with a number of handcuff tie tacs, was at the end of the bar telling one of his lewd jokes to a couple of long-haired Federal narcotics agents dressed in leather jackets.

There was a hangout such as Ling's in most major cities, and Carr figured he could name most of them. Like the others, Ling's was an air-conditioned, secret grotto where the detectives came to take alcoholic vows, join bureaucratic plots, make threats, swear vengeance, bitch about the court system, talk lustfully about women, and rehash cases for the fiftieth time. The only taboo subject was informants.

True sipped his drink and looked smug. "Go ahead and say what you're thinking," he said. "But I'll tell you right off you didn't have to buy me a drink to tell me you don't want me for a partner. You've heard the stories, and you'd rather not have me for a partner. . . . Go ahead and say it. I've heard it before."

Carr lit a cigarette and waved out the match. "I *have* heard the stories," he said.

True turned and faced Carr. He spoke through clenched

204

teeth. "Well, they're *true*," he said. "I've ended up in a beef with every agent-in-charge I've worked for. When they screw me, I tell 'em to get fucked—right to their face. That's why they've been sending me around the horn. In the past eighteen months I've been stationed in Detroit, Providence, Miami, and now Los Angeles. My wife's a schoolteacher. She couldn't take it and filed for divorce. But I'm going to keep going. I can take everything they can dish out. . . . *Fuck them!*" He glared at Carr for a moment, then turned back to his drink. "So if you don't want me for a partner, just say so," he said to the bar mirror. "I don't really give a rat's ass."

Ignoring the remarks, Carr casually loosened his tie. Starting with finding Ralph Smith's body, he recounted the facts of the case, trying not to omit any detail. He spoke clearly, without hesitation, for at least twenty minutes. When he was finished, he lit another cigarette and blew smoke in the air. "As far as working with you," he said, "I have no problem with that. Yes, I've heard that you are a bolshevik. I've also heard that you are a stand-up guy, a good backup man. That's what I'm looking for. I don't care about your other problems. In fact, I'm not even interested."

True's expression was unchanged. "How do I know No Waves didn't assign me to this case so you can keep book on me? Headquarters is building a package of reprimand letters on me so they can fire me. How do I know you're not going to set me up?"

Ling brought more drinks. Carr didn't speak until he walked away. "Because I have no reason to," he said. "Besides, I hate No Waves' guts. I worked for him here in Los Angeles and he had me transferred."

"Then why did he assign *me*, out of all the agents in the office, to be your partner?" True stirred his drink.

"Because he's in a power play for promotion with Delgado," Carr said. "He assigned you because he figured you were the worst man for the job."

True tugged an ear. "I don't see what you mean."

"You have to look at it from No Waves' point of view," Carr said. "If the investigation fails, his bureaucrat's mind sees two possible scenarios. One, because of your bad personnel package, Delgado and I use you as the scapegoat. We write you up to cover our failure. If this happens, No Waves would have the ammo to fire you, something none of the other SAIC's have been able to do; thus a feather in his cap. Two, No Waves gives you the choice of taking another transfer or writing a memo to the chief on how poorly Delgado directed the investigation. In this scenario, Delgado is hurt and No Waves has helped put himself in line for promotion."

The young agent leaned back in the seat. "And if we make an arrest and solve the case?"

"Then No Waves takes credit for a major case solved in his district," Carr said. "He puts out a press release, and transfers you on the next list, as he had planned to do anyway. No big gain, but then again, no loss. In other words—" Carr drew his palm across the bar—"no waves."

True finished his drink and looked inside the glass. "Looks like I get screwed no matter what happens in this case," he said ruefully.

Carr shook his head. "Wrong," he said. "If we make the case, Delgado will take care of you. He will get you off the merry-go-round. I can guarantee it."

Someone plunked coins in the jukebox, and soft music filled the tiny pub. Neither man said anything for a while.

True broke the silence. "You have a pretty good reputation," he said. "The parole office gave me the address of Grady Parks's print shop. It's on Crenshaw Boulevard. . . ."

The neighborhood was transitory. It was made up of apartments that people abandoned when the rent was overdue and little shops that were traded between finance companies; not a ghetto area, though, just a place where car repossessors made good bucks. The City of Angels . . .

Carr pointed at a sign over the door of a small storefront. It read:

PARKS PRINTING

True pulled the sedan to the curb.

The print shop was sandwiched between a beauty-supply

store, with wigs and shampoo bottles in a display window, and a run-down movie theater that had been turned into a revival hall. The marquee read:

THE HOLY MINISTRY OF
THE REVEREND AND MRS. ANTHONY C. EISENTROUT
MIRACLE HEALING SERVICES DAILY

"The print shop looks closed," True said.

"Let's watch for a while," Carr said. He took off his coat and threw it in the back seat.

Three hours later a young black man wearing white pants and shirt, wide-brimmed hat, and belt, rings, bracelets, and a necklace approached the door of the print shop. He knocked a few times. The door was opened. The black man looked both ways at the street and went in.

"He looks wrong," True said.

Carr nodded. "He *is* wrong. Name's Dorsey. I arrested him four years ago for forgery. He burgles mail trucks on the first day of the month for the Social Security checks."

Less than a minute later the man came out, stuffing something in his shirt pocket. Doing a sort of heel-and-toe walk, he strode down the sidewalk to a silver Mercedes sedan. He got in the driver's seat and started the engine.

"Follow him," Carr said.

True gave him a puzzled look and pulled into traffic. He drove around the corner and headed west on a residential street.

"Take him at the next stop signal," Carr said.

True raised his eyebrows. "If you say so."

A light changed to red. The Mercedes pulled up and stopped.

Carr jumped out of the sedan and ran to the driver's window. He had his badge in his hand. "Federal officer," he said. As Dorsey reached for the gearshift, Carr swung open the car door and pulled him out by his collar. Dorsey swung at Carr and missed. Carr punched him solidly in the stomach. Dorsey fell backward against the Mercedes. Carr threw his best right-hand punch. The man's head snapped to the side. He fell to the street.

207

Carr leaned down and pulled a driver's license out of his shirt pocket. It was counterfeit. It had Dorsey's photograph and a name and address in Orange County.

Carr twisted the man's arm into a hammer lock and walked him onto the sidewalk. True got in the Mercedes and pulled it to the curb.

"Where'd ya get the license?" Carr said.

"I don't know nothin' about any mutha-fuckin' license," said the black man.

True stepped out of the Mercedes. He held a blue-green U.S. Treasury check by the tips of two fingers. He approached, and Carr showed him the driver's license. "Same names," True said. He looked at the prisoner. "I guess you were on the way to the bank."

"I want to talk to my mutha-fuckin' lawyer," Dorsey said.

"You won't need one," Carr said. "You can go. We'll keep the check and the license." He dropped his arm.

Dorsey's eyes darted back and forth to each agent. He backed up toward the Mercedes. "Thanks, man." He got in the car and drove off.

True's jaw was open. "Why'd ya let the bastard go?" he said. "I don't get it."

"If we took him downtown, we'd end up doing the same thing. The U.S. attorney would say we had no probable cause to believe Dorsey committed a crime. Hunches are no good in court. Therefore, stopping him and searching his car was illegal."

True shook his head sadly. "You're right, come to think of it," he said.

"Now let's go see Grady Parks."

Carr knocked on the door of the print shop. True stood behind him.

"Who's there?" Parks said.

"Federal officers," Carr said. "Open up, Grady."

"Do you have a warrant?"

"Don't make us kick it in," Carr said.

Grady Parks opened the door a few inches. A middle-aged man with a salt-and-pepper ponytail, he wore nothing but swimming trunks and red-and-blue joggers' shoes. He had the wiry, rippled frame of an athlete. With the exception of his head and eyebrows, he was hairless.

"I thought you got transferred to Washington, D.C.," Parks said.

"I did. I came back because I missed you, Tarzan." Carr shoved the door with his shoulder and knocked Parks to the floor.

"What's this all about? It's been three years since I printed money! I'm clean!" Parks stood up and adjusted his ponytail.

The printing machinery in the shop was scattered among a mattress, bean-bag chairs, barbells, and a clothes rack. A stereo set was on shelves next to a full-length mirror. There were teeth-marked watermelon rinds sitting on top of things.

Carr took the counterfeit driver's license out of his pocket and showed it to Parks.

Parks shook his head. "Okay, so I needed a little extra cash and made up an ID for somebody." He stuck out his wrists. "So send me back to Terminal Island. I don't give a shit any more. I haven't been able to get any of my legitimate customers back since you people arrested me. I'm living in this sweatbox to make ends meet. I don't even have an apartment, no air conditioning. I might as well go back to the joint. I've been so depressed I can hardly keep in shape. . . . Go ahead, put on the cuffs."

Carr sauntered over to a photo enlarger. He picked up a stack of counterfeit driver's-license forms and tore them in half. "I want to know where to find Freddie Roth," he said.

"Why should I . . . ?" Parks's hands fell to his sides.

"Give me an address and we take a walk," Carr said.

"You mean I don't have to . . ."

Carr turned on his heel. "What part don't you understand?"

Parks pointed to a drawer in a metal filing cabinet.

True opened the drawer, looked in, and nodded.

Parks reached in and pulled out an electric hot plate, a stack of papers, and, finally, a three-ring notebook. He flipped pages. "Here it is," he said: "9910 Bakersfield Street, El Monte. Space 101."

True took the notebook. He copied the address on a piece of paper and stuffed it in his coat pocket.

Carr approached Parks. He stood directly in front of him and whispered into his face.

"If you tell Roth we're looking for him, we'll come back and make a case on you and you'll go back to the pen. That's a promise," he said.

"I don't want him to know any more than you do," Parks said.

Nothing was said for a few moments. True was looking around the room. He removed the top from a metal can. It was filled with watermelon rinds.

"I haven't eaten anything except watermelon for over a week," said Parks. "I wanted to lose a couple of pounds. Dr. Ashlocke's melon diet."

True put the top back on the can.

The agents went out the door, walked to the G-car, and got in.

"How do we know it isn't him?" True said. He started the engine.

"We don't for sure," Carr said, "but if he had printed securities, he would have been paid enough for the job that he wouldn't still be making phony licenses at twenty bucks a crack."

"Maybe," True said.

Carr set his suitcase down in front of Sally's apartment door. A note that said "Charles" was Scotch-taped to the door handle. He pulled it off and read:

Key in usual. Back in a sec.
Love, Sally

Carr ran his fingers across the top of the door frame and felt the key. He opened the door and went in. The apartment was just as he remembered, a mixture of old and new: oversized sofa pillows, a tiny roll-top desk, an oil primitive in shades of rust, grass-mat wallpaper. "Eclectic," Sally had described it. The place was spotless, and a stack of magazines on the bookshelf was squared exactly.

Carr set his suitcase just outside the bedroom door and took off his coat. He pushed open a window. A breeze smelling faintly of wet beach sand and salt filled the room.

Near the pier in the distance was the apartment house he had lived in before being transferred. Looking back, he thought it perhaps *was* odd that they had never moved in together permanently. He wished he had written.

There were footsteps. The door opened. Sally, a wiry woman in a purple jogging suit, rushed in with a bag of groceries. Her gray-streaked hair was in a jogging bun, and she had a golden tan that few women over forty would dare. She put the bag down on the table and brushed his cheek with a kiss.

"Would you believe it's been a year," she said almost casually, hurrying back to the grocery bag. She began stuffing things into the refrigerator.

"It doesn't seem that long," he said.

"I've been busy as a bee since I've seen you. Really *over-loaded* with projects, not to mention *two* conspiracy trials that lasted three months each. I was putting out hundreds of pages of transcript every day . . . stenotyping in my sleep!" She floated to the sink and washed a cauliflower. "I hope you like vegetables. I'm off meat altogether, and now I have more energy than you can believe." She dropped the cauliflower into a pan and ran water. "I went to a health-food seminar a few months ago. . . . I've totally lost my taste for meat. I need less sleep."

She closed the refrigerator door and crumpled up the grocery bag furiously. She stuffed it into a container under the sink.

Carr looked out the window again. People milled on and off the pier, killing time. "I'm not very good at writing letters," he said.

"I would never have guessed." Her tone was sarcastic. She chopped at an eggplant and tossed the pieces into an aluminum wok.

Carr walked up behind her and wrapped his arms around her waist. His tongue was on her neck.

Sally dropped the knife. "You didn't even miss me," she breathed.

"Yes, I did," he whispered.

Sally turned to face him. "I hate that part of you," she said.

Their tongues met. Sally's arms squeezed him tightly. He picked her up and carried her into the bedroom.

"Thank you for leaving the suitcase there when you came in," Sally said.

"Yeah, sure." On the bed he unzipped her jogging shirt and gently pulled it off her arms.

They were at the dinner table. The kitchen smelled of vegetable steam and soy sauce. Carr finished eating and poured himself another glass of wine.

"In the morning it's nothing but natural grain, nuts, and yogurt for me," Sally said. "Did you know that most popular breakfast cereals are *fifty percent* sugar?"

"No kidding." He gave a nod.

"But you don't really care about such things. You're just humoring me. You always have."

"I . . ."

She raised a hand. "There's no need to say anything. I'll even change the subject. Who will be your partner while you are here?"

"Young fella named True . . . Buck True."

"He's a troublemaker. You should have seen what he pulled in the courtroom last week. It was a counterfeit case, and he was being cross-examined by Arthur Bailey . . . you know, the attorney that wears all the rings?"

Carr nodded.

"Bailey's whole case was based on discrediting True because the defendant had confessed to him. When he was cross-examining, True kept lowering his voice—almost to a whisper. Bailey kept asking him to raise his voice, until finally the judge broke in and said, 'Agent True, is there something wrong with your voice?' True pulls his collar down and shows a scar to the jury. 'Yes, your honor,' he said. 'I was shot in the throat in Vietnam.' The jury loved it. You could see them smiling and nudging one another. Ringo Bailey went crazy with objections, but it didn't do any good. During the rest of his testimony, True's voice seemed to have miraculously recovered. The judge was absolutely *livid*. Afterward he called True into his chambers and told him he didn't like shenanigans in his courtroom. True said, 'Is it true that you and Bailey were once law partners?' The judge threw him out of the chambers and complained to the special agent-in-charge. It was a real *scene*."

Sally pointed at the vegetable dishes. "Would you like anything else?"

Carr smiled. "Yes. Some of the first course, please." He took her hand.

"I hate to leave dishes," Sally said as he led her into the bedroom.

$/7

The Oasis Motel was one of many in a long desert block of credit-card signs and swimming pools surrounded by copper-toned sales leaders and secretaries who were just in for the weekend. Everyone was wearing the latest in bathing suits, straw hats, and sunglasses.

Larry Phillips pulled into the parking lot.

Freddie Roth was standing in front, looking out of place in a pair of workman's overalls and a baseball cap. He got in the back seat of the car.

"This is Melba," Larry said.

"Pleased to meet you."

"Is everything ready, Mr. Greenjeans?"

"You betcha, Scary Larry."

They laughed.

Roth pointed straight ahead. "Keep going on this highway, but take a few turns on the way just to make sure you ain't being followed," he said.

After driving in and out of a few motel and supermarket parking lots with Roth staring out the rear window for a tail, the printer gave directions to a place at least six miles out of town.

It was a large ranch-style house that needed painting, situated on an enormous desert lot, with a detached garage in the rear. The closest structure was a service station a half-mile south on the main highway.

214

Larry swung into the driveway and hit the brakes.

"Wait till ya see how I got things set up," Roth said proudly, giving a toothy yellow smile. He hopped out and waved them to a door in the side of the garage. Unlocking a padlock, he ushered them into sweltering darkness that smelled of motor oil. He pulled a string on a fluorescent light.

Roth pointed to the maze of printing equipment like a ten-year-old to a new bike.

An offset press stood in the middle of the garage, clean and oiled. Other machinery rested against the walls.

"What's all this stuff?" Larry said, motioning across the room.

"Camera, plate maker, light table, paper cutter. Everything I need," Roth said. "It's all top-of-the-line equipment. I spent the whole five grand you gave me."

"Mercy," said Melba. "Where do you engrave the plates?" She leaned on the formidable-looking aluminum light table.

Roth pushed his glasses back on his nose. "They only do that in the movies," he said. He removed a green work apron from a hook and put it on. "I use offset printing. I'll take a picture of the T bill and make a negative. Then I burn the negative onto a lithographic plate, then I . . ."

"Mercy," Melba said.

"Well, it's printing a picture of a real one onto paper." Roth beamed and turned to Phillips. "Of course, this time it's printing a picture of one onto *real* paper. I'm gonna love it." He rubbed his hands together fiendishly. "It'll take the rest of today for me to make the negatives. You two can wait inside the house. Might as well take advantage of the place; it costs a hundred a day for the rent. Guy that owns the place is an old friend of mine from Terminal Island. He does big junk deals here. You can see the Feds coming a mile away. No need to go to the store or anywhere else. It's better that way. We all stay here till it's done."

"I agree, Freddie. It's the best way," Larry said in the manner of an executive.

Larry leaned back in a recliner chair and thumbed through his book on Chinese porcelain. In the living room there was also a television set and a threadbare sofa surrounded by knickknack shelves containing ceramic figures of horses, dogs, and little country boys playing guitars.

Melba turned on the television and flopped down on the couch. "I know why you and I ended up together," she said.

"So do I," he said. "I told the bellhop to send up a broad." He turned a page.

The TV flickered on.

"*That's* not what I mean," she said. "I mean how we sort of just teamed up afterward."

"Uh-huh . . ."

"It's because you are a Pisces and I'm a Leo. They go together," she said. "I believe in the signs. When I was eighteen I tried to get in the navy. This recruiter told me that I could take my baby daughter with me, except for boot camp, if I would just go ahead and sign up for four years. My horoscope that day said, 'A trip with a loved one.' Can you believe that?"

Larry got up and opened the refrigerator. He took out a Coke, popped open the can, and sat down again.

"Why did you want to go in the navy?" he said.

"Because I thought it would be good for me. . . . I never did get around to enlisting though. My ex-husband stole my daughter and went back to Texas. I ended up on the hotel circuit. My girlfriend got me in. She showed me what to do, what to carry in my purse."

Larry turned to a photograph of a blue-and-white porcelain bowl. The caption read: "Imperial Porcelain. Sung Period, A.D. 960–1279."

"You're not listening to me," Melba said.

"Yes, I am." Larry spoke without looking up from the book.

"Why can't we just pass the Treasury bills here? Why do we have to take them to Europe?"

"Because over there we can get rid of 'em all at once. People get caught because they pass bills one at a time. You pass one at a bank, somebody ends up calling a cop. You end up doing federal time for one bill. That's the mistake they all make—passing bills one at a time. It's the same thing with funny money. . . . I'm going to make a one-shot deal—big enough that I will be set from here on out. One deal, only one risk."

216

"Mercy," she said. She was leaning back staring at the television. The picture was snowy.

Nothing was said for what must have been a half hour. Suddenly she spoke, as if she didn't care who heard her. "I keep thinking of poor Ralph . . . how weird it was to talk to him in that bar. It was like being in a movie with him. He was the only one who didn't know what was going to happen next. That stewardess idea was a perfect excuse to not see him for a few days at a time. How do you *think* of that stuff?"

Larry put the book down. He rubbed his eyes with both hands. He turned to Melba. "I *always* have the perfect excuse. You just do exactly what I tell you and you'll never have anything to worry about." He smiled strangely.

Melba sat up. "I wish you wouldn't have shot him." Her voice was thick.

Larry got up and walked to the sofa. Standing over her, he spoke in a fatherly tone. "You're anxious right now because we're waiting for our project to get off the ground. This is understandable. It is a natural reaction. Would you like to relax and feel at ease?"

She nodded.

He took off his wristwatch and held it in front of her eyes. "Look at the watch, Melba, and, as you do, your eyes will become tired and you will want to close them." He moved the watch closer to her face. "And now they will close." Her eyes shut. "And you will relax and begin to sleep. Relaxing more and more with each and every breath you take. More and more relaxed . . . you will enter into peaceful sleep and nothing will disturb you. Noises will only make you go deeper into a restful, peaceful sleep." Her head drooped.

Larry went back to his chair. He picked up the book and found his place.

Melba breathed deeply.

Larry paced outside the garage, hiding his hands in his pockets from the morning desert chill. The clackety-clack of the press filled the air like the snapping of bolts. Since they had arrived, Freddie Roth had been out of the garage only to catnap.

Suddenly the noise from the garage stopped. Roth slung open the garage door and strolled out, wiping his hands on a bluish rag. His T-shirt was smeared with black and red ink. "It's done . . . all of it," he said.

Larry walked past him into the garage. Stacks of counterfeit Treasury bills covered the workbench like a colorful blanket. He felt blood rush to his limbs, to the top of his head.

Roth pointed at the stacks. "Everything is ready to go," he said. "All the serial numbers are on. Just barely had enough paper for the last few. Made it, though. One hundred pieces. And your passports came out perfect."

Larry picked up one of the phony bills and examined it closely. He put it down. "Good job, Mr. Greenjeans."

"I guess it's all up to you now, Scary Larry. They're just toilet paper unless you can cash 'em." He wiped his forearms up and down with the rag. "This wasn't my fastest rush job ever," he said. "I once did some General Motors stock in six hours and forty-seven minutes—and that included burning the plates. Had a guy that needed 'em real quick and was willing to pay the price. Funny story—the way it ended up. The poor guy got ripped off when he tried to peddle them. He was sitting in a motel room on Hollywood Boulevard waiting for the money man, and two hippies kicked in the door, tied him up, and took the bogus. But that's not the worst part. They tied him up so well, you know, handcuffs, gag—the whole bit—that he couldn't untie himself. Maid found him the next day in the room. Poor guy had choked to death on the goddamn gag."

Roth picked up a portable hair dryer and plugged it into a socket above the workbench. It hummed on. He waved the hot air across the bills as he spoke. "This'll dry that ink up real nice." His voice seemed to blend with the sound of the hair dryer. "There's nothing I ain't seen when it comes to phony paper. I've been in the business for over thirty years." He flicked the dryer to slow speed and continued. "There's one thing you've got to remember. Whatever scam you've got figured, you ain't the first to think of it. Everything has been done at least once. Guys sit in the joint for years just planning a caper, adding little bits to it with every lap on the yard. . . . I know that's what you've done. I knew when you made a point to make friends with me in the joint that you had something planned."

He picked up one of the counterfeits with two fingers and held the hair dryer close for a few seconds. He dropped it onto the dry pile and continued. "I don't know how you plan to cash the T bills, and, as a matter of fact, I don't really *want* to know. But my guess is that you're planning a one-shot deal. Now that's fine—well and good—but take some advice from old Mr. Greenjeans: don't get greedy, and remember that it's not your enemies you have to worry about, it's your *friends*. They will end up fucking you every time. Don't trust anybody. Since you had a list of serial numbers for me, I figure you to be setting up a bank switch or a phony-collateral loan deal. That means you have a potential of scoring anywhere up to a million bucks after everything is said and done—maybe more. Well, the point of this whole thing—" he picked up one of the T bills and wiped something off it with the corner of a rag—"the point is, when you're talking about that much money, *everybody* wants into the act. People start frothing at the mouth to get in on the caper. Everyone wants to cut the fat hog in the ass. . . . What I'm telling you is to watch out for people trying to move in on you. Your scam is complicated and you need people to do things. Do I have that right?"

Larry nodded.

Roth turned off the hair dryer and tossed it onto the workbench."Well, be damn careful of those people. Keep the planning to yourself and don't trust anyone. And, most of all beware of federal snitches. They will be everywhere in a thing like this. There's too much money involved. The Feds will be willing to pay big money to bag you."

Larry picked up one of the bills and compared it with the genuine bill that was clipped to an easel next to the workbench. He couldn't tell the difference.

Roth droned on with his grammar-school lecture.

As an experiment, Larry focused on the red seal on the Treasury bill and drew a vivid mental picture of a Freddie Roth with a hair dryer for a head, warm advice surging from his mouth. He closed his eyes for a moment, opened them. He gave Roth a pat on the shoulder and walked out of the garage.

In the house he took the .32 automatic out of a drawer and put it in his belt under his shirt.

Melba walked in from the kitchen with a cup of coffee.

"Do you want some breakfast?" she said.

"Pack everything. It's time to leave."

It took close to an hour to pack bags, put them in the trunk of the Chevy, and wipe every item in the house for fingerprints.

Larry told Melba to wait in the car.

He walked back into the garage. Freddie Roth was squatting on the floor next to a can of cleaning solution. He was scrubbing an inked press roller with a wet rag.

"I guess it's time for you and me to settle up," Roth said. He put down the roller and stood up, wiping his hands on his pants. His eyes got bigger when he saw the look on Larry's face.

"I mean, if you don't have it all right now, I'll trust you for a few grand. I know you're good for it." He spoke as if he needed to swallow.

Larry looked at the workbench.

"They're all dry now," Roth said. "Everything is ready. I can wait here if you have to go somewhere to get your money. I can wait here with the bills. Any way you want to . . ."

Larry pulled the gun out and pointed it at him.

Roth folded his arms across his chest and shook his head. "I never thought you would rip me off. I don't know why. I guess I had confidence in you. . . . You conned me. Go ahead, take the phony paper and go. This ain't the first time I've been ripped off. I'm no cherry. The least you could do is give me a few grand for the job. You could owe me the rest." His lips were quivering.

Melba came to the door of the garage. Larry glanced back at her. "Get down on your knees, Freddie," he said.

"You don't have to tie me up. Just take the bills and go. What do you expect me to do—call the cops about not being paid for counterfeiting government bills?"

"I want you to get down on your knees, Freddie. Everything is okay. Everything is fine. Please obey me. I want you to relax."

Roth dropped down on his knees.

"That's fine. I want you to look at Melba and don't turn your

220

head." Slowly, Larry walked around Roth and stood behind him. "Continue to focus on Melba."

"There is no need to do anything foolish," said Roth. He was shaking.

"I'm just going to tie your hands. I'll call somebody to come untie you an hour after we leave. Everything is fine. Everything is okay. Please put your hands behind you."

Roth had a disgusted look. He put his hands behind his back.

"That's fine," Larry said.

He put the gun an inch away from the back of Roth's head and pulled the trigger. The blast threw him forward violently.

Melba backed away from the garage, her hands covering her eyes. "Lordamercy!" she shrieked.

Freddie Roth was on his back, his hands and feet shaking uncontrollably. He moaned and sat up suddenly, his hands seeking the top of his head.

Larry fired five more times, aiming carefully to make sure each bullet entered the brain. Roth's body struggled and twisted for life. In a few moments the moaning and kicking stopped.

Larry walked to the workbench, picked up the Treasury bills, and stacked them carefully in a small cardboard box with the passports. He took one last look around, recalling that due to good project planning and careful attention to detail, he had made it a point not to touch anything in the garage. He took the box to the car and placed it in the trunk. He closed the trunk lid and got in the driver's seat.

Melba was sitting in the passenger seat staring at the floor.

Larry started the car and drove toward Los Angeles.

It was dark and humid. A nearby freeway was a cacophony of whizzing metal and tires, a sound that people living nearby had probably gotten used to.

True parked the sedan on the dimly lit street in front of the trailer court. "I guess we have nothing to lose," he said.

Carr took his gun and handcuffs off his belt and shoved them in the glove compartment. He got out on the passenger side and headed down a graveled passageway illuminated only by tiny trailer windows. Odors of junkyard earth and fry-pan cooking mixed with the sound of beery conversation.

Carr found Roth's trailer. A light was on inside. He knocked and got the butterflies. To him, the feeling was related more to concentration than fear: a general gearing up, a desire to make things work.

A fiftyish woman with a flaking complexion peeked out a crack in the door. She was wearing a housecoat. "Who's there?" she said. Her voice had the hollow tone that people get from smoking or drinking too much.

"Is Freddie home?" Carr said.

She undid the door latch and walked to the sink. She came back to the door pushing a set of uppers into place. Her housecoat was almost the color of her gray-rooted black hair, which, oddly, hung almost to her waist.

"He's on a trip," she said.

222

"That kind of puts me in a bind," Carr said. "I was supposed to drop something off to him and I'm leaving for Miami in a couple of hours."

"What're ya s'posed to drop off?"

"Some money I owe him."

The woman opened the door and stepped back. "Wanna come in?" She smiled.

Carr took three steps to a sofa.

"You can just leave the money with me," she said. "It's okay. I'm his . . . uh . . . wife." The false teeth clicked as she spoke.

Carr ran a hand through his hair. "Sorry, but Freddie told me to give *him* the money. I don't want him to get pissed off at me. You know how it goes."

"What's your name?" said the woman, tossing her hair over her shoulder.

"Charlie. I'm a friend of Grady Parks."

She shuffled past Carr to the television and turned down the volume.

"Sit down," she clicked.

Carr sat down carefully on the grease-stained sofa.

"He's never mentioned you." Her eyes were on the television. "How much money do you have for him?"

"A hundred bucks."

The woman's eyes came to life. "I think I remember him telling me that somebody was going to bring over some money and that I should keep it for him. Yes, now I remember him telling me that." She gave her chin a rub of sincerity.

"No offense, but I did that once and next time I saw the guy he told me his old lady never gave him the money," Carr said.

"Oh, you don't have to worry about . . ."

"Could you just call him up? If he tells me to leave it with you, it's fine with me."

"I ain't s'posed to call him where he is now." The woman stuck her hand inside the housecoat and adjusted a breast.

Carr stood up and went to the door. "Well, I think I'll be on my way. When you see Freddie, tell him I'll be back from Miami in a couple of months."

"Hold it," said the woman. She was out of the chair and tapping a rigid finger on Carr's chest. "I want that goddamn money! It's Freddie's money and I'm his old lady. That son of a bitch left me here for the weekend without a dime. He's afraid I'll go out and get laid or something." Her teeth clicked furiously.

Carr opened the door. "Like I said, you aren't getting the money unless I hear his voice. You can either call him up or not. I don't care."

"Okay!" Clack. "I call him up, since you want to be an asshole about it." She grabbed the phone from the sink and put it to her ear. "If he says I can't have the money, I'm going to set a match to this goddamn trailer and leave him for once and for all." She dialed.

Carr stepped close as she dialed.

She was reading a number from a coffee-stained envelope next to the phone. He took the receiver from her hand and put it down. "I'm sorry," he said. "I'll leave the dough with you. I don't want to cause any trouble between the two of you. Freddie's a friend."

The woman looked at him with a puzzled expression. He took five twenties out of his wallet and put them in her hand.

She looked at the money. "I'll be sure to give it to him," she said with a serious expression.

Carr went out the door repeating the phone number in his mind. At the sidewalk he glanced back into the trailer park, then trotted across the street to a pay phone in front of the junkyard. He dialed the number.

"Good evening, Oasis Motel."

"May I have your address, please?"

"Sure: 11921 Desert Palm Circle."

"City?"

"Palm Springs, of course."

Carr hung up the phone and gave the thumbs-up sign to True.

Carr pointed at the PALM SPRINGS ONE MILE sign, and True steered into the right lane.

The discussion had centered on why Freddie Roth was in Palm Springs.

Carr was adamant. "It's his M.O.," he said. "He always prints

224

in some out-of-the-way place. Years ago he ran off a load in a barn in Coos Bay, Oregon. He bought a press in Los Angeles and put it in a U-haul trailer and drove all the way to Oregon to print. He's paranoid."

"He should be," True said. "His sheet shows he's been convicted of counterfeiting seven times in the past eighteen years."

Carr leaned back against the head rest, holding the steering wheel with stiff arms. "But what a craftsman—the portrait, the scrollwork—a real artist."

At the Oasis Motel, True rang the registration-desk bell and waited. A fortyish man in a Hawaiian shirt came out of an office. His hair was as white-blond as his face was tanned.

Carr showed his badge. The man nodded without smiling.

"Do you have a man named Roth registered here?"

The desk clerk ran his hand down a rack of five-by-eight cards. "No. I think he checked out," he said, looking at the cards.

True handed him Roth's photo.

"That's him," said the clerk. "I remember now. He checked out day before yesterday. Stayed here almost a week."

"Anybody with him?" Carr said.

"Don't b'leeve so. I b'leeve the man was alone. Never saw him at the pool. He was gone most every day. Drove an old red clunker. A Ford with a U-haul trailer on it . . . What did he do?" The clerk gave a curious grin.

"Big-time counterfeiter," True said with a wink.

The man laughed. "Sure," he said. "I'll b'leeve that. And I'm the King of Sweden."

"Do you still have the phone bill for his room?" Carr said.

The man went into an office and came out moments later. He handed a sheet of paper to Carr. "You can have it," he said.

Carr looked at the sheet. The phone numbers had the area codes for Los Angeles and Las Vegas.

The man returned to his office.

"There's a pay phone," True said, pointing at a booth outside the glass-fronted door. They almost rushed to it.

Carr deposited a handful of change and dialed a Las Vegas number listed on the bill. A man answered.

"Andy's."

"What kind of business are you in?" Carr said.

"This is Andy's Printing Supply House."

"Thanks. Wrong number." Carr hung up the phone.

"Bingo," he said. "Freddie's setting up a printing plant."

"He's probably running the press right now," True said.

Carr ran his hand through his hair. "Now all we have to do is figure out where."

They went out the door and got back in the sedan.

"It doesn't make sense," True said. "Why would he stay in a motel for a week if he was going to set up his printing plant?"

Carr leaned back in the passenger seat and spoke to the windshield. "Maybe he got somebody to lend him a place but he couldn't get it until the weekend, so he bought supplies all week."

" He couldn't store any supplies at his trailer park. That's for sure."

"A red Ford. That's all we've got to go on."

True exhaled. "So I guess it's take a look-see at every red Ford in Palm Springs."

"There's nothing else," Carr said.

True stopped at a red light.

Red Fords seemed to be everywhere. To Carr, the phenomenon was normal and familiar. Neither he nor True discussed it. They understood that when an investigation centers on a particular clue, the investigator will, without a doubt, find it—more than once.

He remembered searching the streets of Los Angeles years ago for a twenties passer with a star tattoo on the back of his right hand. As if a curtain had been raised on a new world, it seemed that every bar, alley, and coffee shop was filled with star-tattooed skin. Carr gave up looking while sitting in a barber chair. He noticed that his barber of ten years had a star on the back of his hand.

Carr pointed across the street. "There's another one."

True shot across two lanes and pulled into a gas station. An attendant was washing the front window of the Ford. The man in the driver's seat wore dark clothing.

226

True and Carr approached the pickup cautiously. The man inside wore a policeman's uniform.

They turned and got back in the sedan.

True looked at his watch. "Four o'clock. He's probably just going on night duty."

A few minutes later a red '58 Ford full of teen-agers pulled in front of them from a high-school parking lot. Carr shook his head.

Carr and True searched for Freddie Roth's Ford until 3:00 A.M. and ended up renting a room at the Oasis Motel, at the government rate.

Carr was underneath his pillow, shielding his ears from True's bitter snoring, when the telephone rang.

"Special Agent Carr?"

"Speaking."

"This is Detective Contino, Palm Springs Police Department. You still interested in red Fords?"

"Yes."

"One of our patrol officers just found one parked in a back yard a few miles out of town. It's registered to somebody named Roth at an address in El Monte."

"We'll be right there. What's the address?"

"Eleven nineteen Fremont Road . . . but don't hang up till I give you the zinger. The owner of the car is there, too. *He's* parked in the garage. Somebody blew his brains out."

"Goddamn."

The phone clicked.

Carr and True were there within fifteen minutes.

There was no streetlights on Fremont Road, the only illumination being the red, white, and yellow lights of the army of emergency vehicles that filled the driveway and street in front of the wood-frame house.

True parked behind a patrol car, and they trudged down a driveway.

The garage overflowed with detectives in casual clothes and sleepy-eyed uniformed cops. Flash bulbs popped and police radios echoed into the chilly desert blackness. The body of Freddie Roth was lying next to a printing press, face up.

In the glare of the garage's naked light bulb, Roth's grayish features glistened like a plastic mask. Oddly, the look frozen on the puffy face appeared to be one of disgust, or perhaps dissatisfaction, rather than fear.

"Ink on the hands," True said. He stared at the corpse.

A man of Carr's age was standing in the corner of the garage making a sketch in a notebook. "I'm Detective Contino," he said, without looking up. He had a blackish tan which lent credibility to his continental appearance: form-fitting sports shirt, pleated European trousers, eyeglasses with Italian frames. "Is this the guy you were looking for?"

Carr stepped closer to the body. "That's him."

"Who is he?"

"A counterfeiter," Carr said. "An old-timer. Just out of Leavenworth."

"There's no counterfeit money here," said the detective. He took off his glasses and rubbed the bridge of his nose. "We've done a complete search. I waited to pull the press apart until you guys got here. Figured you'd know where to look for clues in it."

True stepped to the workbench. He hesitated before picking up a screwdriver.

"Go ahead," said Contino. "We've already dusted for prints."

True picked up the tool and leaned over the press. He shoved the screwdriver into the roller area and popped a rectangular rubber mat off one of the rollers. He held it up with thumb and forefinger. The look on his face was one of concern. The words *United States of America* and *Treasury Bill* were visible, barely, in the inky scrollwork design across the top. He handed the mat to Carr.

Contino held up a flashlight as Carr examined the image. "One Hundred Thousand Dollars!" said the detective. He glanced at the other policemen who had gathered around.

True dug his hand into a trash can next to the press and pulled out a handful of paper cuttings. "It's been printed and cut. We missed it." He looked at Carr.

By the time the sun came up, Freddie Roth's body had been carted away, and the rest of the garage, Roth's Ford, and the

228

ranch house had been searched, researched, and searched again.

Carr, his shirt sleeves rolled up, sat at the kitchen table inside the house and waited for Detective Contino to get off the phone.

True sat on the sofa and fiddled with the plastic envelope containing the rubber blanket roller. At his feet was a plastic trash bag containing printing-press scraps. It had a large "Evidence" tag attached to its sealed opening.

Contino mumbled on about trajectories, bullets, and postmortem lividity. He sounded exhausted.

Carr turned his chair around to face True. He thought aloud. "They're going to have to set up a bank caper to down the T bills."

True kicked off his shoes. "I'd say so. Unless there's a liquor store that gives cigarette change for hundred-thousand-dollar government bills. Ha ha ha." He leaned back on the couch.

"*Any* bank will check out the serial numbers of the Treasury bills before they cash them," Carr said, "to see if they have been duly issued and if they are on the stolen list."

"So what else is new?" True put his hands behind his head.

"So to make the scam work he would have to use the serial numbers of *genuine* Treasury bills," Carr said.

True sat up. "That means he had to have an 'in' at a bank to get the serial numbers."

"*And* to get a sample Treasury bill for Freddie to copy on his trusty offset press."

Carr grabbed the brimming plastic trash bag at True's feet. He ripped off the evidence tape and poured the entire contents of the bag in the middle of the living-room floor. He dropped to his hands and knees and sorted through the scraps of paper.

"You're right! Serial numbers!" True said. He scrambled off the couch and dug through the pile.

Contino hung up the phone. He stood over them. "What the hell are you people doing?"

They didn't answer.

"That was the coroner," he said. "Bullets are from a .32 automatic. Roth had been dead for about twenty-four hours when we found him. That's about it, except that the files show that this house is leased by a local dope pusher. The word is he loans the place out for dope deals now and then. I doubt if he's involved. Makes too much money selling weed. He supposedly does a Mexican hay run once a month. . . . Really, what the hell are you doing down there?"

True jumped up off the floor holding a scrap of paper in his hand like a gold nugget. "Got one!" he said. He handed it to Carr.

"Nine digits," Carr said. "It sure *looks* like a serial number." He reached for the telephone.

Carr sat in the conference room at the Los Angeles field office, a chamber containing an executive-size table, at least twelve chairs, and ashtrays. The walls were bulletin boards with hastily scribbled surveillance diagrams and photographs. He was so tired he felt like crawling up on the table and going to sleep.

"Let me do all the talking," he said.

True yawned and stretched. "I wonder why he's making us wait?" he said. "I saw him sitting in his office when we walked in. He was reading his pipe catalogue."

"Protocol," Carr said sarcastically.

A few minutes later Special Agent-in-Charge Norbert Waeves entered the room with a carved Meerschaum jutting from his teeth. He wore a short-sleeved white shirt and a red necktie with a rifle-and-pistols pattern. The white shirt had ball-point-pen marks around the pocket. He was spare of frame, with the bony arms of a man who would rather smoke than eat. A tinge of freckles and curly hair made him look a little too young to be a boss.

As if it was a practiced gesture, Waeves adjusted his trousers and heisted a bony buttock onto the conference table. "What do you see for the *big picture* in this case, Charlie? Sort of a *dry well* at this point, wouldn't you say?" He puffed sweet smoke.

Carr sat up. "We still have a lead," he said. "If we can trace the serial-number scraps we found . . ."

Waeves made a stream of smoke exit from the bowl of the pipe. Grasping the edge of the table with both hands, he hoisted the other half of his rear end onto the table. "Sort of a *long shot*, wouldn't you say? I mean, it's not like the cow isn't out of

230

the barn. . . . Don't get me wrong . . . great investigation on your part . . . certainly nothing personal . . . but at this point there's not really a lot we can do. Really no need for you to stay out here on TDY just to run out gumshoe leads. I'm sure there are much more important things for you to do back at headquarters." His hands were squeezing the table.

Carr said nothing. True fidgeted in his seat.

"You might as well grab a flight back," Waeves said. Three rapid puffs came from the pipe.

"This is a headquarters case, and I have orders from Delgado to stay out here until all the leads are run out," Carr said without inflection.

No Waves acted as if he hadn't heard the remark. He took the pipe from his mouth and pointed it at True. "I take it you've been getting along with Buck?" He gave a half-grin. "He's sort of our *problem child*." He laughed.

True's face grew suddenly red. "What kind of a remark is that?" he said.

"Just a little funny! You shouldn't take things so personally. You're much too defensive." Another pipe smile.

True stood up. "Just a *funny*, huh? Well, *fuck you!* How's that for a real knee slapper?"

No Waves glared at him for a moment and slid off the table to his feet. He adjusted the pipe to the other side of his mouth and walked out of the room.

True put his fingers on his temples. "Here comes another insubordination beef," he said.

"You shouldn't have said it," Carr said.

"I know it. But just the sight of that prick . . ."

The wall phone rang. Carr walked over and picked up the receiver. It was Delgado.

"I just spoke with the people at the Federal Reserve Bank. The serial number matches a genuine Treasury bill that was issued a couple of years ago by the San Francisco Fed and sent to the United Merchants Bank at 14211 Wilshire Boulevard in Los Angeles. Call me when you find out anything."

Carr hung up the phone and wrote the bank address down on a piece of paper in his wallet.

Emil Kreuzer had been in bed for a half hour or so when he remembered the article.

He swung his legs over the side of the bed and rubbed his
eyes. Naked, he got up and found his way into the living room
of the darkened apartment. He turned on a lamp and picked
through the newspaper strewn over the sofa until he found the
article. It read:

ROCK IDOL PLEADS TO TAX RAP

Los Angeles recording star Rexford Epps of the Purple Anteaters
rock group pled no contest to tax evasion charges today in Los
Angeles Federal Court. Epps's Beverly Hills defense attorney,
Martin Robinson, a specialist in tax cases, stated that the rock
star's problems stemmed from a misunderstanding. . . .

Kreuzer tore the article from the paper and turned off the
lamp. He went back into the bedroom and put the article on top
of the dresser next to his wallet and change.

Tracy rolled over in bed. "What time is it?" she said.

He looked at the clock. "It's one-thirty, *Liebschen.*" He clicked
the light on next to the bed. "I can't get to sleep . . . too much
on my mind," he said.

Tracy shielded her eyes from the light. "Why don't you smoke
a joint," she said.

"I have something else in mind, *Liebschen.*" He pulled the covers off her.

She sat up, dressed in a cotton nightgown that looked as though it could use a washing. "Do I have to put on the stuff?" she said matter-of-factly.

"You know how I like it, *Liebschen,*" he said perfunctorily.

Tracy looked at him sleepily for a moment. She yawned, tapping her palm to her mouth a few times, and got out of bed. Dropping to one knee, she picked up a pair of boots and a matching leather vest with buckskin fringe from the floor. She pulled the nightgown over her head, dropped it, and sat down on the bed naked. Her eyes still half closed, she pulled on the boots and shrugged on the vest. It had no buttons. Without a word she walked into the bathroom and came back with a large jar of Vaseline. She set it on the bed.

Kreuzer crawled onto the bed. "I'll try not to make it last too long," he said. "I know you're tired."

The next morning Kreuzer got off an elevator wearing a black suit and striped tie. The door in front of the elevator said, MARTIN L. ROBINSON, ATTORNEY AT LAW. He took two deep breaths and opened it. To a svelte receptionist in a green tailored suit, he handed a card that read:

> DOCTOR ADOLPH CROSS
> CROSS PSYCHIATRIC CLINIC
> 13 RENNWEG
> ZURICH, SWITZERLAND

She ushered him into an office decorated with mahogany panels, lithographs, and diplomas. A bay window behind an oversized and uncluttered desk looked down on the Beverly Hills business district.

She handed the card to a gray-haired man sitting behind the desk, who had a tennis tan and cultivated sideburns. He stood up, introduced himself, and gave a fishy handshake.

Kreuzer replied in his clearest nondialect English and sat down in a zebra-striped chair in front of the desk. "It's about

233

my friend's wife," he said with a sad expression. "Or should I say my deceased friend's wife? He passed away; only fifty-five years old, too." He put his hand on his chest. "The heart," he said.

"I'm sorry," Robinson said, with a few sympathetic blinks.

Kreuzer nodded appreciatively. "My friend was a very wealthy man," he continued. "The oil business. He married a younger woman a few years ago; he was in bad health even then. She was an airline stewardess . . . half his age . . . lives here in Los Angeles now. The family has had problems since he passed away. The bulk of the estate is made up of a number of valuable pieces of art, mostly Chinese porcelain, that he had collected over the years, and that he kept in his chalet in Switzerland. . . . Am I rambling?" Kreuzer said.

The lawyer nodded and blinked a few times. "Please go on," he said, fiddling with a fountain pen.

"I am acting only as a friend of the family in this matter."

"I take it there is a legal problem. . . ."

"Yes and no," Kreuzer said. "What it really boils down to is that my friend's wife is a very unsophisticated and, frankly, somewhat dull young woman. She has offered to sell the collection of porcelain to a reputable Swiss art dealer. They have been negotiating on a price. She retained an American art expert named Prescott to help her dispose of the art. A very reputable and honest man, I must add. I have checked his references myself. But every time he gives her advice, she questions it. She is absolutely paranoid about paying taxes on the money coming into the United States. It should be over a million dollars, by the way. At this point my friend's family is at wit's end because nothing can be settled until she sells the porcelain collection. . . . I have come to you because of your reputation as a tax lawyer. I propose that you act as an adviser to her and Mr. Prescott in tax matters. My only purpose is to expedite the transaction. The family members I represent are willing to pay you a retainer to have the matter taken care of once and for all."

The lawyer made notes on a yellow pad. He looked up. "I take it you are aware that my retainer is fifteen thousand dollars?" he said.

Kreuzer held up his hands. "That will be no problem. . . . It's

234

a million-dollar sale. That is, if you will take the case . . ."

"I'll take it," Robinson said. He smiled. "I think I recognize the outline of the problem."

"Our retainer will be deposited in your name at the United Merchants Bank here in Beverly Hills. You can call Mr. Arbogast—the bank manager—to arrange payment."

Robinson nodded. "Fine, fine." He wrote something on the pad and looked up. "I'll need to know who the client is."

Kreuzer shook his head. "That's what has made the whole thing so difficult up to this point. . . . She demands anonymity."

The lawyer raised his eyebrows and shrugged his shoulders at the same time. He exhaled. "I'd better talk with the art dealer, Mr. Prescott."

"I hope you don't think my taste in art is too mundane, Mr. Prescott," said Martin Robinson, motioning to the prints on the office walls. He gave an ingratiating, sitting-behind-the-desk-in-my-fancy-office smile.

Larry Phillips was sitting in front of the desk. He crossed his legs. "Frankly," he said, "many of my colleagues in the art world actually prefer prints for their offices." He resisted the urge to wring his hands.

"That makes me feel better," Robinson said. Another lawyer smile. "Uh . . . about the art collection itself . . ."

"A collection of antique Chinese porcelain." Phillips emphasized the last words.

Robinson made a note on a yellow pad. "Period?" he said.

"Excuse me?"

"The porcelain . . ."

"Yes, of course," Phillips said. "The Sung period, around 1000 A.D. The collection is made up of blue and white bowls, all bearing the Imperial mark . . . all were fired in an Imperial kiln." Having said this, he held his breath. Please don't ask any more questions, he thought.

"The buyer?" Robinson continued to write. He didn't look up.

"A Mr. Tessier. He is a well-known Swiss art dealer. Highly regarded." He tried to speak effeminately.

Robinson tore a page off the pad and set it aside.

"I know you must think that this whole business is extremely unorthodox," Phillips said.

Robinson put his pen down and folded his hands. "You really can't expect me to represent a client without knowing her identity. . . . Please try to understand my position, Mr. Prescott. Considering the total picture, at this point I'm going to have to demand to know the identity of the client or I can't go any further. You can be assured of my complete confidence and discretion."

Phillips assumed a thoughtful expression and stood up. He took a few steps to the bay window. He waited a few seconds before speaking, for the proper effect. "Dr. Cross only told you *part* of the story. This thing is a time bomb. . . . The porcelain collection belonged to Hayden Murdock. Yes, *the* Hayden Murdock, of Murdock International Oil. Mr. Murdock died a few weeks ago of a heart attack at his chalet in Switzerland. I'm sure you read about it. . . ."

The lawyer nodded.

"He was there with my client, an ex-airline stewardess who was his . . . well . . . mistress. To be candid, she is an uneducated, low-class female whose only attraction to Murdock was youth and good looks. . . ." He turned to Robinson. "The problem is that Murdock did, before his death, give her the porcelain collection, as a gift. Dr. Cross is a friend of the Murdock family and is trying to see to it that Murdock's gift to the woman is kept secret. The sale of such a collection, though not the biggest ever in the art world, will certainly be one of note. Everyone in the art world knows he owned it. Cross is just trying to help the woman dispose of the collection discreetly, without besmirching the Murdock name. . . . As you may know, Murdock's wife is now running the corporation. The mistress—her name is Melissa Rogers—has retained me to help her with the sale. She has no idea that I have known Dr. Cross for many years *and* that I went to school with Hayden Murdock's son. Frankly, I have no desire to see the Murdocks get hurt in this affair."

Robinson looked pleased. "As I see it, the object of the game is to sell the porcelain collection in the most expeditious and discreet manner possible."

"Exactly," Phillips said.

"First," Robinson said, "there is the matter of a retainer, since I am representing Miss Rogers's interest in the matter. Fifteen thousand is my usual fee." He had a haughty expression.

"I can personally vouch for her payment of that amount on the day of the transaction, but she doesn't have a dime at this point." Phillips shook his head.

The lawyer nodded and pressed a button on an intercom. He told the secretary to bring a retainer form.

She came into the room almost too quickly and handed a printed piece of paper to Robinson. He wrote fifteen thousand on a blank line and handed the form to Phillips. Phillips made a show of reading the form. He set it on the desk and signed "L. L. Prescott."

"Due to the unusual circumstances, I'll set up a trust account in my name for purposes of the transaction," Robinson said matter-of-factly.

Phillips's heart beat faster. It always happened.

Robinson continued. "Once Ms. Rogers and the buyer agree on a price, have the seller contact me for payment instructions. I will guarantee the security of the transaction and also its confidentiality. The trust account is a safety feature for both parties. My retainer will be deducted from the selling price once the amount is deposited in the account. And, although there's no need to discuss it, I see no reason why the entire transaction should come to the attention of the IRS." He winked.

Phillips winked back.

They both made polite laughing noises.

Phillips made his exit from the office building and walked around the corner to see if he had been followed. He trotted across the street and got in the passenger seat of the car and shook hands with Emil Kreuzer. "The greedy shyster came up with the idea of a trust account all by himself!" He giggled. "He hit me for another retainer and went right into a fuckin' trance! He figures an easy thirty grand. The bastard had dollar signs in his eyes!"

They belly-laughed to tears, caught their breath, and laughed again.

The secretary plunked down in the zebra-striped chair, leaned back, and closed her eyes. She made no move to adjust her dress below her knees. "I phoned Mr. Arbogast at the bank. No problem. He said Cross's retainer fee would be in any day," she said. "I called a couple of art dealers. A Sung period collection *would* be worth over a million dollars." She sat up. "Where are you going to take me for lunch?"

"And Murdock?" Robinson said. He was looking at her thighs.

"The newspaper morgue had an article a month ago," she said. "He died in Switzerland of a heart attack while on a skiing trip. Everything checks out."

"I don't believe the stewardess story," he said. "They just don't want to pay tax on the sale of a million-dollar art collection. Can't blame them." He stood up and stretched. "I wonder if I should have asked for twenty-five G's each. They didn't bat an eye at the fifteen."

"I'm hungry," said the secretary.

The motorcycle repair shop was small: a wooden-planked showroom, walls covered with posters of half-naked women astride Hondas and Harleys. Larry Phillips leaned on a display of helmets and face masks to speak with the bearded owner, a pot-bellied man wearing baggy jeans and an undershirt that just missed covering his navel. "I'm getting ready to take a trip," Phillips said.

"Who sent you in?"

"Emil Kreuzer."

The man pushed back what could have been a shower curtain, and they stepped into a room filled with greasy tools and motorcycle parts.

"Right on. Whataya need, brother?" The man belched.

"A briefcase," Phillips said.

"To carry big things or small things?" The man surveyed him carefully.

"Small things."

The heavy man reached under a worktable with rough, grease-stained hands and pulled out a cardboard box. He opened the box and took out a black leather briefcase. He

238

flipped it open. "This is X-ray and dog proof. There's no way to find the hidden compartment unless they rip the whole thing apart piece by piece. And they don't do that unless a snitch calls up the Customs pigs and gives 'em your name, rank, and license number. The price is four hundred bucks. It's a lot of money, but what you're paying for is safety." He picked a screwdriver off the workbench and loosened a small screw at the base of the latch. Gently he lifted the corner of the lining inside the case and revealed a compartment almost an inch deep and a foot square. "See?" he said. "Slicker'n shit."

"I'll give you two fifty," Phillips said.

The bearded man's face had no expression. He reassembled the briefcase and put it back in the cardboard box. "I ain't hungry, pal. This is just a sideline for me. A legal one. My lawyer told me. He says what people put in the compartments is their own mother-fucking business. Don't matter to me if it's snow, skag, funny money, or, for that matter, kangaroo shit. . . . I'll take three fifty, and before you counteroffer like the tight-ass bastard that you appear to be, you can just truck right on down the road."

Phillips reached into his pocket and counted out some bills. He handed them over.

"Bon voyage, brother," said the motorcycle man.

$/10

The bank was full of customers.

Carr stood in a group of men and women at a customers' table in the middle of the bank lobby and feigned filling out a deposit slip. He looked at his watch.

Less than twenty feet away, the telephone on a desk marked WILLIAM ARBOGAST—BRANCH MANAGER rang. The fat man sitting at the desk picked it up.

"Yes, this is Mr. Arbogast. . . . Treasury Department?" He swallowed. "Yes, certainly. I'm available this morning. May I ask what this is all about? . . . Oh, *I see.*" Arbogast's puffy face changed from a pink to a white tinge, which was most noticeable just in front of his ears. His pencil became a tapping drumstick. "Yes. I'll be expecting you." He hung up the phone, swallowed again, and took a deep breath. Both hands wiped his forehead.

Casually, Carr walked out of the bank.

True stood in front of a phone booth across the street. Carr waved at him. True looked both ways and trotted across the busy street.

"He freaked out," Carr said.

"Maybe he's just a generally nervous person."

"You never know."

They walked into the bank and showed their badges to Arbogast. Politely, he ushered them into a conference room and

240

pointed to chairs around a heavy, polished table. They sat down.

"You said your questions would be of a confidential nature," he said, unbuttoning his coat. "You know what gossips bank people can be. . . . Well, how can I help you?"

"We'd like to check on some Treasury bills that you have in your vault for safekeeping," Carr said.

The look on the banker's face was one of resignation. He could have been reading from a TV script. "Is there some problem?" he said. His jugular vein was throbbing.

"Yes," Carr said. He handed Arbogast a piece of paper. "This is the description of the Treasury bill in question. We'd like to see it."

Arbogast looked at the paper. "See it?"

"Yes, take a look at it."

"Now?"

"Yes, now."

"Sure, why not?" The heavy man got up and left the room.

True made the okay sign to Carr.

Arbogast slouched back in the room a few minutes later with a Treasury bill in his hand. He handed it to Carr. "Is there some problem?" he said again, with a controlled "you're barking up the wrong tree" expression.

Carr examined the bill for a moment. He looked up. "There sure is," he said. He stared into the other man's eyes.

"What is this all about?" Arbogast said. He sat down again.

"It involves someone taking this Treasury bill outside this bank for a few days."

Arbogast put a fist to his mouth and gave a dry cough. "I'm afraid I don't see what you mean."

Carr snapped a finger against the bill. "I'm afraid you do," he said. "We're here to clear the matter up. If you help us, we will make your cooperation known to the United States attorney. You have no criminal record. You're a solid citizen. All this is in your favor. There're always lots of people involved in these kinds of schemes, and the person who wins the race to the witness stand is usually the one who fares the best. Be assured that someone *will* crack. In every case like this that I have handled over the past twenty years *someone* has cracked. Right now you're on the inside track. We're giving you the chance to be the first, to do the best thing for yourself and your wife and kids. All we want to know is: Who borrowed the T bill?" Carr held it up with two fingers.

"I don't know what you are talking about," Arbogast said. His expression was deadpan, as if he knew a smile or a frown wouldn't work.

"You just said that because you probably saw some Holly-wood queer say it in a movie," True said.

"I don't really appreciate your attitude," Arbogast said. He spoke as if he had been practicing the words. "And I *don't* know what you are talking about. I really *don't.*" He shook his head.

Carr stood up and walked to the door. True followed.

"We'll be back tomorrow morning," Carr said. "But by then it may be too late for you. You may have lost the race. Everything will be down shit creek for you from there on." He turned the doorknob. "If you change your mind tonight, you can call me at the Federal Building. The number is in the phone book. My name is Carr."

The fat man was staring at the wall as they walked out.

The Treasury men strolled out of the bank and got in the car. True started it up and drove a block down the street. He made a U-turn to face the bank.

Carr took the binoculars from the glove compartment and held them up to his eyes. He turned the focus knob. "Wouldn't it be funny if he *wasn't* the right guy?" he said.

True snapped open the glove compartment and adjusted the radio to the surveillance frequency. "It would be even funnier if he *is* the right guy and doesn't call us tonight," he said. "Tomorrow morning when we don't show up at the bank he'll know we were bluffing, that we don't have any evidence. We'll look like two donkeys. We'll have showed our hand for nothing."

"Don't be such a goddamn pessimist," Carr said.

It was a little after 6:00 P.M., and most of the bank's employees had gone home, leaving the bank parking lot almost empty.

Carr held the binoculars up to his eyes. "Here comes our boy," he said.

True started the engine.

William Arbogast trudged across the parking lot and got into a red Cadillac. He started the car and drove out onto Wilshire Boulevard. He blended in with a column of automobiles edging onto a freeway a few feet at a time. The agents were less than a block behind.

The hurry-up-and-stop freeway ride lasted more than an hour. Going south, they passed through gray industrial areas that finally blended into Orange County's geometric sea of stucco structures and manicured lawns. Billboards posted along the freeway touted three-bedroom houses in areas named Prestige Ridge, Hearthside Manor, Elegance Village.

The Cadillac sped off the freeway and wound its way into a residential area made up of two-story homes with three-car garages. It passed a group of T-shirted youngsters riding expensive-looking imported bicycles. It pulled into a driveway and stopped. The garage door opened automatically, and Arbogast drove in. The door closed.

A few minutes later a handsome blonde woman parked a new Lincoln in the driveway and carried groceries into the house.

True stretched his arms. "Maybe he acted nervous because he's just a nervous guy," he said. "Maybe we're off base. Logically, it could have been anybody working in the bank."

"You're right, Buck."

Carr slid the front seat backward.

True got out of the car and stretched his legs. He got back in. "Did I tell you what happened in Providence?" he said.

Carr shook his head.

"The agent-in-charge called me in and said he wanted my daily reports handed in *typed* instead of *printed*. So I spent four days and typed every one I'd ever submitted. *Orders* is *orders*, right? I take 'em in in a big pile, hand 'em to him, and he tells me that he didn't mean that I should type the ones I had *already* handed in. So I tore the whole stack up right in front of him and threw 'em in his wastebasket. He says, 'You're nuts.' "

"Did you tell him to get fucked?" mumbled Carr.

"No. There were three other people in the room. But I called him up that night at his home and told him. . . . I was transferred the next day."

A loud "pop" came from the area of Arbogast's house.

"What was that?" said True.

"It sounded like a shot."

"Probably a kid with a firecracker."

The blonde woman flew out the front door of Arbogast's house with her hands flailing. She screamed hysterically. *"He did it!"* she shrieked. "Call a doctor! Blood all over! Blood all over!" She tore at her hair. "Oh, *no!* NOOOOOH."

True started the engine and sped down the street into Arbogast's driveway.

Carr jumped out of the vehicle and showed her his badge. Screaming jibberish, she pointed to the house. Carr ran for the front door.

True grabbed the woman's arm and sat her down on the grass. Neighbors ran out of the tract houses.

Carr entered the house cautiously. There was a smell of carbide. He pulled his .357 from the cross-draw holster. The well-furnished living room was in order. He crept through it into a bedroom. William Arbogast, dressed in a business suit, was lying on the bed with his head on a pillow. His hand gripped the butt of a blue-steel revolver pointing into his mouth. A highway of blood and tissue chunks extended out of the back of his head across a bright yellow bedspread. There was a bullet hole in the headboard.

Carr put his gun back in its holster. He picked up a phone on the nightstand and dialed the police.

It was almost midnight and everyone except Carr had left. A small army of uniformed policemen, homicide detectives, coroner's deputies, and police photographers had come and gone. The end of William Arbogast's life was now the subject of reports, summaries, sketches, and color photographs, which would be typed, copied, and distributed to police officials, who would review, sign, and initial each copy before filing.

Carr sat at the kitchen table with Sherri Arbogast, a stunning blonde with the legs of a show girl. She had stopped crying only long enough to pull tissues out of a Kleenex box sitting between them.

"My husband overdid everything. He *ate* too much. He *drank* too much. He *gambled* too much. If he bought doughnuts, he

244

would buy three dozen, and we would end up throwing most of them away. If it was wine, he bought a *case*." She closed her eyes and massaged her temples.

"How were the finances?" Carr used a brotherly tone.

She pulled the last Kleenex out of the box and dabbed both eyes again. "He was desperate until a couple of months ago, and then things eased off. I think he borrowed from a loan shark or something. He wouldn't talk about it. . . . We don't own one single thing in this house. I'll have to go to work. God, how I hate the Las Vegas casinos. Everything is money, money, money. My husband was a sick gambler. I should have known something like this would happen. I walked in from the store and he's lying on the bed. He never did that. He said, 'I need some rest.' I walked out of the room and then there was a shot. It was so *loud*." She rubbed her temples again. She looked at Carr. "Were you just driving by?"

"Uh, yes, just driving by. We saw you run out of the house," he said.

The woman put her head down on the table and sobbed. She caught her breath and sobbed some more. "My husband had gambling debts," she cried. "*Big* gambling debts from playing craps in Las Vegas. He would get telephone calls and he would rush out of the house at all hours. He was so worried, he'd get up in the middle of the night and eat sandwiches." She slammed the heel of her hand onto the table.

"Who did he owe?" Carr said softly.

She sat up and wiped mascara-streaked tears from under her eyes. "I don't know exactly—the casinos, the Mafia or something. Up until recently he was making payments to some creep named Emil. He was a go-between—a bagman or whatever they're called. He used to meet him at the race track. He's some kind of a half-baked stage hypnotist. He called here once. He has a German accent. I hate the casinos, the atmosphere, everything about it. I hate Las Vegas. I hate Nevada. Everything was money, money, money."

The front door opened and closed. True walked into the kitchen with a small cardboard box containing hamburgers and coffee. He sat the box on the kitchen table.

"Thank you but I'm not hungry," Sherri said, forcing a smile.

"Would you like us to drive you to a friend's house?" Carr said.

"No. I'm going to stay here tonight and pack. I'll move tomorrow."

"You sure?"

She nodded. "Thank you for being so kind."

Carr avoided her eyes. He nodded, and the woman put her head down on the kitchen table.

Carr got up quietly and followed True through the living room and out the front door. They got into the G-car.

True started the engine and headed back toward downtown Los Angeles. "Did you get it out of her?" he said matter-of-factly.

"Arbogast was owned by a Shylock," Carr said. "The bagman is somebody named Emil, a stage hypnotist."

It was almost closing time, and Ling's Bar was starting to clear out. Ling was telling the joke about the two sperms again.

Carr sat at the bar listening politely, hoping he would have enough energy to laugh at the familiar punch line. True was reading an *L.A. Times* with a flashlight.

A Mexican woman with a beehive hairdo sat at the end of the bar, giggling as she fought off thigh gropes from the drunken FBI agents sitting on either side of her.

"I've found him!" True said. He folded the newspaper and set it on the bar in front of Carr. He focused the flashlight on the article.

It was an advertisement in the entertainment section. It read:

THE ORCHARD LANES
The San Fernando Valley's
Finest Bowling Establishment
Featuring Doctor Emil Kreuzer,
Master Hypnotist
Three shows nightly
in the Winners' Lounge
No cover, no minimum

"You're right; how many stage hypnotists could have the name Emil?" Carr said. He headed for the pay phone on the wall next to the bar and dropped in change. He dialed and a phone rang.

"Del?"

"Huh? Charlie? Wait a minute till I wake up. . . ." A few seconds passed. "Okay, go ahead."

"The bank manager drove home from the bank and committed suicide after we interviewed him. Blew his brains out."

"You can't be serious."

"I am."

"Christ . . . any publicity?"

"No."

"Thank God."

"Apparently he had gambling debts. . . . I need a headquarters name check on a bagman named Emil Kreuzer, K-r-e-u-z-e-r, who was squeezing him. If Kreuzer has an arrest record, would you teletype it to the field office as soon as you can?"

"I'll take care of it," Delgado said. The phone clicked.

Carr hung up the receiver. He sat down at the bar again. "We've got to get a hook into Kreuzer," Carr said.

Sitting in the coffee shop across the street from the Federal Building, Carr read each page of the teletype carefully and handed it to True.

The arrest entries were listed as follows:

Date	Agency	Offense	Dispo
4/15/56	L.A. Sheriff's Dept.	Lewd conduct/ minor	Dismissed
3/11/58	Los Angeles PD	Grand larceny	Sentenced three years
1/3/64	Philadelphia PD	Hypnosis without license	$300.00 fine
3/3/67	Tampa, Fla. PD	Prac. med. no license	20 days
11/12/69	Albuquerque PD	Bunco/grand theft	Dismissed interest of justice
12/7/70	San Francisco PD	Statutory rape	State prison one year

5/19/74	Phoenix PD	Hypnosis no license	Dismissed
7/15/76	Los Angeles PD	Lewd conduct w/minor	Dismissed
2/28/78	U.S. Treas. LA	Counterfeit securities/Fraud by wire	Dismissed

Another page was titled "Organized Crime Strike Force Intelligence Summary." It read:

Kreps Emile aka Emil Kreuzer aka Dr. Adolph T. Michaels, aka Dr. Richard Edward Croft/male, Caucasian, 5'10", 210, brown eyes, brown hair.

1. Kreuzer is currently a bagman in extortionate credit transactions for Las Vegas OC figure Victor King (see index A1421).
2. Performs occasionally as stage hypnotist; has affinity for underage females.
3. Kreuzer believed to be involved as coconspirator in 1977 advance fee confidence scheme involving Los Angeles confidence man L. T. Phillips (see index Y4567).
4. Currently employed as stage entertainer at Orchard Lanes Bowling Alley. Victor King loaned money for Orchard's first mortgage.

Carr handed the last page to True and waved to the waitress for more coffee.

"All the beefs since 1974 were dismissed. Are you thinking what I am?" True said.

"Yep. Looks like in 1974 he may have learned the benefits of being a stool pigeon. Things are looking up."

The bowling-alley parking lot was almost full.

It was past midnight, and the desert basin that was Los Angeles had finally cooled off. A breeze rolled an empty beer can, a few inches at a time, along the asphalt. Carr sat behind the wheel of the government sedan and waited for Emil Kreuzer's last show to end.

True walked out of the bowling alley and got in the front seat of the car.

"The last show just started," he said. "During the break a

248

young chick came into the bar and sat at a table with him for a few minutes. A *real* young-looking gal. *Jail bait*."

"A blonde with a Little Orphan Annie hairdo?"

"Right."

Carr pointed to a row of automobiles on the left. "She came in that silver T-bird right there." He opened the door and got out. "Beep the horn if anybody comes."

True nodded.

Carr glanced around and strolled to the Thunderbird. He tried the door. It was unlocked. He got in the front and closed the door. His hands rushed to the glove compartment. Nothing but two flashlight batteries. He stuck his hand under both seats. A woman's wallet. He flipped it open. Photographs of teen-agers, a change purse, a poem cut out of a newspaper, a high-school student-body card stamped "Freshman" in the name of Tracy Andrews, an envelope addressed to Mr. and Mrs. John C. Andrews, 1419 Gardena Circle, San Pedro, Calif.

A horn honked. There were people coming out of the bowling alley. Carr folded the wallet and stuffed it back under the seat. He got out of the automobile and closed the door quietly. He hurried back to the sedan and got in.

"What's it look like?" True said.

"How old are you when you are a high-school freshman?" Carr said.

"If you are female, you're not old enough to know better."

It was almost two hours before Emil Kreuzer walked out of the front door of the bowling alley with Tracy Andrews. He had his arm around her waist. The couple got in the Thunderbird. They drove out of the lot.

Carr and True followed them to a neon-lit motel on Ventura Boulevard that had an "Adult Movies in Every Room" sign. Tracy waited in the Thunderbird while Kreuzer rented a room. He returned to the T-bird, looked around once, and walked her to the room. He unlocked the door and ushered her inside. Carr couldn't tell whether it was Kreuzer or the girl who pulled the blinds. The number on the door was 109.

Carr got out of the car and jogged to a pay phone at an adjoining gas station. He dropped a dime in the phone and dialed the police emergency number.

A few minutes later a black-and-white police car cruised into the motel lot, shining its spotlight on first-floor room numbers. The spotlight hit 109 and was turned off. A police officer lumbered out of the driver's seat and slipped a night stick into his belt. He was followed by a younger centurion with gorilla arms, who got out of the passenger side. They sauntered to the door, positioned themselves on either side of it. The younger man knocked three times with his night stick.

"Police officers! Open up."

The door stayed closed.

A voice came from inside. "What seems to be the problem, officers?"

"Open the door!" said the policeman with gorilla arms.

"Will you just tell me what it's all about?"

"We're looking for a thirteen-year-old girl runaway."

"I'm alone, officers. You must have the wrong room."

"Okay!" said the policeman with gorilla arms, pulling his gun out of his holster. "Sorry to have bothered you!" He stepped back and karate-kicked the door handle. The door flew open. The officers rushed in, and there were the sounds of slaps, screams, and furniture breaking.

Minutes later a handcuffed and barefoot Emil Kreuzer was ushered out of the room in his shorts. He had a bloody nose. High-schooler Tracy Andrews followed him in tears. Everyone got into the police car.

Carr and True sat at a round desk covered with mug shots of black men with goatees.

The police squad room was empty except for a pockmarked detective interviewing an old woman with a fresh bandage on her forehead. The tone of their discussion was subdued, perhaps sad. The woman kept touching a red spot on the bandage and looking at her fingers.

The policeman with gorilla arms walked into the room with a clear plastic bag containing a wallet. He set it on top of the mug shots. "Says he's a doctor. A hypnotist. Nothing much in his wallet to speak of. His story is that she's a whore and he paid her, says he didn't know her age." He pointed to a door. "She's in the other interview room telling a policewoman how they're engaged to be married."

Carr opened the plastic bag and looked in Kreuzer's wallet. Credit cards, cash, a piece of paper with telephone numbers, some wallet-sized photos of teen-age girls. He took a small note pad from his coat pocket and wrote the numbers down. "Okay if we talk with him?" he said.

"Knock yourself out," said the policeman. "I told him we got a call from a friend of her father's who'd seen her at the bowling alley and taken down his license number. Just like you said."

"Thanks," Carr said.

He got up and walked into the interview room. True followed. Emil Kreuzer took his feet off the table. Carr showed his badge. "Treasury agents. My name's Carr. This is my partner, Cecil True."

"Treasury?" Kreuzer sat up in his chair. "What's this all about?"

The agents sat down at the table. "Victor King. We understand you do errands for him."

Kreuzer showed no emotion. "Who's he?" His stomach paunch moved lewdly as he spoke.

There was silence for a while.

"What's your bail?" True said.

"Two grand. A bondsman is on the way. I'll be out in an hour. . . . How did you know I was here?"

"We were here on something else," Carr said. "Just happened to see your name on the booking list downstairs."

"I guess with that prior kiddie conviction you might end up doing a little time for this one," True said.

The hypnotist stared at each man separately. He blinked nervously.

"The old conviction was a completely trumped-up case. I was framed by a San Francisco detective. He got the gal to give a phony statement and say that I came on her tits; stuff like that. The whole thing was bullshit. The cop framed me because he hated my guts. That's the truth whether you believe it or not." His jaw was set.

"So you've never met Victor King?"

He stopped blinking. "I didn't say that. I meet a lot of people. I'm an entertainer. I don't remember every son of a bitch I meet."

"How about a banker named Bill Arbogast?"

Kreuzer's eyes were focused on a wall. He was silent for a few moments.

"I might know who you are talking about," he said.

"How well?" Carr said.

"I think I met him once."

"When?" Carr said.

Kreuzer put both hands flat on the table. His fingers were outstretched. "And if I answer that, you Feds say where, why, and how, and on and on we go. I know the game. Maybe you should check my record. You might see that I cooperated with you people a couple of years ago. Cleared up a major securities-fraud case."

"And Uncle Sam is eternally grateful," True said sarcastically.

"Very funny . . . but whether you know it or not it *was* a big case and I was a *paid* informant. Maybe you'd better check. There's an Agent Kelly in the L.A. office who'll vouch for me."

"I'll do that," Carr said. He left the room.

The gorilla-armed policeman sat at a desk writing a report.

"What kind of a case do you have?" Carr said.

"A zero," said the policeman. "They were nude when we went in the door, but there's a problem with the bitch's parents. I just called 'em and they won't file a complaint. Her stepfather isn't interested—something about she was old enough to make her own decisions. The 'doing her own thing' line. Refused to come over and pick her up . . . I'm sure the district attorney will kick the case." He shrugged.

Carr lifted a phone and dialed.

"This is Charlie. Ever heard the name Emil Kreuzer, a snitch in a fraud case a couple of years ago?"

"Sure have," Kelly said.

"How about a rundown?"

"He's a double-crosser. It was a phony-stock case and he was in the middle of it. He gave us just enough info to keep our interest peaked. The old line of shit, telling us how he was 'working on it' trying to get some 'names.' 'Get back to ya in a day or so with more'; the usual snitch crapola. He was good at giving little tidbits that were impossible to corroborate at the time. Then boom! Suddenly a bunch of old people start making complaints about being ripped off in a securities scam. Kreuzer's name comes up as being one of the prime movers in the operation."

Carr made notes. "Was he prosecuted?" Carr said.

"The U.S. attorney declined to prosecute him because in trial he would have had the defense of acting as a federal informant during the course of the crime," Kelly said. "The prosecutor was worried about losing a case, because a federal judgeship had just opened up and he was in line for it. As it turned out, he didn't get it anyway. He was aced out by old Judge Hollingsworth's oldest kid."

"Who were Kreuzer's associates?" Carr said.

"A young con man named Larry Phillips. He was the front man and ended up with a two-year shot in Leavenworth. Smooth operator. There was also a guy who printed the phony stock certificates. He was missing for a long time. They finally found his body in a public dump in Azusa a year later. Head shots. No way of knowing whether his death was connected to the case or not . . . Oh, just remembered something else. Kreuzer likes to ball teenyboppers. Need anything else?"

"Yes. Don't tell No Waves I called."

"I wouldn't tell No Waves if his house was on fire," Kelly said.

"Thanks." Carr put the phone down. He walked back to the interview room and opened the door. "It checks out," he said. "Kreuzer was on our side in a securities case a while back." He closed the door and sat down again.

Kreuzer smirked. "Now maybe you fellas will level with me. What is it you really want? . . . For all I know, I've been framed."

Carr took off his coat and hung it on the back of the chair. He offered a cigarette to Kreuzer and he accepted. They both lit up. Carr rested his elbows on the table. "We're interested in Victor King," he said.

"I'm interested in getting this case dismissed, squashed for good."

"So show me some cards, dealer," Carr said.

Kreuzer lowered his voice and furrowed his brow. "How

253

about paper rip-off at the Printing Office in Washington, D.C.? I've heard rumbles."

"If you can put that one together, I'll get the case dismissed for you. That's a promise," Carr said.

"All I have at this point is that Victor King may be involved in the theft. I can find out some more in the next few days."

"Sounds good," Carr said.

"Of course, if I solve the case for you, I'll expect a cash reward as well," Kreuzer said.

"Of course."

Most of the passengers on the jumbo jet were sleeping. Those who weren't ambled along the narrow aisles stretching or waited in lavatory lines.

Larry felt cramped.

Melba noisily folded a copy of the airline flight magazine in half and underlined another name. "Angelo Colantonio," she said. "That's damn sure *Eye*talian." She copied the name on a cocktail napkin under three other Italian monikers.

Larry looked at the magazine. The name was in an article entitled "People on the Move."

"Now practice writing them," he whispered. "Each one in a different style."

"I hate paperwork," she said.

Shortly after the sun came up, the FASTEN SEAT BELT sign came on, and Larry felt the DC-10 begin its descent into Zurich. The captain said something over the intercom about enjoying one's stay in Switzerland.

Larry nudged Melba awake and whispered final instructions. "Don't act overly nice," he said, "and don't act overly put out if they want to search the luggage. Just act sleepy."

"Okay, *okay*," she said. "You've told me a hundred times. I'm not *that* dumb. Mercy."

The plane landed and taxied to the ramp. He handed her the

briefcase and moved among the stream of passengers struggling through the front exit door.

At the Customs checkpoint, a red-cheeked Customs officer tossed Larry's suitcase onto a stainless-steel table and opened it. He stuck his hands into the clothing as if it were bread dough and then said, "*Danke schön.*" Another uniformed man stamped his passport. Larry moved on among the crowd of tourists.

Standing behind a short, chrome-pipe fence, he watched the officer wave Melba past the checkpoint with a broad smile.

She slinked up to him, grinning. "Didn't even have to open the briefcase," she said. "He was staring at my tits the whole time." She was still talking proudly of the feat when they got into a taxi.

"I have a question," she said.

"Uh-huh."

"What if I would have got caught?"

"Then you would have just told them that a man asked you to carry the briefcase and that you didn't know what was in it. You don't even have a key to it. They can't prove intent. You'd have nothing to worry about."

She closed her eyes and leaned back in the seat. "Mercy," she said softly.

The hotel lobby had a dignified, almost austere look. Everything—the sturdy carpet, the polished ornamental wood on the walls, a mural of the Swiss Alps—looked as if it had just been cleaned.

At the fastidious registration desk Larry showed his passport and signed Lawrence Hess on a card. He handed it back to a bespectacled clerk, whose nails appeared manicured.

The clerk said, "Just a moment, sir," and opened a drawer. He took out an envelope and handed it to Larry. "A message for you. Enjoy your stay." Smiling, he motioned to a bellhop.

In the room Larry opened the envelope. The note read: "Welcome to Zurich. I will call you tomorrow at 10:00 A.M. Glanzmann." He dropped the note in the wastebasket.

He undressed and lay down on the bed naked, resting his hands behind his head. "I don't like this setup. Sitting here in this room with the bill. Waiting like a sitting duck," he said.

Melba stripped to her panties and sat down at the dresser and brushed her hair. Her heavy breasts moved rhythmically with each stroke. This went on for at least fifteen minutes.

"I'm peeking at you in this mirror, honeybunch," she said, "and I see someone with a little ol' starter-upper. . . . You always get turned on when you're pulling some shit." Still brushing, she turned to face him. "You must be thinking about money right this very minute." She giggled.

"Shut your mouth and get over here, you goddamn whore. You stupid bitch. You rotten hillbilly cunt."

"Now you're talking, cowboy," Melba said. She stood up and pulled off her panties.

The next morning Larry finished a breakfast of rolls, coffee, and eggs and set the tray on the floor next to the bed. He fluffed up a pillow and leaned back.

Melba sat at the dresser, pecking slowly on an American portable typewriter a bellboy had delivered. She copied from an airlines magazine propped up on her overnight bag. She stopped typing. "Can't there be just *one* tiny mistake?"

"What did I just tell you?" Larry said to the ceiling.

She ripped the paper out of the typewriter. "Well, goddamn it all to *hale, sheeyit, fuck*." She put another piece of paper in the machine. "These Eyetalian names aren't easy."

The phone rang at precisely 10:00 A.M.

Larry plucked it from the polished nightstand.

"Hello, Mr. Hess?"

"Yes," Larry said.

"Glanzmann here. Could we get together for lunch today? I could come to your hotel."

"Noon?"

"Fine. I'm looking forward to meeting you."

Larry put down the receiver.

The white-tableclothed dining room was decorated with oil paintings of men in brightly colored military uniforms and other eighteenth-century outfits. Bowls of artificial flowers, which looked real enough to sniff, were on every table.

Larry Phillips handed Glanzmann an envelope. He removed a bottle from a silver ice bucket and refilled the man's wineglass.

The banker opened the envelope and unfolded the letter discreetly, as if someone might try to read over his shoulder. He was a short, red-cheeked man in a woolen suit and a stiff-collared shirt. The ensemble might as well have been stenciled "banker's uniform." His face was angular and fastidiously well shaved. Perhaps it was this feature that reminded Phillips of his father, the diplomat, a man who could waste an hour shaving his face.

"These are the only other persons besides myself who would have access to the account," Phillips said.

Glanzmann pushed the letter toward him. "Is this pronounced *Col*antonio?"

"That's correct."

"I see."

"They would identify themselves by their signature," Phillips said.

"Of course . . . And the amount of the initial deposit for the account?"

Phillips lifted the wine bottle and poured. He spoke matter-of-factly. "I'm going to open the account with one hundred U.S. Treasury bills in one-hundred-thousand-dollar denominations. This is to be changed into Swiss francs." He avoided looking directly at the other man.

Glanzmann lifted the wineglass. He drank. "Piesporter Goldtröpfchen," he said. "I really prefer the German white wine. Unlike so many Swiss, I have no prejudice against the Germans."

A tuxedoed waiter served plates of veal decorated with pimento and parsley, and rushed away.

"*Guten Appetit*," Glanzmann said. He hoisted his knife and fork and began eating.

"The Treasury bills were kept in a Canadian bank," Phillips said, "and, frankly, the U.S. Internal Revenue Service found out. I'm sure you are familiar with the IRS interest in casino . . . uh . . . funds."

"I believe it's called skim money." Glanzmann smiled.

Phillips gave a furtive glance at the oil paintings for effect.

"Relax, Mr. Hess. You are in *Switzerland*. Your deposit, from whatever source, for whatever reason, is not illegal in this country. We are familiar with these types of transactions and guarantee complete confidentiality. I can open a numbered account for you. This guarantees that no one outside myself and certain key bank officers has knowledge of the transaction. Future access for you or your colleagues requires only presentation of the number and an authorized signature." He took a bite, chewed, and swallowed. "American tax investigators are not even allowed inside our bank offices. We make them wait in the lobby when they come around asking questions. Sometimes I get the feeling these silly bureaucrats come to Switzerland just for the free trip. They *know* we never answer their questions." He stuffed another chunk of calf in his mouth.

Phillips gave a cogitative nod.

"When do you intend to deposit the securities?" Glanzmann said. "So I can have the proper papers ready."

"I'll bring them to the bank tomorrow morning. I need to make a call to Las Vegas for final instructions. I'm sure you understand. My organization expects the account to be mobile, functioning. We may, on occasion, have special requests for funds."

"We handle such things routinely," said the banker.

Emil Kreuzer bowed deeply to the scattered applause. The curtain closed.

He walked off the stage and sat down on a musty sofa. The last thing in the world he felt like doing at the moment was roaming the barroom tables to make obligatory small talk with the audience of bowling-shirted yokels.

Tracy Andrews, the braces on her teeth gleaming because of the bluish stage lights, came in the side door, carrying a drink. In the silver cocktail dress (a color similar to that of her wired teeth), she almost looked twenty-one. She sat down next to him on the couch and sipped her drink. "The bartender told me to tell you that Tommy Luchese is waiting outside for you and has two guys with him."

Kreuzer suddenly felt nauseous. He could feel his heart beating in the tips of his fingers.

"Who's Tommy Luchese?" she said.

Kreuzer jumped up and began rubbing a fist into an open palm. He walked to a pay phone hanging on the wall in the corner and paced back and forth a few times in front of it.

"Are you okay?" whined the teen-ager.

He found a dime in his pocket and dialed a number.

"Hello," said Victor King. He sounded sleepy.

"This is Emil. Sorry to wake you up, but I just wanted to let you know that I have the money, all of it. You can send someone to pick it up tomorrow."

"Tommy is looking for you tonight. Give the money to him," King said.

"I'm on stage tonight. I don't have the money *with* me. Have Tommy meet me at Hollywood Park tomorrow before the first race . . . in the clubhouse. I'll have the money then, as God is my witness."

There was another silence. Kreuzer felt like throwing up.

"Have Tommy call me," King said finally. "I'll give you the last postponement for old time's sake. Have the money tomorrow." He hung up.

Kreuzer put the receiver on the hook. He picked up the drink and tossed it down without taking a breath. He took a pen out of a side pocket of the tuxedo jacket and grabbed a cocktail napkin off the floor. Holding the napkin against the wall, he wrote "Tell Tommy to call Victor King immediately" on it and put the pen back in his pocket. Folding the napkin, he gave it to Tracy, who was at his side, whining, wanting to know what it was all about.

"Give this to the bartender," said the hypnotist, "and bring me back another drink, *Liebschen*. . . . Tell him to make it a double."

"Victor says today is it. No more fuckaround," said Tommy Luchese with glaring wolf's eyes.

Kreuzer thought he looked like a two-dollar tout in his off-the-rack hound's-tooth coat, someone who didn't belong in the clubhouse.

"I'll meet you in the bar next to the hundred-dollar windows at the end of the fourth race," Kreuzer said. "I'll have the fifteen

G's. I'm waiting for someone to bring it right now." He looked at his wristwatch.

The swarthy man adjusted something inside his coat. "Be there," he said.

"Okay, I'm impressed," Kreuzer said sarcastically. He returned to his table in the dining area and sat down.

The blonde with braces was combing her hair. Her make-up was overdone. "What's a furlong?" she said.

Kreuzer looked to see if the man was gone. He told the girl he would be back in a few minutes.

"You're not even listening to me," she said.

He picked up his cocktail, got up, and took the elevator to the general-admission area.

Carr stood next to a line of barred windows with signs that read: $5 WIN–PLACE–SHOW. People (who all seemed to be wearing hats) shuffled and trotted through a cement prairie dotted with hot-dog wrappers and parimutuel tickets to line up at the windows. The sport of kings, thought Carr, kings who breathe a prayer on the dice in Las Vegas, hoping to win enough money for a tank of gas to get home.

True slouched against a cement pillar a few feet away eating ice cream.

A door marked CLUBHOUSE—MEMBERS ONLY opened, and Emil Kreuzer stepped out, carrying a plastic martini glass. He ambled through the crowd to Carr's side. He whispered, "The guy who stole the government paper is about thirty-five years old, medium build, brown hair, and wears glasses. He may have done some time in the federal joint." His eyes surveyed the milling crowd. He finished the drink and tossed the glass in the trash can. He took a racing form out of his pocket and turned the pages.

"What was he in for?" Carr said, keeping his eyes on the faces in the crowd.

Kreuzer spoke from the side of his mouth. "Unknown at this point. I expect to have more for you in a couple of days." He looked up from the racing form. "It would help if you could give me some leads . . . like run a few things by me and maybe something would ring a bell." He circled a number on the form.

"We have nothing to go on at the moment," Carr said. "Zero leads. The people in D.C. are still trying to figure out how much of the paper is missing, believe it or not." Carr shook his head disgustedly. He put a cigarette in his mouth and lit it without looking at the other man.

"You can count on me," Kreuzer said. "It's just a matter of time. . . . In the meantime here's one for you. Tommy Luchese is in the bar next to the hundred-dollar windows. He's wearing a hound's-tooth sports coat and a shoulder holster. I understand you Feds are looking for him."

"Thanks for the bone," Carr said.

"I'll call you the moment I get something on the paper thing." Kreuzer gave Carr a buddy pat on the arm and headed back toward the clubhouse entrance.

Carr walked briskly toward the hundred-dollar windows. True caught up with him. "Ever heard the name Tommy Luchese?" Carr said.

"There's a wanted poster in the field office. He escaped from Terminal Island six months ago. He was in for dealing bogus Series E bonds."

Carr stopped in front of a crowded bar. He stared.

"Goddamn," True said. "That's him . . . the one in the sports coat." He talked out of the side of his mouth.

"There are too many people," Carr said. "We'll wait till he leaves and grab him outside. Go tell Track Security what we have planned. I'll keep an eye on him."

True took off at a run.

Luchese looked at his watch. He glanced up and surveyed the crowd. His eyes fixed on Carr.

Carr turned his head to avoid eye contact. He looked back and Luchese was moving, weaving, through the crowd. Carr followed. At the cement ramp leading to the parking lot Luchese looked back at Carr and broke into a full run. There were screams as he knocked people down clawing his way through the crowded passageway.

Carr sprinted behind him along the ramp. He dived across a turnstile gate and caught an arm around the man's neck. Then they were both on the ground, and something hard hit the side of Carr's head. He saw stars for a moment and squeezed harder on Luchese's neck. They rolled into trash cans. People were yelling.

"Break it up, you two," screamed a man with a high voice, "before someone gets hurt!" They were in a forest of feet. People were falling down.

"Police . . . police . . ." groaned Carr.

Luchese twisted and pulled the gun from his shoulder holster. Carr pulled backward on his neck with all the strength he could muster. The gun went off with a frightening hollow sound as it ricocheted off a trash can. People wailed and ducked for cover.

Carr's ears were ringing. True slammed through the pile of trash cans and got his hands on the gun. He gave a violent twist, and Luchese yelped. True wrenched the gun from his hand. Suddenly an army of blue-uniformed security men was helping to squeeze handcuffs on the young crook's wrists.

True pulled Luchese to his feet. A trail of blood from the crook's nose to the point of his chin began to dot the hound's-tooth coat.

Luchese sat in the back seat of the government sedan next to Carr. "How'd ya know I was at the track?" he said. He forced a little gust of air through his clotting nose.

Carr didn't answer.

"You don't have to answer that, cop. There was only one person who knew I was there . . . Emil Kreuzer." The dried blood on his upper lip cracked when he smiled.

"Who's he?" Carr said.

The telephone rang, just as Emil Kreuzer knew it would. He got up from the couch and turned down the volume on the television. The phone rang again.

Tracy put down the bottle of nail polish she was holding and started to get up off the floor. She blew on her hands. "Want me to get it?" she said.

Kreuzer shook his head. He let the phone ring twice more before he picked up the receiver.

"What happened to ya?" said Victor King in a serious tone.

"I met Tommy at the track today and paid him the money, just like I told you I would. I told you you had nothing to worry about."

"Tommy is in jail," King said.

"In jail!" screamed Kreuzer. "Did you get the money I gave him?"

"Somebody fingered him at the track," King said.

"Don't pull that shit on me! I paid Luchese. If he says any different, he's a goddamn liar and I'll tell him that to his face!"

There was a silence for a while. Kreuzer's temples throbbed.

"I'll check into it further," King said.

"You do that. You just do that. That punk isn't going to double-cross me! I won't stand for it."

The phone clicked. Kreuzer put down the receiver. His hand was shaking.

Tracy blew on her fingers. "Who was that?" she said.

He walked to the cupboard and took out a bottle of vodka. He spun off the lid and took a swig directly from the bottle.

"Emmmiiilll," whined the teen-ager, "who *was* it?"

"Shut the fuck up," he said under his breath. "Someone from the lounge," he said.

The county jail's prisoner-reception area smelled like dead skin. Carr told Tommy Luchese to stand in front of a barred door. He dug a key out of the change in his pants pocket and removed the handcuffs.

The other new fish, at least half of whom were black, stood and squatted behind the steel bars of the arrival tank. Sheriff's deputies, wearing uniforms one shade darker than the pale-green walls, stood on the other side of the tank putting on rubber gloves in preparation for the usual intimate greeting.

True leaned on a counter in front of a one-way mirror and filled in the booking form. He finished and stuffed the form through a slot in the window. The jailer inside the booth said, "One comin' in," in singsong fashion.

The prisoners pulled their hands off the bars to avoid the heavy tank door as it slid open on a metal track. Carr shoved Luchese inside the tank. Slowly, with the sound of metal on metal, the door returned to its original position.

The agents went out into a hallway and removed their revolvers from a gun-locker box. They put the guns into their holsters. "Did Kreuzer say anything about the paper scam?" True said.

Carr shook his head. "A ration of crapola: 'the guy you're looking for has brown hair and is medium height; I'll have more for you in a coupla days.'"

"At least that's something."

Carr shook his head. "Wrong. It's nothing."

"You don't believe him?"

"No, I believe him."

True followed Carr out the door and into the parking lot. He had a serious expression. "I don't get it," he said.

They got into the sedan, and Carr started the engine. "Kreuzer is jerking us off," he said. "He's telling us facts that are probably true, but not substantial enough to follow up on." He drove a hundred yards, to a chain-link gate, and held up his badge to a TV camera attached to a steel post. The gate opened and he drove out.

"I still don't get it," True said.

"If he's right in the middle of the scam, he could be giving us just enough info to cover himself if he gets caught. He could say he was a federal informant and was involved only because he was helping us. A jury would probably buy the story."

They pulled up at an intersection red light. There were bail bondsmen's offices on all four corners. A signboard on a roof of one of the offices showed a pair of bright-pink clasping hands. FRIENDLY SERVICE—24 HOURS A DAY was written in huge gothic-style letters.

"So what are we gonna do?" True said.

Carr took a right turn toward Chinatown.

$/12

Ling's was almost empty; the only patrons left were regulars—cops and investigators with the alcohol habit, sipping the drinks they would be sorry for in the morning.

"Where do we go from here?" True said.

"We're going to follow Emil Kreuzer twenty-four hours a day."

"What do you think he is going to do?"

"I don't know."

The bar phone rang. Ling picked it up. "Charlie! For you," he said. He set the phone on the bar in front of Carr.

"I figured I'd find you in your old hangout," said Jack Kelly. "An inspector from D.C. flew in today. He's been hanging around with No Waves all day. He checked True's personnel file. Thought you might want to know."

"Thanks."

Carr handed the phone back to Ling. He looked at his young partner. "I'm guessing an inspector is going to give you a surprise interview tomorrow when we check in at the field office. No Waves has probably written up a formal insubordination charge."

True rubbed his chin nervously. "Jesus. What should I say?"

"Let's discuss it," Carr said. He ordered another round.

• • •

The atmosphere in the field office the next morning was harried. Phones rang and special agents, dressed in the Los Angeles uniform of short-sleeved white shirts, wing-tipped shoes, and black leather holsters containing revolvers with rubber grips, buzzed from one part of the office to another, gossiping and making bets on what would happen to Buck True. Most of the money was on "termination for cause."

Carr sat on a hard-backed chair in the interview room and stared at Norbert Waeves's pistol-and-rifle necktie. The inspector, a thirty-five-year-old Ivy Leaguer, who, Carr knew, had spent his career at a desk in headquarters, made notes with a pen that looked almost too big for his hand.

"What do you recall of the discussion?" said the fair-face inspector.

"Not a lot, really," Carr said with a thoughtful expression. "I was preoccupied with this case I'm working on. I wasn't really listening. . . . I do remember SAIC Waeves telling Agent True something about him being a troublemaker . . . something like that."

No Waves' mouth became a straight line.

"What were his exact words?" said the inspector.

"He said, 'True, I've had it with you. You're so stupid. I doubt if you know what your own name is.' "

"Did True have any response?"

"Yes. He said, 'My name is *Buck True*.' He raised his voice when he said his name."

The inspector looked at No Waves sheepishly. "Could he have said the words *Fuck you?*"

Carr answered immediately. "Definitely not. He said, *'Buck True.'* I remember that distinctly. He said, 'My name is Buck True.' "

Waeves slid his chair back violently and stormed out of the room. He slammed the door.

The young inspector stared at his notes. "You can go now," he said under his breath.

Carr and True left the field office, each carrying a pair of binoculars.

As if No Waves might have bugged every part of the Federal

Building, neither man spoke on the way down in the elevator. They checked out a government sedan, and Carr steered out of the underground parking lot down Spring Street and into a steel stream that was the Hollywood Freeway.

True smirked. "Boy, did we fuck them!" Roaring with laughter, he slapped his knee. "No Waves was fucked at his own game—and that pussy inspector! Ha ha ha ... Say, how come you're not laughing?"

"Because you are a dipshit."

"What did you say?"

"You heard me."

"What's wrong? You're the one who made up the story for me."

They passed by Echo Park and got off at Vermont. Carr headed north, past food stands and small, dingy shops.

"That's right. If I hadn't, they'd have proved insubordination and your career would be over. . . . Your problem is that you don't understand people," Carr said.

"Like who? Like that backstabber No Waves?"

"He's a jerk," Carr said, "nothing more, nothing less. You and I stuck our necks out this morning for nothing. For absolutely nothing. Sure, the beef will be nonsustained, but No Waves will get back at you eventually. He'll figure a way—and that pogey inspector will help him. Unless you wise up, you're on your way out. Not just another transfer. I mean *out*. They'll sit up nights figuring ways to fire you. You're going to have to learn to keep your big mouth shut."

Carr steered right and passed well-kept apartment houses on Los Feliz until they blended onto a steep one-way road toward Griffith Park.

The younger man's face was red. "Look, if you don't like working with me . . ."

"I don't like working with any *dipshit*." Carr turned for emphasis. "Particularly one who's got a martyr complex."

"Yeah, well, *get this*. I was in the navy for four years. I swore that when I got out I wasn't going to take any shit ever again. That means from you or anybody else. So, fuck you!"

Carr slammed on the brakes and threw the sedan into parking gear. He jumped out and ran around to the passenger door. He

268

ripped open the door and pulled True out by his necktie. With an open-handed flashing blow, he slapped him in the face. True flew backward into the dirt.

True scrambled to his feet swinging. Carr back-pedaled and, keeping his hands open, cat-slapped him again. True threw a right hook. Carr blocked it with an elbow and administered three more lightning-powerful slaps. The younger man lost his balance and fell into the dirt again. His face was fever red.

With a thrust of his hands and feet he was up and diving at Carr. Carr side-stepped to the right. He slapped again. True slammed into the door of the sedan. Carr caught the junior agent's neck in the crook of his arm and choked. True went to his knees. Carr pulled the handcuffs off his belt and snapped one onto a loose wrist. He snapped the other cuff around the sedan's passenger-door handle and stepped back.

True caught his breath and struggled violently. "You're nuts!" he screamed. He pulled violently at the door handle.

Carr was breathing hard. He leaned against the fender of the vehicle. "If you get fired, do you know who will get your little gold Treasury badge?"

"Take these off, goddamnit. . . . You're nuts."

Carr waited for an answer.

"Okay, *who?*"

"Some asshole *just like No Waves* . . . That's what you don't understand, Mr. Shit-for-Brains. He will have *won. You* will be selling pencils door to door, not *him.*" Carr hoisted himself up on the fender. He loosened his tie.

True slumped down next to the sedan, one arm still attached to the door. Both men sat without speaking for a few minutes.

Carr sauntered to the trunk. He opened it, dug into an old flight bag, and pulled out a pint bottle of Scotch. He slammed the trunk and walked to the side of the sedan. He stood in front of True and loosened the bottle cap. He took a healthy swig from the bottle and wiped his mouth with the back of his hand. "From now on I want you to start doing a lot of listening and not too much talking."

"How do you know I even *want* to work with you?" True tugged at the handcuffs.

"You have to," Carr said. "No one else wants to work with

you." He stared at True for a moment and handed him the bottle. The younger man shook his head but took a drink. He handed the bottle back. Carr twisted the cap back on and returned it to the trunk.

"You've got a handcuff key in your pocket," Carr said. He got back in the car and waited until the red-faced True dusted off and got back in the sedan. They drove off without speaking.

The restaurant was a checkered-tablecloth operation with a four-seater bar in the corner (wine and beer only). The walls were decorated with black-and-white Olympic-auditorium photos of a flexing, bald wrestler wearing a foot-wide championship belt. Each photo bore the inscription "Prince Nikola of Serbia." The only differences between the photos and the man wearing a form-fitting T-shirt behind the bar were grayer eyebrows and perhaps twenty pounds around the midsection.

The good tables in the place were the ones at the front window, which provided a view of Santa Monica beach and the picturesque, if run-down pier. At Sally's insistence, Carr had called ahead and reserved one.

The menu had been chicken smothered in paprika (Carr had eaten Sally's, too, because she said most chicken ranches added steroids to the feed), roast potatoes, string beans, and cheese strudel.

Prince Nikola of Serbia came to the table wiping his hands on an apron. He filled the wineglasses. "Maybe they transfer you back someday?" he said to Carr.

"Maybe," Carr said.

The wrestler picked the credit card from the table and shoved it into Carr's shirt pocket. "The dinner is on me," he said, slapping Carr roughly on the shoulder.

Carr reached for the card. "No, Nick, I couldn't. . . ."

"Shawdup," said the Prince of Serbia on his way to the kitchen.

Sally took a sip of wine. "I could get a promotion if I transferred to Washington, D.C. Plenty of openings for court reporters from what I've been told."

Carr finally said, "Oh, really," knowing that it wouldn't sound right. She was going to start.

Sally folded her hands on the table. "How does that sound to you? You know, me coming to D.C.?"

"Fine, sounds great. . . . That was really nice of Nick to buy us dinner."

Sally was staring out the window. The just-after-dusk ocean was steel gray. The waves were more plodding than powerful and, though slightly more than the width of a football field away, seemed distant. They could have been in an aquarium. "Nothing has changed," she said after a while.

Carr lit a cigarette. "There really is a possibility I might get transferred back to Los Angeles," he said.

"Even if you did, nothing would be any different between us, would it?" She continued to look at the ocean.

Carr fidgeted in his seat. "I don't know," he said.

Sally looked him in the eye. "I promised I wouldn't do that . . . 'putting you on the spot,' as you call it." Her tone was bitter.

The walk back to Sally's apartment was strained, Carr resisting the urge to take her hand for fear of being regarded as condescending. They made little bits of white-flag conversation.

In the apartment, Sally went directly to the sink and ran water into a small coffeepot. Carr sat down on the sofa like a stranger. He wanted to take off his shoes, but didn't.

After a few minutes he got up and went into the kitchen. Sally was standing at the stove. She turned away from him and wiped her eyes.

He put his hands on her shoulders and turned her around. Her head found his chest. "I'm so lonely," she said.

"Don't cry . . . I . . ."

Sally squeezed her nails into his back. "Please don't say anything," she said.

It was foggy, and the Zurich sky was as gray as most of the downtown buildings. The streets wore a film of early-morning rain.

Larry Phillips got out of the taxi across the street from the bank. He looked around.

The bank building itself was an imposing structure with a domelike roof and heavy glass doors. The formidable entrance reminded him of the administration building at Leavenworth,

271

though he quickly dismissed the thought as immature, an "anxiety reaction," as Emil would say.

He walked up the steps on the balls of his feet.

Glanzmann was waiting in the marbled lobby. He ushered Phillips into a comfortable conference room decorated with a heavy oak table and leather-covered chairs. They sat down.

Phillips took the stack of T bills out of the briefcase and handed them to the banker.

Glanzmann put his glasses on. He examined the securities carefully, holding them up to the light, flipping a finger at a corner here and there. Arranging them like a deck of cards, he counted the bills out loud. *"Acht und neunzig, neun und neunzig, hundert."* He stopped counting and looked up. "Everything seems to be in order."

"How long will it take you to authenticate the bills?" Phillips said.

The banker hesitated for a moment. "Two working days. It's just routine procedure for such a large amount. It's not that we don't ..."

"Of course," Phillips interrupted. "Call me at the hotel when the authentication is complete. My people will need to know that the account is in order before I leave Zurich."

Glanzmann tapped the edge of the stack until it was even. He placed the bills in a folder. "Certainly, Mr. Phillips. This is quite a large transaction."

"Las Vegas is a large transaction."

The banker laughed politely.

The discotheque was a cavern of artificial light and shadows.

Larry sat with Melba in a corner booth sipping wine. Because of blaring rock music, they screamed whenever they thought of something to say.

Melba had worn her tightest-fitting sweater and she was braless. "When can we go back?" she said. "There's nothing to do over here " Her words were slurred. She picked up the wine bottle and filled her glass again. "Zurich sucks." She put the wine bottle down and fidgeted in her seat.

"Another day or so," he said.

A spindly blond man wearing a T-shirt, red scarf, and trousers tight enough clearly to outline his genitals sauntered over to the table carrying a leather hand purse. He said something to Melba in German and put out his hand. His eyes were red-rimmed.

Melba looked puzzled. "I don't understand a word of that Mexican you're speaking, honey," she said.

"He wants to dance with you," Larry said.

The man smiled. "Hello, American people." His accent was guttural.

"Why not?" Melba said. She took the man's hand and blended into the crowd of couples on the dance floor. She took clumsy, drunken steps.

After a while they came back to the table. They were holding hands. "This is Gerhard," she said. "I can't even pronounce his name." They snuggled into the booth. "He's high on somethin'," Melba said, giggling. They all laughed.

Larry ordered more wine.

Gerhard held his thumb and index finger an inch apart. "I speak little English," he said. His smile was stuporous. He turned to Melba and began counting her fingers. She giggled again.

The music was electronic waves. Hours went by. There was more wine, and Gerhard ate pills, which he took from a matchbox in his handbag, and sang "You Are My Sunshine," in halting English.

They finished another bottle of wine, and Larry ordered more. By 3:00 A.M. Gerhard had his arm around Melba.

The music stopped suddenly and the musicians headed for the bar.

Melba put her hand over her mouth, because she had been yelling. She laughed.

Larry reached across the table and tapped Gerhard on the arm. "Say, how would you like to fuck her?" He pointed a thumb at Melba.

The man nodded, smiling.

"I knew you were going to say that," Melba said, her words blending together.

They took a taxi to the hotel and used the rear elevator to get to the room. Gerhard had popped two more pills on the way, using the wine in a half-full bottle he carried as chaser.

Inside, he stripped to a pair of elastic briefs and lay down on the bed. He swigged more wine.

Melba glanced at Larry. He nodded. She pulled the sweater over her head and tossed it on the floor. She stripped off her other clothes and climbed on the bed.

Gerhard pointed the wine bottle at Larry. "He will remain?" he said, with an amused smile.

Melba pulled down his briefs and grabbed his limp penis. She giggled. "Gerhard's not hard," she said.

Larry turned off the overhead light and closed the curtain. He undressed carefully and hung up each piece of clothing in the closet. Pulling the dressing-table chair closer to the bed, he sat down and felt the texture of harsh woven material on his bare buttocks.

On the bed the blond man made little pleasure grunts as Melba's head plunged between his legs. Wet sounds.

Larry felt a tingling in his cock, but did not touch himself. He closed his eyes. By the time he was erect, the bed was a sea of squirming arms and legs, redness, body heat, and hair. He rose from the chair and got on the bed.

The bank conference room was neat and still. The musty odor of seldom-used furniture reminded Larry Phillips of a mortuary sitting room.

"I'm sure you'll be happy to hear that the Treasury bills have been authenticated through banking channels, and the account is now in order," Glanzmann said. "Things are how the Americans say—A-OK?" His fingers made the American sign. The banker was trying to be American-style casual, just as he probably would act prim if he were speaking to a German or a Dane.

"That's good," Phillips said. "Because my organization needs some cash very soon."

"How much?" The banker stopped smiling.

Phillips opened a leather-covered notebook he was carrying. He pretended he was checking figures. "One point three million," he said. "We will only need the money for a few days, so

I propose to borrow the amount, using the Treasury bills as collateral. Does the bank have any problem with this?" He spoke as if he was in a hurry.

"How . . . in what form . . . would you want the money?" Glanzmann said. His brow was furrowed.

Phillips looked up from his notebook. "You can just wire-transfer the amount into our account in Los Angeles. That would be perfectly acceptable."

"The interest would be rather high, even for just a few days." Glanzmann had a troubled expression.

"Within six days we will wire-transfer the amount of the loan back to you. A few days later I'll be in Zurich with a large amount of American currency for deposit. These transactions will take place once a month or so, the year round. . . . I prefer not to go into any more detail. . . . I'm sure you understand."

"I will have to get approval for such a large loan."

Phillips gave a look of annoyance. He glanced at his wristwatch. "I'd like to have the approval before I leave the bank." He bit the inside of his lip.

"*Ein* . . . er . . . just a moment, Mr. Hess." The banker got up and left the room.

Phillips closed his eyes and took a deep breath. He pictured Glanzmann rushing back into the room with detectives dressed like his father, Glanzmann pointing at him as the steel teeth of handcuffs devoured his wrists. His shirt collar felt too tight.

Fifteen minutes passed. Perhaps the one point three was too much. Should he have asked for five hundred thousand?

The door opened. Glanzmann came in with some papers. He sat down at the table and filled them out. "No problem with the Treasury bills as collateral. I just had to get approval." He pushed the papers gently toward Phillips.

Phillip's tone was sarcastic. "I should hope not. Ten million in bills as collateral for *one point three*?" He signed the copies with a flourish and stood up. "I will call you from Los Angeles with instructions to initiate the wire transfer," he said.

"As you wish."

Walking down the steps of the bank, Larry realized that perspiration had soaked through the underarms of his suit coat.

$/13

Carr looked at the dashboard clock for what could have been the thousandth time. It was 4:00 P.M. The day had been spent waiting for Emil Kreuzer to leave his beach apartment. A grim-faced Agent True, his right cheek tattooed with finger-shaped welts, sat behind the wheel. He hadn't spoken all day.

They were parked on a narrow street made up of apartment houses similar to Kreuzer's—two-story, wood-ornamented places with minuscule balconies. The front yards were dotted with signs that read ADULTS ONLY—NO PETS and, considering the uniform look of the young people around, Carr's boredom flashed a vision: a sign that read TANS ONLY—NO LOOSE-FITTING CLOTHING. The automobiles parked nearby were sports cars with surfboard or ski racks.

There were no vacancy signs, a fact Carr figured was due to the proximity of portholed pubs along the Marina Del Rey pleasure-craft harbor, youth-oriented lounges where everyone ordered Margaritas and lied with impunity about owning a boat or having placed in last Sunday's 6.2 jog.

"I guess I was the one who was off base yesterday," True said. "So I've got no hard feelings."

Carr held the binoculars to his eyes. "That's good."

True gritted his teeth.

"Here comes our boy," Carr said.

True started the engine.

276

Kreuzer got into a white Mercedes sedan and revved the engine. He backed out of the driveway and wound through the residential area onto the Pacific Coast Highway.

"He's heading toward the Marina Freeway," Carr said. "Don't lose him."

The Mercedes took the freeway on-ramp and accelerated into the fast lane. True stayed two cars behind. Two miles later the sports car swerved across two lanes of traffic and took the exit marked "San Diego Freeway South." A few minutes later he exited from the freeway at Century Boulevard. The green signs pointed toward Los Angeles International Airport. A block later the Mercedes pulled into a coffee-shop parking lot.

True swerved the sedan into a gas station across the street and parked. Carr lifted the binoculars.

Kreuzer got out of the car and looked around. He checked his watch. A bearded man with a gold earring walked out of the coffee shop. The two men spoke, making few gestures, for almost a half hour. Kreuzer looked at his watch again. He patted the bearded man on the shoulder and climbed back in the Mercedes.

The bearded man straddled a Harley-Davidson motorcycle and started the engine.

Carr took out a pen and wrote the motorcycle's license number in his notebook.

The Mercedes continued east on Century Boulevard with the motorcycle close behind. The vehicles passed over a small bridge into a swirl of airport traffic. The agents were three cars behind.

Kreuzer pulled the Mercedes into an area marked "International Arrivals" and parked. He locked the sedan and walked across the street to the terminal building. The bearded man parked his motorcycle a few spaces away and began rolling a cigarette.

Carr jumped out of the sedan and followed Kreuzer at a safe distance.

Kreuzer went in the glass doors of the terminal.

Carr ran across the street and into the terminal area behind him. Kreuzer had disappeared into the maelstrom of rushing tourists and baggage porters. Carr focused on face after face. He rushed from one ticket line to another, until everyone started to look the same.

True dodged through a group of women in saris and ran up to him.

Carr slammed fist into palm. "I lost him!" he said. He pointed. "You take the airlines down that way. Start checking flights. . . . He didn't have a suitcase."

True took off at a jog.

Carr continued to move through the harried crowd. Finally, he left the terminal building. Kreuzer's Mercedes and the motorcycle were parked in the same places. The bearded man leaned against a light pole in the corner of the parking lot.

True came down the sidewalk from the baggage area, walking briskly. He spoke out of the side of his mouth: "He met a man and a woman who arrived on a flight from Zurich. They're picking up their baggage." He turned his head to the side. "There they go."

Kreuzer gestured excitedly as he led the man and a strawberry blonde across the street and into the parking lot.

The agents returned to their sedan at a full run. With the binoculars Carr saw the three get into the Mercedes. Kreuzer drove out of the lot and back onto Century Boulevard.

They followed. In the rearview mirror Carr saw the bearded man casually walk toward his motorcycle. He went the other way.

The Mercedes took the most direct route to Beverly Hills. The agents were two cars behind it the whole way.

It pulled up at the front of the potted-plant entrance of the Chez Beverly Hotel. Carr used the binoculars again.

A doorman in a purple uniform helped them out of the vehicle. They entered the glass doors with an army of bellhops.

Carr put the binoculars down. "Drive around to the back," he said.

True accelerated out of the lot and around the corner.

Carr pointed to an alley lined with the hotel's trash cans. He told him to park. They got out of the sedan, and Carr led the way between two garages. Using an empty trash can as a ladder he climbed onto the roof of a garage. True followed.

On the roof an overhanging tree provided cover for a binoculars' view of the hotel's sun-drenched balconies. "Every room with a view," Carr said in singsong fashion.

Less than ten minutes later Kreuzer opened the sliding glass doors and walked onto a balcony. "Third floor," Carr said. Kreuzer was followed by the younger man. They talked animatedly. A few minutes later the strawberry blonde came out in dark glasses and a bathing suit. She sat in the chaise longue.

"Cantaloupes," True said.

Kreuzer walked back into the room. He returned wearing only his trousers and carrying a telephone with a long cord and a towel. He sat down at a dainty table.

The younger man went in and came out minutes later in bathing trunks. The two men spoke seriously to one another. Kreuzer made chopping motions with his hands for a while. He held a towel over the telephone mouthpiece and dialed.

The younger man looked at the woman and held a vertical finger to his lips. He picked up an extension phone from the table and held his hand over the mouthpiece.

A woman's voice. "Law offices."

"Mr. Robinson, please," Kreuzer said in his deepest German accent. He wrapped the towel tighter around the telephone.

"I can hardly hear you, sir," the secretary said. "Please hold the line."

The phone clicked.

"Hello, Mr. Tessier," Robinson said. "I take it you have finally agreed upon a price with Mr. Prescott?"

"Yes. One point three million. But I have certain reservations regarding the transaction. Mr. Prescott has asked me to forward a cashier's check for the one point three million to the trust account before I actually receive the collection. This is not acceptable to me. I fear the possibility of damage or theft to the items between the time I send the check and when I actually take physical control of them." Kreuzer puffed up his German accent. "At this point I *must* be assured safe delivery. I want to take possession of the collection simultaneously with my payment. My people demand this."

"I see," Robinson said. "Mr. Prescott should be at his hotel by now. He arrived at the airport a short while ago. I will speak with him and . . ."

"May I call you back in a few hours?" Kreuzer said.

"Yes, of course, Mr. Tessier. I m sure something can be worked out," Robinson said.

Kreuzer hung up the phone. He looked at his partner. "What do you think?" he said.

"I think Robinson is a farmer," Larry Phillips said.

Melba laughed and shook her head. "You guys are really cold."

The phone rang a minute later. The men switched phones. It was Robinson.

"I'm having problems across the pond," Phillips said. "I couldn't sleep a wink on the flight back."

"Tessier just called me," Robinson said.

"He wants immediate delivery," Phillips said. "But that's not the biggest problem. My client is driving me *crazy*. She wants the deal over with like *yesterday*. I'm just tearing my hair out over the whole thing." He smiled at Kreuzer and jerked a cupped hand up and down.

"Will Tessier wire-transfer cash?"

"If he could take immediate possession, he'd probably go for it."

"Fine. Where is the collection at this moment?"

"We have it in a bank safe deposit vault in Zurich. My colleague Mr. Hess is there."

"Then I propose we have Tessier wire-transfer the full amount while he's at the bank with your colleague looking at the collection. When the amount reaches the bank here in Beverly Hills, you phone Zurich and acknowledge receipt of the money; and Mr. Hess then releases possession to Tessier directly." Larry, holding the phone to his ear, stood up and pumped his arm lewdly.

"Sounds acceptable to me," he said in a businesslike manner. "I will speak with my client and get back to you." He hung up the telephone carefully.

"We're getting close to the walkaway," Larry said.

Kreuzer nodded proudly. "I can feel it, too," he said.

280

"What's the walkaway?" Melba said.

"That's when you pick up one point three million dollars in cash and walk away with it," Larry said.

Melba laughed.

Carr let the binoculars drop to hang around his neck. "They haven't scored yet," he said.

"What makes you say that?"

"If they had scored, they wouldn't be together. They'd have gone their separate ways already. If not that, they'd at least be popping champagne bottles and jumping around doing a jackpot dance. Right now they're talking turkey, staying in the same room. They're watching one another real close, making phone calls, building up to the score."

"Taking a lot for granted, aren't you, Charlie?" The young man was smirking.

"Get the camera out of the trunk of the car," Carr said. "Toss it up to me and then take a position across the street from the front of the hotel."

True scrambled off the roof.

As the day wore on, Carr, a camera as well as binoculars hanging around his neck, could see as well as feel the heat waves shimmering off the white-graveled roof. In the partial shade of the tree branches, he leaned back against an air vent. As he rubbed his gravel-indented knees, his mind drifted to a hundred such uncomfortable places—roofs, ladders, vent openings, storefronts, bus benches, airport waiting lounges, shopping centers, fast-food stands—where he had watched people do both normal and abnormal things. Watching people work their way into prison.

So far, Kreuzer and the younger man had done nothing but stroll on and off the balcony making phone calls.

The woman was still sunbathing, eyes closed, resting on the chaise longue. Suddenly, without opening her eyes, she leaned forward and unfastened her bathing-suit top. She shrugged it off and tossed it on the table. Reaching down into a purse, she removed a small plastic bottle and squirted something on her hands. She rubbed her heavy, cocoa-nippled breasts until they glistened. She got to her feet and pulled off the bottom of her swimsuit. Sitting down again, she rubbed oil over the whitish skin of her crotch.

Kreuzer was standing at the sliding glass door watching. He said something to her, and she turned her head and looked at him. She may have nodded.

The woman got up and walked past him into the hotel room. Kreuzer pulled the zipper down on his trousers and stepped into the darkness of the room.

After a while, the woman walked back onto the balcony and picked up a towel from the table. She wiped between her legs and dropped the towel on the floor. She returned to her position on the chaise longue, leaned back, and closed her eyes.

As was usual during a Los Angeles August, it didn't cool down much even when it became dark.

By midnight Kreuzer and the others had enjoyed room service twice. They had been lounging and watching television in the suite since 7:00 P.M., the curtains wide open.

Carr was hungry, thirsty, and had a headache that felt as though a screwdriver were stuck in his right eye.

The lights in the suite went out. He stood up and stretched. Using the trash can in the alley as a stepladder, he climbed off the roof.

He unsnapped a Handie-Talkie from his belt and pressed the transmit button. "Sixteen Lima four to Lima nine," he said.

"Go ahead, Sixteen," True said.

"They went to bed. Let's head for the field office."

Carr sat at a squad-room desk covered with hamburger wrappings and empty Coke bottles. Between bites he had phoned the Department of Motor Vehicles and learned that the license-plate number on the motorcycle was registered to someone named Clyde Reno.

True's feet were up on a table. He made an offer of another Coke by holding it up. Carr shook his head.

An intercom on the wall buzzed. The duty agent told Carr he had a call on line six.

"Two A.M.," True said. "Maybe it's a broad." He laughed.

Carr picked up the receiver and punched the line-six button. "Agent Carr."

Emil Kreuzer whispered, "I'm working on that thing we discussed. . . . I may have to hang up any minute."

"Where are you?" Carr winked at True and motioned him to pick up an extension line.

"Uh . . . San Francisco. I've been breaking my balls to put this case together for you. The main player involved in the paper theft is a guy named Larry. I don't have a description of him yet. The case looks big. It looks like this Larry may have had something printed on the paper already."

True gently picked up another phone receiver and held it to his ear.

"Any idea what was printed?" Carr said.

"Some kind of government bills. Sorry I haven't been able to get back to you sooner. Just wanted to let you know I'm still on the job for you. This thing looks big. I should be able to find out more tomorrow."

"You've got to get me some more details," Carr said in mock desperation.

"Trust me," Kreuzer said.

The phone clicked.

Carr put the receiver down.

"That sneaky son of a bitch," True said.

Jack Kelly burst into the squad room holding a wet photographic print by its corners. "It's Scary Larry! It's him for sure." He dropped the dripping print on the desk in front of Carr and pointed to the younger man standing in a casual pose on the Chez Beverly Hotel balcony. "He's an above-average confidence man. Careful. Plans his moves. He's patient, and sly to the point of being paranoid. Kind of guy who says he'll meet you at nine o'clock and shows up at seven-thirty to get the lay of the land."

Carr nodded.

"And something else. He always carries a piece and he isn't afraid to use it."

Carr picked up the phone again and dialed Washington, D.C. Delgado answered.

"This is Charlie. I . . ."

"I was just going to call you," interrupted Delgado. "We may be too late."

"How do you mean?" Carr said.

"I just learned that main Treasury received a bank teletype ten days ago requesting authentication on over ten million dollars in Treasury bills with serial numbers similar to the ones you found in Freddie Roth's printing trash."

"Was the bank teletype from Switzerland?"

"How did you know?" Delgado said.

"We followed Emil Kreuzer to the airport today. He picked up a man and woman who got off a flight from Zurich."

Nothing was said for a few moments. Delgado spoke in a somber tone. "I've got to get off the hook on this case, Charlie. Notifying a foreign bank that they've taken a loss won't cut it. We've got to *clear up the case*. The secretary of the Treasury himself has been poking his nose in. Wants to appoint a commission to review security procedures, a 'place the blame' operation. Run by a bunch of twenty-five-year-old prick lawyers. He's even threatened to turn the case over to the Secret Service. I want to get off the hook, Charlie."

"I'll see what I can do," Carr said. He hung up the phone and rubbed his chin in thought. He stood up and walked to a filing cabinet. He pulled open a drawer marked "New Info" and looked under the *R*'s until he found a file marked "Reno, Clyde Darnell." The folder was stamped "Smuggling suspect."

Carr sat down at a desk and opened the folder. Stapled to the upper left-hand corner was a booking photograph of the bearded man Kreuzer had met with.

The other side of the folder was a computer printout which read:

1. Customs U.S. Port of Entry San Juan: Arrestee Washington, Amos P. named Reno as manufacturer of false-bottom suitcase seized from him upon arrival at San Juan Airport. Suitcase contained one pound cocaine (ref case # 121-9431W).
2. Customs U.S. Port of Entry Calexico: Subject's name found in address book of Castro, Juan Adolpho, Columbian national, arrested smuggling Columbian-produced marijuana/light aircraft pilot.

Carr turned the page. Reno's arrest record was a three-page laundry list of robbery and assault. The last entry read:

Date	Agency	Charge	Disposition
5/1/78	L.A. County Sheriff's Dept.	Murder	Acquitted

"Buck," he said, "I want you to go over to Sheriff's Homicide and find out about the murder beef. Talk to the detective who handled the case—call him at home if you have to. I want to find out what kind of guy Reno is, what he's into. . . . In the meantime, I'll finish up here."

"See you at Ling's when I get done," True said. He put on his coat and headed out the door.

$/14

Carr slipped in the back door.

Ling's bar was full, and the tune coming from the outdated jukebox was as familiar to Carr as the well-worn bar furniture.

Carr did the long-time-no-see routine with a group of florid-faced detectives slumped in a booth covered with empty glasses, excused himself, and went to the bar.

True arrived a half hour later. He sat down, and Carr motioned to Ling for a drink.

The young agent took a note card from his coat pocket, reached over the bar, and found Ling's flashlight. He focused the light on the card. "Here's the story," he said. "Clyde Reno, aka Cowpoke, owns a motorcycle-repair shop in Pico Rivera, but the sheriff's dicks say he earns his living by rigging boats, cars, and luggage for smugglers; makes false-bottom suitcases, stuff like that. His murder beef goes like this: a year ago, two enterprising dope pushers, the Garcia brothers, hired Reno to rig a carrying spot on the frame of a camper truck. The Garcia brothers took a trip to Sombreroland and scored a load of Mexican brown heroin. Coming back, they crossed the border at night through Tijuana and drove up through San Diego. Just outside of town, a car pulled them over with a red light. Some campers across the road saw a man with a beard get out of a car, walk up to the camper. He ordered the Garcia boys out of the camp-

286

er and blew them away with a .45. The bearded man drove off in the camper. Clyde Reno stood trial. The campers couldn't positively ID him because he shaved his beard, and he got three Hells Angels to testify he was with them on the day it happened. Reno beat the rap." He picked up his glass, stirred the ice with a finger, and drank.

Carr rubbed his chin in thought. "Buck, I want you to catch a couple hours of sleep and set up on Clyde Reno before the sun comes up. Whatever you do, don't lose him once you start surveillance." He finished his drink and set it down. "I think these people are getting ready to score."

"Tell them to wire the money *immediately*," Robinson said, leaning his back against the bay window in his office.

Larry Phillips was sitting at the lawyer's desk, holding a telephone to his ear.

"Go ahead, sir," said the operator. "Mr. Glanzmann is on the line."

"Hello, Mr. Glanzmann," he said.

"Is this Mr. Hess?"

"Yes. Good morning," Phillips said, speaking loudly. "You may proceed with the transfer immediately as per my previous instructions. The recipient bank is the Merchants Bank of Commerce and Industry, Beverly Hills, California. The account of Attorney Martin L. Robinson. Account number 421564." He enunciated each number carefully.

"Four two one five six four?"

"Yes."

"The money will be on the wire within thirty minutes." Glanzmann hung up.

Phillips spoke to a buzzing sound. "Yes, Mr. Hess, you may deliver the goods. That's right: *deliver the collection*. Good-by." He hung up the phone.

Robinson looked pleased. He rubbed his hands together. "Will a bank cashier's check for the amount be agreeable to your client?" he said.

Phillips picked up the phone again. "Let me find out," he said. He dialed Melba at a phone-booth number he had memorized. "Hello, Miss Rogers, this is Mr. Prescott. The money is being transferred by wire to a bank here in Beverly Hills at this very moment. When it gets here, shall I have the bank prepare a cashier's check for you or . . ." He waited a few moments for effect. "Cash? I'm not sure that's feasible." He looked at Robinson. "Just a moment, please." He put his hand over the mouthpiece and shook his head in a distressed manner. "She wants it in *cash*," he whispered.

Robinson had a look of disbelief. "You mean over a million dollars in *actual* cash? A very bad idea. Unheard of."

Phillips offered the phone. "Please, would you talk with her."

The lawyer took the phone receiver as if it was diseased. He held it to his ear. "Madame, this sort of transaction is extremely risky. . . . Uh, yes, I'll . . . well . . . but . . . Could I suggest another . . . All right. I'll see what I can do, Madame. Certainly. It's your money. No one's questioning that." The lawyer held the phone out from his ear. "She hung up." He shook his head. "She wants *cash*. She wants the whole amount in *cash*. Christ, it'll fill a suitcase." He put the receiver down for a moment, then picked it up again. He dialed a number and asked to speak with the bank manager.

"Art, this is Martin. You know that trust account I opened up a couple of days ago? I have a special request. . . ."

Phillips strolled to the opposite end of the room. The sound of the lawyer's voice was like a record. Following the suggestions of the hypnotist, he thought. He sat down on the sofa. The conversation had lasted more than twenty minutes. He looked at his watch.

Robinson hung up the phone. He was sweating. "We will have to pay for an armored car run from the main branch in Newport Beach. They will have the one point three in cash by tomorrow at 4:00 P.M. He said the wire transfer was coming through on the teletype right as we were talking." He ran both hands through his hair and exhaled. "Your client is an extraordinary one, I must say."

Phillips held his hand perpendicular to his chin. "I'm up to here with the woman," he said. "Just up to here. I can't wait until this is over."

• • •

288

Larry woke up because Melba was massaging his penis.

Kreuzer's bearlike snores floated through the open door of the adjoining room.

"Lately, I've been doing Emil more than I have you," she whispered. Her hand cupped him firmly. "I don't mind doing it, though, as long as you want me, too." She pumped gently. Larry stretched his legs. "Emil made a phone call in the middle of the night," she said.

Larry pushed her away and sat up in the bed. "What did he say?"

"I couldn't tell. He was whispering. I think I heard him say something about government bonds."

Larry got out of bed and pulled on his trousers.

"Don't you want me to finish?" Melba said.

"No," Larry said. He dressed and strode into the next room. He shook Kreuzer's shoulder roughly. "Wake up," he said.

The husky man rolled over and rubbed his eyes. "What time is it?"

"Who did you call last night?"

Kreuzer got up. He swung his legs over the side of the bed. "What's wrong?"

"Who did you call last night?"

He rubbed his eyes again before answering. "I remembered I had to call a guy in Las Vegas—uh, a pit boss; works midnight to eight. Only time I can reach him is late."

"What does he have to do with government bonds?" Larry said. He shoved his hands in his pockets.

"As a matter of fact we discussed bonds—some hot City of San Francisco bonds. He's peddling a package of them. I told him I would call him back to tell him yes or no on the deal. I told him no." Kreuzer rubbed his face roughly with both hands.

Larry glared at him for a moment. "Let's get this fuckin' deal over with," he said. "I'm tired of this hotel room."

Kreuzer gave him a fatherly smile. "We all get a little uptight right before the walkaway. It's called an 'anxiety reaction.' This is very normal."

Larry turned and picked the phone receiver off the night-stand. He dialed and asked for Attorney Robinson.

"Mr. Prescott here," Larry said.

"Glad you called," said Robinson. "The money will be ready at the bank at 4:00 P.M. Can you meet me there?"

"See you at four."

Larry hung up the phone.

Kreuzer sprung out of the bed in shorts and grabbed him by the arm. "We're almost to the finish line, my friend! Take it easy." In quarterback fashion, he gave Larry a buttocks pat. He walked into the bathroom and closed the door.

Carr leaned back in the seat of the sedan with the binoculars. He focused on the glass doors of the hotel's entrance. Kreuzer, Phillips, and the girl were standing at the cashier's desk. Phillips signed something and they walked out of the hotel. The doorman handed him a set of keys. He opened the door of a new dark-blue Cadillac. The three got in. Phillips handed the doorman a tip.

Carr turned a radio knob to frequency T and pressed the microphone switch. "They're loading up," he said.

"Reno is still doing sixty-five in a pickup truck," said True. "He's going west on the Santa Monica Freeway. Okay. Off the freeway at Robertson. He's heading north toward you."

Phillips started the engine. He slid the Cadillac into stop-and-go Wilshire Boulevard traffic.

"We're moving," Carr said into the microphone.

True's voice boomed from the radio. "Reno's pulling into an empty lot. . . . It's two doors down from a bank. . . . Okay. He's parked, sitting in the pickup. Just staring at the bank."

"Roger," Carr said. He tossed the microphone down on the seat and steered in and out of a parade of luxury cars. Phillips turned south on Robertson and less than a mile farther pulled into a bank parking lot. Carr found True parked in an alley across the street. He waved. The young agent got out of his vehicle and climbed into the passenger seat.

"Whataya figure?" True said. He was out of breath.

Carr didn't take his eyes off the bank. "This is it," he said. He pulled his .357 magnum out of its holster and spun the chamber. He stuffed the weapon back.

"There's four of 'em," True said. "Shouldn't we call for a backup?"

290

Carr stared across the street. "No," he said.

Larry Phillips turned off the engine and straightened his tie. He turned to Kreuzer. "Stay in the car. I'll come out with the money and put it in the front seat between us. We'll drive around the corner, split the take, and go our separate ways. Agreed?"

"Agreed," Kreuzer said. He looked pale.

Phillips got out of the car and looked around the parking lot. He took an empty suitcase out of the trunk and walked carefully toward the bank's glass door. He opened the door courteously for two face-lifted matrons and followed them in.

The interior of the bank was peso-colored marble. Robinson sat at a desk with a well-dressed man wearing smoked eyeglasses. "Mr. Prescott!" The lawyer strode silently across thick shag carpeting. The man followed. Robinson introduced him as the bank manager. They shook hands.

"Everything is in order, I take it," Phillips said.

"We strongly recommend you use an armored car, Mr. Prescott. This is really . . . unheard of," said the lawyer.

Phillips threw up his hands. "I'm just following my client's instructions," he said. "This whole thing has been an *experience*."

Everyone's head shook. The banker motioned him to a desk.

Phillips sat down and signed the name L. L. Prescott on at least eight forms.

The banker examined them and stapled them together.

"Please come this way, Mr. Prescott."

Phillips picked up the suitcase and followed him into a well-lit vault. There was a wheeled steel cart that was covered with stacks of bills. Phillips felt cold perspiration running between his shoulder blades. Relax, deep relaxation, he thought.

It took a half hour to count and stack it in the suitcase. Phillips could barely close the lid.

He handed Robinson a ten-thousand-dollar stack. "Would you mind being paid in cash? My client prefers . . ."

"Certainly." Robinson looked at the banker and back to Phillips.

Phillips pulled ten hundred-dollar bills from a stack and stuffed them into the banker's shirt pocket. "We appreciate your discretion. We really do."

The banker's eyes darted to the vault door.

"It's something for the family," Phillips said.

The three men smiled.

Walking across the lobby of the bank, Phillips pictured the suitcase falling open and the money spilling at his feet. Handcuffs tore through his wrists, and his hands, bloody, spurting, fell onto the pile of money. A visual hallucination, he thought.

He opened the glass door of the bank and walked out. He stopped and looked both ways. Across the street and two doors down, a sedan with two men in it was pointed out of an alley. He kept an eye on the vehicle as he walked toward the Cadillac.

Kreuzer reached over and opened the passenger door for him. His face was ashen.

Larry put the suitcase between them in the front seat. "I got it. Let's get the hell out of here," he said.

"Mercy," Melba said.

Kreuzer pulled the headlight switch and fumbled with the ignition key. The engine turned over.

"Why'd you turn on the headlights?" Larry said.

A bearded man was at the passenger window. He pointed a gun at Larry's face.

"It's Reno. He pulled a piece," screamed True. "It's a rip-off." He grabbed the door handle.

Carr grabbed his arm without taking his eyes off the Cadillac.

"What are you waiting for? Let's take 'em!" True jerked his arm away and pulled his revolver. He reached for the door handle again.

Carr grabbed his arm in a vicelike grip and jerked him back violently. "Not yet," he said.

Larry Phillips held his breath.

"Easy, brother," said Reno. He held the revolver with both hands.

Emil Kreuzer pulled the key from the ignition. He grabbed the suitcase and scrambled out the driver's door. He ran to the pickup truck and got in.

Larry's hand was on his automatic.

There was the sound of gunshots.

292

Carr released True's arm. He floored the accelerator, and the sedan flew across the street and into the bank parking lot.

The strawberry-blonde woman jumped out of the Cadillac screaming.

Reno fired, and her body slammed against a parked car. She flopped to the asphalt like a doe. He turned and fired at them. Windshield glass sprayed into Carr's face.

With a rolling motion Carr was out the driver's door and in a shooting crouch. He fired four times. Reno fell backward, a hand clutching his groin. He raised his gun hand again.

From the other side of the sedan, True fired until his revolver clicked. Reno's body flipped over and quivered.

The pickup truck roared directly at them. Carr fired twice into the cab. With a deafening crunch, the machine sideswiped a row of vehicles and smashed through the glass door of the bank. The agents ran through the broken glass and pulled open the doors of the cab. Emil Kreuzer fell out with both hands covering a bleeding forehead. He moaned as True snapped handcuffs on his wrists.

Carr rushed back to the Cadillac and looked in. Larry Phillips was lying on a leather seat dashed with blood and pink-and-white tissue. He turned away.

There was a sound of sirens and of people screaming and running.

The field office buzzed with activity.

Carr, sitting at a squad-room desk covered with paper cups, wrote the last paragraph of his investigation report. It read:

Suspects Phillips, L., Reno, C., and Rivers, M. were pronounced dead at the scene (reference is made to the attached Coroner's Report). At 2000 hours Interpol Bern (Switzerland) was requested by teletype to seize the counterfeit Treasury bills from the victim bank in Zurich.

True had a phone to his ear. He swung his feet off a desk and jumped up. "You've got to be kidding," he screamed into the mouthpiece. "There must be *something* you can charge Kreuzer with! . . . What does that have to do with it? . . . He was *there*, wasn't he? He tried to flee with a suitcase full of *money*. How's that for evidence of criminal intent? *Any* jury would convict him on that evidence alone. . . ."

Carr got up and stretched. He ambled out a door into a hall-way. Television cameramen in casual clothes lugged heavy cameras and sound equipment into Norbert Waeves's office. Carr took a few steps and stopped just outside the open door. No Waves was bathed in light. He was holding Larry Phillips's suit-case open to show the money. "I ordered my agents to stop the suspects if they attempted to leave the bank parking lot," he said, using his deepest voice. "At this time the suspects resisted arrest, and we were forced to use our weapons. The shooting that ensued resulted in mortal wounds to three of the four suspects. Although we are still checking, at this point I am of the firm belief that these suspects were closely associated with organized-crime elements. . . ."

Carr continued on down the hallway and took a drink from a water fountain. He returned to the squad room.

True was still standing, his face flushed. He was almost biting the phone receiver. "In *that* case," he said, "*here's* a legal term I *know* you'll understand: *Fuck you!*" He slammed the receiver down so hard it bounced off the desk. He turned to Carr. "The U.S. attorney's office says to cut Kreuzer loose, to let him *go home.* They won't prosecute because they're afraid he'll take the stand and say he was working as a federal informant. . . . Can you believe that?"

Carr sat down at the desk. He picked up a pen and wrote the last two sentences of his report.

United States attorney's office has declined to prosecute suspect Emil Kreuzer due to lack of sufficient evidence to prove criminal intent. Case closed due to lack of any further investigative leads.

He put down the pen and paper-clipped the report to the surveillance log and the prisoner-information sheets. He tossed the sheaf of papers into a typing-pool basket. "You can't get everybody," he said. He got up and walked to the door of an interview room.

True followed.

Carr opened the door and they strode into the soundproof

room. It contained a small table, three chairs; the walls were made of thick acoustical plasterboard.

Emil Kreuzer lifted his head from the table. It was a turban of bandages.

"Sorry to keep you here so long," Carr said, "but you know how those young federal prosecutors are. . . . My partner here had to do a lot of singin' and dancin' to convince them not to prosecute you on a conspiracy charge."

Kreuzer stuck out a hand to True. "Thanks a lot, man. I really mean it," he said.

True shook hands numbly. He looked at Carr with a blank expression.

"It was just a mix-up," Kreuzer said. "The deal went down so fast, there was no time for me to get to a phone and let you know what was up."

"At the bank, we didn't even know it was you in the pickup truck," Carr said. "We had been following Reno because somebody had told us he was going to make a big score. Incredible, the way it turned out." He shook his head in mock disbelief. "Can we give you a ride home?"

Kreuzer stood up, smiling. "Thanks anyway," he said. "I think I'll just grab a taxi. . . . You'll be hearing from me in a day or so. It's Victor King the loan shark. I'll have the goods on him . . . I mean *the* goods. Names, dates, and places; the whole schmear."

"Sounds good," Carr said.

Kreuzer walked to the door and paused. He turned around. "Stop by the bowling alley some night," he said. "The show is on me."

"Promise you won't hypnotize me?" Carr said. They smiled at one another strangely. Kreuzer shuffled out the door.

True let out his breath. "I don't know how you do it," he said.

"It's easy."